Elyse Kelly

THE DARKEST THIRST

A VAMPIRE ANTHOLOGY

THE DESIGNIMAGE GROUP, INC.

ISBN: 1-891946-00-5

THE DESIGNIMAGE GROUP, INC.

Printed in the U.S.A.

10 9 8 7 6 5 4 3 2 1

Acknowledgements

Reconciliation, © 1998, Michael J. Arruda.

The Debauched One, © 1998, Edo van Belkom.

Snare, © 1998, Sue Burke.

Mercy, © 1998, Margaret L. Carter.

Abba's Mark, © 1998, Stirling Davenport.

Nocturne A Tre In B-Double-Sharp Minor, © 1998, Robert Devereaux.

The Boy Next Door, © 1998, d.g.k. goldberg.

Trailer Trash, © 1998, Scott T. Goudsward.

Before A Fall, © 1998, Barb Hendee.

Waiting For The 400, © 1998, Kyle Marffin.

For The Love Of Vampires, © 1998, Deborah Markus.

How Brando Was Made, © 1998, Paul McMahon.

The Covenant Of Il Vigneto, © 1998, Julie Anne Parks.

On Line, © 1998, Rick R. Reed.

The Alberscine Vigil, © 1997, Thomas J. Strauch, Previously published in Stygian Articles, 1997, Jeremy Johnson Editor.

The Bleeding of Hauptmann Gehlen, © 1998, William R. Trotter.

Contents

D a r k   H i s t o r i e s

Mercy	Margaret L. Carter	3
Before A Fall	Barb Hendee	15
Abba's Mark	Stirling Davenport	31
The Debauched One	Edo van Belkom	41
The Bleeding of Hauptmann Gehlen	William R. Trotter	51

O b s e s s i o n s

The Boy Next Door	d.g.k. goldberg	79
Waiting For The 400	Kyle Marffin	87
On Line	Rick R. Reed	111

T h e   H u n t e d

Trailer Trash	Scott T. Goudsward	125
Snare	Sue Burke	137
How Brando Was Made	Paul McMahon	149

R e d e m p t i o n

The Alberscine Vigil	Thomas J. Strauch	161
Reconciliation	Michael J. Arruda	185
The Covenant Of Il Vigneto	Julie Anne Parks	197

A r t s   &   L e t t e r s

Nocturne A Tre In B-Double-Sharp Minor	Robert Devereaux	209
For The Love Of Vampires	Deborah Markus	227

The Darkest Thirst

The Darkest Thirst

The thirst for immortality. The thirst for revenge. The thirst for redemption. The unquenchable thirst of dark desires. The darkest thirst of all...the thirst for blood.

In this anthology you're invited to drink from the darkest imaginings of sixteen horror writers - familiar genre names offering unfamiliar twists on time-honored legends of the undead, and emerging new talents with equally new takes, twists and tweaks on those dark creatures of the night.

Vampire tales freed themselves from the constrictions of black-caped noblemen and crumbling Balkan castles long ago. So in this anthology you'll be taken for a tour through history's dark side among Celtic raiders, Caribbean slave traders and WWII partisans. You'll find the darkest desires of the undead revealed behind the protective mantle of religious propriety, nearly invisible inside middle-America's trailer parks and concrete canyoned offices, lurking in the eerie cyber-space of modern technology...perhaps even hidden behind the familiar face of the friend sharing tea and conversation with you. You'll share the obsessions of the enraptured victims, the fear of the hunted, the triumph of the hunter, and the grim justice both earned and eluded.

You're invited to discover the pains, punishments and pleasures of the darkest thirst of all...

The Darkest Thirst

DARK HISTORIES

Mercy

By Margaret L. Carter

The fleece that she lay on chafed her damp skin. Whenever she stirred in pain, the straw in the mattress crackled. The spare, tight-lipped face of Gilda, her husband's sister, floated above Jocelyn in a bodiless blur as the birth-pangs racked her. The older woman's hand alternately wiped her brow with a wet cloth and rubbed her belly with a salve meant to ease the cramps. Hadwin, Jocelyn's husband, paced outside.

Her labor had already dragged on, far into the night. Her head felt heavy with the aroma of the candle and the smoke from the banked hearth-fire. Gilda propped her up to take another sip of the honey-flavored mandragora potion. Then an uproar of men's rough shouts – strange voices – burst through the haze of her travail. A truncated shout from Hadwin in the door-yard. Jocelyn moaned aloud and clutched Gilda's arm. "What happened?"

Half a dozen men swarmed over the small room. A bearded face loomed over her, with a voice bellowing, "Help yourself to the other one, lads, this one is mine!" She knew instantly who the man must be, though she had never seen Udolf the Red before. So called for both his habits and his flame-colored beard, he led a band of masterless men, stripped of their homes and goods by the Normans.

Jocelyn knew better than to expect clemency from the outlaws. In the wavering candlelight she glimpsed three of the men ransacking the cottage's single room and loft for whatever stored food they could carry. After one glance at the corner where Gilda shrieked in the hands of two others, as still another ripped the older woman's bodice, Jocelyn closed her eyes.

Thus the stab of pain at her neck came as an unexpected shock. A man's weight on her chest crushed her ribs. She struggled for air and writhed against the grip that pinned her arms to the mattress. The hot mouth at her throat withdrew momentarily, and Udolf said, "Don't waste your strength, little mother. I need it all." His breath smelled like rotten meat. Again his teeth fastened on her. She shuddered through alternate waves of heat and cold, punctuated by the rhythmic pressure of labor pains.

A scream from Gilda startled Jocelyn into opening her eyes. Udolf grinned down at her with wolf-like fangs, his lips smeared with a dark stain. His eyes glowed like live coals. She had heard whispers that Udolf the Red was no true man, but a demon in human flesh. Now she believed it.

Shifting her gaze to the shadowed corner, she saw Gilda standing upright, her kirtle in shreds, in the grasp of two smirking robbers. Her faded brown hair straggled loose from its braid. Panting, Gilda glared at Udolf and said, "How can you slaughter a woman in childbirth?"

Udolf said with a hoarse laugh, "Let no man claim that I can't show mercy." After ripping at his own arm with those bestial teeth, he twined his fingers in Jocelyn's hair and forced her mouth into the crook of his elbow. She choked on hot, bitter fluid.

His voice, seeming to echo from a distance, said, "There, now she won't die."

A moment later, the men tramped out, and silence fell. Jocelyn felt Gilda's hand clasp hers. "Gilda – where's Hadwin?"

"Not now, sister. Think of your child."

Then he's dead! Before Jocelyn could gather strength for tears or prayers, a squeezing, rending sensation overwhelmed her. Seconds later, she heard the cry of an infant, yielded to the lightheaded relief at the momentary absence of pain, and felt a gush of liquid between her thighs. Then she knew no more.

The familiar odors of smoke and the rushes strewn on the floor filled her nostrils. Jocelyn lay with her eyes shut, trying to remember why the silence of the room troubled her. She heard only the snap of twigs on the fire and the breathing of one person. *Where's my baby? Why don't I hear him crying?* Him? She didn't even know whether she had birthed a boy or a girl. And her husband –

Sweet Jesu, no! Hadwin is dead! Memory flooded back – Udolf, the outlaws – Opening her eyes, she stared up at the familiar soot-blackened underside of the thatched roof. *So they didn't burn us out.* Doubtless Udolf practiced thrift, leaving the village intact to produce more booty for him at some later time.

Tears stung her eyes and trickled, searing hot, down her cheeks. When she raised a hand to wipe her face, she realized she was lying on her mattress on the floor in her usual corner, loosely swathed in a length of cloth. She felt chilled despite the low-burning fire under the cauldron. As she started to turn on her side, a cramp seized her. She clutched the hollow curve of her abdomen. The emptiness burned. *Where is my baby?*

Beside the hearth-stone under the roof-hole in the center of the room, Gilda huddled on a stool, fingering the beads of her rosary. No sign of an infant. The details of the dim cottage looked strangely sharp, the fire a dazzling miniature sun, the candle's flame a shining spear-point. Still stranger, a rippling pink halo surrounded Gilda's body. Blinking, Jocelyn focused on her sister-in-law's face, marred by a bruise along the jawline. Gilda dozed over her prayers. Jocelyn tried to speak, but another pain wrenched her stomach and choked off the words. When the spasm passed, she heaved herself to her feet.

Gilda jerked awake, sprang up, and crossed herself over and over. "No – you're dead – saints and angels save me –"

Jocelyn leaped like a cat, grabbed Gilda by the shoulders, and gave her a brisk shake. "Stop that!"

Clasping the wooden beads in her left hand, the other woman swung the rosary like a whip, striking Jocelyn's bare shoulder with the crucifix. When Jocelyn only gazed at her in bewilderment, Gilda gave a low moan, dropped the talisman, and backed away to sag against the wall. Her bruised face looked clay-pale in the candlelight. "Your eyes – they glow –"

Jocelyn stared at her sister-in-law. What caused the rosy light that shone around her? *Is it something new?* Jocelyn wondered. *Or am I seeing what was always there?* "Stop raving, Gilda. Talk sense."

"You never woke again after – after the baby came. You died this morning. Father Martin baptized the child and anointed you. I washed your corpse and laid you out myself. We buried Hadwin today, and you're to be laid beside him tomorrow." As if the act of speaking calmed her fear a little, she edged away from the wall, righted the overturned stool, and sat down. "You can't be alive. You were cold, I tell you – stone cold!" Her voice rose to a shriek, then fell silent.

Suppressing her own fear and anger, Jocelyn pulled up the only other undamaged stool, not too close, and said, "That's madness. Don't I look like a live woman to you?" But she knew some terrible change had possessed her; if nothing else, her altered vision proved that. "Udolf – he did something to me. He said I wouldn't die."

A rapid nod from Gilda. Jocelyn saw her throat convulse several times before she could speak. "Some folk wanted you buried at the crossroads with a stake in your heart. But Father Martin wouldn't have it."

The Norman priest sent by the new Bishop was more tolerable than most of the interlopers; at least he spoke the Saxon tongue. "Wouldn't he? Why not?"

"Said it was nothing but foolish old wives' tales, and he wouldn't stand for having your body desecrated." Gilda added with a sickly smile, "He was wrong, wasn't he?"

Don't the Normans know about the walking dead? Jocelyn wasn't sure whether or not to be thankful for Father Martin's contempt for their country lore. If she had been snatched from death only to walk the earth as a demon in human shape – *But I don't feel like a demon! I'm still myself.* "Never mind Father Martin. Where is my baby?"

Gilda merely gaped at her, open-mouthed.

Jocelyn dug her nails into Gilda's shoulders. When droplets of blood oozed from the skin, the scent rising like incense in church at Easter, Jocelyn let go and stepped back, shaking. Another cramp racked her. "Is my child dead? Tell me the truth!"

Gilda shook her head. "No – not yet –"

Jocelyn clenched her fists at her sides. "Where is he? She?"

"He – Father Martin christened him Edward."

Jocelyn's eyes blurred with fresh tears. The saint whose name their parish church bore – perhaps it would serve as a charm of protection. "Where is Edward?" she whispered.

"I took him to the fairy stones."

"You did *what?*" Jocelyn gulped deep breaths, struggling to remember that this was her husband's sister, not an enemy she could strangle.

"The christening didn't help – everyone still thought he was a changeling. A devil's spawn. No wet nurse would have him. I begged every nursing mother in the village. He would have starved to death. This way is faster."

"How long? When did you take him?"

"This evening at sunset. Please, don't kill me –"

"Why would I kill you?" Turning from Gilda in disgust, Jocelyn started for the door. A glance downward, though, reminded her that she was clad only in a white winding sheet. "My clothes?" she hissed.

Gilda extended a tremulous hand toward the chest in the corner. "They didn't take our clothes – too shabby to barter for coin."

Jocelyn flung open the chest in the corner, pulled out a smock and her one kirtle of threadbare russet, and hastily dressed. She didn't see her shoes and decided the robbers must have judged them worth stealing. Thinking of her baby lying on the bare ground, she blinked back tears and snatched up her well-worn, gray cloak.

Gilda watched, mouth agape. "What are you doing?"

"Going to find my child, of course. Don't worry, I won't trouble you again – sister." Without another word, Jocelyn rushed from the cottage, leaving the door swinging behind her.

Before Udolf's invasion, fear would have kept her from setting foot anywhere near the fairy stones. Now, skimming over the moor at a pace that should have exhausted her within minutes yet left her unwearied, she allowed herself a bitter smile. Compared to such as Udolf, elf-haunted ruins merited scarcely a qualm.

Crickets chirped in the weeds; glancing toward the sound, she glimpsed tiny blue-green sparks. Through the scent of the heather, she caught a whiff of musty odors – rabbits, a fox – *How do I know that?* she wondered. Moths flitted in the hedgerows that bordered the fields; they, too, glittered with greenish light. Under the hedge a larger patch of light, red as an autumn sunset, arrested her attention. She froze, inhaling the scent that hovered around the vague shape. *Rabbit!* She hissed through her teeth. The rabbit darted out of its shelter.

Driven by a need that overrode thought, Jocelyn pounced on the animal. A scarlet mist clouded her vision. Seconds later, a hot, salt-sweet liquid poured into her mouth. She found herself kneeling on the ground, her teeth gnawing into the rabbit's side. Jumping up, she flung the furry corpse away from her. *I drank its blood! What am I? Walking dead – demon –*

Jocelyn shook herself and wiped the smear of blood from her lips. No time for such thoughts now. She had to get to the ruins and save her child.

She found the place easily enough, marked by dozens of tumbledown stone rings. A few of the beehive-shaped huts still retained their roofs. Poised on tiptoe, she listened. She heard no sound aside from the burr of insects in the weeds. *Is he dead? How long can a newborn babe live without milk?* She had no idea. She began a slow circuit of the ruins, suppressing the urge to call his name. *Edward.* At less than two days old, he could hardly answer.

A weak cry, more like a kitten's mew than a human voice, emanated from one of the roofed huts. She dashed inside it. The deeper darkness foiled her sight for no more than a few seconds. Her eyes adjusted, to reveal a squirming bundle on a stone slab in the middle of the small chamber.

Falling to her knees, Jocelyn ran her hands over the swaddled body. The tightly wrapped bands of cloth were soaked. "He's alive!" Sobbing his name, she scooped up the baby and hugged him to her breast. Why hadn't she thought to bring fresh swaddling clothes? *I'll have to take him home and* –

No. She'd forgotten that she had to stay away from her former neighbors. If anyone except Gilda knew she had revived, they would pound a stake into her or chop off her head, then abandon Edward to the wild beasts – or the Fair Folk, if such really stalked here. *Then we'll go somewhere else, where nobody knows us. But I must think first – must rest.*

After stripping off the wet cloth, she wrapped the baby in the cloak she had brought. That would soon get soiled, too; she would have to scrounge supplies from somewhere. When she rocked the baby in her arms, he momentarily stopped crying. She gazed down at him, squinting through the rosy glow that outlined his shape. A fine brown fuzz covered his head. He yawned, exposing toothless gums, and turned his head to nuzzle the coarse fabric of her bodice. With a frustrated wail, he stared up at her as if in reproach. In his deep blue eyes, tiny sparks gleamed.

What's that? Something else I see because my own vision has changed? No, she had glimpsed no such fire in Gilda's eyes. *Udolf's blood has tainted him, too! No wonder they thought he was a changeling!*

But surely the baptismal water must have canceled any taint. This was no time to worry about that, anyway. He was starving. Jocelyn tugged down one shoulder of her loose kirtle to expose her left breast. When she stroked Edward's cheek as she had seen new mothers do, he again turned to root at her bosom. His mouth clamped onto her nipple with startling force. Hissing, she hugged him tighter.

After a moment's hard sucking, he pulled his head back and screamed. She pressed him close again and coaxed him with incoherent whispers. When she switched him to the other side, he tried to nurse on the right breast but almost immediately gave up, with an outraged cry.

Moaning, she rocked back and forth, while scorching tears trickled down her cheeks. *No milk! I can't feed him!* Of course dead breasts couldn't nourish an infant, and Jocelyn knew she was somehow dead, although she walked, spoke, and felt. Anger at Udolf twisted her gut like

9

a physical pain. She paced the confined circle of the stone hut, jiggling the baby to quiet him. "Don't worry, I'll get food for you. You wait here, I won't be long." She laid him on the rock platform, hoping he would tire himself and stop crying. She reminded herself that people feared this place too much to come near it, especially at night. Edward would be safe for now.

When she crept near the village on the side farthest from her former home, she found she would have to cross the stream near the mill. She hesitated, recalling tales that witches and demons couldn't cross running water. *Surely I'm not a demon – Gilda's crucifix didn't hurt me.* Lifting the hem of her kirtle, she stepped into the stream. The rapids chilled her bare feet but didn't hurt. She paused to rinse her hands and face and smooth her tangled hair.

As she stalked toward the miller's substantial cottage, a rank smell filled her nostrils. A dog, with its muzzle gaping in a snarl. It warily approached her, ears back, tail waving stiffly, and let out a warning bark.

"Quiet! Hush!" She flapped her hands at the shaggy, black-and-white mongrel. When she gazed into its eyes, it sank onto its belly, glaring up at her. "Yes, that's it." She cringed at her own whisper, which sounded too loud in the silent darkness. To her surprise, the dog rolled on its back, exposing its nearly hairless abdomen.

This beast, too, was surrounded by a luminous halo. Its wet-hair smell no longer repelled her. Entranced, she sank to her knees beside the dog and bit into the tender skin of the underbelly. Again, salt-sweet elixir trickled into her mouth. She sucked until the thunder of the dog's heart-beat ceased to pound in her ears.

When she stood up, her stomach no longer cramped. She noticed that the reddish light had faded from the animal's body. *That glow must have been his life, and I stole it!* No longer distracted by the hollowness at her core, she recognized the mongrel as the miller's watchdog. *Later, Mother Mary help me, I'll do penance later.* At the moment, she blessed the dog for lending her strength to do what she must for Edward.

She slinked up to the miller's house, large compared to hers. He kept two cows, both with calves beside them in the byre. Now thankful for the chance encounter that had disposed of the watchdog, Jocelyn edged nearer to the fence. The livestock stood huddled next to the house. So Udolf and his men had contented themselves with easy, though poor, prey instead of risking an attack on this better-guarded holding. *Cowards!* The cattle shifted their feet and flicked their tails, while the geese rustled in their pen. "Hush," Jocelyn whispered. "Please be quiet – oh, please."

The geese settled down, and the cows turned their wide, dark eyes upon her. She bent over to crawl through the fence, then laid her open palm on the nearest cow's flank. "Good lass, sweet lady, I won't hurt you." She ran her hands over each animal in turn, humming a barely audible lullaby, until each one's head drooped in slumber. If this power came from Satan, Jocelyn would risk her soul to use the magic to feed her baby.

Glancing around, she caught sight of a wooden bucket in the corner. She knelt in the dirt to milk one of the cows, who stood in a doze until Jocelyn finished the job. The tightness in her chest eased after she had set the bucket on the other side of the fence and slipped away with it, safely out of earshot of the miller's house. At least she had milk now, even if she wasn't sure how she would get it into the baby's stomach.

On her way to the stream, she glimpsed something white fluttering in the dooryard of a neighboring cottage. A quick inspection revealed two smocks drying on a gate. *How careless,* she thought, *to leave laundry out all night to be dampened by the morning dew.* The cloth was just what she needed to replace the soaked swaddling bands. She rolled up the garments and hurried on her way.

By the time she came in sight of the fairy stones, the sky was turning gray. Something stung her arms and face, like heat from standing too close to a fire. The growing light made her head ache. She quickened her pace and scurried into the shelter of the hut.

Her throat tightened with fear when she realized she hadn't heard a cry from Edward. One glance, though, showed her that the life-halo still clung to him, like the haloes around the plump child-angels in the windows of the church at Highmarket. Was the pink glow becoming weaker, paler? When she picked him up, he woke with a feeble whimper. Her hands shaking, Jocelyn tore one of the smocks into strips and swaddled him, then covered him with a dry corner of the cloak.

While he lay on her lap against the far back wall of the hut, out of reach of the creeping daylight, she twisted a spare scrap of cloth into a nipple-like shape and dipped it in the milk. The baby sucked avidly, complaining whenever she had to remove the cloth to dip it again. With painful slowness she fed him, until at last he dropped asleep. She laid him against the wall, snugly tucked in the cloak. She covered the bucket with the remaining smock, to protect the milk from flies.

"Tonight we'll go away," she whispered. A strange heaviness weighed on her limbs; she was not immune to exhaustion, after all. "Tonight when we're rested, and nobody will see us. We'll go to Highmarket, where nobody knows who we are." She knew they couldn't stay in one place long, for a solitary beggar woman with an infant would attract too much attention. And how could she handle the usual field chores of a wandering laborer, if the sun burned her skin? But she would think of something, and meanwhile she had to get away from here, where people knew her as a "demon." Perhaps she could work her way south to still larger towns, maybe even to Londinium.

She lay down with the baby, huddled in the deepest of shadows, and sank into oblivion.

She woke to Edward's thin cry. She sat up quickly, a cold grip clutching her heart and stomach. Sucking a deep breath, she looked wildly around the cramped space. *What – where am I?* This time memory flashed back within seconds.

Gathering up the baby, she gazed at his face. The sun had recently set, and as twilight yielded to darkness, the sparks she had noticed in Edward's eyes became clear again. When strangers saw that, might they reject him as a changeling, too? On the other hand, they wouldn't know he had been tainted by Udolf's blood at the moment of birth. Given the proper hints, they might see the baby's bright eyes as a miracle, a blessing from his patron saint.

Setting that worry aside, she uncovered the milk pail and began the slow process of feeding him. The milk smelled a little sour but not repellently so, and Edward didn't seem to mind. When he had finished, Jocelyn wrapped him in fresh rags. She noticed a deeper, brighter hue in the light that surrounded him. His life-glow, as she had come to think of it.

Thank God, he's getting stronger. Mentally invoking the Holy Name caused her no distress, no more than the cross or the running stream. She wondered what other beliefs about Udolf's kind might prove false.

As she stared at the baby, she became aware of a sound drumming in her ears. A rhythmic throb that lured her to lean close and absorb it, like inhaling the fragrance of a newly opened rosebud. *His heart,* she realized. *I can hear his heartbeat.* Cold teeth gnawed at her insides.

I'm hungry.

She realized her lips were brushing the baby's forehead and skimming over his cheek to his throat. With a convulsive shudder, she thrust him away from her and leaped up, backing toward the doorway. "No – I won't – Blessed Virgin, don't let me –"

Dashing outside, she fell to her knees in the tall grass. Her fingers, clawlike, kneaded her abdomen, as if she could crush the hunger pangs like a nest of wasps. "Please don't let me hurt him!" She would have to find another animal to drink from. Abomination, yes, but better than killing her own child.

The feel of another presence, like a chill wind, cut across her misery. She scrambled to her feet and rubbed the burning tears from her eyes. A tall, dark figure glided toward her over the moor.

When it came close enough for her to distinguish the fiery eyes, she knew who it was. Udolf the Red! Alone this time, without his band of robbers. Jocelyn retreated into the hut.

He called to her from outside, in a low voice that nevertheless echoed in her head. "You can't hide from me, little mother. And what are you afraid of? I've come to help."

"Go away and leave me alone!" She wrapped her arms around her chest to subdue the shivering that possessed her.

"Leave you to blunder along the way you probably did last night?" Udolf stepped inside, bending to keep from hitting his head on the arch. "You should thank me for coming back. I wasn't sure you would rise, but here you are. You're a strong one."

He has no halo! He's a walking corpse! The thought roused a surge of anguish. *And so am I!* Jocelyn backed against the stone slab. "What do you want from me?" Her mind reeled with images of the night of Edward's birth and the terror of staying trapped in that nightmare forever.

He grinned with his wolflike teeth. "To teach you our ways. Isn't it my duty to show kindness to a widowed goodwife?"

"I don't want anything from you!" Her fingers curled into claws.

"Our band could use a strong fighter like you – a spitfire Saxon wench with a proper hate for the Norman scum."

Brazen liar! "You don't fight the Normans. You ravage your own people."

"You begrudge supplies for my men? They have to eat. After all, they're only human, not like us." He inched closer as he spoke. "Well, we can talk about that later." His glowing eyes darted around the room. "A clever wench, too. You've brought food."

It took her a second to realize how he stared at the baby, who lay on the ground, fretting. Udolf was already striding toward Edward when she woke into action.

Grabbing the only weapon at hand, the wooden bucket, she flung it into his face. The dregs of the milk splashed in his eyes, and the blow cut open his forehead. His eyes went blank with astonishment. The pungent aroma of his blood permeated the air like a crimson fog. As he stumbled, Jocelyn leaped upon him. Her weight bore him to the ground, his head crashing against the stone wall as he fell.

Her lips twitched back from her teeth. A maddening heat tingled in her jaws. She ripped into Udolf's neck. Blood spurted, flooding her mouth with an intoxicating flavor like potent mead. Rainbow hued lightnings flashed in her head. Thirst drowned all thought, and she gorged until the flow slacked to a trickle. Faintly she heard choked cries from Udolf and felt his body heave under her, but she ignored those distractions.

When she stood up, sore from bruises and scratches he must have inflicted before losing consciousness, the robber lay still. She couldn't tell whether he was dead. Since he had no life-light to begin with, its absence told her nothing. Staggering to Edward's side, she picked him up and swayed with him until he stopped whimpering. "We have to leave here," she whispered. "Right now!"

Outside, she gazed up at the waxing moon. She would have a clear night for her walk to Highmarket; they ought to reach it before dawn. The baby squirmed in her arms. His warmth reminded her of the ravenous need that had ruled her only moments before. She swallowed the sob that rose in her throat. "I can't take care of you, can I? You could never be really safe with me."

In the market town, where nobody knew the baby's origin, surely some family would take him in. Someone would give him the home he needed, instead of a vagabond life with a mother who had become a demon-beast. *I'll leave him at a church. The priest will find him a haven, even if it has to be a convent.*

And what of herself? Jocelyn's future stretched before her as barren as a winter field, but Father Martin preached that self-destruction – even if she'd known how to destroy herself – was a sin. Once she had provided for her child, she would have to do penance for what she had become. Perhaps that way she would find rest.

She kissed the baby on the forehead, settled him firmly in her arms, and started walking.

Before A Fall

By Barb Hendee

The fortress often grew cold at night, but Christopher seldom noticed. He sat at a small table working on yearly accounts. The door opened, but he knew who was there and didn't bother looking up.

"Christopher?" a troubled voice said.

Two things made him raise his head quickly to a lovely olive-skinned woman wearing a tan dress. First, Margaritte rarely used his given name, preferring to support the illusion that he was the lord and she served him. Secondly, because in the seven years he'd known her, she'd never once sounded troubled.

"What's wrong?" he asked.

Her eyes wouldn't meet his as she searched for words. "I think we have a visitor roaming the villages."

"Has someone been feeding carelessly?"

"No."

Standing up, he felt an unaccustomed nervousness creep in. "Margaritte, has one of the peasants been killed?"

"No, I'm not sure, but I heard . . . ." She trailed off. "You'd better come."

The hovel Christopher entered was warmer than Creale – his fortress – but still chilly from the autumn air. However, he only thought such a thing because several people in tattered rags stood shivering. He so rarely interacted with the peasants who served him, that for a moment he said nothing at all. He counted one sickly looking man and two middle-aged women staring at him in fear, all taking in the sight of his green tunic and long, wool cape. These people hadn't called on him, and they certainly didn't want him here.

The sight of Christopher made most serfs cower. Neither handsome nor ugly, the two words most often ascribed to him were tall and solid. Though born in Italy, he had a French nose with a small bump at the bridge. His short, black hair and beardless face, combined with a cold, businesslike manner and the sword at his side, projected the aura of a professional soldier.

The peasants stood, almost on guard, in front of the reason for his visit. Lying on a makeshift bed mat, a half-conscious teenage girl tossed and moaned, crying out once or twice. Her teeth rattled, and occasionally she made a gargling sound.

"My lord," the man said, as both women lowered their eyes.

Margaritte stepped from behind Christopher and walked through the room, sitting down next to the girl. She touched the girl's wrists and head, then turned back toward him with a slight nod. But he already knew the truth and didn't ask her any questions.

"What is wrong with young Eliza, my lord," one of the women dared ask.

"How long has she been like this?"

"Since last night, after Saint Catherine's feast," the woman answered. "We couldn't find her." She paused. "The mead was flowing, and then Mark saw her lying in the field. She won't eat. She won't drink. She won't talk. She has no fever, but tosses and cries as if out of her head."

Christopher nodded. Then he walked over and picked up the girl. She bounced once in his arms from the force of being lifted too quickly, and he pulled her to his chest. Margaritte tucked a torn blanket around her shaking form. The old man stepped forward.

"What are you doing, my lord?" he asked.

"She's ill. I'm taking her back to Creale for proper care."

A woman began to weep. "No, please don't take her . . ."

He gazed at her tears briefly and then left the hovel, carrying the girl. Charity allowed him to forgive the woman's ignorance and attempt to contradict him. Such a display was quite pointless. No one could stop him – and he knew it.

Back at the fortress, Christopher sat facing a large bed watching Margaritte feed the girl, Eliza, from her own wrist. In any other setting, they might have been mother and daughter, except of course the elixir used to nurse Eliza was blood, not milk or spoon fed mutton stew. Margaritte surprised him. On occasion, his only undead companion displayed brief flashes of compassion, but he couldn't focus on her gentle care of the unfortunate creature right now. He was angry.

Christopher Travinne liked order. He didn't like uncertainty or any scrap of existence falling outside his control. Received into the quiet world of night dwellers a scant hundred years ago, he'd worked hard to attain his current position and considered himself somewhat unique. In his early years as a vampire, he disappeared from mortal view, living with his sire in Italy. As time passed, a driving ambition welled up inside him to dominate mortals on their own terms; he would never rule from the shadows, relying only on his unnatural powers. As a mortal, he had fought in the first Crusade against the Seljuk Turks. But recently, the French/English Crusades to retake Jerusalem provided a new opportunity, and he quickly distinguished himself in the ranks of Lord Roger Martel, who served King Philip II.

Christopher trained a small band of men and earned a reputation as a night raider, slaughtering more infidels than any knight under Martel. While Jerusalem was not recovered, Christopher was among those who gained favor for his military abilities. Of course, he could not ride all day with the main body of soldiers – but found methods to escape gossip. Due to the great age and power of his sire, he could withstand daylight for short periods of time, even several hours on cloudy days, although it tired him, and his troupe found nothing odd about traveling at night, since they usually attacked under the cover of darkness. Besides, Christopher claimed Italian bloodlines and many from that land were known to prefer night life, where revelry often did not begin until the moon rose.

Upon returning to France seven years ago, he was considered Lord Martel's favorite and after swearing vassalage, was appointed a fiefdom between Dijoin and Orleans of four hundred acres. These were Martel's own lands, given to him by Philip, but Martel preferred living in his family home nearer to court and so granted Christopher Travinne the honor of retaining such holdings.

Christopher took his position very seriously. It was an important rung upon the political ladder. He collected rents and protected the people under him.

Now, watching Margaritte with Eliza, *his* serf, he felt almost powerless. This past week seemed to bring one tragedy after another. Four days ago, the parish priest, Father Edward, vanished, and so far, none of Christopher's soldiers managed to locate a trace of him. He'd been a good priest, slightly corrupt, who minded his own business and looked over the peasants well.

And now some half-witted vampire had turned a peasant girl only to leave her lying in a field – without a word. Christopher kept expecting her eyes to clear and her shivering to stop, but even after feeding from Margaritte, she looked lost and a bit mad, unable to speak.

"What's wrong with her?" he asked.

"I don't know. I've never seen anyone respond like this." Margaritte shook her head, a few stands of dark hair falling in her face. "It's as if she's caught somewhere between mortal and immortal. Come look. What do you think?"

Christopher stood up and went to the bed. Eliza's hair was red-brown, and through dirty streaks on her face he could see a pale complexion. She might even be pretty when cleaned up. But everything about this situation felt wrong to him. He didn't believe peasants should ever be turned, and nothing in her manner or appearance gave him a clue as to who was responsible.

He turned to leave. "I'll put some guards on night patrol."

Margaritte's eyebrows raised. "What good will that do?"

"Make the serfs rest easier until I find out what's happening." He motioned to Eliza. "You'll take care of her?"

"Of course."

※※

Two days later, past midnight, the mystery solved itself. Margaritte was with him on the ground floor of Creale, sitting in the cavernous hall his guards used for eating and gaming in the evenings. It was heated by an open, central hearth bordered with stone, and the floor was strewn with rushes which Margaritte often had replaced. Now the guards either slept in their barracks or patrolled the villages.

"Eliza's starting to talk," Margaritte said, "but still doesn't know, or understand, what happened to her. She drank some mead at celebration and can't recall anything until waking up in my arms yesterday. I'm not sure how much to tell her yet."

Although unable to express it, Christopher felt profound relief that Margaritte was handling this unpleasant situation. He honestly wasn't sure he could. While the hearth had died down, embers glowed against the side of her face, making her flesh appear warm. For the hundredth time, he thanked fate for her presence.

Years ago, upon his arrival to take over Creale, he'd been astonished to find the house overseer a vampire with goals of her own. Unlike him, she preferred whispering in Lord Martel's ear and sought to create a safe haven by making herself indispensable. In a world where a vampire alone in the streets might be caught feeding – and burned by mad peasants – a home and a disguise and a protector were all necessities.

Christopher, on the other hand, sought a world with financial and political advantages. He would obey his undead sire without question if the need arose, but he didn't want help from anyone and raised himself to a position of power through deeds. Margaritte had thought him vain at first and treated him with absolute disdain, but after a tenuous beginning, the two found value in each other and now depended on the other's counsel.

There were nights when he believed he may already possess everything he ever wanted: power, respect, wealth, a comfortable haven, proxy ownership of numerous serfs for his own purposes, and even the pleasant companionship of his own kind.

"What do you think is wrong with the girl?" he asked.

"I don't know. That's the strange part. It's almost as if she is incomplete, half-turned, but I've never seen anything like this before."

Before he could question further, Corin, one of his men, appeared in the doorway. "I'm sorry to disturb you, my lord, but there's someone asking admittance."

"At this hour?"

"He's a monk."

Christopher stood up. "Show him in."

Perhaps a member of the clergy had word of Father Edward. By the time Christopher turned around, Margaritte was gone. He knew she would listen from somewhere in the shadows. That was her way.

Waiting to greet his visitor, Christopher suddenly realized he sensed only Corin coming back into the hall. He could smell Corin's warmth beating just beneath the skin, but the other entrant was a heatless form, another vampire, wearing the white habit of a Cistercian monk.

"Go back to your post," Christopher told Corin immediately. Then he looked impassively at the Cistercian, waiting, not racing to conclusions.

"I'm Father Luke of Clairvoux," his visitor said in a soft tone. "I've come to offer my services."

"Services?"

Father Luke came forward, pulling a letter from his habit. "Yes, I have a letter of introduction from Bishop Cresieme of Gascony. I wish to serve as pastor of Creale's flock until word of your missing Father Edward becomes known."

Christopher remained where he was, arms at his sides. "Does the letter name you as his successor? Give you leave to take the parish?"

"No." Luke almost smiled. He was smaller than Christopher, thinner, with light brown hair and greenish-yellow eyes. His narrow, slightly pock-marked face hid all trace of emotion besides gentle concern. "It only confirms my credentials and recent ordination. I hoped you would assist me in establishing a place here."

Inside the hearth lay nothing but dying embers. Christopher's arms left his sides, and he crossed them over his chest. "And how would I do that?"

"Quite simply really. You write a letter to the Roman Curia expressing your wish to have me instated. Your Lord Martel is nearly worshipped in the French court, and you are his voice here. My superiors would be pleased to grant his wish."

With no idea what to make of the situation, Christopher dropped the polite pretense. "I can tell you're young. You haven't even lived out one lifetime yet, have you?"

"Is that important?"

"Yes, if you want my help."

Father Luke's face flickered slightly at the word "help." Christopher wanted to give him hope.

But Luke only answered, "Yes, I am still young . . . although that means little. I've honed my powers rapidly and lack neither drive nor ambition. This parish above all others is the place I wish to serve."

"Why?"

"Because clergymen don't rise in status through good works, they rise from generous donations brought to the church. Your lord is one of the richest men in France. You will invite me to supper when Lord Martel visits you, and I will do the rest . . . I can be very persuasive."

Either this upstart whelp was quite clever or quite foolish. Christopher couldn't tell which. "Why are you telling me this? Why state your plans so openly?"

"To show good faith." Luke held both hands out, palms pointed upward. "We will be joined by land and lord, and I keep nothing from you."

One move too far, Christopher thought. "All right. Did you kill

Father Edward?"

For the first time, Luke hesitated, then smiled again. "He was inconvenient."

"And that girl I've got upstairs? Did you turn her?"

"The peasants need church protection to keep them safe from such evil. Fear of the unknown is a good weapon."

"Then why not just drain her? Or why not turn her and stay to assist? To teach?"

Again, the monk faltered, as though weighing how far he should go. "Because I wanted you to know what I am capable of. I drained her blood and then fed her some of my own, but not enough. She'll be locked forever between two states of being – never quite sure where or what she is. Life could become very unpleasant for your serfs if I'm not pleased. There is no act I won't commit, no commandment I won't break. I wish to serve in this parish."

The disgust and anger inside Christopher slipped into his voice. "Do you threaten me? I earned my position through deeds, not by tormenting those who can't defend themselves. You seek power without earning it, hurting the weak to create an illusion of strength."

His sudden change of demeanor threw the monk off balance.

"I have worked within the confines of the church long enough to earn ordination," Luke almost stammered. Then his confidence returned. "Helping me brings no harm or hardship to you. Indeed, it can only strengthen your place here. Imagine what might happen if the church sent out a true holy man."

For an answer, Christopher walked over to the wall and took down a polished long sword. "I would throw myself onto a burning pyre before putting an irresponsible pup like you in charge of this parish. Do you understand?"

The blank, stunned expression on Father Luke's face was almost amusing. Apparently he thought his hand well played and deadly serious. Christopher did not.

"Get off my lands before I take your head and fling it from the tower. I'd do it now, but I don't need any more missing clergy to explain," Christopher said in dismissal. "If I see you again, or if you cause any more grief, I promise it will be the last time."

The monk took two steps back in confusion. He seemed to find Christopher's reaction unbelievable.

"You think you can just send me away?" Luke asked. "You think it's that simple? My lord . . ." his voice echoed with sarcasm, "You should reconsider both your decision and your tone, or you may end up on that burning pyre yet."

It was Christopher's turn to be openly surprised. "You think to frighten me?"

This fool didn't have a wit in his head. Christopher was the acting lord of Creale. His word was the law, no matter what he ordered. What did some greedy little undead charlatan think he could do?

Sword pointed casually, he moved toward Father Luke, determination coloring his face. "Get out."

For the time it takes a candle to flicker and die, the monk's eyes narrowed as if he planned to fight. Exactly how remained a complete mystery to Christopher, but then the small invader turned to flee. Christopher chased him as far as the outer door. There he stopped but remained watching until his visitor ran past Corin and disappeared into the night.

Corin blinked. "Did you just run off a Cistercian?"

"Yes, and if he comes back, don't talk to him. Come get me."

"Do you think he'll come back?"

"No."

Fear of excommunication made almost everyone terrified to stand up to the clergy. Christopher knew Corin would gladly follow his order, and so he went back inside to the main hall and called out for Margaritte.

"Did you hear all that?"

She stepped in from nowhere, holding her dress off the floor, a thoughtful expression on her face. "Yes, every word. You handled it badly."

"What do you mean?"

Her dark hair was now partially unpinned and hanging in long wisps around her face. "Christopher, you pretended you'd help him, and he shared his plans. Then you bullied him into threatening you, and after all that you let him keep his head."

"He's nothing. A foolish whelp, seeking positions he hasn't earned."

She frowned, but walked forward, reached up, and grasped his arm with both hands. Had he not known better, he would have considered the gesture protective.

"You underestimate everyone," she said. "It's your only real weakness."

"Stop worrying. He's gone."

But she only gazed at the empty doorway and didn't answer.

A week later, Christopher rode home after feeding, and his world seemed back to its usual state of comfortable control. He and Margaritte were both careful about feeding, establishing no patterns, leaving no obvious marks, rarely killing, but rather allowing peasants no memory of the event.

The only hindrance to perfect order at Creale was the girl, Eliza. Although she grew more coherent every night, and Margaritte was teaching her to survive, both older vampires knew something wasn't quite right and discussed it at length.

He was astonished when Margaritte suggested he write to his sire in Italy, seeking information.

"I've heard stories of those half-turned, but know little of their existence. Only someone much older might offer us help," Margaritte said.

Christopher refused, almost angrily. He would rather see Eliza as an immortal invalid than ask his sire – or anyone else – for assistance. Fierce independence was part of his nature, and he understood that about himself. But, at the same time, concern grew in the back of his mind. Eliza's welcome here might soon become a problem. The population of his lands supported two blood drinkers adequately. Three were too many.

Such were his thoughts that night as he rode home. Reaching the bridge to Creale, he noticed a small crowd standing, waiting. When he pulled up his horse, faces turned to see him and figures cowered away. Out in front was someone he vaguely recognized . . . oh, the sickly man from Eliza's hovel. Corin said he'd come several times inquiring about his daughter during the day.

Whatever was wrong, it would be better if the guards handled it. He had no call to speak to them and was about to turn his horse toward the stable when Corin came jogging across the bridge, his skin pale. Christopher dismounted quickly.

"What's happened?"

Corin shook his head. "Too much to tell, my lord. After you left, that Cistercian monk came with a group of Benedictines and Norman guards. They'd already been to the villages asking questions. The priests all went upstairs to the girl's room."

"What? You let them in?"

"My lord." Corin stared at him. "They are men of God."

Christopher left his horse standing and moved quickly across the bridge. Hissing sounds from the peasants followed after. He couldn't begin to speculate why his home had been invaded by the clergy.

Several of his guards, including Corin, fell in behind him as he entered the main hall. The size of the group had not been exaggerated.

Father Luke, four Benedictine priests, and seven Norman guards stood awaiting his arrival. Margaritte was nowhere in sight.

Christopher took off his gloves. "Can I help you?"

One of the Benedictines, an aged man wearing a wooden cross, said, "Yes, you will come with us to Anjou tonight."

"And you are?"

"Father Ramarre of Anjou. We will leave now."

The situation was becoming obvious, but Luke had a shock coming if he thought Christopher would let himself be arrested. "I have duties here, Father. I'm afraid traveling is out of the question."

"Do not resist," Father Ramarre said, "Or you and anyone who assists you is in danger of excommunication."

"What am I charged with?"

"Conspiring with the devil. You corrupted a young girl and made her join with you in black arts. She has already confessed to drinking your blood, and her father attests you took her from his house after stealing her soul."

A mix of discomfort and anger hit Christopher as he turned to Luke, the white-robed Cistercian vampire. "What did you do to her? Did you threaten her? Did you promise her safety if she'd sign a confession?"

"She spoke willingly without torture," Father Ramarre answered coldly. "We only wish to question you, examine you before a tribunal. Some say there is no life in your body. Others say you live only at night. This, combined with testimony from the girl, warrants investigation. You stand guard over many poor souls, and we must be cautious. If you are innocent, you have nothing to fear."

"Perhaps you ought to investigate your own people before nipping at my heels," Christopher answered, pointing at Father Luke. "He's the one who brought these 'charges' to your attention, is he not?"

This was a dangerous game. Making accusations would not pull all attention off himself, nor save himself, but he had no other recourse at the moment. His words had no effect on the Benedictines; moreover, they did not seem to even hear him. Several of the Norman guards stepped forward, but the leader's face was lined in worry. Arresting Lord Martel's vassal in his own fortress could have repercussions later. Disobeying the clergy could warrant excommunication.

Christopher looked at Corin and saw the same battle in his eyes. He had a duty to his lord, but must obey the church. At the same time, Christopher knew if he ordered his men to fight, such an act would only make him look guilty.

He cast a glance of hatred at the Cistercian, then turned his full attention onto Father Ramarre, holding the priest's gaze tightly. "I don't think you want me in Anjou," he said. "I think you have made a mistake."

Resorting to unnatural powers annoyed him since he was the fortress lord and should simply be obeyed, but no other options remained open. His ability to mentally dominate mortals was quite honed even though he only used it to feed.

However, again, Father Ramarre did not appear to even hear his words and nodded to the Norman guards. Father Luke's mouth twisted slightly at the corners. Christopher tensed in surprise. What was happening? Some undead whelp's mental control could not possibly be this strong.

Corin looked at his lord hopelessly as if to say, "What do I do?"

If Christopher fought, he would look guilty. If he escaped – which he was capable of – he would look guilty.

"Stand down," he said to Corin. "Just send word to Lord Martel. He is staying in Orleans this month, and he will deal with this matter. These priests will know their error soon enough."

When Martel and King Philip heard of this, Father Luke would have greater concerns than simply acquiring a parish.

Hearing audible sighs of relief from his men, Christopher allowed himself to be led away.

A week later, he rolled over on the floor of his cell, knowing a demand for his release would not be long now. He hadn't fed, but wasn't suffering yet. The darkness of his cell pleased him, and except for the filthy conditions, he had no complaints. He knew he wouldn't be here long. Neither the Benedictines nor the Cistercians could accuse a lord with his connections of devil worship and expect a tribunal to come to fruition.

"How are you faring, my lord?" a quiet voice whispered.

He sat up. "Margaritte?"

She stood at the door of this cell, her olive complexion a little wan. "You actually look well."

"How did you get down here?" he asked and then realized it was a stupid question. Margaritte blended with the shadows.

"I came in with the women who bring food, slipped away, and put your guard to sleep." She paused, rattling something in her hands. "Come, quickly. You have to get away from here."

He blinked. "I can't run. If I do, I'll lose everything."

"If you stay, they'll burn you."

"Shhhhh," he whispered, walking to the door. "Stop. They aren't going to burn me. What news has come from Martel?"

"Christopher, will you listen to yourself." Her expression grew hard. "Have you been playing the mortal lord so long you've forgotten what you are? No life pounds in your veins. Father Ramarre hasn't attained permission from the Papal States to examine your body yet, but he will. The Benedictines have already examined Eliza, and they are frightened."

"Eliza? Where is she?"

"She's here. Didn't you know? They took her away before you even got home that night."

Hatred for the Cistercian monk kept growing inside him. "He's going to let them burn his own progeny? I can hardly believe that, even of him."

A sound clicked, and Margaritte opened the door. In her hand was a ring of old, rusty keys. "Hurry. We'll have to get her."

How could he make Margaritte understand. "Don't you see? I can't run. Lord Martel will act soon. We have to follow mortal laws if I'm to retain a mortal position."

He noticed she wore the dusky blue dress he'd always liked. She shook her head, wordless for a moment.

"You've been released from vassalage," she said. "Corin will hold Creale and the lands until Martel appoints a suitable replacement."

Confusion made Christopher step back. "What are you saying?"

"You are alone. Martel had no choice. The Benedictines have a signed confession from a girl who wasn't even tortured. I think Luke promised her protection and afterwards had her arrested, or maybe she can't help but obey him. Then the priests caught her drinking blood four days ago from a rat in her cell, and they hold you responsible. Creale's parish priest has disappeared, and the peasants are afraid. Your liege lord can't help you. King Philip can't help you. They both want to distance themselves as far from this business as possible."

Shaking slightly, Christopher walked over to his only piece of furniture – a small bench – and sat down. "I have nowhere to go. No horse of my own. I have no money but the few coins in my pocket. Margaritte, where will we go?"

She looked away. "I can't leave Creale. I've worked too hard for my position there. It's my home now."

"Even you?" he whispered.

Holding out a brown hooded cloak, she said, "Put this on. We'll have to get Eliza, and then take all memory from the guards. I know of a door on the ground level."

He remained sitting, unmoving.

She walked over and shook him. "We have to go now! And I need your help to get us all out."

"I have nothing."

"You have your body intact."

"My face is known among the important nobles," he said. "I can't go back to the military."

"Then do something else for fifty years." She paused. "Maybe you could ask help from . . . those in Italy."

"No," he snapped. "I'm not crawling to my sire."

She knelt down. "We'll, you're going to need help from someone. For now, can we not please just leave this place?"

He stood back up, numb and uncertain. "Show me where to go."

❖

Past midnight, the Cistercian chapel at Anjou stood empty save one occupant. Christopher stood in the doorway watching a single white-robed monk who was busy lighting more candles to read by. This was a plain, humble chapel, adorned only by a wooden cross at the front alter, white candles, and a few benches, not a place suitable for an ambitious soul like Luke of Clairvoux.

"Bless me, Father, for I have sinned," Christopher said.

The vampire monk's head jerked up from his book. A flicker of surprise crossed his face and disappeared just as quickly. He kept his emotions well guarded. Even Christopher would grant him that. Luke's eyes lowered to the plain short sword his visitor was carrying.

"Where did you get that?"

"Took it from a sleeping guard," Christopher answered.

"Your little Margaritte got you out, then? That crossed my mind, but I thought in the end she'd let you rot. I've met her type. She's a coward you know, fooling herself with noble airs." He looked around. "Where is she now? In the corner perhaps?"

"No, she's gone back to Creale, to live with everything else that matters to me." Christopher entered the chapel calmly. "You've taken it all. There's nothing left."

Luke faced him in defensive pose, holding one hand up with fingers curled slightly. "And you think destroying me – not that I'm saying you could – will gain your position back? Your power? The trust of your liege lord?"

Christopher stopped right in front of Luke, feeling so dead inside he no longer even hated. "No, but you're going to disappear like Father Edward. You have a few things of value that I want."

"Like what?"

"Like your monk's habit."

As those words left Christopher's mouth, something solid slammed into the back of his head, pitching him forward. He hit the ground and rolled halfway back up, in time to see a bench continue flying across the room to collide with the cross. His head began bleeding.

"You think everything can be accomplished with a sword," Luke spit, pock-marked chin tight with anger. "I could have fought you at Creale, but chose to run just so I could see the look on your face when Martel abandoned you. Pity, I missed the moment didn't I, or you wouldn't be here?"

Moving faster than most mortals can see, Christopher lunged at him, aiming the sword point at his throat. Luke tripped backward, but managed to stop the blade in mid-air, holding it by some invisible force a breath away from his collar bone. Christopher's shoulder strained to push through, as he labored for focus, for balance. Having never fought anyone who could move objects through the air at will, he half-expected burning candles to come flying at him and the image was frightening. He struggled to ignore any thought besides driving through Luke's defense. An expression of concentration on the monk's pock-marked face grew intense, as if holding off the sword expended great energy. Perhaps he couldn't focus on anything else.

Christopher kicked him in the side hard enough to crack ribs. At that moment, pressure on the blade released, and Christopher jerked it up high, swinging it back down with practiced control.

Luke's head rolled across the chapel floor.

His murderer stood over him for a while, not feeling triumphant, not feeling anything at all. Dark blood spread outward in a growing pool, but Christopher suddenly lifted the body so its neck pointed downward. He didn't want more blood on the habit.

The night wore on quietly at St. Gregory's Abby in Edinburgh, Scotland. Father Bernard loved the peaceful solitude of late hours more than any other time. While his brethren slept, he sat comfortably in a chair cushioned by blankets, reading the works of St. Augustine. A rotund man of pleasant nature, he could not help but give all his daylight hours to needs of others, and being blessed with the good fortune of needing little sleep, he considered the time of darkness his own.

His reading was interrupted when the outer gate's bell rang. Someone sought admittance. "So late," he thought, closing his book. As far as he knew, none of the brethren expected company.

Cool air touched his face as he left the warm abbey, lifting his white habit off the muddy ground. Upon reaching the gate, he opened it to an odd sight. Standing before him was a tall, travel-worn, Cistercian monk holding out a piece of parchment. Behind the monk, a tired-looking, red-haired girl sat on an equally exhausted horse. Wrapped in blankets, she gripped the horse's mane as if to keep from falling.

"My son," Bernard sputtered. "What are you doing on the road at this hour?"

"Forgive me, Father," a low voice, with a slight Italian accent, answered, "We were so close, I decided to push on."

"Were you traveling here? To the abbey?"

Handing him the parchment, the stranger said, "Yes, I am Father Luke of Clairvoux. I have a letter of introduction from Bishop Cresieme of Gascony." He gestured to the girl. "My sister is not well. We seek refuge."

Father Bernard glanced at the letter, understanding dawning in his mind. This newcomer could not be more than twenty-seven. Someone of his age with a written introduction from Bishop Cresieme could only be a political climber, probably the second or third son of a lord. How road weary he looked, and how sad. Not sad as if he'd suffered an unpleasant journey, but as if all the fight inside him had withered away. Poor child. The political arena was no place for good men or scholars. Bernard knew that well enough from his own younger days.

"Come in," Bernard said. "I'll find you something to eat."

"No, we need rest. I only wish to keep my sister here a short while, until I can arrange to send her to . . . my family in Italy."

"Of course, we seldom have women visitors, but there is a private room in the north wing. That should do."

Relief flooded the stranger's face. "Thank you, father."

"And how long do you plan to stay with us?" Bernard asked, finding this man more interesting with each moment.

"As long as you'll have me. I heard in France that your abbey trains scribes. My Latin is excellent, and although difficult to believe, I have a very fine hand. I once kept accounts for a French lord."

Noting old – unusually old – battle scars on the man's hands, Bernard longed to hear his story, but never asked the secrets of another.

"You wish to stay at the abbey indefinitely?" he asked. "We are a remote group out here. There is no chance of meeting important patrons or bishops."

"That doesn't matter. I no longer care for such things."

Ahhh, there it was. This young monk waged a political battle and lost. Now he wanted a place to lick his wounds. Father Bernard had no intention of dismissing him. Ambitious souls who learned from their mistakes only grew and prospered under scholarly pursuits. But in the same thought, it would be foolish to simply accept him as well.

"My son," Bernard said sympathetically, even though the two were of equal rank. "Some like you come here, seeking peace and a quiet place, only to change their minds in a matter of weeks and go running back to France or Italy, hoping for power and wealth. We are simple monks here, with no expectations beyond the joy of each other's company and our work transcribing. We are a humble brethren. Do you understand humility? Can you accept it?"

"Yes, Father," came a soft answer. "I can."

"Good then. Bring your sister."

Bernard reached up and patted his new brother's back, noting it was very cold and thinking he must find extra blankets.

Abba's Mark

By Stirling Davenport

The sky was so dark and the storm had been raging for so long that most of the crewmen didn't know if it was morning or night. The bosun, who should have rung the ship's bell, was occupied in the stateroom below with a bottle of the Captain's brandy. The log book stood open to the date October 31, 1679, but the page had only one notation: "Still bloody raining."

The barrel chested, red-headed Captain Malcolm Broadwharf was on deck, lashing another slave to the mast.

The first mate called out, his voice barely carrying over the gale. "Goddamn the fates that brought this evil upon us! More sail, boy!"

The cabin boy scampered up the rigging to let out the fouled sheet. He shouted into the wind, "It wasn't God who sent this storm, it was those blackamoors. They're witches and devils, all of them. And killing one more won't help."

A few hours later, a small rowboat washed up onto shore, carrying seven passengers. Five of the men were dark-skinned and chained together. The sixth was Captain Broadwharf. The seventh was a dainty, ebony-skinned woman whose hands were bound with rope, the ends of which were tied to the Captain's belt. The rest had drowned, still praying for salvation, and they were the lucky ones.

From the northern tower of the stone keep overlooking the harbor, a tall, handsome man in a black velvet coat and fine silk hose watched with a spyglass. He was not given to haste, and did not seem the least surprised at the unannounced visit. Smoothing his long black hair, he descended the staircase.

The keep loomed like a giant crag upon the island, as the small party labored in the continuing rain up the meandering path of seawalls to the ornate double doors. A wizened butler led them into the great hall, and two burly servants immediately herded the chained men down the corridor and out of sight.

"Come to the fire, Captain," said a voice. The master of the house stepped out of the shadows and bowed gracefully. His eyes were on the woman, as he greeted the bedraggled seaman.

"You made good time. I'm sorry, however, that your cargo did not fare as well."

The Captain scowled. "Did you order the storm for my benefit or your own amusement, Baron?" He spat on the marble hearth. "The cargo may be small, but they're in good health, not counting the lice and the scurvy. Remember last time? The whole lot drowned, and I was forced to sell you half my crew. Now, you'll pay me extra and build me a new ship, or I swear on the bones of my mother, I'll never set out for Bermuda again."

His host laughed mirthlessly. "I've made you a rich man many times over, my friend, but I can spare the gold. My ship wrights will start tomorrow. It'll be the last of my timber, though. If you want another, you'll have to wait for the trees to grow back."

The palsied butler helped the Captain out of his wet jacket, and the Baron snapped his fingers. Another frail servant hurried up with a box of cigars, which he offered to the Captain.

All this time, the slave woman stood silent in her sodden rags, like a wet dog dripping on the polished floor, her eyes burning coals and her fists clenched.

"Did you save this one for me?" the tall man asked the Captain, his heavy-lidded gaze still trained on the woman's. His high cheekbones and chiseled mouth hardened his youthful good looks.

"I ought to know your tastes by now," said Broadwharf, grinning. "She's a bit used, but all the better, eh?" He gave a gravelly laugh.

The Baron's eyebrows rose at the gleam of hatred that sparkled in the woman's black eyes. "An interesting specimen," he said.

Captain Broadwharf roared. "Don't waste your time, Baron. She's stubborn and half-witted. Barely understands the King's English."

The Baron said, "Oh?" Then, in an exotic dialect, he drawled something unintelligible to the Captain.

The woman blinked rapidly, then gave a quick nod, which seemed oddly dignified, given her ragged appearance.

"Taylor," the Baron said to the butler, "Put this one in the green room, will you? Unbind her, but lock the door."

The Captain unhooked the rope from his belt and handed it to the butler. "And which room do I get, your Highness?" he said with a mocking bow.

Unfazed, the Baron said, "Your suite overlooks the harbor. You'll be able to watch your ship being built."

When the Captain had changed and ordered a fire in the silver grate, he sat with his cigar and a bottle of claret, while his host paced near the window, sipping from a goblet of his own private stock. The Baron pulled the drape aside and watched the moonlight on the harbor.

"It is a lovely view, if I do say so myself," he said in a voice that was velvet with a reflected mystery from the night a few inches away.

"Right now, I don't care if I never see another ocean," said the Captain. "You can't imagine the trouble I go to for you, dragging these brutes out of the jungle, braving the storms and bad navigation and finding this tiny spot that doesn't appear on any nautical map anywhere on the globe. Where are we, anyway? You always promise to tell me, but you never do."

The Baron only smiled. "Like you, I found the Triangle by accident."

"No accident brought me here," snorted Broadwharf. He took a long drag on his cigar. "Unless you're slipping."

"Tell me about this new girl you brought me."

"She's a savage, like the rest. Spirited, though. Her mate came down with the misery three days out of port. Fever and the heaves something awful. She kept begging for water. Made a damn nuisance of herself, so I did them both a favor." He flourished an invisible cutlass.

"Hm," said the Baron. "An act of unusual charity."

The Captain laughed. "She paid for it in my bed. Sure, she hates me, but she fears me more. These savages are cowards and idiots. We have to chain them, or they'll jump into the sea and drown themselves."

The Baron moved from the window. "You're not afraid of her working in my kitchen, Malcolm, after you've murdered her husband?"

The Captain froze, not at the question, but at the uncommon use of his first name. But he barked, "I'm afraid of nothing!" He stubbed out his cigar. "If a goddamn storm can't kill me, no slave bitch will. Enough have tried. I'm the devil's own son, I'll wager." He laughed until he was stricken with a fit of coughing.

"Very well," said the Baron. "It will be an interesting experiment. My cook had the misfortune to die recently." He gave an enigmatic smile and left in that curious, cat-like way he walked. The Captain's cough echoed behind him.

Broadwharf stayed on the island for several weeks, enjoying the soft bed, scented baths, and the Baron's store of claret and cigars. He made the slave woman take the first bite of every dish she served him, but eventually he began to relax. In fact, he had never eaten so well. He was amused to see that the Baron insisted on calling his new cook *Abba*. As usual, his host was absent at meals, but in late evening he would invariably join the Captain for a drink.

Abba herself was overwhelmed just to have a bed to sleep in, pleasant work to do, and an employer who treated her with a chilly kindness, all of which were preferable to her life on Captain's Broadwharf's slave ship. She never saw the Baron during the day, but at night she often accompanied him to the cellar under the kitchen, to hold the lantern while he chose a bottle from his private stock. It was a strange kind of burgandy that smelled awful, but she had no experience in such things. There was a small, wooden cabinet on the wall at the bottom of the cellar stairs, to which the Baron had the only key, and she longed to know what it contained.

If her mind had not been burdened with anything more weighty than curiosity, Abba would have been content. However, she never saw the men who had been brought with her, and suspicions about the Baron tormented her. She remembered bits and pieces of legends told by the village elders, things that reminded her of him.

And with this, her thirst for revenge on the Captain consumed her night and day. Broadwharf was never unarmed, else she might have spilled hot water on him or attacked him with a carving knife. Unfortunately, she'd seen what he could do with his cutlass.

The new ship was now ready, and the Captain had announced at dinner that he'd be leaving on the next tide. The Baron had graciously agreed to sell him a dozen men from his own dungeons. The Captain had objected to the price, but he had little choice. Besides, he well knew that the Baron's dungeons included many a sailor who had washed up on these shores.

Although Abba was provided with the means to prepare even the most elegant meal, the butler supervised all the food gathering. The door to the garden was locked, and her bedroom bolted from the outside every night. If there was poison anywhere, it must be in that cabinet in the cellar.

She had thought of stealing the keys from the Baron, but the only way she could think of was to seduce him and seize them while he slept. She could not bring herself to get that close to him, and besides, he frightened her.

Tonight she had served roast lamb with scallions and olives, mint jellied consommé and strawberry leaves. Not being a native of this particular country, her first culinary attempts were not felicitous, but the Captain now ate every bite of his meals. Tomorrow might be her last chance, and time was running out. Intent on her thoughts, she dropped a crockery dish, which broke on the hard wood floor. One piece had wedged itself under the sideboard, and as she pulled it out, her hand touched something else—a rusty key. Her heart beat faster.

Quietly, she unbarred the cellar door, and darted down the stairs. With shaking fingers, she fumbled the corroded implement into the lock of the cabinet. As the key turned, a voice seemed to grate like rust, "Beware."

She shivered, ascribing it to her imagination. Cautiously, she peered inside. There were rows and rows of stoppered vials. She couldn't read or understand any of the strange symbols on the labels. She took one filled with dark blue liquid, and quickly shut the cabinet. The keyhole groaned, "You'll be sorry."

She made a sign with her fingers, nipped up the stairs and leaned, gasping, against the cellar door.

From the shadows by the window, the Baron cleared his throat. "Are you going to use that?"

Abba jumped. With shaking fingers, she set the vial down on the work table and backed away.

The Baron moved to the table in the center of the kitchen, his face illuminated by the firelight. He smiled with one side of his mouth. "Fermented lizard toenails, very rare. It will paralyze him nicely, for a few minutes, but he'll come out of it hopping mad, and probably score you with that fancy sword he wears."

Tears came into her eyes.

"I know your trouble. We are the same, you and I," he said. His eyes gleamed.

She shook her head.

"You do know what I am. I can help you."

She made the sign again with her fingers.

He whispered, "My kind are not evil. We are creatures who bear unspeakable burdens, thrust without mercy into a hostile world. The hunger, the despicable thirst is a constant affliction, and we must employ the most noble restraint against it."

He moved closer. "By pretending to be human, we can kill, we can torture, and we have the godlike power to execute justice. But true companionship is denied us. Loneliness is our final punishment."

She realized she'd been holding her breath and let it out all of a sudden.

He stared out the window for a moment, then looked at her with his black, hollow eyes. "The long years will stretch before you without number, as you, too, draw the helpless sailor off his course and lure him to your lair. Eventually, you, too, will feel the need to bare your soul even to one of your prey, these frail humans, so that you may see some poor creature shed a tear for you."

"Me? But I'm not ..."

He gave a feral smile, the long incisors gleaming.

"Don't be afraid," he whispered. "You're one of the brave ones. You have the mark."

"What mark?" she hugged herself.

"Let me tell you a story. When I was young, before I had become resigned to my fate, I shunned the company of humans, and sought the wilds. In my naive way, I could not bear to prey upon those I had from my childhood considered my fellows, even though I now had far superior powers of body and mind." He examined one long, yellowed nail. "In the hills above my birthplace were old caverns used by early humans when they were little more than savages. I made my home in one of them. There were all sorts of creatures to feed upon."

She felt sick, and steadied herself against the sink. The Baron raised one eyebrow and smiled with the mouth that had tasted the blood of rabbits and frogs.

He continued. "One day I chanced upon a snake. I could tell by its coloring that it was poisonous. The most dangerous ones are the most beautiful, you know. Fitting, isn't it?"

She nodded, swallowing.

"They say that death from a snake bite is very painful. The poison gets into the bloodstream and causes hallucinations and slow destruction of the whole organism." He folded his long-fingered hands. Abba's eyes went very wide.

"That was a turning point for me, the day I fed upon that snake's blood. I embraced my nature and became what I truly am. You may judge me for making bargains with men like Captain Broadwharf, but I pay good gold for my nourishment, and some of my victims find death preferable to enslavement. I ask you. Who is worse, me for feeding my natural hunger, or him for selling his fellow creatures to such a monster?"

Abba was afraid to move.

"You see? We understand each other. If you were bitten by a poisonous snake, would you wish to die very slowly, enduring the pain and fighting the hallucinations? Or would you accept the visions and long for a quick and easy death?"

"I...I would choose the slow death, hoping..."

He nodded. "Of course you would. Either way, you are one of the brave ones."

She shook her head. "No..."

He smiled that cruel smile again. "You are the kind of fool who would get close to a poisonous snake."

He reached out his velvet-covered arm and the lace ruffles at his wrist brushed against the bare skin of her neck. His talons stroked her cheek. "If I kissed you with my venom, what dreams would come into your mind, I wonder? Maybe I can guess."

His voice was hypnotic, his eyes were like whirlpools of dark ecstasy. She was overwhelmed suddenly by those eyes, which contained a mysterious reality that could sneak up on you in the dark, a magical lair of spiders and serpents, a place where demons might lurk in every corner. And yet, he transmitted to her a strange exultation, a sense of eternal life, in which nothing could kill her, nothing could hurt her ever again.

She could almost imagine that she herself was a spider, a black widow, perhaps. She felt the fur along her arms, the great faceted eyes able to see into the hidden recesses of the night, and in her mind was etched the lust for vengeance, an unholy hope, an idea so monstrous that it captured her in its web and enwrapped her with its sticky fluid. The vampire's words played in her mind, *We can kill, we can torture, and we have the godlike power to execute justice.*

The Baron laughed, and his delight made him seem young again. With lightning speed, he bent down to her neck, and two fiery needles slid under her skin like knives into butter.

She moaned and would have collapsed but he held her up, his lips soft against her skin, his teeth embedded in her flesh. The poison cauterized her bloodstream like a drug, and through the haze of pain, she swam in a river of colors.

Her dead husband's smiling face came into view and she could smell the fragrance of his skin, hear his gentle laugh. He called to her, using the secret name he'd always used.

Then an icy current swept him away from her, and he was lost in the maelstrom, to be replaced by the leering face of Captain Broadwharf.

Hatred clogged her throat, like an undertow of deep green and black sucking her down, pulling her struggling soul beneath the surface of her consciousness.

Losing control of all past and future, she plummeted to the bottom of the river of time. Her last memory was of the Baron lifting her in his arms with a satisfied expression on his ageless face.

She awoke in her bed above the kitchen. The pine dresser stood against the plain green wall. Pale sunlight floated from the casement window, and she covered her eyes. She was wearing her shift. She didn't remember putting it on, only a vague and terrifying dream.

Slowly, she sat up and her head throbbed. There was a burning itch at her neck which no amount of scratching seemed to ameliorate. She stumbled to the window, and pulled the cord tying back the drapes. They fell heavily, blotting out the sunlight.

She hurried into her underclothes and blue cotton dress and apron. If it was morning, her place was downstairs. She smoothed back her wiry hair and tucked the ends into the string that bound it on her neck. She gave a quick look in the glass, and gasped. There was the rumpled bed, the braided rug and chamber pot. But where was her own image?

The stillness in the room was terrifying, and Abba leaned closer to the mirror and rubbed it with her sleeve. The scene was unchanged. It was no trick of light, no dream. An awful realization filled her, and she remembered – what she was and what she could do.

Her enemy was moments away from total destruction. She could have screamed with joy, and the anticipation of his annihilation flooded her senses. But the poison in her bloodstream gave her a new calm. She could see with an uncanny foreknowing the days that would follow, and once again, the image of a black widow came into her mind. This time, her furry arms and legs were stuck to the strands of her own web, and the more she struggled, the more entrapped she became.

Abba steadied herself against the wall, then made her way down the circular stairs to the kitchen. On the work table, behind the mangoes, tomatoes and pineapples, was the vial of dark blue liquid. She passed the table, and went to the door leading to the garden.

Closing her eyes, she surrendered to the new strength that filled her. Pushing with all her might, she forced the door open, and the lock gave way.

Stumbling, covering her eyes, she followed the path down the terraced hill to the shoreline. The sound of the waves reminded her of home, and the crashing surf filled her ears. Her senses were keener than they had ever been. The sound was deafening. When she reached the water, she took off her shoes and dress, and clad in her bloomers and undershirt, began to swim.

Her work-honed body was strong, and she soon reached the ship anchored in the sunlight. She wasn't even tired. Spider-like, she easily climbed up the side and came aboard. The planks of the new deck gleamed. Her nostrils were filled with the smell of salt water and wood polish.

She could hear the sounds of men working. Broadwharf's new crew. One was polishing the wheel. His feet were hobbled with a length of chain, and his hands were loosely shackled, as well. She came behind him and tapped him on the shoulder. The man turned and regarded her with astonishment.

"Can you navigate?" she asked, shielding her eyes from the sun.

The man nodded.

She grasped the chain between his hands and, concentrating, broke it in half. She bent down and did the same to the one at his feet.

"I'm the Captain now. Set sail."

Late that night, Abba came up on deck. One of the crew was busy at the helm. She leaned her back against the mast and folded her arms. The sheets luffed in the breeze, and the moonlight floated on the water like a sparkling veil. A deep hunger burned in her veins, but her soul was at peace for the first time since she'd left Africa.

The Debauched One

By Edo van Belkom

"He's a very dangerous man, this Rasputin," said Felix Yusopov, the Czar's nephew by marriage and a prince in the Russian Imperial Court.

"Dangerous, without question," replied Grand Duke Dmitry, a cousin to the Czar. "But a man? I think not."

Yusopov laughed. "Don't tell me you've started to believe his demagoguery as the ladies have."

"No," said Dmitry. "Nothing like that."

Yusopov looked at the Grand Duke and noticed the grip of fear in his eyes. "What it is, then?"

"Something worse."

"Tell me."

"I fear," Dmitry began, "that Rasputin is not a man, but...*nosferatu.*"

"A vampyre," Yusopov scoffed. "Come now, you can't expect me to believe such nonsense. Rasputin is an odd, unsophisticated peasant who is dangerous yes, perhaps even crazy... but a creature of myth? A legendary beast? I'm sorry, but I can't allow myself to believe it."

"Can you allow yourself to at least listen why I think it?"

Yusopov, realizing he might have been somewhat impolite, nodded. "Of course."

Dmitry smiled as if satisfied that his theory would at least be heard. "Come here," he said, motioning Yusopov to a corner of the large and elaborately decorated library. On a baroque, gilt-edged oak desk he had several leatherbound volumes open, and others with places marked in them with red or green ribbons. "I have been studying these texts for several weeks, searching for information about the legend of the *nosferatu.*"

"And you came up with?"

"Many interesting things that can perhaps explain the source of Rasputin's power over the Czarina."

Yusopov sat down in a chair across the table from Dmitry. "Tell me."

Dmitry nodded, and opened one of the books on his desk. "It is no secret that Rasputin's body has a foul odor about it. We've all come to the conclusion that it is because he does not bathe, but I have another explanation."

Dmitry leaned forward and began reading from one of the open books.

"There are a number of ways of distinguishing a vampire – notably by the loathsome stench of his breath. Bloodsuckers naturally have a charnel smell about them..."

"An interesting coincidence," said Yusopov.

"Possibly, but what of his eyes. Surely you have noticed how piercing they can be, how hypnotic..."

"Yes."

Dmitry closed the book he had read from, placed another on the table before him and began to read. "Some had diabolical smiles on their faces, while others – perhaps most terrible of all – had their eyes fixed and open so that they seemed to be staring at the terrified onlooker and watching his every move."

"Again, it is interesting," said Yusopov. "But it is hardly anything I might call proof."

"Perhaps, but if Rasputin does not possess the hypnotic eyes of the *nosferatu,* then how can you explain his strange power over people, peasant and nobleman alike. How would you explain his absolute dominance of the Czarina?"

"I'll admit that that is something which has confounded me for years. I suspect it has everything to do with his ability to heal her son, Czarevich Alexie."

"Yes!" Dmitry hissed, raising a finger as if in exclamation. "And have you never thought it strange that of all the doctors and men of science in Russia, the only one who can heal the boy's hemophilia, is a semiliterate peasant."

"I have never been able to make sense of it," admitted Yusopov.

"Because you've never considered the fact that Rasputin is *nosferatu.* Who else would be so utterly qualified to heal a malady of the blood than a vampyre? Who else would even consider using such a unique talent in order to gain a position of power within the Imperial Court?"

Yusopov said nothing.

"Who other than a *nosferatu* would profess to be a monk, then go through life as a drunk and unabashed lecher? What other creature would revel in being called Rasputin, a name which literally means 'The Debauched One?'"

"An interesting argument, Dmitry," said Yusopov between puffs on his cigar. "But it is *all* speculation. You have no proof."

"Yes." The word came out almost as a whisper as Dmitry's shoulders slumped, as if in defeat. "That is true. None of this is proof, only speculation in support of a theory."

"And that theory is?"

Dmitry's spirits picked up at this. "I believe that Rasputin is a direct descendant of Count Dracula himself."

"Vlad Tepes?"

"Yes, Dracula was very active in Eastern Europe for many, many years. I propose that Rasputin, one of Dracula's own children, was forced underground during one of the crusades against the Turks. There, he lay in waiting until the political climate in Eastern Europe changed. When things had finally stabilized, he rose from his crypt and set his sights on a position of power, choosing the Imperial Court of Russia as his starting point. Then, using his mystic powers, he befriended the Czarina and used her trust in him to ascend to a position which made him one of the most powerful – and most hated – men in all of Russia."

"It's too fantastic," said Yusopov with a wave of his hand. "It makes sense only by wild stretches of the imagination. You can't really expect me to believe it all. Rasputin is nothing more than a simple peasant named Grigory Novykh, a man who simply got lucky."

"Rasputin only masquerades as a peasant," Dmitry said, his voice rising in frustration. "How else could he have entered the Imperial Court? Certainly not as a nobleman, our bloodlines have been too closely documented. The only way he could ever attain a position of power within the court – something which his kind craves almost as much as blood itself – is to enter the Court as a simple peasant and earn the Czarina's trust."

Yusopov shook his head with finality. "You have proven nothing, and I'm sorry, but I have no choice but to dismiss it all as an interesting theory. Nothing more."

"You're being foolish to dismiss my claim so easily," said Dmitry as he stared at the prince. Then his eyes narrowed slightly. "I know of your plans to kill him."

"Who told you of that?"

"That's not important. It matters not to me that you kill Rasputin, indeed there are many who will applaud your efforts. What is important to me is *how* you kill him."

"Really?"

Dmitry nodded. "Yes, for he is not a man and he can not be killed in the usual ways."

Yusopov laughed. He'd really had enough of this. "Rasputin *is* a man. He has lived like a man, and he will *die* like one!"

❋

It had taken weeks of planning and days of preparation, but as Prince Felix Yusopov looked over the elaborate supper table covered with numerous poisoned delicacies, he knew he had done well. Rasputin's fondness for sweets and cakes was well-known in the Imperial Court and it seemed almost too easy to use that weakness against him. Any one of the cyanide-laced cakes contained enough poison to kill a man. And since Rasputin would likely eat more than one, his death was imminent.

The invited guests arrived around four in the afternoon, the guest of honor among them.

"Rasputin!" Yusopov greeted the man. "I'm honored that you could join us today." The prince loathed to shake the man's filthy hand, but did so to maintain an air of propriety.

Rasputin nodded, taking off his coat. A pungent odor accompanied him, trailing behind him as he walked past Yusopov toward the supper table.

Yusopov greeted the other guests, all of whom were members of the Imperial Court, and all of whom were aware of the plot to kill Rasputin. Of course, Grand Duke Dmitry was among them. He stepped through the door with a carpetbag in hand, looking quite anxious over Yusopov's plans.

Yusopov took the duke's hand in his and shook it. "I hope you will be able to relax this evening, Dmitry. I assure you everything has been taken care off."

Dmitry sighed, but said nothing.

At last Yusopov led the men to the supper table where Rasputin was already gobbling down cakes.

"Ah, Rasputin," said Yusopov. "I see you've already decided to sample some of my hospitality. I trust they are to your liking, they've all been made from a special recipe in your honor."

The men in the room laughed nervously at the brazenness of Yusopov's comment.

"Is very good," said Rasputin. "But a little dry. Perhaps some wine?"

This is all too easy, thought Yusopov. *Much too easy.*

"Of course," said Yusopov. "I've uncorked some of my private stock for the occasion." He gestured to several decanters on the table. "Drink as much as you like, there's much more where that came from."

Rasputin smiled appreciatively.

Yusopov returned the smile, knowing that Rasputin would be hard-pressed to stop drinking the wine until all of it was gone from the table. He smiled as well, knowing the wine had similarly been laced with cyanide.

"Now, if you'll excuse us," said Yusopov. "There is a family matter we must talk of briefly in private. I trust you'll be all right until our return?"

Rasputin downed a glass of wine and nodded. "I have everything I need right here."

"Excellent," said Yusopov, leading the others out of the room. He stopped at the door, and turned back to face Rasputin. "Some music, perhaps?"

Rasputin nodded eagerly.

Yusopov wound up the newly acquired phonograph and placed the needle on the record. Then, with the muted sounds of *Yankee Doodle* filling the room, Yusopov and the others nervously headed upstairs.

⁂

As they waited in an upstairs salon in silence, *Yankee Doodle* finished playing on the phonograph. They all listened carefully for any sound, then inhaled a collective gasp as the record began to play again.

"He's not dead yet!" came a whisper.

"How can that be?" came another.

Grand Duke Dmitry simply laughed.

"He has to be dead," said Yusopov. "How could anyone ingest so much cyanide and still live?"

The record played through, then began again.

Yusopov had to see for himself. He rushed down the stairs and came upon Rasputin pouring himself yet another glass of wine.

Rasputin looked at Yusopov, staring at him with those piercingly hypnotic eyes of his. Then he emptied his wine glass in a single gulp, and slammed the empty glass down hard on the table. A sly grin appeared on his face, and then he laughed.

It was a mocking sort of laugh, the type Yusopov had come to despise over the years. It was a laugh that was an affront to the Czar and his Imperial Court. It was a laugh that said, "Here I am, Grigory Novykh, a simple peasant with more power than a court full of princes and dukes."

Prince Yusopov had had enough of it.

Without hesitation he pulled a revolver from inside his jacket and shot Rasputin in the chest.

Rasputin slumped forward in his chair, but remained seated.

Yusopov took a deep breath. At last it was done. He turned to head back upstairs only to find the others on their way down.

"What's happened? We heard a shot!"

"He's dead," said Yusopov softly. "Perhaps we should now discuss how we might dispose of the body."

They turned around and headed back upstairs, a sense of relief washing over them.

All except for Dmitry. He lingered on the stairs and mumbled under his breath, "If the cyanide wouldn't kill him, what's to say a bullet will?"

◈

Yusopov came back down the stairs twenty minutes later. It was decided that they would dump Rasputin's body into the Neva River and then deny he was ever at Prince Yusopov's palace.

But when Yusopov reached the supper table he was shocked to find that Rasputin's body was gone. There was no blood on the floor where he'd been shot and no trail of blood leading out of the room.

Frantically the prince searched the adjoining rooms for a body, but Rasputin was nowhere to be found. Yusopov ran out into the courtyard and stopped suddenly as he witnessed something beyond belief...

It was Rasputin lurching toward him like a walking corpse.

Yusopov watched in horror for several long seconds as Rasputin came toward him with outstretched hands. He was trying to say something, but the words came out sounding like agonized moans.

The prince fumbled to reach inside his jacket and had to take several steps backward to prevent Rasputin from getting a hand on him.

At last he had his revolver out. It wavered in the air uncertainly for several seconds...

And then fire suddenly erupted from its barrel as he squeezed the trigger twice.

Rasputin was hit in the chest with both shots.

He groaned one last time, then fell forward, face first onto the stone slabs of the courtyard.

Yusopov stood over the body, the gun still shaking in his hand. He was looking for further signs of life. There were none, but neither were there signs of death.

And as he stood watch over the corpse, waiting for it to get up and walk, he recalled the words of his good friend Grand Duke Dmitry.

He is not a man and he can not be killed in the usual ways.

Yusopov believed that now, believed too that Rasputin was *nosferatu* and had to be treated as such.

He ran back inside shouting, "Dmitry! Dmitry!"

"Yes," answered Dmitry, running out into the courtyard. "Are you all right?"

"I believe you now!" said Yusopov.

Dmitry simply looked at the prince and nodded slightly as if he found little or no satisfaction in being right.

"I've shot him twice more," said Yusopov. "But I don't think he's fully dead." He put a hand on his friend's shoulder. "Tell me how can we kill him?"

❖

Grand Duke Dmitry rifled through the carpetbag he'd brought with him. He'd turned Rasputin's body onto its back and was now emptying the contents of the bag next to the prone body.

The wooden stake was a foot long and made of oak, as thick around as a man's arm at one end, as sharp as a needle at the other. Dmitry held the stake firmly in his left hand while he reached into the bag with his right. The mallet had a hardwood handle and a large and heavy steel head.

Dmitry firmed his grasp on the two items then looked at Yusopov and the other men in turn. "Hold him down!"

At another time such a statement might have seemed silly. After all, Rasputin had eaten poisoned cakes and had drank poisoned wine, *and* he had been shot three times in the chest. However, none of the men hesitated and each of them did their best to make sure they had a firm grip on the body.

Dmitry placed the point of the stake against Rasputin's chest, in the middle of the triangle made by the bullet holes, and raised the mallet over his head.

He took a final deep breath, then brought the mallet down against the stake.

There was a sharp sound of metal and wood smacking together.

And then Rasputin's eyes popped open, as if the sound had awakened him from nothing more than a deep and pleasant sleep.

The men gasped in shock, but none let go their hold.

Rasputin's eyes darted back and forth, first to Yusopov, then to Dmitry. The realization of what was happening put a sudden fire into the vampyre's eyes. They were aflame with anger, bent on revenge.

Rasputin's hands rose up, despite the men's best efforts to hold them down.

Undaunted, Dmitry raised the mallet once more and struck an even harder blow against the stake.

The point of the stake broke bone, punctured muscle, and then finally, pierced Rasputin's heart.

The vampyre's mouth opened wide in terror and the air was filled with the horrifying sounds of his agonized scream. His hands became lifeless and fell back to the ground.

Dmitry was still not satisfied however, and continued to pound the stake until the thick end was almost flush with Rasputin's chest.

When it was done, Dmitry dropped the mallet and pulled himself away in order to catch his breath.

"Is he dead, now?" asked Yusopov, still holding Rasputin's shoulder down.

"Yes," Dmitry nodded. "Now, yes."

They decided that their plans for the disposing of the body would remain unchanged and in minutes they had the body wrapped in a curtain and loaded onto a wagon.

By the time they reached the shores of the Neva River on the outskirts of St. Petersburg, the night had grown dark. Together, the men lifted the bundled corpse out of the wagon and carried it down to the water.

Without a word, they coordinated their efforts and managed to throw the body into the deep part of the river. With any luck it would be carried a long way before resurfacing, maybe even all the way to the Baltic Sea.

Dmitry let out a final deep sigh of relief.

Rasputin, the *nosferatu,* was dead at last, and mother Russia was safe from his corruption. "Let us get out of here," he said. "We have some celebrating to do."

Days later a little boy walked the southern bank of the Neva River on his way to a neighboring farm. At a sharp bend in the river he saw something at the water's edge.

He scampered toward it.

It was dirty and in tatters as if it had been torn to shreds. Still, the boy recognized the stained red and gold material as being an old carpet, or perhaps a curtain from one of the larger royal estates upriver.

He stepped over it and saw something else further down the bank. It was a piece of wood. But although it was just a short piece it didn't look much like a branch.

He picked it up.

It was heavy, and smooth... and sharp like a spike.

The boy traced his fingers along the smooth edge of the wood, starting from the point and moving back to the thick, rounded end. The piece was also stained, and the thick end looked as if it had been clawed at much in the same way as the curtains had been. There were dozens of scratches and gouges in the wood that looked like they might have been made by...

The claws of some beast.

A sudden chill came over the boy and he dropped the piece of wood, then stepped away from it. He looked at it a few moments as a shiver of fear moved up his spine, then he knelt down, picked it up and threw it into the river. It bobbed on the water's surface several times, then started floating westward, out toward the sea.

The Bleeding Of Hauptmann Gehlen

By William R. Trotter

On the map of the Balkans, there is a place where the borders of Hungary, Romania, and Yugoslavia come together like slices in a pie-graph. Until the descent of the Iron Curtain, the actual borders were mostly academic references on a map – a matter of operetta guardhouses and candy-cane gates on the few good roads, sudden bouquets of trilingual signs; otherwise nothing.

Race after race, army followed by army, had washed through these fog-shrouded passes since the days of the Scythians – the tides of centuries, each leaving its own trace on the palimpsest of regional history: Mongol, Magyar, Serb, Slav, Turk, Byzantine, Slovak.

And, for a time, German.

Shortly before dawn on September 8, 1944, Hauptmann Rudolf Gehlen was awakened by the diffident prodding of his orderly, by the slash of a flashlight across the darkness that Gehlen was reluctant to leave.

"Sorry to wake you, sir, but you're wanted at headquarters right away."

As always happened when he was suddenly pulled from sleep, Gehlen felt a reflexive kick of adrenaline – a memento branded into his nerve synapses one morning in the Ukraine when he had come up from the sleep of total exhaustion to discover a T-34 covered with Soviet shock troops filling his vision at a range of thirty meters.

He traversed an anxious twilight into full consciousness. Outside were no shellbursts; his ears did not register the whine of straining tank engines. Through the window, he could see violet paling into lemon, a clear autumn dawn preparing to receive the sun. Against it, the eaves of onion-domes of the Hungarian district capital of Szeged stood as black and sharp as silhouettes cut from paper.

While the orderly moved discreetly to one corner of the room and began to make coffee, Gehlen swung out of bed and thrust his feet into waiting boots.

"Any idea of what's going on?"

"No sir," replied the Feldwebel, "but there was a lot of coming and going from the radio room a little while ago. Maybe the Russians have started their offensive."

"Christ, let it be anything but that – we only got here two days ago. Have Oberleutnant Kammler and Captain Lupescu meet me in my office in ten minutes."

Gehlen pulled on his tunic, lit a cigarette to cover the taste of sleep, downed a cup of coffee, and went outside. In the not-unpleasant chill of dawn, he realized that his fears were unfounded. If the Russian attack really had started, a brushfire of urgency would already be crackling through these sleepy streets. But he saw few lights, less movement. From the railway depot came the smell of sausages frying; on the station plat-form, sentries paced slowly beside a train pointed east, canvas-shrouded tanks hulking on its flatcars; a nervous trickle of steam pissed-forth from a leaky coupling hose.

Gehlen walked past the station and turned into the rabbit-warren of former municipal offices which housed his temporary headquarters. Whatever was happening, he hoped it did not mean they would have to move again. Two days had not been enough.

Not after the six months his battalion had spent fighting partisans in the mountains of northern Yugoslavia. At least, it had been a battalion when it was originally formed, back in March: an "einsatzgruppe", a composite unit manned by the flotsam of the Eastern Front – burned out survivors of decimated units, swept up from the replacement depots all over eastern Europe and sent in to conduct operational sweeps against Tito's formidable guerilla army. And now, depleted from a battalion to the actual strength of a company – like a knife grown too dull to use – they had been withdrawn and sent north to Hungary, to the backwater garrison town of Szeged, ostensibly for rest and recuperation, but in reality to form part of the dwindling manpower pool from which reserves could be drawn to plug the gaps that would result from the new Russian offensive. That attack was expected to begin any day now, before the autumn rains turned the tempting, armor-ripe plains of Hungary into a sea of mud.

It was all there on the map that hung behind Gehlen's desk: the red line poised ninety miles to the east, just on the far side of the Carpathians' crest. When the Red Army was ready, when it had caught its breath from the summer's terrible squandering of blood and supplies, it would surge through those passes like a flood bursting through a funnel – through the gorges, pouring down the meadowed valleys, out on to the plains which led to the Austrian heartland of the Reich, a target which beckoned Stalin's marshals even as it had once beckoned the armies of the Golden Horde.

The door to Gehlen's office stood open. The reek of stark, black tobacco met him as he stepped through and saluted his executive officer, lieutenant Hans Kammler.

"Good morning, Hans. Sorry to wake you so early, but something's come up. Lupescu, would you close the door?"

A hulking figure rose from the corner nearest the door and moved to follow those instructions. Captain Lupescu was a raw-boned man with coarse, shaggy brows. He affected a vast peasant moustache that drooped over his entire mouth and had an unpleasant tendency to display bits of whatever its owner had eaten for his last meal. Lupescu commanded a detachment of Romanian Fascist auxiliaries, members of the Iron Guard, who had been attached to the Anti-partisan force in June.

As effective troops, Gehlen rated the Romanians only a slight cut above the Italians. Liquored-up, or if the odds were strongly in their favor, they fought savagely; otherwise, they skulked, dragged, made excuses. The Wehrmacht veterans who comprised the rest of Gehlen's unit had come to despise the Romanians and always gave them the least important role in any operation. Lupescu pretended that his national honor was insulted, but he never volunteered his people for a more dangerous part of the field. Nor did he do anything to discipline the bestial excesses of his men during periods of lull, when their favorite pastime seemed to be the wholesale rape of Serbian women.

Gehlen would have sent Lupescu away long ago, but he was under strict orders to keep the Romanians attached as an example of inter-allied cooperation against the common Bolshevik foe. Those orders had not changed, but the situation certainly had: three-quarters of Romania now lay behind Soviet lines, and Lupescu's former superiors now dangled from the street lamps of Bucharest. Lupescu's men would be killed by the Russians if they fled east, shot by the Gestapo for desertion if they went in the opposite direction; for the time being, they clung to the status quo.

Gehlen read through the sheaf of message paper he had been handed, moments before, in the teletype room down the hall.

"Well, gentlemen, it looks as though we're going to have to play fire brigade once again."

"Mother of a whore," growled Lupescu. Kammler said nothing, but his lips compressed around the butt of his cigarette.

"We've been ordered forward into this mountain pass...just here." Gehlen turned and put his hand on the map. He pointed with the two fingers that had been fused into a single digit when his Panther tank brewed up on the third day at Kursk, the day he had won his Iron Cross. Dawnlight now streamed through the dirty window pane and lit the maimed hand cruelly. The other visible wound, the long pink furrow that disfigured one side of Gehlen's face, was turned into shadow.

"We've had a platoon of engineers working round-the-clock to fortify this pass – minefields, bunkers, antitank barriers, the lot. The job really requires a company, but a platoon was all that could be spared in this sector. I don't have to tell you how vital those fieldworks will be when the Reds decide to start moving again.

"Well, they've been up there for three days, but they haven't had an easy time of it. Two nights ago, they were fired on at long range and took some casualties. Later that night, their perimeter was infiltrated and a man was taken prisoner – just pulled out of his foxhole and dragged screaming into the night. Most unnerving."

Gehlen paused to offer a cigarette to Kammler. He did not glance at Lupescu, who noisily lit one of is own, fouling the air not only with the wet-dog stench of cheap Russian tobacco, but with the spray from a wracking, porcine cough as well.

"Yesterday, they had to mount guard while they worked. Needless to say, that slowed them down and not much got done. Late in the after-noon, they radioed for permission to withdraw. It was refused – if they left, whoever had fired on them could just walk in and take over the pass. So they were ordered to dig in defensively, to hold on for one more night, and told they could expect reinforcements this morning – that was to be us.

"Starting at about 0300, they began sending hysterical signals. First, it was sniper fire again...then they were under heavy attack. There was evidently some hand to hand fighting. Either their radio was hit, or their position was completely overrun, because they went off the air suddenly about an hour before dawn.

"It seems clear that they ran into some partisans – probably not a very large band, or they would have attacked on the first night, instead of weakening the engineers first. Our job is to get up there and rescue the survivors, if any; after that, we track down the guerillas and finish them off."

"I wasn't aware of any partisan activity in that region, sir," said Kammler.

"There hasn't been anything serious until now. But with the Reds so close, it's not surprising they've come to life. We could even be dealing with Russian parachutists, although it seems unlikely they would be wasted by dropping them into such a remote area. They could also be Romanian deserters, or maybe a Communist cadre that's been lying low for years. Hell, it could even be some of Tito's people, straggling up from Yugoslavia – the border's terribly vague all through that area, as you know.

"Whoever they are, let's make quick work of them so we can get back here and get some rest. I want all elements loaded into the trucks in thirty minutes, with rations and ammo for three days. Lupescu, you ride in the halftrack with me, in case we need a translator."

The fog was starting to burn off in the low places, ninety minutes later, as the small column of vehicles, led by Gehlen's halftrack, crossed the border into Romania. Massive whale-backed hills rose around them, their elevation not great but their rolling area enormous; the lower slopes and valleys close to the road were covered with fields gone to rot. A blue mountain river twisted between groves of birches, their turning leaves aglow like hard-candies held up to the sun. Farm houses were few and usually deserted. Occasionally, a motorcycle growled past, carrying a dispatch rider from the front. Just beyond the border, a crossroads village of twenty houses swept by in a flurry of pariah dogs, stick-thin children, and kerchief-hooded crones who watched the convoy with eyes as sullen as autumn rain.

Ahead, the road took the first long curve that moved it from the plains into the lower escarpment of the Carpathians. Across the horizon, stark and heavily shadowed in the slanted morning light, stretched a rampart of mountains. Cultivated land yielded to deciduous forest: shapely pines and rugged, solitary hemlocks on the lower slopes, thick carpets of spruce on the higher elevations. The road began to twist and snake, the looming ridges on either side often blocked the solders' view and closed them in with the reverberation of the vehicles' engines.

On a narrow hairpin curve, with the halftrack's outer wheels scraping dirt into a fog-tattered gorge, Gehlen leaned over an armor-slab and watched the scenery unroll like a Chinese scroll: a huge arc of mountain spine fading in and out of vision as a stately drapery of rain slid over its contours, thick as a bolt of grey silk.

"Reminds you of a Gustav Dore engraving, doesn't it?" said Kammler.

"I'm not familiar with the name," said Gehlen.

"A nineteenth century artist who loved to draw wild and romantic landscapes – such as that one out there."

"Mmm. You'll have to show me one of his paintings...sometime," said Gehlen dryly.

The exchange was typical of the casual conversations the two officers had with one another. Kammler was a good enough soldier, but he remained a civilian at heart, not a man born to that iron trade. Gehlen, however, came from a family with deep historical connections to the officer caste. He had joined the Nazi Party coldly, apolitically, strictly to further his own military career. While Kammler still had qualms about killing – viewing it mainly as a part of the equation which might ensure his personal survival – Gehlen had none at all. For him, the act of killing, or the infliction of pain, were not matters that admitted of degree. He felt contempt for those who sought to practice war yet deluded themselves by thinking that death had nuances either of barbarity or decency, the way colors had shades or radio waves had different frequencies.

Gehlen knew better. He had been to where death lived and danced, and he had seen that there were no degrees, no subtleties, no fine distinctions: pain raised to the provence of madness was a pure state of being beyond a threshold as absolute as any imposed by mathematics.

When Gehlen had clawed his way out of his Panther tank in the cauldron at Kursk – with machine gun ammunition bursting from the heat, blobs of liquified steel splashing inside the turret, with the gunner cut in two at the waist but still very much alive when the flames boiled up in his face and welded him to the turret-wall – when Gehlen himself had tumbled from an open hatch enveloped in a cloud of living fire that flensed his flesh like the teeth of an animal, he had learned the final lesson of his chosen profession.

All hesitation, anything of pity or compassion that two years on the Russian front had not already taken out of him, were gone by the time he returned to active duty after Kursk. Added to his professional competence – which had marked him as a leader from the beginning of his career – there was now, in the conduct of his anti-partisan operations, a cold purity of timing, a lucidity of purpose, a honed and refined ferocity of act, which made him brutally successful. His men sensed the gulf that separated him from themselves. Their respect for his competence was reinforced by the powerful fatalism which radiated from him, a force that was felt impartially by friend and foe alike.

The same respect could be seen even in the pain-dulled eyes of the captured partisans whom Gehlen tortured with the same abstract professionalism, the same cold purity of will, that he applied to his battlefield tactics. Strong men, motivated men, dedicated cadre – Communist and Chetnik alike – had, in the end, whispered information to Gehlen that, under the ministrations of any other interrogator, they would have taken to the grave.

Ten miles from the pass, the truck just behind the half-track – an old Italian Fiat long overdue for retirement – broke down on a grade that was too much for its exhausted radiator. The convoy was blocked for several hours before repairs could be effected.

These delays, along with the narrowness and roughness of the road, prevented the convoy from reaching its destination until late afternoon. There had been no sounds of firing on the wind, and no further radio communications had been received from the engineer unit.

Gehlen halted the halftrack when it rounded a spur and he saw stacks of concertina wire piled beside two abandoned, burned-out trucks. He ordered Kammler to stay with the heavy machine gun on the halftrack and give cover. Gehlen dismounted, motioned for a squad to follow him, and set off slowly with a Bergmann submachine gun held lightly in his hands and two stick grenades thrust into his belt. The sun hung between two western ridges, flooding the forest with ruby light. As he stepped past it, the stack of barbed wire glowed like a delicate coil of garnet glass. Behind him, loud and hollow, echoing in the trees, came the sound of Kammler cocking the bolt of the MG-34.

Thirty meters down the road, Gehlen found the first body: an engineer corporal with two small-caliber entrance wounds in his back. The man appeared to have been dead since early morning. On his face was not the usual stunned expression of a man feeling the impact of bullets; instead there was a frozen mask of terror, as though he were fleeing from something worse than a quick death.

They found the rest of the engineer unit strewn-about farther down the road and up on the slopes of the narrow ridge where they had dug in for the night. There had been a firefight; some men had died in their foxholes, piles of spent cartridges glittering around their bodies. Most of them appeared to have died from the expected causes; grenade bursts and bullets. But on the northern crest of the little perimeter, where the besieged men had emplaced their only machine gun, it was a different story.

Gehlen thought he had seen every variety of corpse modern warfare could produce; he could read the caliber and nationality of death by the appearance of its effects. But he had not seen anything like this before. There were two battered torsos in the foxhole. On one, a black, broken melon of a head still hung, attached by a thread of cartilage; twisted segments of limbs lay at a distance down the slope, as though they had first been ripped from the bodies, then flung savagely away.

Now Gehlen began to understand the expression on the face of the first corpse. He turned to Lupescu, who was staring at the darkening forest with an expression of brute misery.

"These men look like they were mauled by a bear – do you have any idea what could have done this?"

The Romanian shook his head.

"Herr Hauptmann?" said a corporal, kneeling by the sandbags and pointing down toward the trees. "It looks like someone was dragged out of this position – see those marks in the dirt? Maybe he's still alive down there."

Thirty meters downslope, in a flattened tangle of underbrush, they found the last body. When Gehlen turned the corpse over, there was no sign of life. As he moved the body, the bloodstained field jacket pulled away from one shoulder, revealing a large bruise on the neck – a swollen, grape-colored crescent.

Lupescu's indrawn breath became a hiss: "Nosferatu!"

Two Romanian soldiers, sullenly lugging another body to the rear, overhead that exclamation. Dropping their burden, they scrambled down, examined the corpse's discolored neck, and began to jabber in awe-struck whispers, crossing themselves furiously.

"What the hell is the matter with your men?" barked Gehlen.

Lupescu pointed at the corpse, his finger trembling in the fading light like a short pale wand. "We must leave this place at once. This was done by a vampire."

It looked for an instant as though Gehlen were about to strike him. On the slope behind them, a German soldier raised his Schmeisser and held it on the three Romanians.

"Listen to me, Lupescu!" Gehlen leaned close to the man's face and spoke in metallic tones: "These men were killed by partisans, not by ghosts! And those same partisans are still somewhere out there in that forest, maybe close enough to see and hear us. Now I want you and your men to get to work cleaning out these positions. It's almost dark, and we don't have time to indulge in superstitious rubbish! If I hear another word about vampires, from any man in your unit, I'll disarm him and throw him out into those woods alone! Do you understand me?"

"Jawohl, Herr Hauptmann," snarled the Romanian. Lupescu turned to his two countrymen, both of whom had remained kneeling, clutching their weapons, staring at the forest with wide white eyes, and began kicking and pushing them back up the hill.

Kammler approached out of the twilight shadows, saluted. "We've got all the bodies together in a gully by the road, except for this one. No trace of any partisan casualties, as usual; they must have taken all their dead and wounded off with them."

The two men smoked a last pre-dark cigarette and listened to the muffled chuff of entrenching tools on the ridge behind them, watching the gloom gather in pools under the trees.

"Will they hit us tonight, do you think?"

"Yes, if they're still out there. It's too dark for us to go back down the road – they could be all over the trucks before we even saw them. We'll dig in here, extend the perimeter to cover the vehicles, and we'll probably be all right. We're much stronger than the engineers, and we've got mortar support. At first light, we'll track them down and try to finish them. Can't be much more than thirty or forty men, otherwise, they would have finished off the engineers in one attack instead of whittling them down first."

Kammler gestured at the bloodstains on the sandbags, just visible as inky patches of stiff cloth. "And what do you think tore those men apart?"

Gehlen's shrug was barely visible.

"Perhaps some wolves came by, after they were dead."

"Captain, you used to hunt before the war. So did I. We both know that no wolf was responsible for those mutilations."

"All right then, lieutenant, I don't know what killed them. But unlike our Romanian comrades, I don't for one minute believe it was something that can't be killed by our own bullets!"

The two officers crushed their cigarettes, then took up the body with the bruised neck, its flesh cold and papery in their grip, as though the skin would slide away like film, and carried it to the gully where the other bodies were stacked. By the time they were done, it was full dark. Cold rations were opened, extra flares lined up on the edges of foxholes; the waiting began.

They started to draw sniper fire just after midnight. Gehlen enforced strict fire discipline: grenades were thrown in reply, but no weapons were fired, no flashes gave away their positions or hinted at their strength.

The assault came at 0300. It materialized up the steep northern slope, close to the place where the dismembered bodies had been found. Flares sizzled into the sky; by their sickly white-green light, it was possible to see undulating shadows flickering between the trees. Because the treeline was so close to the top in that direction, Gehlen had anticipated an attack from that quarter. Two machine guns had been sited to lay a crossfire on that very approach, and their fire broke up the attack before it could do more than lap at the ridgetop.

Thirty minutes later there was another attack; this time, the partisans came in from two sides at once. Gehlen ran from side to side within the defensive perimeter, shouting encouragement, firing bursts from his own weapon, directing the fall of mortar shells. The attacks were determined, but as yet Gehlen was not seriously worried – his estimate of the enemy's strength seemed close to the fact: forty men, fifty at the most, about a pla-toon operating on either flank. The attacking force was neither numerous enough, nor possessed of sufficient firepower, to overrun his veteran unit as they had the lightly armed engineers. It would start growing light in about an hour, and then they could turn the tables and take the offensive against these bandits.

Suddenly, the volume of fire grew wild, redoubled in intensity. On the eastern flanks, Gehlen saw some of his men falling back. Grenades popped in a string along the ridgecrest. Then he saw a group of howling figures lunge from the flame-stabbed forest, bayonets leveled, and tumble into a slit trench where three of his men had stood their ground. Rifle butts rose and fell; flarelight danced on steel; shadows knotted and writhed; men screamed. Beyond, more figures came from the forest, firing as they ran.

Gehlen ordered the mortars to fire starshell; as the flares burst above the contested position, he saw an entire squad of partisans surge into the broken perimeter. He took in the scene in adrenalized slow motion: the running guerillas, in ragged uniforms, their faces filled with a desperate raging determination to get at close quarters, where the defenders' advan-tage in fire power would not matter, and in the center of the charge, a figure that seemed larger than the other men, and very different. The color-leeching flarelight burned bone-white on his protruding cheeks, his eyes glowed amber within two pits of darkness, and his teeth were bared in a cry so keen and piercing that it could distinctly be heard above the clatter of the guns, the shouting, and the crack of exploding grenades.

The figure led his men deeper into the German position; even as bullets began to find them, he propelled them – as much by the force of

his example as by the ferocity of his physical presence – toward the center
of the defense, toward the two mortar pits, near the place where Gehlen
knelt as though mesmerized. The spectacle of these charging men,
doomed and savage, like spectres of vengeance rising from the forest itself,
held his gaze and, for an instant, paralyzed his will.

Discipline reasserted itself quickly. Gehlen took over an MG-42 from
its wounded gunner and aimed it toward the charging men. The salvo of
starshells died, but the partisans were now so close that they were clearly
visible from muzzle flashes alone.

Just as Gehlen brought the sights to bear, the partisans reached the
mortar position. The gun crews defended themselves with pistols and
entrenching tools and several attackers fell. The tall skullfaced man who
led them leaped into the gun pits. Then the melee became too mingled
and confused for Gehlen to risk firing.

Now the screams began, tinged with madness. Knotted shadows
boiled in the mortar pits. Another flare went off, and by its light Gehlen
could see a severed arm, trailing a ribbon of bright arterial blood, spin
through the air. The screaming rose in a crescendo. The tall partisan stood
upright, clutching a booted leg. Dark and shiny as claret in the putrid
light, blood streamed over the big man's torso and bubbled from his
mouth.

Seized by fury, Gehlen pressed the trigger and the machine gun
bucked. A dervish of flame danced around the flash-suppressor and a
stream of tear-shaped tracers lanced out and struck the big partisan full in
the chest. Gehlen could clearly see the tracers striking the body, the rounds
impacting and fading like coals falling into a well. The figure shook from
the impact, but did not fall. Instead, he pulled on the booted leg and a
living German soldier came up from the heap of bodies, yelling like a mad
thing. Gehlen fired another, longer burst; again, the tracers went into,
were absorbed by, the body. Although he had been hit by at least a dozen
rounds, the partisan loped back into the forest, dragging his screaming
prisoner behind him.

Then the apparition was gone and a vibrating silence descended over
the ridge. As the last flares sputtered out, Gehlen saw several of the
Romanians pointing, white-faced, toward the spot where the bizarre figure
had vanished.

Lupescu scuttled across broken ground and slid into Gehlen's
position, his breath hoarse and his moustache bristling. He gestured
fiercely at the forest.

"Now will you believe? That was the creature! You saw it, Captain!

You saw the bullets strike – enough bullets to kill ten men!"

Gehlen said nothing. From out in the forest, at an unknowable distance, came a scream that was scarcely human in its timbre; Gehlen was reminded of the foamy-mouthed horses that had run past him on the road to Smolensk, their bellies ripped by shrapnel and their insides unwinding into the mud like long purple snakes.

Lupescu made the sign of the cross and huddled, shivering, in the bottom of the foxhole.

There were no more attacks.

Thirty minutes before dawn, before anyone could spot them, about half of the Romanian unit crawled out of its positions, overpowered a German sentry, and stole a truck.

Gehlen sent a patrol out at first light. Twenty minutes later it returned, bringing in the body of the German soldier who had been dragged away. This time, the light was good, the wounds were fresh, and there was no mistaking the reality of what they were seeing: deep puncture wounds in the neck, the flesh brittle and paper-colored, the eyes and mouth open in a rictus of terror.

Men gathered around the corpse. The Romanians huddled in a knot, hardly daring to look at the confirmation of their childhood nightmares. Gehlen observed them with inner dismay; the braver ones were the ones who had taken the truck, willing to take their chances between the Gestapo and the Russians; this lot that had stayed behind were ready to piss their pants with fear.

Still, Gehlen had to admit that the circumstances had affected his own men as well. Hardened men, veterans of the Eastern Front's endless horrors, they now stood together uneasily, whispering among themselves, remembering how their bullets had struck the tall partisan without effect, glancing furtively at the mortar pits where torn limbs and shattered torsos lay under a hastily thrown tarpaulin.

Gehlen lit a cigarette to cover the trembling he felt in his own hands. He had commanded men in combat for three and a half years, and he knew the signs of imminent collapse; knew that, in a veteran unit, it usually came with one sudden, unexpected turn of the rack. These men were getting close to the edge, close to the moment when discipline and experience would be subverted by blind instinct.

Choosing his words carefully, Gehlen spoke to his wavering troops: "All right, all of you, come close and take a good look! This is reality, it seems, and not a fairy tale, and we must deal with it as a reality. Somewhere out there is the monster that tore your comrades to pieces, took their life's blood from their veins while they still lived. Monstrous, yes! but whoever, or whatever it is, it wears the uniform of a partisan – it is the enemy, and it must be dealt with as an enemy. That part of the equation has not changed: it's still a matter of you killing him before he kills you. Man or monster, it's our duty as soldiers to kill him, and kill him we can!"

Gehlen watched the men carefully as he spoke. On their faces he read respect for his leadership – proven a hundred times in their presence – and their trust in the cool tactical skill with which he hoarded their lives in combat; yet plainly visible, too, was growing doubt that there was any power in their weapons, any tactic within their ambit of experience, which could prevail against such a strong and terrible foe.

"Lupescu, is it true that these creatures can move freely only at night?"

The Romanian shrugged, as if to say: the legend itself has proven true, so why not all the peripheral myths that go along with it? "It is said that they must return to the earth before sunrise, yes."

"To a coffin, right?"

"A coffin, a grave, a vault...whatever."

"And if they are found thus, during the daylight hours, they are vulnerable, they can be easily killed?"

"So it is said."

Gehlen smiled grimly at his men. "If it helps, just think of this as a new weapon in the enemy's hands. Like all new weapons, it calls for new tactics to counter it. Man or demon, we *can* kill this thing – if we behave like soldiers. If you panic, if you give way to your fears, then we'll all end up like this poor bastard at my feet. Now, Kammler, bring my mapcase over here. Squad leaders, gather around me, and I'll show you how we are going to do this thing."

"The rest of you, take the identification badges from the dead, stack all the bodies in that gully near the road, and burn them."

Gehlen's plan was clean and logical, and its very simplicity reassured his men. The creature had last been seen about one hour before dawn. Given its strength, it could probably have moved at the speed of a running man for most of that time. After a few calculations, Gehlen took a pencil and drew a radius on the map, with their own position at center.

"This represents the maximum distance he could reach before daylight. If the legends are correct, we'll find him holed-up somewhere inside this radius, in his box. There's a dirt road connecting the only two villages inside this circle: here and here – presumably, the only places that would have graveyards. The rest of the band may not be with him, but you can be sure they're not too far away. First we find the vampire, then we take care of the rest."

The operation went smoothly. Dismounting from their vehicles, just beyond earshot of a small village named Birsava, Gehlen's men surrounded the place silently and efficiently. The village lay huddled on steep slopes around a plateau; radiating down from it were terraced fields, now gone wild. The huts were built in tiers along the mountainside, facing west, where the contours of the land afforded the maximum sunlight. Aside from one half-starved dog, nothing moved in the village; the inhabitants had fled, their hearths grown cold.

Just off the village square was a small stone-walled church; behind it, an old graveyard. Sunk back into the hillside were a number of family vaults, mossy with age. On guard at the entrance to one such crypt were two partisan soldiers. Both men were emaciated and showed signs of exhaustion. One, indeed, was nodding asleep over his rifle; the other smoked and stared, hollow-eyed, at the landscape.

Two shots cracked. The sleeping man slumped over, dead; the other man's shoulder sprouted a rosette of blood and he fell sprawling to the ground. There was no return fire; as Gehlen had predicted, the rest of the partisans had gone farther, beyond Gehlen's "radius of daylight".

Inside the vault was a coffin, and within that, a tall grey man with dove's-belly skin drawn tight over protruding bones. His lips were the color of dried plums, and old blood, like a wash of rust, colored his chin. His foul-smelling Romanian army tunic was holed by numerous bullet-strikes, but the blood caked there did not belong to its owner, for there were no visible wounds in the creature's flesh.

"Kill it! Kill it now!" shrieked Lupescu when he beheld the figure pinned under the beam of Gehlen's flashlight.

"Cover it again," ordered Gehlen. When the coffin was shut, he opened the vault door and pointed to a farm hut whose shuttered windows faced west, overlooking the blue serrations of a half-dozen lower ranges.

"Carry the coffin up there, to the house", he ordered several men standing nearby. "I'll be there in a while. Lupescu, let's see if we can get any information out of the wounded man."

When the coffin was brought out into the daylight, Lupescu's men began to moan and cross themselves. One young man went to his knees, fumbled inside his tunic, and held forth a battered crucifix as four German soldiers, cursing the weight of the soil that lined the coffin, struggled past on their way to the hut Gehlen had singled out.

"Why don't you kill it?" yelled Lupescu.

Gehlen stared icily at the Romanian officer. He permitted months of accumulated contempt to soak into the tone of his voice before he quietly replied: "Because I want to ask it some questions first."

Enraged, Lupescu turned and kicked the wounded partisan in the stomach; the man vomited over his own boots. Gehlen made an angry gesture and Lupescu stalked away, kicking at tombstones, turning often to glare at the hut where the coffin had been taken. Gehlen offered the wounded partisan a cigarette. The man's eyes, glassy from shock, were nevertheless as hard as gunmetal; no wavering of will flickered there as he accepted the cigarette, no hint of gratitude.

Gehlen hadn't expected any. Hours ago, he and this man had been trying hard to kill each other. That comradeship which civilians liked to imagine existed between foes when they were not actively shooting at one another might sometimes exist in North Africa, where gentlemanly generals fought set-piece battles, but on the Eastern Front, the very idea was ludicrous.

Gehlen waved for Lupescu to come near again; glowering, the Romanian did so. "Translate for me, Lupescu. We'll give him a chance to do it the easy way, first."

Gehlen began with the question that both he and the partisan knew was the only one that really mattered.

"Where is the rest of your unit?"

The partisan returned his stare woodenly and said nothing. Lupescu drew back his fist and cocked a questioning look at Gehlen. Gehlen nodded, permitting him to rain blows on the partisan's face until he drew blood from a crushed nose. A dull moan escaped the man's lips; otherwise, Lupescu might as well have been pummeling a block of wood.

Gehlen was not surprised; he had met this partisan before. In the Prippet Marches, in the mountains north of Sarajevo, in the forests along the banks of the Drina. The man was molded from familiar material: a strong, sweat-simple peasant, his flesh an alloy of hardship and endurance, all dross emotion and all illusory hope long since burned away. He had been treated cruelly by his enemies, harshly enough by life itself; in exchange, he would offer barbarity for barbarity. Moreover, this man had been left to guard his..."comrade"? Surely not "friend", not that thing in the coffin! Tired and careless, he had been surprised, wounded, captured. In this man, therefore, there was not only iron purpose but now, also, shame. He expected to pay with his life for his carelessness – indeed, that would be his atonement. Oh yes, Gehlen had met this man on numerous other battlefields: you could torture this man to death and he would not tell where his people were.

Suddenly, a thought came to Gehlen. He rose and gestured toward the hut where the coffin had been taken. "Lupescu, come with me – I want to discuss a few things with you regarding our unusual prisoner."

Lupescu spat on the ground. "The only thing you need to know is that you'd better kill that damned thing before nightfall. If you don't neither I nor any of my men will be here at sunset. I promise you that!"

Ignoring this insubordinate outburst, Gehlen turned toward lieutenant Kammler: "Hans, I'll send another Romanian down to translate. Keep asking questions, although I doubt it'll do any good. I'm going to see if there isn't another way to obtain the information we need."

Kammler tried to relax while waiting for the new interpreter. His prisoner, exhausted and in great pain, was not about to hurl himself at the Walther pistol Kammler held in his lap. He tossed a pack of cigarettes to the ground and indicated by gestures that the Romanian should help himself. There was a barely perceptible nod.

Gehlen was right: this man was not likely to divulge information of military value. But Kammler still wanted very much to talk to him, about other things – about his "comrade" in the coffin.

How unfortunate that Kammler had left his Leica back at his billet in Szeged! Would anyone believe him if, after the war, he told them that he had actually seen a vampire? More: that he had fought a pitched battle with a band of partisans led, actually commanded, by such a creature? Here was knowledge indeed! In the midst of the routine horrors of guerilla warfare, he had stumbled upon the confirmation of one of Europe's oldest, most fearful legends.

A Romanian private appeared, saluted, got down on his haunches. Kammler gave the man a cigarette and, through him, began to question the wounded partisan.

"What is your name?"

"Gheorghe Stanescu."

"What was the other man's name?"

"The man who was killed outside, or the other?"

"The other."

"Before he was changed, his name was Mihai Maiorescu."

"How long has he been 'changed'?"

"Since early this summer."

"Where did it happen?"

"In the mountains. Deep in the mountains."

"How was he changed?"

"He was bitten. How else?"

Thinking of the corpses burning in the gully, Kammler asked: "Do all who are bitten change?"

"No. If the one who is bitten dies of fear, or if the heart stops before the feeding is complete, he does not change. If the blood is drained and none returned, he dies and does not change. Only if some portion of the blood is recirculated into the victim will the change take place."

"How is it that this happens some times and does not happen other times? How did it happen with Mihai?"

"He willed it to happen. Most of those who are bitten would prefer to die rather than face eternity in that form. Others, a few, actually seek to become one of the undead. That desire need not be spoken – from the blood itself, the vampire can read the heart. And if the vampire chooses, the blood-seed will be passed back into the victim's body, and the change will take place."

"Why would Mihai choose to become what he is?"

The Romanian laughed mirthlessly. "In order to kill Germans. The change gives great strength, invulnerability to bullets. In his present form, he has slain many of you, and he will go on killing until you have left our country."

"Why does he hate us so deeply?"

"He hates all Fascists. Before the war, his father was a socialist, a professor, who opposed the Iron Guard. When the Germans came, the Iron Guard puppet regime put his father into a camp and he died from the treatment he received there. The shock of that news, in turn, killed his mother. Mihai fled to the mountains and eventually became a partisan."

"But is he not also a danger to his own comrades? What if he needs blood and there are no enemies close at hand?"

"It is necessary from time to time for one of us to open a vein. We take turns. But Mihai is a man of great discipline, and it is no longer necessary for him to feed every single night."

"You called him 'a man'?"

"Yes, damn you, a man! For all that has happened, he is still that."

"What will happen when the war is finished here?"

"When the last Fascist has gone from our country, we will have a priest come and bless Mihai, so that his soul will be freed from damnation, and then we ourselves will slay him in the prescribed manner and bury him will full honors. When those things are done, he will know peace."

In the corner of his vision, Kammler saw two men climbing out of the halftrack and staggering up the hill to the stone hut, burdened with something heavy and unwieldy.

He returned to the questioning, but the partisan would not speak further. He wondered what to do next, then he saw Lupescu coming down the hill from the hut, loping with an incongruously lighthearted gait, a leer on his face. He ran over to where the partisan sat, hunched in misery, grasped the man's hair and pulled him up savagely.

"Come on, guerilla pig! Come up to the hut and see how we deal with vampires! You send devils to fight for you, eh? Well, now you'll see how Captain Gehlen handles devils!"

With Kammler trailing behind, Lupescu half-kicked, half-dragged the partisan up the slope toward the hut. The afternoon sun beat full on the mountainside, imparting a bronze stillness to the air.

The darkness inside the hut was, at first, impenetrable. A scent, both feral and sickly, tickled at Kammler's membranes. He blinked rapidly, trying to adjust to the gloom. Gehlen turned up the flame in an army-issue gas lantern and hung it from a nail in the timbered ceiling.

When he beheld the rest of the room, the wounded partisan groaned and slumped to the floor.

"Tie that man up," ordered Gehlen.

A plank table stood against the far wall, leaning at a 45-degree angle to the floor. The vampire lay flat against its surface. All four limbs, the neck, and much of the torso were wound tightly with chain taken from the winch on the halftrack; thick as a man's wrist, the links had been forged strong enough to pull six-ton armored vehicles from the mud of the Eastern front.

Lupescu was twitching and rubbing his hands; the mingling of fear and sadism had brought a fever to his skin. Gehlen was as cool, as businesslike, as he'd been during the most routine interrogations of the previous months. Kammler's skin prickled at the sight of the figure bound against the table, its skin shading from liverish purple at the lips to fish-belly white on the stomach, where the chains dug deeply into the paper-textured skin. A carved wooden crucifix, hung from the wattle wall behind the table, added a ghastly touch of irony to the tableau. Huddled together in one corner, smeared with grease from carrying the chain, two German soldiers smoked nervously.

"Get anything out of the wounded man?" Gehlen asked.

"Nothing about his unit, no."

"I didn't think you would. He's a peasant, and he already expects to die. We shoot him, he goes to Heaven – bang! Like that! Even the Communists revert to that kind of thinking at the end. No information from him, not this side of the grave...

"On the other hand," Gehlen gestured toward the bound giant, "that one already *is* on the other side of the grave. And yet, he lives...forever, or so I am told. Eternal life must be a very hard thing to part with. Lupescu also tells me that if a vampire dies without being shriven by holy rites, it goes straight to Hell. All things considered, I think the vampire has more to lose than the wounded man. All I need to know is the location of that partisan camp. And I believe this creature can be induced to tell us where that is."

Gehlen went to the shuttered window and unfastened the wooden clasp that held it shut. Then he placed a square of wood – a lid torn from an ammunition crate – over the opening so that only the bottom inch of the window remained uncovered. With a bayonet's point, he reached under the lid and pushed the shutters open.

A thin, flat ray of sunlight, cloudy with dust and flies, fell upon the vampire's chained feet.

Its eyes opened, rolling with incomprehension, red as coals, their pupils deep as mineshafts driven into a mountain's heart. A bubbling sound was heard, like the first percolations of a coffee pot. The pale flesh on the creature's feet began to wrinkle and darken; hairline cracks appeared in the skin, and from them a red-black fluid oozed up like tar sweating from pavement on a blistering day. A smell of char and corruption, worse than burning flesh, bled into the air.

The thing on the table screamed. The massive chains dug through skin, sank deep into knotted muscles. Its body slapped against the planks.

Gehlen covered the window and darkness returned. The vampire sobbed for breath – a sound like a file going through old, soft iron. Gehlen motioned for a soldier to hold the covering lid across the window. Then he walked over to the table, and, through Lupescu, spoke to the creature that glared at him with a hatred that no animal, nor any normal man, could have manifested.

"Listen to me, whatever you are. I have a chaplain outside – a priest. You must surely know that I will kill you in the end, no matter how long it takes. All I need to know is the location of the rest of your partisan group. Just that. It need only be a single word, if that word is on my map. Speak that word, and I will send for the priest. He will cleanse your soul and you'll be allowed to die quickly. If you do not tell me, you will die unblessed. And until you tell me, I shall give you a foretaste of the hell that awaits you if you die unshriven."

The creature spoke, its voice thick and clotted, as though layers of rust blocked the air that sought to move its vocal cords: "A hotter Hell waits for you, Fascist dog!"

Gehlen motioned and the soldier at the window raised the covering so that the shaft of sunlight, now brighter and more direct, fell on everything from the knees down.

Flesh liquified, steaming and bubbling. It boiled away until bone gleamed through, sudden as a smile. The creature howled and the table thundered with its convulsions. The chains around its straining thighs half-vanished into mealy flesh; bones cracked. One of the soldiers near the door doubled over and retched.

"That's enough for now," ordered Gehlen.

Darkness blanketed the room again, though fire still danced on the retinas of the watching mens' eyes. Gehlen's voice was once more cool, sympathetic, confident.

"Where are the partisans encamped? Tell me, and the pain will stop. Tell me and I will bring in the priest. Tell me and you will know peace, salvation. Die in silence, and your soul will know everlasting torment."

The thing that had been a man said nothing, but the fear in its eyes deepened.

Gehlen walked to the covered window. From the brightness seeping through around the lid's edges, it was obvious that the sun was now directly opposite the window, its light pouring full against the hut.

"Hold the lid tightly," Gehlen ordered. He then stabbed the bayonet into the wood and pushed, working the blade back and forth until a coin-sized hole had been punched through. A needle-thin column of sunlight pierced the reeking gloom. Taking the lid in his own hands now, Gehlen moved it so that the sunlight played slowly, teasingly, across the figure on the table, burning arabesques into its torso. Finally, he aimed the beam at the face. At the sunlight's touch, one bulging eyeball popped like an egg yolk. The vampire thrashed and roared, the chains plowing furrows in its neck and shoulders.

Gehlen covered the knothole and left the soldier holding the lid. He bent over the vampire's ruined face, nostrils flaring against the stench that rose from the creature's wounds.

"Shall I call for the priest?"

Its will broken by fear and agony, the vampire nodded.

"Then tell me where the partisans are camped."

The creature's voice was like the rattle of a broken gourd: "In the village of Cuvesdia."

From where he had fallen to the floor, the wounded partisan began to weep.

Gehlen smiled and spoke clearly into the creature's ear, while Lupescu translated in hoarse tones.

"I will go there and kill them all. Thank you for the information, monster."

Gehlen unfastened the clasp of the Iron Cross that hung at the throat of his tunic.

"By the way, I lied. We have no priest, vampire. Now go back to the Hell that spawned you."

He placed the medal directly above the heart.

With the sound of white iron being quenched in water, the cross sank into the thing's chest, vanishing in a smoking welter of liquefaction. It reached the heart. The vampire screamed until its vocal cords burst. Its neck snapped against the chain. From somewhere deep inside the bubbling cavity of its chest came a thin whistle of escaping air. The mangled body went limp. It was finished.

Gehlen turned to the shaken men around him: "Get everyone ready. That village is only four miles away – if we hurry, we can take care of this business before dark."

"What about the other partisan?" Kammler asked.

"Shoot him, then join me in the halftrack."

Kammler led Gheorghe to the edge of the forest, pistol in hand. The man seemed to be in shock. Kammler was glad for that; it would make this unpleasant business a little easier. He raised the Walther to the back of the man's head while they were still walking. At that instant, as though he had read Kammler's mind, the wounded man lunged desperately to one side. The pistol banged harmlessly.

With startling energy, the partisan turned and butted Kammler in the chest, sending him sprawling. Kammler retained his grip on the weapon, however, and he fired twice as he struggled to his feet. At the second shot, blood flew from the partisan's head. The man toppled into a leaf-choked gully and vanished. There followed a receding sound of movement through the underbrush.

Kammler decided not to waste time searching for the man. In those thickets, it might take quite a while, and every minute counted if they were going to mount their operation before dark. Besides, the fellow was gravely wounded now and could hardly survive for long. Kammler holstered his sidearm and jogged back uphill to rejoin Gehlen.

Once in motion, the plan unfolded smoothly. Gehlen deployed his men around the village like a noose. Figuring that the partisans would try to flee in an easterly direction, he sent two machine gun teams to cover that route, effectively bottling up the whole village. Then Gehlen's mortars – to which the lightly armed guerillas could make no reply – methodically worked-over each house in the village. When the partisans and their families sought to flee from burning buildings, they were gunned down. Resistance died quickly. Under no illusions as to their own fate but hoping that, by surrendering, they might bring mercy to their wives and children, the men ceased firing.

Gehlen had decided that there would be no survivors – an object lesson for anyone else in this region who was contemplating resistance. The men were disarmed and herded together in the village square. A scythe of machine gun fire cut them to pieces. Gehlen himself moved through the heaps of bodies, administering the *coup de grace* with his Luger.

The Romanian soldiers were by now all but uncontrollable. Gehlen turned away in disgust when they set upon the captured women, but he did not try to stop them. In an hour, the conquerors' fury spent and the last groaning victims dispatched with single bullets, silence returned to the valley.

There was little in the village by way of loot, but some backwoods brandy was located, just before sunset. A bonfire was built, food prepared, sentries positioned, and the vehicles drawn into laager. Gehlen knew it had been a grim, exhausting day for his men, so he permitted them to relax around the fire, and to get a little drunk.

The first sign that anything was wrong came just before midnight, when the head of Captain Lupescu – who had stepped into the woods to relieve himself – came bouncing, not unlike a soccer ball, into the circle of firelight.

❋

Kammler's last bullet had grazed Gheorghe's forehead, tearing the scalp and flooding his eyes with blood. It was a messy wound, but not lethal. He waited until he heard the engines move off, then he began to lurch through the trees, following the contours of the ridgelines, on hunting trails that few men knew about, trails that cut the distance to Cuvesdia in half.

For the partisan band was comprised wholly of local men, anti-Fascists all; they had fortified the village as their headquarters and had brought their wives and families in from the surrounding countryside. From this base, they had hoped to harass the Germans in conjunction with the imminent Red Army offensive.

Gheorghe was not sure he could outrun the trucks, but he knew their road was long and primitive, and he knew the Germans would have to dismount well beyond the hearing of partisan sentries in order to surround the village undetected. All of that would take time. And if Gheorghe could just get within shouting distance, he might be able to give a precious few minutes of warning – time, at least, for some to escape.

But the fresh blood that kept welling into his eyes made his footing unsure, slowed him down repeatedly as he negotiated steep, rubble-strewn paths. He finally reached a point overlooking the village just in time to see the first mortar shells explode when Gehlen sprung his trap.

Gheorghe forced himself to witness the massacre of his people, to let every shriek, every sob, burn its imprint on his senses. He had far to go, now, and he needed the strength that could be drawn from the total petrification of the human heart, from the total mobilization of the soul's resources in the service of hate.

When he could endure no more, he crawled away, deep into the forest. Behind him, the fires of the burning village stained the twilight sky.

Gheorghe knew that if his wounds went untended, he would soon be too weak to continue; his pain was immense – only his rage kept him in motion now. His journey would be hard – a journey to a certain place in the wildest, least inhabited part of the mountains; a place he might be able to reach before loss of blood forced him to lie still and wait for death. If he could make it that far, there was still one course of action open to him that might deliver his enemies into the hands of vengeance.

So steep was the way that he had to crawl along long segments of the track. The route was not a trail any longer, for no man, under any normal circumstances, had reason to come this way; but it was a direction that was known, by legend, from childhood, to all who dwelt in these mountains. The great somber trees covered him with darkness, and the cool night air soothed the fever of his wounds, as though the peaks themselves welcomed him, understood his mission.

Once he turned and saw, far away, the dying fires of the village. Down there, warmed by the flames, the enemy would be resting, secure and powerful, having overcome – in a single eventful day – enemies both conventional and demonic. At the thought of Gehlen's cold, scarred face, a new wellspring of hatred opened in Gheorghe's pain-wracked body, a surge of primitive strength went through his heavy, aching limbs, and he found the will to resume his trek.

Ahead, jutting black and sharp against the icy stars, loomed a gorge

formed by two towering basalt cliffs. The trees thinned, and now he
stumbled over piles of mossy rubble – the first of the ancient, fallen, stones.

The castle itself had fallen into ruin centuries ago. An overgrown
mound betrayed the outlines of a fallen tower; a trace of wind-scoured wall
could still be discerned, extending from the moon-glistening rocks. Little
else remained. Little else that was visible.

Gheorghe crawled over time-worn stones, toward the utter blackness
where the two cliffs joined together. Here, just as the legends had told, he
found steps that led down into the mountain's heart, to what had once
been the innermost vault of the ancient fortress. Gheorghe felt his strength
ebbing rapidly now – the steepness of the final climb had almost defeated
him. He yielded to exhaustion and pain, toppling, letting his body roll
into the throat of darkness, into a yawning chill, into a place where the
noise of his fall was swallowed by the night the way a stone is swallowed
by a pond.

Gheorghe lay on the floor of the pit. By the feeble luster of fungi, he
beheld the massive bulk of the Old One's tomb.

How long the Old One had dwelt here, not even the legends could
speculate. It was said of him that he had spent ten centuries of nights traveling the world, and had returned here for ten centuries more, to ponder
what he had learned. He fed but rarely now – once, perhaps, in every other
human generation – but his presence lingered in this mountain, a source
of awe and veneration as well as dread.

Gheorghe fought off unconsciousness.

"Old One," he whispered, "I have come to you of my own free will.
I would be joined with you. I would be changed."

Soundlessly, without corporeal form, a presence thickened in the
darkness near him. Resolution mingled with terror in Gheorghe's heart;
part of him longed, even now, to flee this place. Then he remembered the
village. And he remembered the creature that had been his comrade,
Mihai, chained to a table, tortured, and now burning in Hell.

"I offer myself to you, Old One. Take me, so that I may have the
strength to fill the night with the screams of my enemies."

A skein of darkness knotted close to Gheorghe. A thickening of the
air embraced him, held him gently upright so that he would not fall. His
mind felt the caress of something utterly alien. As he surrendered his
consciousness to it, as he felt the darkness shape itself into cool and
powerful arms, embracing him with a manly tenderness, a vision glowed
in his mind, a vignette from the Old One's past, establishing a bond
between the dying man and the thing that had once been a king in these

mountains. It seemed to Gheorghe that he beheld swarthy men in armor made of leather, ancient invaders of these lands, one of the hordes that had brought fire and horror in the long-ago thundering dawn of Balkan history. How the Old One had decimated them, purged them from the valleys and forests, washed the dry stream beds with their blood; when they looked upon him, they looked upon doom itself.

And Gheorghe, borne upon the tide of the Old One's memories – a comrade, now – felt the arms of darkness cradle him tightly, sweetly, as two nails of ice pierced his throat and lodged in the depths of his leaping heart.

His vitality receded like an ebbing tide, drawn up and out until, with the last spark that glowed on this side of the final darkness, he touched the extended hand of Death.

Instantly, the process reversed itself: white as a star, cold as the end of Time, a fire flooded back, outwardly radiating, from that same vanishing point, back through his veins. His flesh sang a wild, fierce song as it was transformed; he moaned ecstatically at the onrush of ebony waves of power, and his mind reeled, intoxicated, at the stately pavane of mysteries, their secrets unfolding within him like orchids carved from black marble.

With knowledge, with reawakening, came thirst; it commingled with his hatred and roared through his body. The wounds in his arm and head now seemed trivial – already, he could feel their tissues stiffly healing. As the tide of vitality crested, prickling his flesh, Gheorghe turned and loped away through the trees, retracing his journey on legs now swift and tirelessly powerful.

On that first night, he had drunk deep, a gluttonous draught of vengeance. Some of the enemy had fled, half-mad, into the forest, but most of them had died by his hand there in the smoldering village, ripped apart. And they had died while firing bullet after futile bullet into his body, while he had laughed redly in their faces.

Now, however, three nights after his transformation, he had learned how to discipline his hunger; he was hoarding it, letting it build slowly and hugely within him.

And on this third night, an hour before dawn, he had heard, far away in the east, the rumble of massed artillery. The Russian offensive had begun. In a few days, a week at most, the battered, once-invincible Wehrmacht would retreat through those passes like an old wounded serpent. And when those long, weary columns of men filled the narrow gorges, he would renew his feasting, extend a hundred-fold the range and scope of his vengeance.

And if he hungered before then, there was always Hauptmann

Gehlen, who had gone quite insane by the end of the second night, and who now lay, drooling and moaning, immobilized by massive lengths of chain, on a table in the windowless room where Gheorghe slept; and from whose body Gheorghe had drawn – and would continue to draw for as long as he could make it last – a bucketful of blood every night.

OBSESSION

The Boy Next Door

By d.g.k. goldberg

"It wasn't any different before I died," I said. In death as well as in life I seem to spend an inordinate amount of time staring out the window at the stream of people flowing past, caught in the corner behind the curtains, as an invited eavesdropper at parties, isolated in a crowd. No, my death has not been much different from my life, merely longer. "I dislike the term undead, it smacks of waffling, a refusal to face reality, an inability to accept what is. I am dead and so are you," I continued.

Bache has heard this all before, he doesn't even reply. He rests his forehead on his forearm and leans against the window. I can feel his anger. I want him to turn and look at me, I am being beautiful just now. He always exudes elegant decadence. Even though Bache does not wear a costume department cape or knee high boots, he seems to swirl and stomp off in eighteenth century disgust whenever I persist in referring to both of us as dead. After so many years I sometimes feel as if his hostility is all I can provoke.

I've really pissed him off this time, he leaves in a fit of high melodrama. It's just as well, romantic pathos to the contrary, I like being alone. I do not restlessly prowl the night seeking signs of other vampires or stalk humans with the hope of giving them the dark gift. I find plenty to do on my own. For decades I read omnivorously, then I wandered the night world of whores, runaways, and psychotics. I spent years drifting through the halls of empty museums. I walked through the dreams of young men. Then, I turned to all night cable TV and strolling the aisles of 24 hour discount stores. Wal-Mart at 2 AM can turn you off the twentieth century. I really think it was Wal-Mart that made me decide I was dead. What is the purpose of immortality when the world consists of plastic?

Lately, I've been watching the boy next door. The boy is gloriously ordinary, I believe I love him.

The great room of my condo runs the entire length of the building, I have those floor-to-ceiling, smoked glass windows favoured by the editors of chic decorating magazines. Editors must have housekeeping services. Keeping all those windows clean is an ordeal. I do my own cleaning. Through my windows, I watch Jamie in his bedroom. My palm pressed to the cool glass, I invade his nightmares. His mother is one of those women who furnishes her house in suites from some chain furniture store. I have never had anything to do with those women.

With Bache stomping off into the night to vent his angst on some unfortunate soul, I am free to sit on the sofa and gaze down on Jamie. I do not worry about Bache. The trite viciousness of the latter half of the twentieth century has made it all so much easier for Bache and me. With people leaving dismembered ex-wives in dumpsters and scattering bits of their neighbors in public parks, what is another bloodless corpse in an alley? No more hue and cry and how did it happen? Is Satan upon us? Nope, wonderful world of Wal-Mart; just two inches in the back section next to advertisements for garden tillers and earthquakes in Korea: "Unknown Woman Found off of Freedom Drive."

Montmartre was never mundane. Berlin between the wars, Covent Garden during the Regency, Haight-Ashbury in the 60's; those were times and places that sang blood-songs and nullified the question of existence. Simply *being* was too electric, too entertaining, too exciting to leave room for the nagging existential issues. Now I exist in neon and cellophane wrapped times. My thoughts are thick with doubt and depression: why get up for an evening? Why not lie in oblivion, waiting for a better time, or at least a more interesting one? I awaken with the dark and watch the boy. His thoughts are so exquisitely average that I am overwhelmed with tenderness.

Before the boy, I would spend the early evenings shopping with Elise. We would mallwalk the first part of the night, scooping up hair ornaments, belts, scarves, crystal figures, enamelled boxes. It suited Elise, her house is full of china figurines, silver miniatures, depression glass vases, and handbags. I am a minimalist, I like eighties chrome and glass, bare surfaces, white walls. Possessions suck the life from me.

When I quit shopping and started watching Jamie, Elise had psychobabble explanations. She said, "Being deprived of motherhood has tainted your undeath, watching over Jamie is your vicarious motherhood." I suspect she videotapes the daytime talk shows. Elise thinks she's mother of the millennium because she had three children before she was given the dark gift. She doesn't like it when you ask her what happened to her children. I suspect Elise feeds primarily on mothers. I do not think about being Jamie's mother.

Tonight Jamie is writing in his diary.

He hides the tattered composition book under his bed with three worn copies of skin magazines and several discarded bags of potato chips. The naked ladies in the magazines are as old as I appear to be. He has loopy, careless handwriting, he writes in a frenzy: "Why don't I have a girlfriend??? What is wrong with me??? I can not think about anything else. I am the only man in America who can not even talk to a girl... I keep coming up with these great plans to talk to one and I end up saying something entirely stupid – telling jokes that no one laughs at or just saying idiot things. What's wrong with me? Why do all the great looking girls have such dorky looking boyfriends? Is it because those guys have nothing to lose (being such creeps)... so they have the balls to go ahead and talk to a girl??" Jamie stops scribbling and stares at the wall. He leans back in his chair, I can see his ribcage beneath his sun-scalded skin. The blue veins in his thin arms climb up to the sweet pulse winking over his collar bone. His glaring Scandinavian hair straggles down between the bird wings of his delicate shoulder blades. He is an odd mongrel puppy, his eyes and hair are Norwegian blue and gold, his skin burnt almond, his cheekbones pronounced. Skin burnt almond, I could lick him like an ice cream till he melts into nothing. No, I do not want to be this slender boy's mother.

What does it mean that he is sixteen? I look to be twenty. Who is there, other than Elise or Bache, that is close to my age? What does age matter when one is dead? And, where is it I count age from? The womb or the grave? I sip a glass of blood and watch the rise and fall of Jamie's chest as he sprawls across the dark plaid bedspread. The naughty boy is touching himself. What would she think, his mother, the provider of plaid bed spreads? I watch him until he finds release. My breath comes in quick shallow pants.

I sense Bache standing behind me. "Home so soon?" I say.

"There's no place like home," he answers. He is idly stroking my hair. "Want him, do you?" Bache has a sinister tone, it is always like this between us: a chess game, each knowing what the other desires and moving towards checkmate. What else can there be after so many years?

How long does it take for the beloved to cease being the other and become the dark side of the self? How many centuries before features once loved blur and bleed into a thing repulsive? How many times can one hear a voice before wishing to obliterate the sound? What happens to a forever love when forever is not a dream, but a sentence?

"I don't know that I want him so much as I want the idea of him." Bache is massaging my shoulders, he has large hands. Jamie's eyes are shut, his eyelashes wet and matted. I put my image in his mind.

"The idea of sweet young flesh or the idea of fresh young blood?" Bache says with menace. His hands slip up to circle my neck. Were we mortal, those competent hands could snap my neck like a flower stem. He can not kill me, I know it, he knows it. To kill me would be suicidal for him, we are each other. There is titillation in the illusion of mortality, I tingle with excitement, I am aroused by our play-acting, the idea that Bache could strangle me is powerfully seductive. I hold my breath. He presses his index finger to my jugular vein, pulse to pulse.

"He is a very pretty boy", Bache murmurs. "Too pretty."

"Too pretty," I agree, licking my dry lips. He rubs his finger up and down my vein with tantalising slowness.

Through the window I see Jamie rouse himself, it is as if our wicked energy has reached out and squeezed his flesh. Aroused and intense, he fondles himself again while Bache mirrors his strokes with his finger on my vein. As all three of us rush towards climax, Bache sinks to his knees beside me, burying his teeth into the sweet spot on my neck. My blood spurts into Bache's mouth, Jamie spurts into his pillow case, and I clutch Bache's dark head to my throat like a baby cradled to the breast.

"We'll have to do something about that boy," Bache sighs. I pull away from him and stare into his dark eyes.

"I think not," I say evenly. Bache remains on his knees, his thick hair falls into his face. "Not that boy," I say. Bache stands abruptly, he tries to hide his hatred, but, I feel the electrical charge of his resentment. "Bache, I will only tell you once more, leave Jamie alone." I do not move my eyes from the window where I see Jamie drifting into sticky sleep. It doesn't seem the time to suggest a run to Wal-Mart. I get up and shut the curtains.

Bache is sulking. He has that peculiar male gloom that men, mortal or immortal, employ to permeate the atmosphere, to punish a woman for her lack of compliance. I think about popping in a video, calling Elise, doing anything to penetrate the sullen silence that dusts every surface in my house. "C'mon then," I say, like I am dealing with a recalcitrant child.

"Let's go out."

We enter the Goth club amidst the silly children in their leather and cheap black rayon velvet clothing, and order drinks to play with. The thoughts of the crowd hover like cigarette smoke. Elise is in the corner dancing pelvis to pelvis with a gaunt young man who will not see the dawn. A dark haired girl in fish net tights, her pink skin clashing with her store-bought ebony hair, approaches our table. She wears cheap earrings that look like spider webs. She attempts to focus her drunken gaze on Bache, "Are ya'll together?" she slurs.

"No," I say. She is thinking how hot he is, how wonderful life is now that she's completely on her own, how oppressive her parents have been. She's thinking that living in mamma's suburban ranch house, she never would have met a man quite so dangerous.

"Yes" he said simultaneously. She is thinking that I must be insane not to grab him. She is thinking about her horrible childhood, the years on dialysis, waiting, waiting for life and freedom. She is thinking that I must not have any idea how beautiful Bache is, how precious the freedom to do as you please. She is certain I have no idea how wonderful it is just to be alive.

The silly twit giggles. She has made our choice for us. We seldom intrude. Bache and I only go where we are invited. She runs her black polished nails up the inside of Bache's thigh. He shoots me a quizzical look as I hummed tunelessly along with the jukebox. "What's your name, love?" he asks her.

"Maggie," she giggles. "But, I'm thinking of changing it, now that I'm a fledgling." Have mercy, a vampire wannabe playing bar-games. Ah, the wonders of medical science! Maggie was rescued from end-stage renal disease when a transplanted kidney gave her a new life. This ludicrous charade is her second chance.

"What name are you thinking of?" I say, feigning interest. There is a commotion by the bar. A young man that looks like an advertisement for a Bible college is glaring at Maggie.

"Why don't you use *her* name?" the young man shouts. He looks out of place among the black and silver of the pseudo-wasted crowd. He is wearing a blue oxford shirt and khakis, his short hair is a non-descript brown. "What about calling yourself April?

"Who's April?" I ask a slim-hipped redhead as she squeezes between my chair and the next table.

"April was his sister," the girl answers. "she used to hang here. She was killed in a hit and run, Maggie got her kidney. She'd been waiting like years for a transplant. It's really cool, Maggie used to be like this really straight, churchy girl. Once she got April's kidney, she went Goth. Now she even looks like April."

I turned back towards Maggie with interest. "So, 'fledgling'" I sneer. "you steal the organs of other mortals to survive?" Maggie goes pale underneath her heavy make-up, spots of bright color appear on her cheeks. She bolts for the door in a blur of black and a jangle of silver, upsetting a table laden with drinks. "You think your life is worth more than April's?" I laugh. "Or do you think you must live her life?" Bache shushes me.

Maggie's blood is an interesting vintage, there is a lingering aftertaste of April.

The next evening I am seated on my perch by the window. "She was like us," I say. "You know, the girl last night." Bache stands behind me, my small shoulders fit easily into the space between his thumb and fingers.

"I know who you mean," he snaps. "She wasn't at all like us, she was insipid." We both wait for Jamie.

"She fed off the other," I say. "She is exactly like us."

"Not like us at all. It was surgery. The doctors did it," Bache sighs. "Besides, she'd have died without the other girl's kidney."

"And?" I say. I wait for Bache to respond, he doesn't. I take a long drink from the crystal goblet, the blood in my glass is cooling rapidly. "She's dead now."

"Yes well, there is that." he says through clenched teeth. Good! I've made him anxious. He sinks to his knees and bares his throat. "Don't you know you can hurt me?"

"Can I?" I say. I feel the mild resistance of his skin as my teeth find the vein. I am gulping Bache's blood in huge, thirsty swallows as I project my image into Jamie's dreams.

The next night and the next, Bache and I repeat the ritual. I sit and watch Jamie moan his desolation and caress his despair. He loses his sweet dreams of the girls he passes on the street. He gives up trying to speak to sunshine blondes and shy young ladies. He shuts his eyes and there I am. He lusts for something that he can not name.

Night after night, Bache tightens his hands around my throat and curses my infidelity. He threatens the pretty boy. Bache will not act. How long can this last? Well, two of us have all the time in the world. But, Jamie is pathetically mortal.

Bache is truly a gorgeous vampire. There is nothing pretty in the harsh angles and sharp contrast of his classic features. I enjoy making him suffer. I send Jamie devastating images, he does not sleep, he does not eat.

Jamie is pale with desire, poisoned with longing for me. Jamie knows in his body what his mind can not grasp, he looks out his window into the dark where Bache and I sit. Jamie wants what he can not name.

"We need him, you know. We need him to go on being mortal." Bache sighs. "He's going to figure it out, you know. He'll show up on the doorstep begging for the dark gift." Bache says. He presses his teeth against my fragile wrist. Bache holds the vision of Jamie in his mind.

"Will he?" I smile. "And, which of us do you suppose will go to the door?" I ask. I am suddenly bored with this bleak eroticism, bored with Jamie, bored with Bache. Both of them seem depressingly similar with their ponderous cravings.

Bache looks into my eyes, I trace the trickle of blood than runs out of his mouth, then slowly lick my fingers. "Both of us, love," he says, "we'll both go to the door." Bache caresses me lovingly. It is too late for all that, I think. Impatiently I move away from him, I need more than he or Jamie can ever hope to offer. I can not endure another moment of this menage. Picking up my purse I hurry out of the condo.

I back out without checking my rear-view mirror. I am actually somewhat fond of traffic wrecks. My traffic accidents annoy Bache. He has a neurotic fear of detection. I run three red lights before screeching to a halt in the parking lot of Wal-Mart. The Muzak is murdering a Beatles song, a cheerful old lady chirps, "Welcome to Wal-Mart," and shoves a buggy at me. I walk down the aisles of can openers, tropical fish food and underwear at funeral speed. A young black man, pants slipping down his buttocks, is teasing a frazzled looking white woman. There is an undertone of menace in his words. The white woman stopped her buggy just inches shy of a black toddler in a sweat suit. She suggested the man pick up his child. He suggests that she "have good insurance if you gonna be pushing that buggy at peoples."

A three hundred pound woman holds up a bright cotton smock against the bulk of her two hundred and eighty pound daughter. The black roots show in the girl's yellow hair, she is wearing an atrocious amount of eyeliner. "That is just the cutest thing," the woman says. The bovine girl sighs. A thin young man with acne snorts at the pair. A skinny woman with olive green sweat pants tucked into the tops of her hot pink socks shoves a pack of disposable lighters into her panties.

They are ugly, mean, stupid, dishonest. They are all petty and trapped. They will live in debt and die in their sixties without ever traveling a few hundred miles from their homes. This year they will each watch approximately 1,460 hours of TV, eat 208 fast food meals, and visit

Wal-Mart 73 times. I am beautiful, immortal, and educated. I speak twelve languages fluently and have visited every country on earth. I will still look to be twenty when their grandchildren are dust. I have all the time I need and more money than I can spend.

And, I would relinquish it all to be like them.

There is ultimately nothing in Wal-Mart I want. The thirst is overpowering. With the hunger ravaging me, my sensibilities crippled, my dreams dulled, I leave the store in a near frenzy. It is not a question of what I want, it has boiled down to need. I am only a few minutes from Jamie.

It always ends this way.

Waiting For The 400
A Northwoods Noir

By Kyle Marffin

"You can stare down those tracks all you want, but it won't make the train come any faster."

How many times had Jess Burton told folks just that? They'd always stand on the very edge of the Monico Junction, Wisconsin depot platform, craning their necks to stare down the line, as if impatient looks could make the train arrive sooner.

And here he was, doing the same damn thing.

Of course, there wasn't a platform anymore. No depot either, for that matter.

The fact was, there weren't even any tracks. They'd been torn up years ago, and the ballasted roadbed was so overgrown with weeds now that it was hard to tell where the old right-of-way ended, and the forest began.

It didn't even seem right to call the little town Monico *Junction* any longer. It went by just plain Monico these days. After all, the Chicago & Northwestern Flambeau 400 cut back to summer-only service after '68. It stopped altogether in '71, when Amtrak took over the passenger trains. And once the copper mines up in the U.P. were all dug clean and the pulpwood trade finally petered out, the railroad donated most of the northwoods lines to the nearest towns. Most of them ripped up the tracks and turned the routes into snowmobile trails. As if that could salvage some of the tourist business that was lost without the trains.

Still staring down the line, Jess cupped his hands over his mouth to blow warm breath into them. It was a cold one tonight. He sensed another howler about to loop down from Canada way, sure to dump half a foot of fresh snow. Those weeds choking the old railbed would just be whiskers stubbling the white crust come morning.

He zipped up his parka, lit a Winston Extra Light, then sucked extra hard. It took that extra effort to drag any flavor out of these low tar/low nicotine nothings. But then, that kid cardiologist over in Rhinelander seemed pretty sure of himself when he'd said that a pack a day at sixty four made it odds-on that Jess'd never see sixty five.

So Jess dragged on that tasteless cigarette, grateful at least for the bit of warmth that seeped into his mouth. The icy wind moaned through the evergreen canyon looming over each side of the old right-of-way. He lifted one of his earmuffs, thinking for a moment that the moaning was really an air horn, and Jess was ready for a diesel to come roaring down that strip of snow between the trees. A bright yellow and green striped E7, maybe, heading up a string of streamlined Pullmans, just about to ease off the throttle for the stop at Monico Junction.

But there was no E7. No string of Pullmans.

It was just the wind.

Jess dropped the ear muff back into place over hair that was thick, but had long ago gone silver-white. He continued to stare down the line though, as if he still expected a train to roll up the tracks that weren't there anymore. Didn't matter if it was cold. Didn't matter if it was about to snow. He just bundled up and made his way down to the old rail line. He'd stood sentry out here on colder nights than this. Waiting. In a way, he'd been waiting for over forty years now, even if he wasn't really here most of that time. Waiting ever since that night, all the way back in '55.

Finishing his cigarette, Jess sat down on a cracked concrete block. Once, it had been a footing for the depot platform. But then, that had been a long time ago.

"Always figured you'd end up working here," old Herbie chuckled as he lugged two suitcases out of the depot.

Jess followed him onto the platform, hauling another trunk, the size of a sofa. "That so? Well, I didn't." Jess eased Herbie's trunk down and leaned against it.

"The hell you didn't," the old man said. "You always hung around the depot when you were a kid, always watched the trains coming and going. I figured you for a real railroader all along. That's why I couldn't be happier it's you that took my job. I hoped it'd be a real train man. And a local boy to boot."

Jess smiled to himself, noticing how the retired stationmaster craned his neck to gaze up the track. Herbie had the train schedule memorized forward and backward, and knew perfectly well that the southbound Flambeau 400 wasn't due for another fifteen minutes. "Well, it was either this or go to work for the paper company," Jess said. "After dodging bullets in Korea for eleven months, I *was* hoping for something a little better than hauling pulp loads." He looked back at the depot, painted in C&NW yellow and green. "But I wasn't exactly dreaming about working for the railroad, either."

"The hell you weren't."

"You think I'm nuts about trains, Herbie, you're wrong. It isn't the trains, it's all the places they can take you to that I like."

"Nothing a man could want that's not right here," the old man said. "Nothing worthwhile, anyway."

Jess didn't argue with Herbie. He just kept him company that autumn afternoon in 1953, talking about the fishing and the hunting old Herbie would miss now that he was headed 'down the line' to live with his cousin in Racine. The Flambeau 400 was right on time that day, like always, and Jess helped the old man load his gear on a shiny, new streamliner. He never saw Herbie again.

'53 rolled right into '54, while Jess settled into the Monico Junction stationmaster's job. The pay was pretty good, especially for the Wisconsin northwoods, where just about everything *but* money seemed to grow on trees. His mother passed on the next winter (Pop had died before Jess was drafted for Korea), so he had the little two bedroom cottage on the edge of town all to himself. He even put a down payment on a two-tone '55 Chevy, with a V-8 that could give one of those new E7's a run for the money.

He didn't go out much. To be honest, not at all. Monico Junction had a market and a hardware store. It had a diner, a gas station and two taverns just off the intersection of U.S. Highways 8 and 45. It had pine forests so deep you could step inside and walk straight for a day before you hit a paved road. It had lakes aplenty with crystal clear water and all the bass and walleye a fellow could catch.

But it didn't have any girls, not really. The pretty ones, they mostly got married right out of high school. The smart ones packed up and rode the train down to Milwaukee. The pretty *and* smart ones made for Chicago while Jess was busy doing his stint for Uncle Sam. The others, the ones who part-timed at the paper mill over in Rhinelander, or sold bait to the tourists along the roadside...well, they weren't quite the dating kind. Not that they didn't try, those paper mill part-timers, the roadside bait sellers, even the ones that got married right of high school and already regretted it. Some said Jess Burton was about as close to 'a catch' as Monico Junction had, a regular trophy mount and as sought after as a record Muskie, and some of the girls giggled behind his back that he looked just like Tyrone Power. Or at least, Tyrone Power with unruly hair and the northwoods flannel shirt and corduroys uniform.

But by the time the summer of 1955 started to cool into autumn, Jess could see his life stretched out before him just like those twin rails in front of the depot platform: straight, plain, a little rusty, and ultimately, vanishing into the woods.

Till that one night, when Nina stepped off the train.

October, 1955. Prime fishing season was just about over, except for a few diehards that still came up on the Friday evening Flambeau 400 "Fisherman's Special" from Chicago. They could dunk their poles for the weekend and ride it back home Sunday night so they'd be at work Monday A.M. But deer season didn't kick in till November, so the trains were mostly empty this time of year.

It was one of those late October Friday evenings that Jess was cleaning off his desk, anxious to knock off and head for the Monico Tap & Table for a burger and maybe a couple of beers. The Fisherman's Special was due shortly, and once it was gone, he could shut down the station.

The train was right on time, and it only paused at the depot for a moment, then pulled away northbound towards the last few stops before the end of the line. Jess logged it into the schedule, shut off the platform lights and locked up the depot before the tail car had even disappeared into the woods north of town.

That's when he saw her.

She stood there in the near-dark on the edge of the platform.

Now the few anglers that rode the train this late in the season usually had a car waiting for them from one of the nearby resorts. The rich ones – fat cats from downstate and Chicago – they had drivers come from their lakefront estates to pick them up. Monico Junction didn't have a taxi service, unless you counted Toby Knutsen, who hauled trash, and for a quick buck might give you a lift in his old Willys.

But the woman standing alone out there on the platform sure didn't look like she was up here for the fishing. And she didn't seem like the type to take a ride from old Toby, either.

With an autumn evening settling over Monico Junction, and the depot lights off, the platform was all dark shadows. And dark as it was, Jess couldn't recognize her. But she was the kind of woman he'd have remembered seeing before. He cleared his throat. "Excuse me, Ma'am, is there anything I can help you with?"

She jumped at the sound of his voice.

"Sorry," Jess said. "I didn't mean to scare you." He tipped his fedora and smiled, not sure if she could see the gesture. "But is there anything I can do for you?"

She fumbled in her purse. "You could offer me a light."

Jess whipped out his lighter. Once it flamed, she stepped closer into the light and held up a cork tipped cigarette in a velvet gloved hand. The lighter glow lit up her fair face, sparkled on glistening ruby red lips. She wrapped them around her cigarette, dragged, and blew a cloud of smoke Jess' way.

He left the lighter going, almost reluctant to return the platform back into darkness. Jess knew he was gawking, but she was just so pretty. City pretty, not like the Monico Junction girls. *Sophisticated* was the word that came to mind. She wore a fancy hat, a kind of beret, with a wisp of netting that veiled half of her face. But that wisp of netting couldn't hide her beautiful features, all made up and just right too, just like the models on the ladies' magazine covers. Dark red hair framed that face, unless it was just painted red by the lighter's glow.

"You'll get burned," she said, and her voice was deep and kind of breathy, the kind of voice the movie stars had, the kind they used in the love scenes before they got kissed.

"What?" Jess finally tore his eyes away from her face. "Oh. Right." He shut the lighter, and the depot platform went dark again. "As I was saying, Ma'am —"

"It's Nina."

"Oh, well, pleased to meet you, Nina. So, is someone expecting you? Can I offer you a ride somewhere?"

"Thanks, but no thanks," Nina said. Jess smelled her perfume right over the cigarette smoke, and it was all floral and sachets, like the cosmetics counter at the Rexall in Rhinelander. "This *is* Monico Junction?" she asked.

"Yes, it is, what there is of it. You have family here...Nina? Friends?"

Jess couldn't see her face clearly anymore, but he heard her snort.

"Yes, I have a friend here. I thought he'd be waiting for me at the station."

"Well, there's no one here but me. And I've been here all day. I was just closing up. I'm the, uhm, the stationmaster, see." A *friend,* she'd said. *He,* she'd said. Jess hoped the darkness masked his scowl. "If you're expecting someone, maybe we could ring him up?"

"No." Nina said that awfully quick. "No, I wouldn't want to pester him. I'm sure he'll be along soon enough."

"Well, it can get pretty nippy out here once the sun goes down. Why don't you come in the station to wait?"

"I wouldn't want to put you out."

"No bother at all." Jess flinched when he felt her gloved hand take his arm. He cleared his throat again, and led her to the depot door. "You know, I have a little something in my desk drawer," he said, fumbling in the dark for his keys. "Just the thing for a cold autumn night."

"Bourbon, I hope," Nina said, and they stepped inside.

It *was* bourbon, and they each had two fingers in glasses that could have used a rinse. Jess offered Nina another, and then another. She sipped each one with practiced ease, while Jess leaped up with his lighter every time one of her cigarettes appeared out of a mother-of-pearl case. When she slipped off her coat, Jess gulped down his whole glass and had to pour himself another. A sleeveless burgundy dress hugged her slim figure, something shiny like satin or silk, and it made slippery, shimmery sounds when she crossed her legs...long legs, pretty legs, ending with burgundy open toed shoes that matched the dress perfectly. Jess had never really seen a woman that looked like Nina, or dressed like Nina, or sounded like Nina, or even smelled like Nina...not behind the counters in Rhinelander's department stores, not in the bars in Seoul, and certainly not in Monico Junction.

"Married? No," Jess said in answer to another of her questions. This Nina was a complete stranger, yet in less than twenty minutes of lounging on the old sofa in his office, she drew him out, had him rattling on about all kinds of things. "I guess I haven't met the right girl yet. Not so sure I plan to stay here in Monico Junction anyway, and getting married would be a pretty good way to cinch that. What about you?"

Nina shook her head from behind her glass. Her deep blue eyes twinkled underneath that mesh veil dangling from her hat. "No," she said. "Lots of...dates. Lots of *bad* dates. Always planned to be hard at work on a bad marriage by now." Nina laughed, a private laugh, and slid another cigarette from her case.

Jess was off his chair in a blink, lighter ready. His hand trembled as

Nina crossed and uncrossed her long legs, nylon whispers screaming in his ears. She wrapped her gloved hand around his wrist to steady the flame, puffed, and Jess was sure her fingers lingered on his longer than they had to. It was only a moment, of course, but it seemed like forever. "Still dating? Come on, a beautiful girl like you? How could you go wrong?"

She smirked. "Maybe when a girl goes wrong, men go right after her."

"Or maybe a wrong girl just needs the right guy." Headlights flickered through the depot windows. Jess heard tires crunching gravel outside. "Suppose your friend's finally shown up?"

Nina stomped out her cigarette and downed the last of the bourbon in her glass. "Thanks for the drink. And the conversation." She slipped on her coat.

"Here, let me walk you out."

"No." Nina blocked the door. "No, thanks, really." She pecked him on the cheek with those red lips. They were soft as velvet on his stubble. "You know, you're a nice guy, Jess. Maybe you should just stay inside."

And then she was gone.

So he hovered by the side window, watching her slide into the back seat of a big, black Cadillac. He tried to make out the driver before the car door closed and the interior light went off. But all he caught was a glimpse of gray hair and a black suit. Then the Caddy peeled out of the parking lot.

Jess went to the mens' room to rinse out the glasses. A red crescent of lipstick colored the rim of Nina's glass. While he held it under the faucet, he touched his cheek with his other hand, and his fingertips came away in matching red. He sniffed them and breathed in faint traces of Nina's perfumy aroma.

That scent would linger in his nostrils throughout a sleepless night.

He saw Nina again Sunday evening. *Saw* her, nothing more. That same black Cadillac roared up to the depot just as the Fisherman's Special was ready to pull away southbound. A tall, dark figure ushered Nina across the platform and helped her on just as the train eased away. Before Jess could even get outside, Nina's *friend* was back in the black Cadillac and on his way.

Jess headed to the Tap & Table after he locked up, stewing over the luster on that Caddie's chrome. Illinois plates, naturally. Probably some honcho from Chicago with a million dollar lodge on one of the nearby lakes. The sort of guy who could keep a woman like Nina happy, could keep her in fancy hats and mother-of-pearl cigarette cases.

He had a twenty in his pocket and a full pack of smokes, and planned on downing boiler makers till the money and the cigarettes were gone. It had been the same Friday night. Saturday too. The beer and bourbon was the only way he could get Nina off his mind.

Cassie – waitress, bartender, and off hours cook at the Tap & Table – poured a shot into a pilsner glass of Blatz before Jess even took a stool. "Not that I don't like seeing you," she said, laying out a cardboard coaster. "But three nights in a row? This is how Toby Knutsen started, you know – boiler makers on a Sunday night."

Jess slapped the twenty on the bar and gulped the drink.

"Suit yourself," Cassie said. "I like to think you're drinking this way 'cause you're trying to work up the nerve to ask me out again." She leaned across the bar, where her smells of dimestore bath salts and a Toni home perm fought to mask the clinging odor of burgers and beers. Fought – and lost. Jeff gulped down his glass and tapped the twenty. "Okay," she said, "You can't blame a girl for trying." Cassie fixed him another boiler maker.

Being a Sunday evening, the T&T was empty. Cassie scrubbed the grill once it was clear that Jess didn't plan on using any of his money for food, any more than he planned on asking her out. By the time Jess started in on his fourth drink, Sheriff Hamm ambled in, a regular rhythm section of jangling key rings, handcuffs and citation books. "'Bout time for a warm-up, Cassie," Hamm called as he dumped his load on the bar, himself on a stool.

Cassie brought Hamm his evening break's usual, a tall mug of black coffee spiked with sweet rum. She whistled at the load of tickets he started to stack in neat yellow paper piles on the bar.

"Yep, Cass, had me a banner day today. Can always count on Sunday to make quota." He blew steam off the coffee and sipped. "It's all those rat race types. Buzz up for the weekend, stay too late fishing or whatever, then try to make up time on their way south doing eighty. Hootched up half the time, and on *my* roads." Hamm always referred to the short stretches of U.S. 8 and 45 that chicaned through Monico Junction as 'his roads'.

Hamm initialed the ticket stubs and made notes in a pocket sized ledger, sipping on his sweet rum-java as it cooled some. "That you *again*, Jess? Third time here in so many nights, ain't it?"

Jess just nodded without even turning Hamm's way. He was still busy remembering the lipstick and lavender scents that lingered in the station.

"Saw you driving home last night," Hamm said. "Friday too. You were drunk and weaving or I was seeing things, Jess. Hate to find that pretty Chevy of yours wrapped around a tree."

Jess lit a cigarette. Maybe the tobacco smell could mask the fragrance still clinging to his fingertips and his cheek for two days and nights now. But he knew Hamm – hell, they'd gone to high school together, hadn't they? Even got drafted together, though Hamm couldn't cut it in the physical *or* the rifle range, and spent the Korean 'conflict' pushing papers in the quartermaster corps in Alabama. Evidently it was good practice, based on the way he neatly stacked his tickets and citations in little piles on the bar.

Yes, Jess knew Hamm, and knew he wouldn't let him alone.

The sheriff hefted his big butt and bigger belly off the stool, winked at Cassie and switched to a seat right next to Jess. "What's with you, buddy? I go for a shot as much as the next guy." Hamm raised his mug for proof. "But it's not like you to drink yourself silly three nights in a row, fella. Anything wrong with the railroad? Those pencil pushers from Chicago hassling you over something?"

Jess emptied his glass and tapped it on the bar. Cassie and Hamm exchanged glances, but she got Jess a refill anyway. Just straight beer this time, though.

"Hamm, you know a big, black Caddie?" Jess asked. "Illinois plates. KW-63-something?"

The Sheriff screwed up his face, probing his head full of plate numbers, addresses and phones. Then that screwed up face screwed up even more. "Yeah, I think I do. Why do you want to know?"

"Well, who's car is it?"

"No one *you* want to know."

"Hamm –"

"One of them Chicago fellows. And not a nice one. Bought that big old place on Twilight Lake, maybe a year ago. Bad customer."

Jess dropped his cigarette in the ash tray and turned to face his friend. "Keep talking."

"What do you want with him, Jess? That's no one to fool around with. Why are you asking anyway?"

Jess looked agitated and he sounded even more so. "Hamm, you tell me about this guy right away or –"

"He's just a bad guy. Nothing illegal, mind you." Hamm shrugged and toyed with his coffee mug. "Make that, nothing I was able to prove. Maybe a gangster. Or something worse. You just stay away from him."

Jess' eyes bored into the Sheriff's and wouldn't let go. "Hamm –"

"Look, it was in the spring, see. I got a call from Ollie Krupa's place, you know, has that little A-frame just the other side of Twilight Lake. Ollie told me to haul ass up there right away. Has a girl there in his kitchen, he says, a girl that just ran through the mud and the rain in the middle of the night and came banging on his door. Ollie had a hell of a time with his Mrs., let me tell you, her thinking this girl came to see Ollie."

"Hamm, what the hell does this have to do with –"

"I'm getting there, Jess." The sheriff took a slow, deliberate sip from his mug, then continued. "I got to Ollie's, and him and the wife got this girl there, all right. Pretty thing, she was. And half naked she was too, down to her skimpies. And young. *Too* young, if you get me. Too young for the getup she had on. And too goddamn young for the bruises she had all over her." Hamm paused, staring across the bar and obviously recalling the sight of that girl. "Took forever, practically all goddamn night, but we finally wheedled out of her that she'd come up from Chicago with another girlfriend, and had been staying up at that big old place across Twilight Lake. She'd been invited, see, by this Chicago fellow, a big timer, she tells us. He paid both their ways, and lots more too."

Hamm shook his head. "She may have been young to look at, Jess, but this kid wasn't young on the inside, get me? She and her friend figured a weekend up in Wisconsin was easier than going five dollars a pop back in the city. Problem was, the girl tells me her friend's dead – *killed* – that this fellow who owns that big old place murdered the friend, then tried to kill *her* too. That she just barely got out with her life."

Even Cassie was listening in now, not even pretending to fuss with the grill and the sink.

"'Course, I went right over. Jeez, but that place gave me the creeps. Looks just like a for real haunted house, if you ask me, and after hearing about tying-up sex shenanigans and rapes and beatings and murder, it looked like that and worse. So this same fellow the girl told me about answers the door, a wrong number if ever there was one. A *Mr. Wolvrik*, he introduces himself as, *Dieter* Wolvrik. Now what the hell kind of name's that? But Dieter, he lets me look just about the whole place over, polite as hell the entire time. There was no other girl, not that I could see. Looked like there'd been one hell of a party, though. Dieter, he admits that he had a girl up from Chicago, just the one he insists. Says he didn't even know her name, nodding and winking, if you get me. That the girl got mad, 'lovers' quarrel' he says, and she hightailed it out of the house without bothering to get all her clothes, but that was all. Well, I give old Dieter the law and order speech, try to put the fear of God and Smith & Wesson in him, point out how we don't need any city slickers from Chicago fancy pantsing underage girls in our town, and how I'll be keeping an eye on him. He listened – oh, old Dieter listened, but I can for goddman sure see that he's just smirking at me the whole time, and damn if I didn't feel that this ugly son of a bitch could've just reached over, grabbed my neck and twisted my head clean off if he wanted to. Just for fun."

Cassie wandered over and leaned on the bar across from Jess. "So, what happened to the girl, Hamm?" she asked.

The Sheriff shrugged his shoulders and downed the rest of his rum and coffee. "Hell if I know. By the time I got back to Ollie's, the Mrs. had given the girl enough clothes to be halfway decent. She'd called up Toby Knutsen and got her a lift to the train station. Jess, you probably sold her the ticket and helped her onto the train back to Chicago. Checked out the name she gave, but it was a fake. No real surprise there."

"And what about Dieter Wolvrik?" Jess asked.

Hamm just shrugged again. "Nothing. Checked him out too, what I could find. Rich guy from Chicago, but not many details. No record." He sighed. "No missing girl. No body. No complainant. Not a goddamn thing to do. And to tell you the God's honest truth, there isn't much I *want* to do about Mr. Dieter Wolvrik. That bastard had eyes that could freeze a bear in its tracks, I swear. Froze *me*, Jess. There was something bad about him, real bad. I don't want to know what's going on up there, and you shouldn't either." And with that, Hamm lifted himself off the stool and gathered up his things from down the bar. "I don't know why you're asking about him, Jess. But my advice is to forget about Mr. Dieter Wolvrik, *and* anyone that's got anything to do with him."

Jess heard Hamm's warning that Sunday night in the Tap & Table, and he heard it again and again ringing around in his head for days and nights after. But hearing it, and listening to it, those were two different things. So the next Friday evening when Nina stepped off the train, they shared another drink in the station, chatting while she waited for that black Caddie to show up. Jess pressed her about Mr. Deiter Wolvrik, but Nina evaded every question.

Two nights of Jess twisting and turning in bed and smelling her perfume later, Nina was dropped off a little early for the southbound train, so they had a good twenty minutes together in the station, sipping on a four dollar and fifty cent bottle of red Chianti that Jess bought special in Rhinelander, just in case. They sat close on the sofa in Jess' office that

Sunday night, sipped the wine and smoked and talked. Sat *real* close, so close that Nina's warmth seeped right through her dress and right through Jess' clothes, and lit him on fire a lot more than the Chianti. He tried again to draw her out about the estate on Twilight Lake, commented on how she was looking a little on the wan side, but she just tap danced around his questions, and got Jess talking about himself again. Jess told Nina about his stint in Korea and the humdrum routine in Monico Junction. Nina told him about the bright lights and the night life in downtown Chicago. Or at least, what she could see of it from her third floor walkup beside the El tracks on the near west side.

Nina kissed Jess just before she hopped on the train that Sunday night, kissed him right on the mouth, nice and long and warm and soft, wet with the taste of Chianti and lipstick, and she told Jess again how he was a real nice guy and that there sure weren't many left like him.

The next weekend, Jess watched the Flambeau 400 pull away north, but Nina didn't get off. He called ahead to the next stations: Three Lakes, Eagle River, Land 'O Lakes, all the way to Watersmeet, Michigan. But there were no pretty girls waiting in any of them, no Nina.

Jess was like a crazy man that whole weekend. Didn't even bother with the Tap & Table, he just bought himself a bottle and sat freezing inside his Chevy, parked in the woods down the way from Dieter Wolvrik's big old place. But he never saw Dieter. Never saw the Caddie. Never even saw a light go on. If Dieter was away, he hadn't taken the train back to Chicago. By Sunday afternoon, Jess got brave, stoked up on his second bottle of bourbon that weekend – that, or maybe just antsy from a sore ass stuck in the Chevy for a day and a half. He went skulking around the estate, but the windows were all shuttered up tight. The doors were locked too, with padlocks and deadbolts, no less. Up here in Monico Junction, where folks still left their screen doors open all night, with nothing worse to worry about than a bear with a taste for kitchen scraps.

But the following weekend, the Fisherman's Special arrived right on time Friday evening, and Nina stepped off, more beautiful than ever in a fancy winter coat with a mink collar, carrying a little satchel with her. Her overnight bag, Jess figured, his fingers clutching the window sill till they almost ripped the wood out of the wall.

But that black Cadillac was idling beside the platform, and she had to get right in, though Jess saw her glancing towards the station, where he stood inside, watching the car pull away, watching Nina watch him.

He could've swore that her beautiful indigo eyes gazed back at him with a look of fear.

No one was more surprised than Jess when he heard the timid knock on his office door that Saturday afternoon. He looked up from his desk to see Nina standing there, beautiful like always.

But a little worse for wear.

Her coat with the mink collar? It was splashed from top to bottom with mud. She hobbled in on a broken heel, her stockings shredded and hanging on her legs like torn skin. Leaves clung to her dark red hair. And dark red was smeared all over her mouth and her chin, making her already fair skin look starkly white. Just lipstick, or a cut lip, Jess couldn't tell. But he didn't waste time deciding. He led her to the sofa. Stoked the fire in the woodburner, then got her a hot cup of coffee. Nina shivered as she gulped it down, holding on to the cup with both hands, both of them shaking.

"I'll kill that son of a bitch," Jess said, wrapping a protective arm around her. "What did he do to you?"

"It's nothing." Nina slipped off her coat, and Jess gasped.

Her dress was torn half off, so her white slip showed through, and even that was ripped so that her brassiere peeked through too . The creamy skin on Nina's arms, on her chest, that silky skin that Jess had been dreaming about since he first saw her, that creamy skin was all pale, froze blue-white, and bruised with ugly, purple welts. Jess hopped off the sofa and stomped back to his desk. He grabbed the phone and started dialing.

"Wait!" Nina dashed across the room. "Who are you calling?"

"Hamm," Jess growled, still dialing. "He's the sheriff, and if he doesn't get up to Twilight Lake before I do, Mr. Dieter Wolvrik's a dead man." With his other hand, Jess slid open the desk drawer and pulled out a revolver.

Nina stopped Jess' hand on the dial. "Don't," she said. "It's not what you think."

Jess cradled the phone and pulled her close, the .38 snub nose still in his hand. "*What's* not what I think? You like what that bastard's doing to you?"

"Of course not." Nina tried to wrestle out of his arms, but Jess wouldn't let go.

"Then, what?"

"I mean...I mean that *he's* not what you think."

"I heard all about your Mr. Wolvrik. He's a gangster or something. Well, I'm not afraid of a thug that needs to bat women around for fun."

She slid the pistol out of Jess' hand and carefully put it back in the drawer. "Is there someplace I could clean up? Where we can talk? This is the first place he'll check. He's going to come right over here as soon as the su-" She paused, and wiggled out of Jess' arms. "As soon as he wakes up and sees I'm gone."

Jess was already pulling his jacket on. He grabbed Nina's mud spattered coat and wrapped it around her shoulders. "Come on."

"What about the depot? The trains?"

"One through freight at 4:30. I'll miss it."

Jess left Nina soaking in a hot bath back at his cottage. He locked the front door, checked around back, checked the windows too. As he walked to the Chevy in the driveway, he eyed up the road both ways, listened carefully for the telltale roar of a big Cadillac motor. But all he heard was the wind knocking the last of the November leaves off the trees.

He sped back into town. It was already getting dark when he threw the Chevy into park in front of the depot, left the motor running and raced inside. He rummaged through the Lost & Found locker and grabbed anything that looked small enough for Nina. Then anything that even looked like ladies' luggage. As he carried everything back outside, he noticed a light snow beginning to fall. Halfway to the Chevy he halted, spun around and ran back into the depot. When Jess returned, he was stuffing the snub nose into his jacket.

Fall was changing into a northwoods winter fast; it was completely dark by the time he got home. He stacked the Lost & Found things by the bathroom door, then went back downstairs to get a fire started in the parlor. Hanging up his jacket, he took the pistol out of the pocket first. That he left on the lamp table right by the front window, nice and close.

Birch bark flamed and crackled to life in the fireplace just as Nina glided into the parlor, an ivory satin robe cinched tight at her waist, hugging her body, parting in front to let her long legs slide in and out. She ran a towel through her damp red hair, all shiny and wet, catching a glimmer off the growing fire.

"Keep a regular dry goods store in that depot of yours, do you?" She stood by the fireplace and finished toweling off her hair, shook it free and raised her arms to run her fingers through it, hiking the flimsy robe higher. The firelight shined right through, silhouetting her entire body.

"Lost & Found," Jess said.

"That's good. I was afraid this is when I'd find out there's a *Mrs.*

Burton." She held her hands out to the fire. "Got anything to chase away the chill?"

Jess nodded and started for the kitchen. He stopped. Turned back and grabbed the .38 off the lamp table, then disappeared down the hallway.

When Jess came back with two glasses and an unopened bottle of bourbon, he found Nina sprawled out on the sofa, firelight painting that shiny ivory robe and her just-as-ivory skin a flickering orange.

"You can put that gun away, Jess." She took a glass and reached in Jess' shirt pocket for his cigarettes, while he opened the bottle and poured them both a drink. Nina lit two smokes and passed one to Jess. "I told you, Wolvrik's not what you think."

Jess slid the pistol out of his pocket and set it on the endtable next to the sofa. "You don't know what I'm thinking, Nina." He sat down, and she cuddled up next to him. They sat there in silence for a while, listening to the birch logs snap and hiss, sipping their drinks while the little parlor grew a layer of haze from their exhaled smoke.

"No, I don't *know* what you're thinking, Jess. But I can guess. You're thinking, 'What did I get myself into? Why do I have a Chicago whore in my parlor?' Close?"

"No, and don't talk like that. But what the hell you're doing with that son of a bitch *is* nagging at me." He held her by the chin, turning Nina to face him. "What gives?"

She turned away. "Do you like working for the railroad, Jess?"

"Huh?" He shrugged. "Not really. No, that's not right. I hate it. The job, the depot, this little town."

"So why don't you quit?"

He shrugged again. "Nothing else to do. A guy has to make a living."

"And how long have you been on the job?"

"Two and half years now."

She turned back to face him, one eyebrow cocked. "Me too."

Nina sipped her drink, and lit another one of Jess' cigarettes for herself. Then she eased down onto his lap, looking up at him while she talked. "Do you remember the first night we met? At the depot? I told you I'd been on a lot of...dates. They aren't dates, Jess, I guess you've figured that out by now. Some girls look at a guy and see their next date. I look at a guy, and I see my next meal."

"Don't talk like that, Nina."

"Well, don't *you* go all innocent on me now, or I swear I'll climb back into that torn dress and hitchhike down to Chicago right now."

"Or back to Wolvrik's?"

"No." She shivered. "Not there."

It started then, on the sofa in the parlor, by the fireplace. Nina eased out of the ivory satin robe, and lay back on the sofa. Jess' eyes should have been riveted on her beautiful nakedness, her beautiful legs and hips and breasts. But instead, they kept lingering on Nina's bruises. With the robe off, with her body naked in the firelight, he could clearly see the patchwork of welts. Some were raw, ragged. On her thigh, inside and just beneath her tuft of soft red hair. On her breasts, and ringed around her nipples. Fresh, sore, ripped right through her tender skin. "What the hell? What *are* those...what —"

But she touched her fingertip to his lips to silence him, pulling him close to her body.

"Nina, they're —"

"Just hold me, Jess. Just love me."

He carried her to his bedroom. He held her. He loved her, just like she asked. And tried to ignore the bite marks all over Nina's pale, naked flesh.

Jess had sex before, of course. Once with Cassie way back in high school. Once in Seoul, which he was still trying to forget. A few more times then with Cassie, after he came back to Monico Junction. But making love with Nina? It was something else altogether. Better than anything Jess had ever felt. Better even than the last few weeks' dreams of what it would be like, and there'd been a lot of those.

After they were done, they lay there in Jess' dark bedroom, watching the snow flurries dance outside the window. He stroked her back and listened to Nina's soft breathing, just savoring the feel of her naked skin on his, her legs knotted in his, her breasts against his chest, her red hair spread across his shoulders. His fingers strayed to one of her bruises, a mean looking, fresh wound, still sticky with blood that hadn't dried.

Nina sucked in her breath, and he yanked his hand away.

"Sorry," Jess said.

"It's all right. Just tender."

"Nina, what does that bastard do to you? What are all these bruises?"

"I don't want to talk about that now. Let's just lay here, Jess."

"Well, I *do* want to talk about it."

She eased off of him and sat up in the bed, pulling the blanket up over her breasts, shivering, suddenly cold. "Could you get us a cigarette?"

Jess scampered out of bed and brought them both a cigarette. Nina sat there with her back against the headboard for a long time, blowing her blue smoke straight up so it hovered over them like a halo. "Jess, it's just like I told you. Wolvrik isn't what you think," she said, not looking at Jess beside her, but staring out the window instead. "Oh, he's bad all right. But he's more than bad. He's...Jess, he's evil."

"I can see that," Jess said, gesturing to her bruises.

She shook her head. "No, I mean *Evil.* The real thing. He's not natural. Not...human." Nina turned away from the window and faced Jess. "He's a vampire. Dieter Wolvrik's a vampire."

Jess said nothing for a moment. Then he burst out laughing. But the laugh dried up in his throat when he saw Nina's face, saw she wasn't joking.

"Nina, come on. A vampire? Bela Lugosi? Dracula? You don't believe that crap, do you?"

She nodded.

"So, I suppose he's got a coffin up there in that estate of his, huh? Runs around in a cape, that it?"

"No. Actually he's usually naked from the moment we get there." That one hit Jess like a hammer. "I've never seen any coffins. And he doesn't have fangs, either. You ever see vampires in the movies with fangs? No. That's just fairy tale stuff, I think. But he sleeps during the day with all the drapes and the shutters closed. Makes me sleep with him. Not that I could go anywhere. He usually has the whole place locked up tight, inside and out."

"But today? How'd you –"

She shrugged her shoulders. "He left one door unlocked. At first I thought it was a trap, that he just wanted to catch me trying to get out so he could hurt me some more. Have an excuse to tie me up or something. Dieter likes to do that." Nina's cigarette was smoked down to the butt. She climbed out of bed and got another, then stood over by the window and lit it. Jess stared at her perfect, naked body, framed there by the pale moonlight filtering inside.

Perfect, except for the wounds.

The bites.

"I made noise before I left. Lots of noise, Jess. I wanted to make sure. But he didn't get up. He just slept up in his room the whole time. I didn't really know what to do then. So I headed for the train station. And you."

"Jesus, Nina. That's three miles cross country from Twilight Lake."

"Really? Felt like more." She pressed her face against the window and looked up and down the road. But there were no headlights out there, no black Cadillacs lurking in the dark. "He drinks my blood, Jess."

"Goddamn it, Nina, then why do you keep coming back?"

"Do you think I want to?" She turned back to face him, tears rolling down her cheeks. "You think I like what he does to me?" Nina trudged across the floor and fell back on the bed, curling up in a ball at the edge of the mattress. "Remember last weekend? I didn't come. Oh, the tickets were there for me. Wolvrik has them sent over each week. Along with an envelope of money. And instructions. Orders, on what he wants me to buy, what he wants me to wear. But I didn't go. I stayed the whole weekend with a friend. Didn't come back to my flat till Monday evening." Her voice choked up now. "Wolvrik was waiting for me when I walked in. He was mad. Real mad. Told me what he'd do to me if I ever disobeyed him again. Ugly things, Jess. Real ugly things."

"Uglier than what he's already doing to you?"

She sobbed. "Yes. Lots."

Jess jumped off the bed and pawed through the darkness for his clothes. "That's it. I'm going over there and finish this right now."

"No!" Nina scrambled off the bed, tripping in the tangled sheets. She fell at Jess' feet and clung to him. "You can't. I'm telling you, he'd kill you. He's not human."

"Bullshit." Jess pulled his legs free and stomped into the parlor. He came back with the .38, checked that it was loaded. "I blew a bear's head off with this once. It was poking around the garbage in back of the depot. Tried to chase it away, but it charged me. One shot, and I swear, half it's head blew off. I don't think Dieter's head is any harder than a bruin's." He climbed into his pants, started buttoning up his shirt.

"All right." Nina's voice was cold. "Kill him." Dead serious. It made Jess' fingers stop halfway up the shirt. "I *want* him dead. I want him to pay. But not with that, Jess."

He looked at the pistol.

"That won't kill him. He's a vampire, Jess. For real. Look at me, if you have to wonder. Look at these bite marks." She lifted one leg and pointed at the ugly wounds on her inner thigh for emphasis. "You have to stake him. In the heart. And cut off his head."

He gulped.

"I'm serious, Jess. I've read up on them. On vampires. Those bullets would go right through him, just like in the movies. You have to get a wooden stake and pound it right in his chest. Then cut off his head. That's the only way. The only way I'll ever be free of him. The only way *we'll* be free."

Jess slowly finished the rest of his shirt buttons. Just as slowly, he found his shoes and tied the laces. He held the snubnose revolver in his hand, looked at it, looked at Nina lying there naked on the bed, beautiful in the pale moonlight. Red hair painted purple by the night. Eyes sparkling just like the flurries glistening on the windowpanes.

He looked at the bruises on her skin.

Jess set the gun down on the mattress.

"You stay here, Nina."

"All right."

"I'll be back."

She nodded. "I love you, Jess." She ran to him and wrapped her arms around Jess' neck. Nina kissed him hard, kissed him long, all wet lips and wetter tongue, her ivory flesh pressed against him. Finally, Jess had to pull away.

"Nina, maybe we shouldn't be seen together when I get back. Have to figure some way to get you back to Chicago."

"Don't worry about it. There's not going to be any trouble. He's a vampire, Jess. Once you do it, he's going to crumble into dust."

"Oh." He mulled that over. "Right. But still —"

Nina approached him again, but Jess backed away, sure if he held her in his arms once more, he'd never get out of there.

"Jess, if anything goes wrong, I promise I'll take the train back to Chicago tomorrow. I'll leave my phone number and address here on the bed. You just call me, and I'll come right back, Jess. I'll be on the very next train and come right back to you. And then we can be together."

He nodded. "Well, if anything *does* go wrong, you call Hamm. Sheriff Hamm. Number's by the phone in the kitchen. He'll take care of you, get you back to Chicago." He paused. "I love you too, Nina. I really do."

She smiled at him.

"Don't forget, Jess. In the heart. Then cut that bastard's head off."

Nina stood at the bedroom window, still naked, shivering from the chill oozing off the glass. The flurries were heavier now, dusting the ground white and starting to cling to the trees. She sipped at a fresh bourbon and tugged on a fresh cigarette, watching Jess plunder the woodpile next to the house. He disappeared into the darkness for a while, and then she saw him return with a straight, three foot long birch branch, one end whittled down to a sharp point.

He carried an ax in his other hand.

She watched Jess start up the Chevy and pull away into the snow.

Nina smiled. She picked the .38 up off the mattress and spun it around on her finger, gunslinger style. Then she took her drink and her cigarette and went straight to the kitchen, where she flicked on the light and found the phone.

"Operator? Yes, can you get me Rhinelander? Triple-A Livery, please. Yes, I know it's late. I'll hold."

❖

Hamm turned off U.S. 45 and spun into a slipsliding fishtail that just missed a tree. He got the old Hudson police cruiser righted, then took it a lot slower as he headed down mainstreet Monico Junction. The train depot was closed. The Tap & Table was dark, Cassie safely home after another night of armwrestling feisty drunks looking for a kiss. Hamm checked his watch. Nearly midnight. The whole town was locked up tight, and he could finally head home for a snack before bed. Which was just as well; the Hudson held up pretty well for all the rough miles it took these past four years, and the town council sure as hell wasn't planning on springing for a new cruiser anytime soon. But this two ton hunk of iron was like a greased weasel on the snow.

Hell of a stupid ass car for the Wisconsin northwoods.

Even taking it slow and careful, Hamm shot through Monico Junction's tiny business strip in a minute. He was just about to make the turn towards home when he caught a pair of headlights whizzing by in his rearview mirror. Hamm grunted as he twisted his big belly around to look over his shoulder. A car sped up U.S. 45, headed away from town. Sped, all right. It was doing eighty if it was moving at all.

Hamm made a fast U-turn, feeling the Hudson spin and quiver on the slick street. He floored it, fishtailed again, then eased off the gas and headed back towards the highway as best he could, keeping his eyes riveted on the two red dots of that car's taillights, a good mile ahead now.

Hamm chanced fifty, then sixty. It wasn't enough to gain on that speeder, but it was good enough to keep the car in sight. "Son of a bitch," Hamm hissed to himself. He knew cars. It was his job. And he knew those taillights belonged to a '55 Chevy, and he knew perfectly well whose it was.

"Where the hell are you headed to, Jess?" Hamm prodded the

Hudson up to seventy, feeling the tires shimmying on the snow slicked asphalt. Then eighty, and at that he could barely keep Jess' Chevy in sight.

"Goddamn, he's going right over there. I don't believe it, he's going up to Twilight Lake." Hamm hit the siren and flicked the switch to start up the red bubble light on the roof. But between the twists in the road, the evergreen canyons looming right alongside, and the snowfall, he wasn't even sure if Jess would see it.

"Damn if he isn't going up to Dieter Wolvrik's, and going to get himself killed." The Hudson shivered when Hamm careened around a tight curve, losing sight of Jess' Chevy altogether. "Jess, you dumb assed son of a bitch, I don't know why you're going there, but that guy's going to eat you for a midnight sna –"

The word caught in Hamm's jowls. The Hudson hit a snowdrift and spun in a full three sixty, at a cool eighty miles an hour. Pine trunks whizzed by in a black and gray kaleidoscope, till the car finally, miraculously, came to a stop. Off the shoulder. In the ditch along the road.

Hamm slammed the steering wheel and scrolled through every swear word he learned in the quartermaster corps. The tires spun uselessly in the snow. So he did all he could and started to rock it – an inch forward, an inch back, another foot forward, another back.

It took forever, or seemed to, at least. Finally the Hudson roared out of the ditch and back up onto the highway, rear tires screaming, belching burnt rubber smoke as the steaming treads melted the snowcover and licked the asphalt. Hamm shot back up U.S. 45, and made a beeline for Twilight Lake.

He pulled up to the Wolvrik lodge, right next to the '55 Chevy. Jess' Chevy. Lights still on, motor running. "Jess, you dumb son of a bitch, why don't you just call ahead and tell him you're coming for him?" Hamm unholstered his service revolver and clomped through the deepening snow to the house. He shivered; the place looked even spookier than the last time he was here.

And, the front door was wide open.

Yellow light spilled out onto the grounds.

"Jess?" Hamm stepped inside cautiously, revolver pointed up at the ceiling, his jangling key rings and cuffs sounding like a sled team echoing in the huge entry hall.

"Jess?" No answer. But Hamm didn't need one. Wet footprints tracked right across the front hall and up the stairs. Hamm followed them, still calling, "Jess? Mr. Wolvrik? I don't know what you two are beefing about, but it's got to be a woman, so what do you say we sit down like men and talk it out over a good stiff belt or two, huh? Jess?"

Hamm reached the top of the stairs.

Heard a *thud.*

Then a grunt.

There – down the hall. Puffing like a steam engine, he ran to the first open door and leaped inside.

"Oh, sweet Jesus," Hamm gasped.

He lowered his gun. "Mother of God – Jess, what have you done?"

Jess Burton looked up from the floor, where he straddled Dieter Wolvrik's body. Or what was left of Dieter Wolvrik. A three foot birch branch poked out of Wolvrik's chest, blood gushing up at the base and spilling all over Dieter's black silk smoking jacket.

Hamm brought the revolver back up to bear on his friend. "You best step away from there now, Jess."

Jess nodded and stood up, the bloody ax still in his one hand.

"Hamm...she said. Said he'd turn to dust."

In his other hand, Jess clutched Dieter Wolvrik's head by the hair, blood still flowing from the neck stump and puddling on the floor.

❖

"You can stare down those tracks all you want, but it won't make the train come any faster."

Jess smiled, hearing old Herbie's voice, hearing his own younger voice saying the same thing somewhere inside his head.

He hefted himself off the stubby concrete block that had once been a footing for the Monico Junction depot platform. Fished around in his pocket and found one last low tar and nicotine cigarette inside the crumpled pack. He lit up, tossed the pack on the ground, right where the twin rails of the C&NW line used to sit. He walked along the old right-of- way for a stretch, but slowly, his tired joints creaking a little. The empty rail line cut a tunnel between the flanking walls of leafless birch and tall pines, a long straight tunnel heading south.

"It isn't the trains, Herbie, it's the places they can take you to that I like."

Places like Milwaukee. And Chicago.

And prison.

Hamm had to take Jess in on that cold, snowy night in '55. He was arraigned in the county seat in Rhinelander. The trial itself was held in Wausau. It was a brief affair. Other than Cassie and Hamm himself as character witnesses, Jess didn't have much of a defense.

Not that anyone in Wisconsin *or* Chicago would miss Dieter Wolvrik very much. His dirty laundry all came out in the trial. An ex-Nazi from Germany, it turned out, a regular SS colonel the War Crimes Commission gave up on in '49. Had a tidy little business going in Chicago: drugs, prostitution, heavy on the latter, with special girls for special men with special wishes. Dieter's own the most perverse – favoring two girls together, bondage games, biting young flesh and sucking the wounds...kinks he picked up in the camps back in the Fatherland. But he had it all cloaked in various layers of legitimate business veneers, and had been doing just fine, thank you.

No, there wasn't anyone to mourn Dieter Wolvrik's passing. Ex-Nazi crooks don't make a lot of friends. Whatever few Dieter may have had, they bid him good-bye the best way they knew how: apparently *someone* looted all his secret stashes and bank accounts not two days after he was killed.

No one to mourn him, not even anyone to claim the body, so Dieter ended up buried in an unmarked grave in the Monico Junction Cemetery, of all places.

The D.A., the county police and the judge all took a liking to Jess. They tried to persuade him to change his defense. *Vampires?* A Nina-no-name from Chicago, that no one could ever locate, even though they managed to track down a phone call made from Jess' cottage that horrible night, a call to the closest thing the northwoods had to a taxi service over in Rhinelander, tracked down the driver who remembered picking up a pretty red head in a blossoming snowstorm, a girl who was dressed in a rag-tag, mismatched bunch of clothes and waited in the snow for him, nowhere near Jess' house, though, but a good two miles away out on U.S. 8. He drove her back to Rhinelander, and left her at the Soo Line station, and that was the last he saw of her.

The Soo station. That was the final slap in the face for Jess.

They gave him sixty years to life, but he was out in just a little over forty. Some armchair liberal in Madison changing the rules, maybe. Or they needed more room for the gangbangers that were crowding out the old timers who were too old to do much damage anymore. Even one who'd taken an ax and a stake to a vampire in 1955.

He ended up right back in Monico Junction. There was no where else to go. Of course, it was just Monico now that the railroad was long gone. Jess pumped gas part time at the tiny Gas 'N Go on U.S. 45, Monico's only business these days. Kept a room on the second floor of the building that used to house the Tap & Table, though that – like Cassie and Hamm – was long gone too.

And on cold nights, Jess Burton wandered down to the overgrown foundation of the old depot. Nights just like this.

Jess hiked his collar up over his neck. He felt a spot of cold hit his already chilled face. A snowflake. Then another, and another. Flurries sifted out of the night sky and started to dust the old right-of way. But he kept walking.

"You just call me, and I'll come right back, Jess."

No, Nina didn't leave Jess a note on the bed that night. No phone number, no Chicago address.

"I'll be on the very next train and come right back to you. And then we can be together."

No note, but no one could ever have convinced Jess that Nina wasn't coming back. Staking and axing a guy, and a nice long prison stint could do a few funny things to a man's head.

Jess kept on walking, lifting his ear muffs every few steps to listen for the moaning from a diesel's air horn.

He kept on walking on his old legs, waiting for the 400.

On Line

By Rick R. Reed

She had promised herself she would limit her time on the computer to less than an hour a day. And now, here it was, a quarter after twelve and Nancy was wide awake, all the books in her apartment read and neatly catalogued on living room shelves, TV turned to low, all sixty channels broadcasting tedious talk shows, infomercials, nature specials and old movies no one wanted to see when they first came out.

Nancy's tiny office, off the dining room, beckoned. It seemed the Macintosh within called on her to forget her resolve, forget the mounting amounts of money her Visa statement detailed each month, the forty and fifty hours of on-line time she could only barely afford and that was only if she subsisted on beans and rice. She knew she shouldn't do it, knew she should head instead into the bathroom where she would brush and floss and then go to bed, where she could lie awake, dreaming of lithe bodies (unlike hers), blonde women with pert, small breasts (unlike hers) and perfect rows of white teeth that lit up a room when the woman smiled (completely unlike Nancy). Perhaps, she thought, rationalizing now and not really caring, such a woman awaited her electronic embrace on "System Up" the service to which she subscribed. When Nancy "chatted" in one of the rooms, she became Raven, the dark-haired, wild-eyed Cuban vixen whose depravity knew no bounds and whose witty repartee would enchant and seduce, inspiring the most fervent love and devotion.

Nancy did manage to will herself into the small bathroom, with its claw foot tub, rusty metal shower enclosure, cracked tile floors and paint-chipped walls. Nancy took one look at her reflection and despaired. She had heard all about self-esteem and knew she shouldn't denigrate herself so, but the woman who peered back at her was not one who could snare a beautiful, nubile young thing. Nancy could have never snared such a creature, even when she was twenty years younger, when she bore an uneasy resemblance to the Nancy of comic strip fame. Now the woman who looked back at her was of healthy proportions (fat), intelligent looking (mud brown eyes enlarged by pop bottle thick lenses, framed in tortoiseshell), and had the kind of haircut she could kindly refer to as sensible (black hair chopped short, just below her ears: Louise Brooks gone sour).

But on "System Up" Nancy could be whatever she wanted, hiding behind a barrage of wit and verbosity, mistress of the clever quip and the alluring line, perfect for quiet, private chats sheathed in the safety and security of instant messages, her own private room (Meet me in the "Mistress of the Night" room) or e-mail.

Nancy did pick up her toothbrush and even decorated its bristles with a ribbon of bright blue gel.

Then set it back down on the little plastic counter beneath the medicine cabinet mirror.

To justify talking tonight, tomorrow Nancy would not visit her on-line service at all. No matter that tonight, she could not afford it, no matter that a good night's sleep might afford her a halfway productive day tomorrow at First National, where she worked as a loan officer. Tomorrow, after all, was Friday and she would have the entire weekend to rest.

So it was no surprise that within minutes Nancy found herself in the tiny bedroom she called her den, seated in front of the Mac screen, watching as the little icons lined up as the system powered up, aiming her toward her destination in cyberspace, where life was beautiful and unfettered by concerns about loneliness, unworthiness and the clock ticking relentlessly downward toward a passing no one would mark.

Nancy pointed and clicked on the System Up icon (a tiny computer with a big, Superman-like "S" on its monitor screen). She waited for the prompt that would allow her to enter her screen name (Raven) and then her password (SapphoXX). Nancy listened hopefully for the electronic voice to tell she had mail and once again was disappointed to see the closed mailbox icon, with its taunting "no mail" message.

Quickly, Nancy moved through the screens until she was scrolling through the Member Rooms, looking for "Chicago f4f" hoping she wouldn't be denied access because the room was full. Nancy was pleased to see there were 15 members in the room (a good number) and within moments, she was in.

The screen was blank. Nancy typed "Good evening, ladies," and waited. Within moments, another message popped up, from a familiar screen name: Flshsinner.

"How you doin', Raven?"

"Looking for love in all the wrong places."

"LOL." (Laughing out loud).

Hmm. This one was easy to amuse. "What brings you out on this cold winter night?"

Nancy waited for a full minute and when she got no response, typed: "I am Raven, mistress of the night."

A screen name she had never seen, TepesAllure, popped up. "I thought I was mistress of the night."

"I don't know if there's room for two mistresses."

Flshsinner joined in. "Uh-oh, a cat fight?"

Nancy typed: "Tepes, there's not enough room. What do you care to do about it?"

A tiny electronic gong alerted her that she had an instant mail message from Tepes. "Listen, bitch, I have more reason to be mistress of the night than you could ever dream."

Nancy responded. "What do you know of my dreams, Tepes?"

"I know they're the only lively thing shedding light in a bland void."

The message chilled her, as on target as it was, with its casual cruelty. Nancy wasn't sure she should go on. "Who knows what are dreams and what is reality? Perhaps my reality is the color and excitement filled world you could only envy."

"I have no envy for the walking wounded, past her prime and desperate."

Nancy swallowed. Her mouth suddenly felt dry. She leaned back and rubbed her eyes. Perhaps this was the CyberGod's way of telling her she should have circumvented her office tonight and headed for the warmth and comfort of her flannel sheets, no matter how many hours she lay awake, tracing hairline cracks in her bedroom ceiling.

"Hello? Raven?"

Nancy caressed the keyboard. "You're a bit on the harsh side, aren't you, dear?"

"Harsh side, dark side. I say what's on my mind. And what's on my mind right now *dear,* is you."

"Why would someone like me be on your mind, when you've obviously decided I have nothing worth your interest?"

"I never said that. Describe yourself."

And Nancy typed in the description that had become so familiar it might as well have been some sort of computer macro. "Long black hair, dark brown eyes, full lips (you decide), 38-24-36. Toned, muscular."

"And I am the Queen of Sheba."

The woman was a first-class bitch. Nancy wondered why she was bothering. She could leave this place by merely pressing the command and "Q" key and be out of here, away from this nonsense, safe in her bed, while visions of Morgan Fairchild danced in her head. Yet, there was a strange allure to her directness, to her refusal to accept any of the crap Nancy churned out, that other women ate up like a kitten lapped up milk. "Well, your majesty, what do you look like? And BE HONEST."

"Honesty is my strong suit, my little lamb. I think you'd agree I look pretty good for my age, which happens to number in the centuries. Think Catherine Deneuve in *The Hunger*. Think elegance and grace. Feline. And don't worry about gym-toned bodies and silicone tits, thank you very much."

Nancy's hungry mind conjured up the image: this fabulous creature at her keyboard, alone in some city apartment (a highrise, where the lights of Chicago's skyscrapers were interrupted only by the dark void that was Lake Michigan). She realized suddenly how easy it had been to sucker in these women who found themselves with one hand between their legs while the other caressed the keyboard as Nancy played up to their fantasies, becoming God's gift to lesbians and the devil's Tantalus to straight men. She *wanted* to believe it was some strange Catherine Deneuve at the other end of their electronic connection. But what was this business about being centuries old?

"Methinks you're a little too enraptured with horror cinema."

"Horror cinema has got nothing on me, my little bespectacled piglet. Horror cinema has managed to get so few of my traditions right as to be truly laughable. But there has been one tradition, rule if you will, they've always succeeded in getting correct."

"And what would that be?"

"I can't tell you that."

"You're quite the mysterious lady, aren't you?"

"You couldn't even begin to guess."

Suddenly, Nancy's spine stiffened as a chill washed over her. The chill was unlike any ordinary chill; It had the feel of icy fingers caressing, just barely grazing the raised bumps of her spine, like long fingernails moving down her back. She wondered where the chill came from and looked up at her screen where the instant message from seconds ago still remained. The words "bespectacled piglet" jumped out, as if highlighted. The description, unflattering as it was, was true nevertheless. "Do I know you?" Nancy typed, fingers beginning to tremble, causing her to have to type the simple query three times before she got it right.

"We've spoken in your dreams."

"Seriously," Nancy pleaded in her electronic voice, the one she thought of until this moment as throaty and seductive. Now the voice was wheedling, whining, a little too low pitched and dense to be heard distinctly. "You seem to have picked up certain of my physical character- istics and I wondered if you were just a good guesser or if you're someone I know." Nancy racked her brain, trying to recall who at the bank she might have told about her after hours "social life."

And came up blank.

"I told you. We've spoken in your dreams. For the last several months, I've visited you there, in that gossamer world, where I found the two of us to be highly compatible."

"And why is that?"

"I can't tell you that."

"What can you tell me?"

"I can tell you that I can see your worth."

"Wonderful." Nancy keyed in, rolling her eyes.

"Would you like to know more?"

"Knock yourself out."

"I don't think you take me seriously."

"Should I?"

"Dead serious."

The word dead floated before Nancy's eyes. Again, she had the prickly sensation of cold, as if something large and icy stood just behind her, casting a black shadow. She glanced over her shoulder and saw nothing more than a painted white bookcase, filled with paperbacks and a framed poster above it: two tabby kittens on a red sweep, one atop the other. Nancy contemplated shutting off the computer and banishing this bitch to cyberspace where she could play mind games with some other unsuspecting soul.

"Feeling a chill, Nancy?"

The room seemed to shift just a little, as Nancy might imagine the movement of a room during an earthquake. Seconds passed while she tried to quell the shaking in her fingers enough to be able to type again. "Again: do you know me?"

"Better than anyone, I'd guess."

"How did you know my name?" Nancy knew she'd never put any real information in her member profile and the only answer must be, had to be, that this bitch knew her. Nancy didn't know how, she didn't know where, but there had to be some way this woman knew who she was. Or perhaps, she wasn't speaking to a woman at all, but one of the young guys who worked at the bank, one of the ones who whispered and snickered when she passed by, nylons swishing, sounding like an insect.

"Your name is written on my heart."

"Oh stop it!" Nancy typed back, weary now of this assault. She wondered again why she just didn't stop, but something kept her fingers glued to the keyboard. And she suddenly realized that something could very well be the simple fact that for the first time, in years, she was feeling a little excitement. For the first time since she could remember, someone was taking an interest in her, no matter how twisted or mocking that interest might be.

"You know you don't mean that."

"Oh what do you know?"

"Everything."

Nancy rubbed her arms together over her ample breasts, trying to dispel the completely unreasonable cold that overwhelmed her. "No one knows everything."

"I know everything about you: all about the loneliness, all about the hours spent in front of the computer or, barring that, the TV or your nose buried in some God-awful Rita Mae Brown novel."

Nancy closed her eyes, feeling as if a bright light had just been shined on her, exposing everything she thought hidden from the world. "You know nothing. I don't know who you are, but you're certainly not right about anything. I couldn't even begin to abide this creature you describe." And then, despair threatening to overwhelm her, typed: "I am Raven, mistress of the night."

"If you're mistress of the night, honey, I'm Hillary Clinton."

Nancy barked out a short burst of laughter. She felt herself backed into a corner and knew no way to get by this, what had she said her name was? TepesAllure...Nancy looked at the screen, thinking that Tepes held some familiarity for her, but in spite of mentally searching her memory banks, could come up with no match for the name. She wanted to ask again who this person really was, but knew she would get no less a cryptic response than she already had.

She changed her tack. "So what brings you to your keyboard

tonight?"

"You do."

"Why me? I don't think we've spoken before."

"Not like this."

Nancy flashed on the few pathetic sexual encounters she had had over the years, encounters she could easily count on two hands, okay one hand. All of them with older, professorial women, who followed her home, satisfied themselves and never called again. Could this be one of them? It had been two years since the last unsatisfying liaison; Nancy had bought her computer within the last year.

"How then, how have we spoken?"

"Your desire speaks to me."

"I'm not horny." Nancy typed, bland, to the point.

"I wasn't talking about that kind of desire, although that sort of exploration does hold its charm, does it not?"

What would Raven say to that question? Nancy wondered. And then berated herself for being such a fool. Things had gone beyond Raven. "I wouldn't know."

"I'm sure that together, we could find out. But let me tell you: your body is not what I'm after, at least not in that sense."

"What then are you after?"

"Your blood."

"What are you, a hemophiliac?"

"You're very funny, Nancy. A hemophiliac, actually, is a fantasy partner of mine. Mmmm...imagine, blood that doesn't clot. Are you getting the picture?"

"You're in the wrong room. There's a vampire chat room. Just go back to Member Rooms, locate it and double click."

"I've located what I want."

"I don't think you have. I have to be getting to bed. It's late and I need to get up early."

"Don't leave. We're just beginning to scratch the surface."

"Go scratch yourself!" Nancy typed quickly and even more quickly pressed the command and Q button to quit System Up. She hit the return key hard when the prompt came up asking her if she was sure she wanted to quit. "Yes, damn it, I'm sure!" Nancy hit the power button and tried to get hold of herself. She was panting, her heart was racing and a thin line of sweat had formed at her hairline.

Later, Nancy found herself awakened from a restless sleep, filled with shadowy images and strange beasts, unidentifiable, lurking around just this or that corner, waiting to pounce.

She sat up in bed, looking down at the silver slats her mini blinds and the full moon outside conspired together to create. She brushed some hair out of her eyes and wondered what it was that had awakened her so abruptly.

Then she heard it. *Gong.* The sound was familiar but seemed to have no place in this restless landscape.

Gong. That chiming again.

And then Nancy recognized the sound for what it was. She lay cautiously back down, thinking the noise had to be a fragment of dream lingering just past wakefulness. If there was such a thing as "lucid dreaming" then perhaps dream images, aural or not, could be a little slower in dispersing than her waking mind could dispel them.

Gong.

And finally Nancy realized she should have become aware of the sound long before, but the sound was so out of place in her little night-quiet apartment that her mind didn't accept it. When the gong chimed again, Nancy arose, putting sheet and blanket warmed feet to a chilled floor, and shivered.

The sound was so familiar because she heard it most every night. It was the sound alerting her that she had an instant message on her computer, as part of System Up's online service.

"God, did I forget to turn off the computer?" Nancy wondered, groggy, thinking with dread of all the hours of wasted time on the system she had used while sleeping.

As she headed toward her den, she knew with a certainty beyond doubt that she had shut things down before retiring. Some sort of glitch maybe? But what sort of glitch would turn the computer back on and sign her on to the service once more?

The door to the den was open. Inside, Nancy could see the pale glow from her monitor screen and the memories of TepesAllure rushed back and Nancy paused at the door, afraid to go inside, for fear of what might be waiting. Perhaps, she thought, anxiously gnawing at a nail that was already bitten down to the quick, someone had broken in and was using her computer.

Perhaps it was TepesAllure herself. After all, she knew Nancy's name, knew what she looked like. Was it really such a stretch to imagine that she knew where Nancy lived and had come to call?

Briefly, Nancy considered tiptoeing back to the living room, where she could dial 911 and report an intruder.

And then what? What if the authorities came out to find a lonely woman who had forgotten to shut off her computer before going to bed?

Nancy stepped inside.

The den was empty.

Nancy sat, feeling weak and dizzy, in front of the computer, where a message flickered on the screen.

"Don't sleep, Nancy, the night is winding down, faster and faster, like water down the drain. Dawn approaches."

"Who are you?"

"I am TepesAllure, mistress of the night."

"I thought I was... oh never mind. What's going on here? What do you want from me?" Nancy's eyelids burned. She needed sleep.

"I told you what I wanted, my dear. I'm simply waiting for you to give it to me."

"My blood?"

"Yes, that hot, pumping life juice."

"Well, let me slit my wrists to make you happy."

"What a perfectly mundane idea. I have in mind a more sensual connection."

"Look, it's late and I don't have time for this." Nancy pulled the plug from her computer, causing the monitor to go blank and Nancy to sigh with relief, or perhaps disappointment. But pulling the plug was the sensible thing to do and Nancy always did the sensible thing. It had gotten her where she was today.

She headed back toward the bedroom.

And froze.

Gong.

Rushing back to her den, where the interior was once more warmed by the glow of the monitor, Nancy froze in absolute terror, her eyes moving from the glowing screen to the empty electrical socket in the wall, back and forth, back and forth. "This has to be a dream," Nancy whispered to herself, a pounding starting at her temples and her respiration coming more quickly. She sat heavily in the desk chair, because she thought her legs would no longer support her.

"You're not rid of me that easily."

"What do you want?" Nancy typed again, weary and nauseous.

"You."

"Then take me," Nancy typed, her fingers hitting the keyboard uncertainly. "Just come over here, waltz through the door and take me. I'm tired." Nancy typed, looking outside her den and making sure her front door was locked with both deadbolt and chain.

No instant message came and Nancy sat staring at the screen, wondering what had happened to TepesAllure. Perhaps Nancy had been too direct. Perhaps she had tired of the game.

Perhaps I'm going insane, Nancy thought, uncomfortable with the feeling that her last thought was most on target.

Nancy typed. "Where have you gone my precious? TepesAllure, you've allured me and left me high and dry. Is that all there is?"

The screen remained blank, taunting her. Isn't this always the way? Nancy thought, shivering and rubbing her hands over her bare arms to warm them. The weird sensation of chill overcame her once more, as if something cold and dark were moving behind her, just out of sight.

But this time, the chill seemed more real. Nancy could have sworn she heard a whisper of movement just behind her. Goosebumps formed on her flesh and her heart began to beat more rapidly. Part of her wanted to turn and look and the other part wanted to remain frozen, staring at her unanswered message on the computer screen.

More whispering movement, then, and a chill that ran up her spine, like a cold draft blowing in. Nancy bit her lower lip. "Please don't make me look," she whispered.

And then, Nancy shuddered because she felt what she could swear was a breath on the back of her neck. Yet this breath did not seem human; its icy chill seemed so far removed from human that it could make her scream.

But Nancy was not the type of person to scream. She was far too sensible for that.

She whirled in the chair, thinking that at last she would dispel this late night nonsense and return to bed. Everything would look different, laughably different, in the morning.

A beautiful woman stood behind her. Nancy froze, voice caught in her throat by an unseen hand, which squeezed, squeezed until all the air in the world vanished. Before the woman came nearer, Nancy knew she had seen this woman before. Had seen her everytime she typed out a description of Raven to some lonely soul out there in cyberspace, who wanted to believe so much that she did.

And then with movement not even perceptible to Nancy's human gaze, the woman was upon her, all fangs and wild, feral eyes, biting and ripping her flesh, drawing her blood from her so quickly Nancy didn't even have time to scream. She heard, through the woman's passionate whisper,

"You invited me in, my sweet. I've been waiting so long."

The last thing Nancy heard was the sound her head made as it hit the hardwood floor, a dull squishing sound.

❖

She had never tried any of the chat rooms before. She likened them to personal ads and phone sex lines, ploys for the desperate and the unattractive, who needed to hide behind a veil of electricity to attract a suitor.

But tonight, Heather was bored. And, as she tossed her long blonde hair over one shoulder, she knew this would at the very least be good for a laugh.

In the Chicago f4f chat room, she typed. "Good evening, ladies."

And a gong sounded. Heather looked up to see the instant message, from someone called Raven.

"I've been waiting for you. In fact, I've been waiting all my life."

THE HUNTED

Trailer Trash

By Scott T. Goudsward

Sure I shot him. He capped off Mickey who capped Rudy. In a way it was like a form of payback. Them vamps, once they get in your skull and brain there ain't no going back. Only way to be sure about it is plugging the possessed guy or tracking down the bloodsucker that put the whammy on him in the first place. I got entranced by them once...

❖

It all started one hot day in August. Momma was in her lounge chair listening to rebroadcasts of the 700 Club. Daddy was under the pickup truck changing the oil and cussing. Every now and then he'd stick his arm out from under to grab his beer. It was the start of a long hot month that I'd never ever forget. My arch nemesis Jimmy Riley was after me that day. He'd chase me through the rows of trailers and I'd have to go stomping through people's little tiny gardens and run over their plastic flamingos and windmills to get away from him. Jimmy was a little bastard and I hated the life out of him. He had red hair and freckles and was missing his front teeth from fighting with his father.

Jimmy chased me out of the trailer park and deep into the woods. I ran all the way down to the river and hid on the banks in back of a huge old tree hanging on by some thick roots. Every time I'd see or hear Jimmy run by, I'd have to hop in the river and then climb in the roots to hide. That didn't bother me too much because it was so hot and the river so cold.

When it came to dusk, I heard Jimmy's Daddy hollering for him.

Even through the rushing water I heard him. Jimmy's family was louder than mine and that spooked me. It got all dark and I started back for the park. I was certain that Jimmy had gone home and I was going to be safe.

I climbed out of them roots and I got the worst chill all through me, just racing up and down my spine. I figured that if maybe I walked faster, the chill might go away to a certain degree, not to mention that I was soaked to the damn bone. I was going back when I heard this snap in back of me, like someone stepping on a branch. I stopped walking, only the noises behind me didn't. I knew it was Jimmy and I was so cold that I didn't give a good Goddamn what would happen to me. So I turned around and I started yelling and swearing, just the way Daddy had showed me to when you're trying to scare someone. That's when the woods went dead. Like all the animals had run off.

I was half expecting to see Jimmy appear out of thin air. I picked up the biggest stick I could find and got ready to smack a line drive down to center field using Jimmy's head. When from out of the trees comes this woman. Prettiest woman I ever saw. She wore skintight leather pants and a white shirt. She had these green eyes that reflected the moonlight, and long blonde hair, half way down her back.

She walks up to me, takes my hand and starts leading me back to the trailer park. I think I should have realized something wasn't right, but she was awfully pretty. We get back to the trailer and Momma is still on her lounge, only the radio is off and she's holding one of Daddy's best belts from Sears. My dinner, a plate full of beans and noodles was sitting off on the lawn. Man I could tell she was pissed. But when Momma saw the lady, she just stopped breathing and her face turned red. I walked up to her and got ready to explain when she raised that belt.

I never saw the lady move, but suddenly she was right there, in front of Momma. She said something to her and Momma just sat down again and dropped the belt. Daddy started to come outside and nearly died when he saw that lady there. I don't know what he was thinking, but I could have guessed pretty easily though.

I went over to him and he just pushed me aside and stepped out. That lady backhanded Daddy so hard that he landed flat on his ass near the pickup truck. I didn't know what to do. I charged her and she swatted me aside like I was a bug.

The lady slaps Momma and splits her lip wide open. It looked like she had been putting lipstick on while drinking from Daddy's moonshine jug. That lady starts hitting Momma and doesn't stop until she falls off the lounge. All the time Daddy is just screaming and screaming. I didn't know why he wasn't moving. When Momma hit the ground she came back so to speak. Momma started crying and screaming and swearing and praying.

Then the damnedest thing happened, that lady bit Momma's throat. There was blood everywhere and that lady was drinking it right from Momma.

Daddy just sort of stopped struggling when that lady came over to him. She had blood all down her shirt and it wasn't white anymore. That lady kissed him full on the lips and smeared Momma's blood all over his face. Daddy being the tactful man he is, spit in her face. She got all mad, I never seen anyone so mad before. It felt like I was frozen to the ground. These giant claws came out of her fingers and she started carving up Daddy. He didn't scream though, until the end when she peeled off his face. Then she came back over to me.

She looked right in my eyes and I could feel something in my brain give out. All I wanted to do was to follow her around, cuddle and touch her and sexy stuff, you know. One morning when she was sleeping I whacked her, did her real good too.

※

She used to make me go in that coffin with her. Sleep in the dirt and everything.

That morning, I smuggled in a chunk of wood, and staked her out. Most fucked-up thing you'll ever see too, because her eyes opened real wide and seemed to glow while she tried pulling that mind control business on me again. But I guess being staked like that paralyzed her mind, too. 'Cause the thing is she couldn't move, she just looked at me.

I crawled out of the coffin and the room was all dark. She had blacked out the windows with paint and then stapled cloth over the frames and boarded them all shut. Me being such a little guy, I had a hell of a time getting stuff done. But I did it. I got the cloth and boards off, then broke the glass with one of her shoes.

But that whole stake thing? All that really does is paralyze them and get them really pissed off. You know her mind was still working but she wasn't at full strength. I got the boards off the window and the sunlight came shooting in like a runaway train. But wasn't it anywhere close to the coffin. And that was the only window in the room, so I figured I was total-ly screwed.

But then it was like a miracle or something, you know? You hear of all them people who like find super-human strength from adren... adrena...

oh, you know what I mean, right? I grabbed hold of that coffin and dragged it over to the window. All the time in my head I could hear her screaming and begging me not to. She damn near exploded when the sun hit her. Wasn't like in the movies where they melted slowly and turned into goo or sand and blew away with the wind. She just exploded and the flame went everywhere.

The rug and walls caught on fire and next thing you know the whole friggin' place is going up around me. But then, I knew I was okay, 'cause there wasn't anymore voices in my head, just mine. So I jumped right out that window and ran like hell.

Halfway down the street, I crashed into this guy with crazy eyes but he had the air about him like he shat money. We hooked up after I explained everything to him four or five different times. Boy that guy could ask a lot of questions, always yapping away. Momma used to have a name for guys like him, *insane.* In-Sane. That's what she was always saying about them guys who preached Jesus on the TV too, *in-sane.* Eric with the crazy eyes, who talked too much he like adopted me or something. I don't call him dad and he never tried any of that sexy stuff on me, or I would've capped him too. But that's how I got hooked up with him.

❖

It all started off pretty simple you know? Just seemed like another job for us to do. That guy with the crazy eyes – Eric, the one I told you about earlier? He organized the whole thing. He gets a team, couple of gun guys, one of them Jack of All trades? Don't know why they call 'em that, none of them are named Jack. But this guy was like that guy from the television, MacGyver?

And he gets some other guy and appoints him leader. One thing Eric has is money and loads of it too. Wipes his ass with hundreds like the saying goes. So the leader guy is uptight and bossy and stuff, and they're all worried about me being on the team; especially that MacGyver fellow because of what happened to me. So he's always staring at me like I'm going to turn heels and go wacky and kill everyone.

We're supposed to go to this house and check it out. Eric's sources told him that there was a bloodsucker living there. Eric being Eric decides that he needs to investigate it for whatever cause he had. The rest of us were there for backup in case things went bad. Or should I say when things go bad? You never know with bloodsuckers.

The house is in this small town in Georgia. Shit, I can't even remember the name. But it was small – I half expected to see rows of trailers, gun and liquor stores, but there's none of that. Wasn't a trailer within miles. We went to the house first, the one where the bloodsucker was supposed to be? Find the bloodsuckers and deal with them, that's what we did. All we know about this place is that there was supposed to be one guy and two women living there.

We pulled up at this house and it's all big and huge, like a mansion. There's no cars, or bikes or anything in the driveway. And it wasn't really a driveway you know? Just like a big half circle that went up to the front of the place and back to the road. Just like one of them drive up windows for McDonald's or something.

We get to the house and Eric had put out something like a jillion dollars for this RV we had. What Eric wanted, though, was to learn about the bastards. You know, find out what they are and how they act and think. I just wanted to kill them, kill all of them for what they done to Momma and Daddy. I didn't give a good Goddamn about any friggin' research he wanted to do.

At the mansion place, the leader guy gets out and starts doing a quick look-see of the place and then we all piled out of the truck and start arguing. The leader guy wanted full control of everything, only no one was listening to him. It was getting us nowhere. After realizing that we have no plan or anything, Eric gets us into a classy hotel and starts making some calls. Surprising how it was in that little town.

This hotel had everything. Eric rents us that penthouse room on top. Shit, the friggin' place even had one of them bottom washers, for after you...you know. When we finally got settled in half the damn people call out beds and are asleep before I can even fart. That leader guy goes downtown and I figure since I'm here and awake I'm going too. Didn't know what those gun guys were thinking taking naps in the middle of the day. We hadn't been on the road that long, and it wasn't like we were going to do a night attack.

He went off to the town hall and I went to the library. That leader guy was lying and fibbing to the lady at the front desk, telling her how we were shooting a movie and needed to scout locations. But he got us copies of the floor plans and stuff. I had no clue why I even tagged along. It wasn't like I could do anything. I fell asleep in the library reading a book on Vampires. I had to meet the leader guy back at the hotel room, on account of he took the truck back and didn't wait for me. I took a cab.

So with all the stuff we had, that leader guy figures it's time to hit. Only he didn't notice that it got dark out. We would of gone and gotten ourselves dead if we went to that house at night. Whether it's a flock of bloodsuckers, or just one, you never want to give them an advantage. You have to hit them when they're weak and powerless, or else your fucked.

So that night we all had steaks and ate real well. One of them gun guys? He was drinking like Grandad used to before he fell down the well and died. And that MacGyver guy kept trying to get me drunk. I didn't have any idea what was on his mind. So I had a few drinks, and it kinda tasted okay I guess, but it burned. Hell, after three of them little glasses I was ready to puke.

I went off to bed, but I think that was the plan all along. To get rid of me so they could figure out what to do. I don't think they wanted me looking over their shoulders asking all my questions. They still didn't trust me. Which was okay, 'cause I never really trusted any hired guns, especially drunk ones with grenades. Oh yeah, one of them guys, the drunk had himself a couple hand grenades. Even though I never seen one up close before I knew what they were, I seen them in movies and on TV.

I slept and they planned. Don't ask me how long either. When I woke up it must of been near dawn. We ate some food and drank a lot of coffee, even me. When we were done with breakfast, they went on talking quietly to each other basically ignoring me till it was time to go. We all carried our stuff out. They tried to dump all their shit on me, but I wouldn't help them. It's their own fault for bringing all that extra stuff.

One thing I'll always remember, is that when your insides talk to you, you better listen up. 'Cause I saw a case of booze that the drunk brought and it was screaming at me to make some bombs out of it. I even had some strips of cloth on me in case we needed some fast bandages. But something held me back. I think it was the way that MacGyver guy always looked at me. Didn't trust him at all, even less than that drunk.

We pulled up to the house, just went right up that driveway and stopped at the front door. That was just plain stupid, if you ask me. But I wasn't being listened to, on account of my age. They all pile out of the RV. The MacGyver guy leaves the engine running and takes point right behind the RV and starts calling the shots, which made the leader guy pretty pissed off.

That crazy drunk guy gets this look on his face and heads round back of the place. The leader has got me on one corner of the house facing the back and Eric on the other side. Here I am the only one with any real experience with the bloodsuckers and they keep me outside. The leader and the other gun guy go up to the front door. It was a double and had some of that thick glass on either side and there are marble columns on the front stoop too.

The leader guy takes a minute to think and knocks at the door, all the numbnuts plans. Like a bloodsucker will come to the door in broad daylight. They start trying the door, checking it and stuff and finally the leader gets pissed and breaks one of them windows. He reaches inside without even looking and unlocks the door. Guess he didn't care much for subtlety, or even the local law. We would have been screwed if a squad car went by.

Meanwhile I can hear the drunk guy muttering over the radio headsets that Eric gave us all. Eric also got some Kevlar vests for us all, but I refused mine. Might be able to stop a bullet, but it isn't going to stop a vampire.

The drunk is saying how he's going in, but the leader just tells him to hush and stay put. 'Bout that time I start getting a little antsy myself and started looking around. The backyard was all kind of weird and there was one of them little gazebo things? Only it was only half painted and what was painted was chipping. The grass was only half mowed. But not like one half of the lawn? It was done in stripes. And one of the windows had a hole in it, like someone had tossed a baseball or something through it. Couldn't see anything through the hole though, 'cause I looked.

I listened to them talk over the radio. That MacGyver guy was always talking, making sure we were all in position and such. Shit, if the bloodsucker didn't know we were coming from the leader breaking the window, then he did from all the talking. I sat on the side grass under the hole in the window and checked myself. Momma always taught me to travel light. Only take what you need, nothing more. I opened my backpack and started checking inside. I had my cross and holy water-filled squirt gun. I couldn't afford one of those battery powered ones, even though Eric was always offering to buy me one. I had made myself a few stakes and had a mallet. I picked up a road flare too, figured that would've been some use.

Then I found my lighter and checked it, making sure the flame still took. Man some of those booze bombs would've been perfect. Just burn the whole place down. That's the only sure way to know for real. Burn them with fire or get them in the sun. Everything else is bullshit. Garlic just makes them smelly, holy water does hurt them but not for long. Crosses are only good if you got faith and that's something I get more and more of each day.

So the leader and Rudy, the other hired gun, go in. I hear from the back as the drunk guy kicks in the back door and they meet in the middle. Silly thing is that the leader forgot the floor plans in the RV and Mac had to bring them in. He does something clever too. There's this winch on the front of the RV? He brings it in, so that when they get one of the blood-suckers down they can just get him hooked and haul him out to the sunlight.

They're all upstairs in the hallway except for Eric and me. Personally I was getting pretty sick of sitting outside. There was nothing at all going on and I was getting bored. Momma always said if you're going to be in something, be right in the middle. I got out my .38 and some other stuff and headed for the back door. I had my .38 in one hand, had my cross and a stake tucked under my belt and my little flashlight. I had my squirt gun out and kept that kind of handy too. It was hard carrying all that stuff, but I managed.

I went in and it was the kitchen. I walked over to the stove, turned it on and prayed for the hiss of gas. But the bitch just started to heat up instead. Inside the oven was all the silverware in the place too. Thought that was odd. But when you're dealing with the undead you should expect anything. I grabbed a handful and stuffed it into my pack. It wasn't really like stealing, since I was going to use it in the hunt for bloodsuckers. I knew it bugged them, just didn't know why.

I could hear those boys rooting around upstairs on account of they were noisy as sin. They came up to the first room and that door was cracked open just a hair. I stayed still where I was. I didn't want a blood-sucker tackling me on the stairs or anything. They went in and it was like a little kid's room, and man that's the worst kind of bloodsucker, 'cause it's like they're too cute to kill. At least that's what Eric tells me anyway.

It was a girl's room, big bed, all frilly sheets and blankets. Little stuffed dolls and animals everywhere, so many it was like being in K-mart. They didn't see nothing though. So the leader went over to the closet, and just stood there staring at the clothes. He whispers over the radio that he sees something inside. That someone is hidden in back of the closet. So he holds up his hand signaling the others to hold up, and then all of a sudden jumps in there swinging the end of his gun, like he was flushing something out. Nothing came though. It was the way the clothes were hanging, made him think there was a person in there.

Next room they came to was all smelly and stuff. That's the only way they could explain it. Shit, we were already exposed so I didn't know why they didn't just start shooting up the place. Would've been easier that way.

I heard over the radio that they heard someone crying through the third door, like a kid crying, but they just wanted to keep going door by door you know? I could tell where they were overhead by the creaking of the floorboards. And every now and again some dust would fall down from the ceiling. They kick the door open and it's the bathroom. Only there's shit all over the place. I mean really, the place was covered in it. The toilet was full and they were starting to go in the tub and sink too. Made me think that maybe the water was off. But then again, vamps don't need the commode, which meant that they had someone else here with them. That drunk guy even went in the room. Walked over and got the window open and then started investigating. Only thing he found was a few hairspray cans and a whole lot of shit.

Then they all lined up in front of that door with the crying behind it. The drunk guy got low and pushed the door open with the barrel of his rifle. Like it mattered now if they were all careful. The leader guy just went in shotgun blazing. There was three folks in there on a couch, two ladies and one man. And that man was the one crying. The two ladies just totally freaked out and ran to the corner when the gun went off. The crying man, well, he couldn't say much after that leader guy blew his face off.

Mac went over with the drunk guy and covered the ladies. The other two were looking at the body and such. Man, they said there were brains and blood everywhere. So MacGyver, he clamps that winch hook through the guy's ribs and Eric hits the motor and starts pulling him out. He zips out of the room and is doing fine until he hits the staircase. That body hit the wall and the hook came out. Eric said it came back to the RV all covered with meat and blood. The body was still out in the hallway, all broken and messed up.

The drunk guy was keeping the two ladies covered while the others ran off to check out that last room. The door was open and it was just a reading room. All full of books. All moldy and musky on account of it had these glass doors which overlooked the side lawn, pretty close to where I used to be. Ain't much use for a reading room for reading the paper on Sunday morning for a bloodsucker.

That MacGyver guy starts downstairs, and the leader and rich gun guy get that body and start to the windows. Only with vamps, you can't trust no one. Those ladies with the drunk, *they* were the bloodsuckers. They whammied him, made him their slave and puts some new thoughts in his head. So the leader and Rudy toss that body out the window and it bounces off the lawn when it hits. And they get all shocked cause it ain't bursting into flames. Hell I could've told 'em that – shit I even tried.

Mickey, the drunk guy gets his machine gun and goes to the reading room. Meanwhile the other two are still waiting for that corpse to explode. He plucks one of the grenades from his vest and drops it. I actually remember hearing the leader guy say "What the hell?" as the pin from the grenade went whizzing by his ear. That fucker went off taking half the room with it. The leader guy goes shooting out the new hole in the wall and hits the lawn. Rudy got knocked unconscious. Then Mickey goes over and shoots him in the back, cause that bloodsucker's still in his head.

Then Mac and Eric run inside too, but its too late you know? I start running when I hear the explosion and I'm not ten feet into the hallway when I see those two ladies coming down the stairs at me. Now, me being raised the way I was, I was told never to shoot a lady unless you're damn sure you're in the right.

I fired a warning shot into the air to make them freeze, and that's when they both started pulling all that vampire magic on me. One of them just disappeared. Sure as the day is long, she turned invisible and was through the kitchen door. I heard this awful racket in there, too. The other one just stopped dead, pardon the pun, and went into the shadows, like she became part of them. I couldn't see her anywhere. The others were all hooting and hollering over the explosion, and how Rudy is dead and the leader is out on the lawn smoldering.

MacGyver comes running down the stairs and knock me out of the way. In the kitchen there's this door I didn't see, on account of it was hid in back of this stack of pizza boxes and garbage. He's in there blocking me out. The drunk is at the top of these stairs looking down and Mac is in the basement walking all around. He says that it reeked of death. And it did, aside from the bloodsucker it was stacked full of bodies.

First thing that Mac said was there was no oil tank or nothing resembling gas. That screwed us again, but at least this time Mac was thinking. Then that lady bloodsucker stepped out of the shadows and puts the whammy on him too. Whispers something that we can't pick up on the headsets.

But next thing I know, there's a firefight on the stairs. Mac is shooting the drunk and the drunk is shooting at Mac. All I know is that drunk had a silencer on his machine gun 'cause I couldn't hear any of his shots. But they both had on one of Eric's vests or something because they weren't hurting each other.

When the drunk guy grabbed his other grenade I knew it was time to go. But just then the chandelier in the hallway comes crashing down and there's no more lights outside the kitchen. So I took my road flare, lit it up and tossed it out. The rugs caught and I was hoping it would move faster, but it didn't. I got my .38 and shot out that kitchen window and dove right through. I heard the grenade go off as I was running and the whole damn house shook. The leader guy crawled across the lawn and got himself in the van. Eric was running balls for toes to it too. I heard the drunk say something over the radio then there was nothing but gun fire. I had this bad feeling that the drunk was dead. That somehow Mac lived through the blast and plugged him. That meant to me, that Mac had killed the drunk on account of that lady vamp putting the whammy on him. And most likely Mac would be coming for us too.

I stayed out on the porch and took real careful aim and prayed I was in the right. When Mac came running out that door, I shot him in the head. One shot, right between the eyes. Didn't have any of that body armor there, did he? No sir. He went down like a ton of dead shit. So I walk over to him and I see him moving around on the lawn, I guess the bullet didn't get all the way through that fat head of his. So I planted another one in him.

Eric got the leader guy into the back and man there was blood everywhere. We got back to the hotel and called up some fancy doctor from the hospital to patch him up. Eric did have some connections, though. Now I'm a little scared you see? For we killed that guy and pissed off his two bloodsucker friends. Sure, we lost half of our group, but people aren't like bloodsuckers. We can let things go. The bloodsuckers will be after you till your days are done. They'll hunt you and stalk you until they find you and then they drain you.

We don't have anymore gun guys and the leader is too messed up to fight. It's just me and Eric. I hope he knows some secret to keep those vampires off us, 'cause if we're still here when the sun goes down, we'll be dead. Personally, I've been through too much to lay down and let them take me. If I have to go I want to go out fighting and kicking and shooting and spitting. Eric would like to get bit I think, 'cause it'll help him learn more. But once he's bit, nothing will matter any more. Those lady bloodsuckers will just take his money and he won't be able to do a thing "cause it'll be like he's their's".

But I'll take us both out before that happens.

This story goes out in the memory of Minda Tillman.

Snare

By Sue Burke

She touched the wine to her lips and enjoyed a single red drop: here was grapes' leap toward immortality.

Hotel banquet hall bars always serve cheap wine, she thought. Still, that single drop breathed sweet fruit – aromas of apples and currants – and left behind a young wine's nip of tannic acid. The spike of alcohol stood out more than ever. In all, she thought, respectable. She wondered if *she* would develop so well in just a few years.

She carried a glass of wine like a prop as she flitted from table to table during the stockbroker conference banquet. Visiting was one way to avoid dealing with a plate of food – and she wanted to greet colleagues she missed now that she worked the nighttime Asian market shift. Seeing them this evening, anew, fascinated her. They seemed so simple, their motives so plain.

They had changed, and so had she. She should have felt sure of herself, but she didn't. Her cocktail dress fit close enough to merit a second glance, short but not too short, elegantly midnight blue and still businesslike, she hoped. Should she have worn her hair up? Black curls rested on her shoulders, soft and simple, probably better than something overdone. She wanted that second glance.

The banquet had just ended and she was still hungry. She watched people sort themselves out, some heading to the bar, some settling in for the band and dancing, others leaving to start room parties. She turned to gaze through a window at shadowed, boxy buildings separated by the lights of snowy parking lots and highways. Deliberately appearing captivated by the suburban landscape, she began to eavesdrop on passing conversations, searching.

She heard footsteps approach and sensed a mind focused on her. She turned. Twenty feet away, smiling, Dan Coytak walked toward her. They worked for the same firm, and though she didn't know him well, he had never struck her as another stuffy stockbroker. His beard sometimes needed a trim, his clothes usually hung too comfortably, his eyes always smiled. And he was healthy-looking. She noticed health now. She smiled back.

"Gwen," he said as he shook her hand. His hand felt warm. "I was hoping you'd come."

She could tell he meant it. Maybe this was an opportunity.

"Our paths don't cross often these days with your new shift," he said.

"They rarely did before," she answered. "Perhaps that was too bad."

"Well," he began, glancing around the room. No one was near them.

Gwen guessed he needed something to say so he could talk with her for a while. She offered a subject. "I know about some good picks on the Nikkei," she said. "Your big clients could be interested. Want to talk?"

"Well, yes, but not about that. About – I know what you are."

How could he know? Her senses surged. If he did know something, she had to lead him astray. A small lie could test it. "An inside trader?" She laughed a little. "Inside information isn't considered so bad in Japan."

"Not that," he said, matter-of-fact, perfectly friendly, but a little hushed. "I know you're a vampire now."

She came to attention. Wine sloshed out of her glass and trickled dark red across her fingers.

"I'm sorry," he said. "I didn't mean to upset you. We should talk privately," he continued – more calmly, probably, than if he had believed she were an insider trader. "I have a room here." He paused, waiting for her response.

Gwen tried to form a plan for what to do with him. She had intended to use conversation to lure him somewhere to charm him out of a pint of blood and then beguile him into forgetting all about it. That worked just fine with people who thought vampires were fantasy. She didn't know what to do with someone who knew they existed.

He was prepared. A smooth trader, he had something to sweeten the deal. "I know you don't have to kill to feed. I want you to have me."

The promise of willing blood stunned her. She hardly noticed as Dan rescued the wine glass from her loosening fingers. She wanted him,

wanted him a minute ago and wanted him even more now that she could
have him so easily.

No one had volunteered for Gwen before, but she'd heard of this.
Humans sometimes thought vampires were enticing, and correctly so.
Vampires apparently emitted some winelike immortal intoxicant. It could
be used – she used it all the time – to seduce victims into compliance. In
a rush of emotions, she nodded, unable to speak.

"This way," he said, grinning at her and touching her arm to guide
her out of the banquet hall. They rode up the elevator in silence while
around them other stockbrokers tittered about bears and bulls and booze.
Dan gazed at her like a precious jewel. Gwen watched him like a hawk
watches a rabbit, wearing what she hoped was a pleasant face to mask
darting thoughts. She wouldn't let him get away.

She couldn't. She had a duty to eliminate any real knowledge about
vampires. Kill if she must, or erase it somehow. She didn't want to kill
him, and she didn't know how to cover up a murder. Controlling minds
mattered more. Night by night, person by person, she was learning to do
that better. But not so well yet.

Anyone watching them would suspect they were having an affair, she
thought as he led her off the elevator. She had sensed another couple on
the elevator with that urgent plan. Dan escorted her down a hall and
unlocked a room. "Please come in," he said, entering first. He took off his
suit coat and laid it across a table cluttered with business paraphernalia: a
briefcase, a computer laptop, neatly arranged papers, and a little memo
tape recorder, with things flagged here and there with Post-It notes, all as
fastidious as his desk at work. But now his mind was a jumble of expecta-
tion.

Gwen paused at the door and took her eyes off him long enough to
find the "Do Not Disturb" sign to hang outside, then slipped the chain
bolt into place – to keep others out, to help keep him in if something went
wrong.

It could. A couple weeks before when she left work in the dead of the
night, the guard at the parking garage offered to walk her to her car. She
accepted, chatting pleasantly, drawing him into her thoughts. "You don't
hear anything, you don't see anything," she commanded in a whisper and
unfolded fangs like a rattlesnake, sharp and slim and hollow.

But he did see. He looked at her and bolted. Gwen responded with
instinct, her feelings turned hard. The chase exhilarated her in a way she
didn't recognize, and she laughed as she sunk her teeth into his neck.
Eventually, his struggles ceased – reminding her, rebuking her that ten

swallows make a pint.

She hadn't been counting. She had taken too many. She snatched out her fangs and eased him down to sit leaning against a car. Before his confused eyes could register her absence, she was back from a vending machine and offering him a cold Pepsi while she mopped blood from his neck with a tissue. The tiny slashes would fade quickly.

"Are you alright? You fainted. We were just walking to my car and you keeled over," she said. Dazed, he accepted a ride back to the guard booth.

Gwen turned back to Dan. Please don't lose your nerve, she thought. Part of her wanted every drop of the guard's blood, of everybody's blood, of the brightest light left to her. She fought that urge every time she tasted it. She wanted Dan's blood – but not all of it, unless something went wrong, unless she had to, unless she made a mistake.

He stood looking at her with anticipation beyond what he might have felt if he had brought her to the room for human seduction. She could sense awe. He had lured a legend to him, and she filled his whole mind.

Notions that big could blot out a lot when hidden, she thought. The vampire of his dreams could snatch up the pieces of his impermissible knowledge and vanish, taking them with her. She could be everything he hoped for. She could lie to his heart's content.

Conscious of how she moved, she set her purse on a dresser, slipped off her pumps – high-heeled shoes never hurt anymore, she noticed – and slid onto the bed, curling one leg underneath her body and letting the hem of her dress frame the other. She tried to see herself through Dan's eyes: Did she look like an immortal vision? The deep blue velvet of her dress sparkled with beads like stars, perhaps romantic enough. She wanted to sit or maybe lounge to emphasize her curves, to shift the hem of her dress a little higher up her thigh, something.

Then she looked at him and felt his adoring eyes like a caress. She was already more than he had hoped for, a long-sought dream sitting on his bed, there for him.

She shouldn't have lost her composure earlier. A vampire shouldn't spill wine at the sound of shocking suggestions. A vampire should be masterful, mysterious, compelling, in control – what he had hoped for, what she could be for him. He had brought her here. The next move was hers, and he was waiting for her.

The next move was obvious: Find out what he knew and start to draw out the knowledge that she needed to steal from him. "How did you know I'm a vampire?" she said.

"I'll make you a deal," he answered – always the dealer. "One question from you," he said, "one from me."

"Fair enough." He probably had plenty of questions. She could pull out everything she needed.

He leaned against the hotel room's desk and started talking. "I've pretty much always thought there were vampires, although I don't know what convinced me first. There's even sort of an underground, a few people who know all about it, and I did enough research on legends thousands of years old to find the footnotes that led me to them. But I didn't like those people. Too many of them are hunters" – Gwen flinched – "and I just want to know."

He shifted his weight nervously as he spoke, but his eyes stayed on her, full of wonder. "The scariest part – they think it's scary, but me ... well, is that it's so hard to tell. They – you – look just like us. It's how you act that shows you're different. Some of it's simple. It happened this fall, right?"

Gwen nodded, smiling encouragingly, but she worried about how simple it could be.

"You took that sudden little health leave and returned to take the Asian shift," he said. "But what I meant by simple: You were suddenly so pale, and you never eat anymore. You don't hit up the snack machines. I've checked, and there aren't any fast-food wrappers in your trash can. You don't even drink coffee."

"I could have turned anorexic," Gwen said, laughing a little. She monitored his every move, heard his heart beat strong and a little fast, felt his mind still focused on her, excited.

"Well...but it's your attitude. More restrained, more alert. You really pay attention to what's going on around you. There's other things, though. Sometimes you hear things other people couldn't, like the way you turned toward me downstairs before I was anywhere near you. And sometimes you're in one place and then another too fast. Sometimes you read things that are too far away for anyone to read."

She made a mental note to watch such behavior. "Is that all?"

"Pretty much. It's little things, but they add up. Of course, I only know what I see at work."

"How long have you been watching me?"

"That's another question," he answered, blushing, and the blood in his face enticed the hungry part of her. "It's my turn. Why did you become a vampire?"

"I met someone who was a vampire. . ." she began. Yes, she had met someone. He had been masterful, mysterious, compelling, loving. She had wanted to be like him, for him. "He showed me what I could do if I let him make me a vampire, how I could make people do what I wanted and make them like me."

Dan's question hurt the more she thought about it, and she had thought about it before. She didn't want to answer it. If she said the real answer, then she admitted to herself things she didn't want to know. If she kept it a secret, she could pretend she had made a rational decision, a successful decision. She sifted, and the whisper of nylons and velvet reminded her of how Dan saw her. She wished she saw herself the same way.

"It's been easier to deal with people," she said. "I can tell what their feelings are, tell what they want – clients, other traders, the staff at the firm. Even over the phone I can tell." She shrugged at the absurdity of telephone telepathy. "It's helped a lot. I'm really doing well."

"You became a vampire just to become a better stockbroker?"

"No, it was to be special," she said harshly, then regretted what she had said. That was too close to the truth. She backed off a little. "For the power. To live forever. To be able to get anything I wanted. That's all." Dan felt unsatisfied, she could tell. He knew that wasn't all. Well, their deal didn't include telling the whole truth.

"My turn," she said. "What do you plan to do with this information?"

"I don't know. I guess that should make you nervous. I know there are vampire hunters, and they say that humans and vampires can't peacefully co-exist. I guess I hope they're wrong. I want to find out." He looked friendly, hopeful.

Gwen thought of the pain she would soon inflict on him, the urge to kill she knew she would feel. Peace? Between predator and prey? Not likely. "Your turn," she said. "What do you want to know now?"

He felt a prick of disappointment, she noted. Probably he wanted her to confirm his hope. Better to stay silent.

His disappointment passed, or at least faded. With a moment's thought, he came up with another question. "What are humans like to you now?"

"Do you mean – " Why wasn't he asking her exactly how a human became a vampire, did she die and get brought back to life, could she fly, did she sleep in a coffin, was garlic really repugnant? Humans made her crazy. She wanted to consume them and she didn't want to hurt them. They fascinated her and they frustrated her. She was closer to their thoughts than ever and farther from their lives than ever. That was the worst part. She didn't know what to say, but she owed him an answer.

"They're so different now. I know what they want. They're, well, simple, most of them. When I was human, it was like everyone was a black box, and I didn't know what was inside. Now I can kind of look in. I know what I'm getting. I can use that to know what to do around them." To manipulate them and to feed. Why not tell him that, too, about feeding? He may as well know what was going to happen to him.

"And I don't mean to scare you," she said, watching his face, "but you said you wanted to know. They're attractive, irresistible really. They sort of glow, not something we can see but something we can sense somehow and we want." Memories propelled her description. "It's in the blood. That's why feeding is so hard, because it's so intense for us, because we feel that glow coming into us, and it's so hard to stop.

"They say killing – if we drink till you die – it's even better . . ." She felt a shiver in his mind and saw a shiver pass through his body. He closed his eyes involuntarily. "I'm sorry. Maybe that's more than you wanted to know."

"It's all right. I asked."

"I lie to everybody now. I can't say what I really know. It hurts sometimes. I can't have friends anymore, human friends. Vampires," she said, "are solitary, I have learned." Solemnly, they studied each other. His eyes had lost their playful smile. Finally she said, "My turn for a question. You know we can kill. I could kill you here. Why are you doing this?"

"I guess I didn't think you would." He wanted reassurance. He had become worried.

"I don't want to," she said. She waited to see if he'd say more or if he hoped she would say something else, maybe something more definite.

"I guess," he said, "I didn't think this all the way through. I just wanted to talk to a vampire. To you. To see what had happened to you. I never got to know you before, and I wish I had, but at least I thought I could talk to you now. I could touch you and give you something that would make you happy."

He was sincere. She felt sorry for him. He would never know how much she was lying to him. He couldn't get what he wanted. . . . but at least she could be kind to him. She slipped over on the bed. "Come sit down," she said, patting the bed next to her. "It's your turn for a question."

He sat close to her, his warmth touching her. "Are you happy?" he asked.

"To be talking to you now? Yes. I don't get to talk like this ever." That wasn't the question. She knew it, and he knew it.

"Are you happy to be a vampire?" he asked again.

"What does happiness mean?" she parried. She couldn't meet Dan's eyes. "I got what I was promised."

"Did you get what you hoped for? What did you hope for?"

"I wanted my life to change, and it did."

She felt sadness rise in his mind, sadness for her. He had finally heard her answer, and it was not what he wanted to hear. The vampire of his dreams was not living her dream, and they both knew it now.

It hurt him. She could feel that. Couldn't she help him? Couldn't she still be kind? A kind idea came to her. At least, she thought, when I steal his memories, I will lighten his heart.

She reached out to loosen his tie and unbutton his collar. Their eyes met again. She smiled. There was some pleasure left in the evening. He smiled back as she stroked his neck and ran her fingers through his beard. He took her hand and kissed it.

"This will hurt," she said. She remembered being bitten herself, feeling fangs pinned in her neck and cold lips against her skin, her own warm blood flowing between them. By offering her blood, she had offered her best treasure. It ached less then than now.

"That's all right," he said.

She unfolded her fangs. "Are you frightened?"

"Of course," he said. His eyes remained steady.

"Are you sure this is what you want?"

"Yes," he said, nodding slightly.

She gently pushed him back to lie on the bed. She leaned over him, looking at his face. Impulsively, she kissed him. His warm lips and wet mouth reminded her of what making love could be like, gentle and sharing. His fingers ran through her hair. He wrapped his arm around her back and pulled her on top of him. He felt warm against the length of her body. She felt his chest rise as he breathed, felt his hands stroking her, felt him stirred by her.

At one time, she would have desired his embrace and cradled his body with hers. Like some phantom, that feeling floated through her mind and mocked her. All she felt now was a human glow against her, felt it pulsing in him, and wanted him only for it. Wanted him for so little, and he wanted her so much.

A fang nicked his lip. She tasted blood, salty and rich, and kissed him harder, a mix of passions, and he responded with human desire. She fought her hunger to give him time and lingered over the promise of blood. She enjoyed the sheer pleasure of touch, so much different for him than her. Finally, almost instinctively, she pulled away from his mouth and lunged at his throat. Her teeth pressed hard for a moment against his skin, then slid in. He tensed and gasped and held her tighter, too close to ecstasy for pain.

As the blood flowed, to protect him, carefully, she tried to keep her mind focused on him and counted swallows. *One.* His skin was moist and smelled faintly musky. The bristle of his beard rubbed against her cheek, and a freshly shaven neck lay smooth beneath her lips.

Two. She heard his heart race. His chest rose and fell with urgent breaths. His muscles tightened and he held her closely, involuntarily. He trembled, and she sensed his elation not only in his own pleasure, but in knowing of hers.

Three. The glow already flowed through her, even down to her fingers as she felt his face beneath the fingers of one hand. The other hand's fingers were clenched around his arm. She wanted more blood.

Four. Once she had been the giver. She remembered the same elation to be able to grant something so valued, so intimate. Finally, she gave everything so she could be the one to take and to treasure those gifts.

Five. The change had been easy. Her mentor had taught her and helped her kindly, but he lost his allure as she found out how little he really wanted. Love? Forget it.

Six. She could barely remember his face anymore. Not that he didn't matter. He mattered as much as anyone – nobody mattered much anymore except in what they could do for her.

Seven. People had become boxes she could look into, rummage around in and take from – simple and flat, prey and objects. Nothing more. Throats that she could drain or spare as it suited her. That's what went wrong. They stopped mattering, but she could still remember when they did.

She was going to choke. She drew her fangs out as steadily as she could – Dan winced as her head trembled – and swallowed, *eight,* just before she began sobbing. Slowly, he took her face in his hands and looked at her, quizzically and sympathetically.

She couldn't bear those eyes that cared so much for her. She turned away. He still held her and gently lowered her head to rest on his chest while she sobbed. He stroked her hair and waited. Like a thunderstorm, her tears fell hard but brief. She lay still for a while. She could sense Dan full of sadness and confusion.

"I'm sorry if I hurt you," he said. "I didn't think this would be so hard for you."

"It's not your fault. I thought – I hoped that when I became a vampire, I would feel towards humans the way I felt toward vampires when I was human, the way I thought vampires felt toward me. I thought I could love humans, love you, love you more than ever, maybe, but I don't love anything anymore. I'm not part of anything anymore. The closer I get to people, the farther away I am. I want their blood, that glow. I don't want them. I suppose if I loved them, I could never take them like I do."

She propped herself up on her elbows to look at his face. He still seemed confused. "It doesn't make sense, but it's true. I don't know how that whole part of me could go away, evaporate and leave me wondering where it went. I don't want to hurt you, but it's like being kind to animals. I didn't know this would happen. I wouldn't have done it if I knew."

"But I can love you," he said.

"Why? You can't get anything from it."

In Dan's mind, she felt that statement fall like the last piece in a puzzle. He still had that sadness for her, but not confusion. He understood her.

She would have liked to keep it that way. The other vampires she met didn't seem to care, and humans had no clue. She would enjoy having someone who really understood her. Sharing that might be a little like love. Sharing was part of love, wasn't it?

But she had her duty. Safety depended on secrecy. No human could be left to know.

Her damp eyes met his. "You're tired now," she said. "Those banquets always do that – too much to eat, too much to drink, and then you have to take a nap."

He did seem tired, exhausted. Too much emotion. This would work. "You need to sleep," she said. "When you wake up, you'll forget about me and about all vampires. There's nothing to know. We're empty, and we don't matter.

"Sleep now." She touched his face. His eyelids drooped, then fluttered as he fought to stay awake. "Sleep." She stroked his cheek, felt the coarse hairs of his beard, touched his lips with her fingertips. His eyes closed.

That was it. He had strived to touch the heart of a legend and found it hollow, and he would never remember.

Gwen stood up and slipped her shoes back on. In the bathroom, she found a tissue and returned to Dan to wipe his blood from his neck. If she had gotten to know him before . . . but it was too late, and her regret was fading fast. Her new self steadily pulled her feelings away from him.

Back in the bathroom, she washed mascara from her cheeks. Undead eyes don't get puffy or red, she noted ruefully.

In a minute, she looked as cool and composed as ever. She picked up her purse, unhooked the bolt on the door, and left with one backward glance. Dan lay sprawled on the bed, the marks on his throat beginning to disappear.

The next morning, Dan woke, still in his clothes. He could remember nothing after the banquet had ended. Had he drunk that much? But he felt fine – no headache, no cotton mouth, no hangover. He checked the alarm clock next to the bed. Only 8 a.m. When was the Sunday brunch?

The conference schedule sat beneath his suit coat on a table. He moved the coat. Underneath, unexpectedly, sat a mini-cassette tape recorder. "Listen to this," said a Post-It note in his own handwriting on the recorder. He couldn't remember writing the note.

Mystified, he picked up the tape recorder. The "record" button was still punched in. Apparently it had been turned on and left on. He tried to rewind the tape. The batteries were dead; no surprise. But he found an opened four-pack – another thing he couldn't remember – with two new batteries still in it. He switched batteries and rewound the tape about halfway.

"This will hurt," he heard a woman's voice say.

"That's all right," his own voice answered.

"Are you frightened?" she said.

"Of course," his voice said – and bit by bit, he remembered a face, Gwen's face, with fangs. He felt those fangs in his neck again, felt his arms around Gwen as she sobbed. . . . He remembered it all.

How could anyone stand to be so lonely? The tape played until it reached its end, and the recorder clicked off. The silence brought him back to the room. He removed the tape, put it in his briefcase, and locked it tight. On Monday, at work, he'd find a reason to stay a little late.

How Brando Was Made

By Paul McMahon

Even after everything I saw, I keep picturing Brando that day he pulled his cheek inside out to prove to McGruff he wasn't chewing snuff on the job. Looked like a firecracker exploded in his mouth. His cheeks were all bitten and pocked with bite marks, and his teeth was stained with blood.

Christ.

There's a whole shitload to explain, I know. Bear with me. I flunked out in eighth grade because I can't write good. That's why I'm saying this in a tape recorder.

We worked at a building site. Condos. "Saint Fresno Heights" it's supposed to be called. If they finish it now.

McGruff was the boss. Stingy, slave-driving bastard. He hired eighteen workers, then broke us up into groups of six. That way, the bastard had three buildings going up at once. And he always kept the groups in competition with each other. You know. See who could get the interior walls up first, see who could get the plumbing in first, that kind of bullshit. While I admit it gets the work done fast, that kind of thing makes safety measures go to shit.

I talked about Brando before, but that wasn't his real name. We called him that because of his habit. He used to chew on the insides of his cheeks something fierce. Sometimes he'd come to work and his cheeks would be swollen out like Marlon Brando's in *The Godfather*. That's why we called him Brando.

That's what was wrong with his mouth the day McGruff accused him of chewing snuff on the job.

✦

I read Brando's diary the night I robbed him.

In a way, McGruff paid me a hell of a lot more than ten fifty an hour. The reason I took that job was the same reason I take *any* job. I get to know the other employees. After a while, because I'm friendly and I listen when they ramble on about nothing, they start to trust me. They make plans for a night out, get excited, and then tell me all about it.

While they're gone I break into their place and take whatever I can sell.

Nothing personal you understand. I just can't see scraping by on one lousy paycheck when I can get so much more out of a steady job, you know?

I don't keep a lot of stuff in my own place. That way I can go to work after I've gotten everything I can and complain that *my* place was busted into. I bitch a lot and tell everyone I'm leaving this filthy, crime-ridden city.

✦

Our group was the only one with a woman. Laura was her name, and Laura was what we called her. The first day on the job, Crusher called her "Babe" and she *accidentally* bashed a two-by-four across his face. He had a black eye for a week.

Let's see. We had Carlos. He was all right for a spic. McGruff hired seven spics, *then* decided to use groups of six. Carlos said getting stuck with the gringos was just his luck.

We had Crusher, who I mentioned. Thought the job was a heap of shit, and he was king of the shitheap. He claimed his friends called him Crusher because he crushed anyone who pissed him off, but I doubt it. He never made a move at Laura after she smacked him.

Then there was Jimmy. He was a big bastard, too. Him and Crusher looked like friggin' tag-team partners. But Jimmy was gay.

First day on the job he told us, and the next day he wore a tee shirt that said: IF GOD DIDN'T WANT ME TO BE GAY, HE WOULDN'T HAVE MADE ME THAT WAY. Crusher read it and laughed and goes: "If God wanted *you* to be gay, He wouldn't have made *me* want to kick your ass for it!"

That made me smile, even though I have no problem with gays. I have problems with gays who think their way of life is everyone *else's* problem. Know what I mean?

This tape recorder is a piece of crap. Fifty dollars and it makes a loud *click* every time I shut it off to gather my thoughts. Piece of crap.

The rest of the group was me, and I've already told you too much about me, and Brando. Brando's real name began with R. Richie, or something like that. I don't know for sure, though, because Carlos started in calling him "Brando" at the get-go. Carlos was a movie nut. I can vouch for that because the night I busted Carlos' place I thought I'd busted a goddam video store.

Didn't keep me from rippin' off his VCR, though.

So, anyway, the night I busted Brando's place I saw this notebook lying open on his coffee table, so I took a close look. Anyone would've. Most of it is scribbled really badly, as if he had the shakes while he wrote it, but I could make out the first line okay.

"I did it. Ramona's dead. If I can just hold on a few more weeks."

He printed it, and still I could barely make out the letters.

The newspaper was on the couch, opened up to the ad for that new punk club, Rokkerzz. Brando had asked me about it that day and I told him the place was great, even though I'd never been there. Then he smiled and said that if *I* liked it, he was definitely going. Tonight.

That's how I got clear to bust his place.

There were at least four pounds of raw hamburger in a colander in his fridge. All the blood from the meat was dripping into a bowl. I didn't think anything of it at the time, but now I *know* that was important.

Me, Brando and Crusher had lunch together the next day. Laura, Jimmy and Carlos were up on the roof, which was a good place for them. They were caught up in one of those soap opera triangles. Carlos had the hots for Laura, and Jimmy had the hots for Carlos. Sick.

Anyway, Brando pissed and moaned about being ripped off for a while, and then got quiet for a bit. Then he says, talking really quiet as if the clowns on the roof could overhear: "Remember that shirt Jimmy had on the other day? About God making him gay?" I nodded, and Crusher poked a sandwich half into his mouth like it was a potato chip. "God makes people lots of different ways," Brando said.

Crusher's hand fell into his lap like someone lopped his arm off. After staring at Brando with his mouth hanging open for a second or two, he said: "Jimmy prob'ly got beaten off by his uncle when he was a kid, and liked it."

Brando shook his head. "They say it don't happen that way."

"You don't know your ass from your tit," Crusher said. "*Queers* say it don't happen that way so they don't have to feel guilty about it. They choose their own way to live, just like everyone else."

Brando said: "What do you mean?" and Crusher turned sideways so he could look Brando in the face. It was hard for me not to laugh because Crusher had a mean face that looked stupid when he tried to think.

Finally he goes: "God only made the *first* life. Atoms or whatever the hell they were. Those atoms grew into fish because they *wanted* to. And then one of those fishes crawled out of the swamp because it got sick and tired of being wet and *wanted* to dry off. See? You make your own decisions about your life. Stuff like that ain't chosen for you."

Brando asked: "Don't you think that first fish was God's design?"

Crusher was quiet for a few seconds, and I wondered what the clowns on the roof were up to. I even thought about going to see, but decided I could at least *stomach* these two numb shits arguing about God and gays.

"Let me ask you this," Crusher said finally. "Do you think it's God's design for grown men to stick their pricks into other grown men's butts?"

Brando shrugged. "Maybe God's got a higher purpose."

"Like what?"

Now Brando stayed quiet for a bit. It was getting past our lunch break, but I kept my mouth shut so I could hear what Brando would say next. I didn't have long to wait.

"Maybe God made gays to help control over-population." Crusher looked a little confused, so Brando shrugged again and said: "Guys can't get other guys pregnant."

Crusher got really quiet. "Yeah," he said. "Maybe you're right."

As soon as we got back to work Brando started chewing on his cheeks again. He winced once, like he bit down too hard, then started sucking really hard.

He never spit anything out, though.

Brando started looking bad as the days went by. I thought he should see a doctor and told him so, but he told me to mind my own business, so I backed off.

Later I saw him chewing on his hand. His left thumb. He gnawed on the skin around the nail until blood ran down his wrist. Then he licked the blood up and started sucking that thumb just like a little kid.

❖

By now I'd already claimed that my own place had been busted. I did a convincing job bitching about it, too. I marched into McGruff's trailer and gave my two-week notice. I only had Laura's place left to bust, and I figured I could get her before I skipped.

Except I couldn't get close to her. Every time I did, Carlos butted in, acting like I was putting the moves on *his* woman. Since Laura always told *him* she had a date, I could never be sure she was really going out.

The last day of my notice was the day all hell broke loose.

❖

That morning, first thing, McGruff told us his delivery company dropped a shitload of stonewall at the bottom of the hill. He throws Crusher the keys to his personal truck and tells him and Jimmy to bring it up. Then McGruff broke us into pairs to complete the upstairs floors. He stuck me with Carlos because I think he was starting to see how Carlos acted around Laura. Our group was always coming in last in those contests against the other groups because that spic kept watching Laura's ass instead of what he was doing.

We got inside and Brando climbed the stairs really slow.

❖

I asked Brando once if he had a girlfriend. He told me he used to. "Her name was Ramona," he said. "She died."

"How?" I asked.

"Murdered," he said. "Somebody cut her head off."

"Jesus," I said, and he shrugged.

"She made me what I am today," he said. Then he smiled at me and there were blood stains between his teeth.

❖

The upstairs floors of Saint Fresno Heights are supposed to be carpeted, so we had to nail down this shitty-looking plywood. Big sheets of it. As soon as Carlos and I got to the room we're supposed to do, though, he decided he had to take a shit and walked off. He stopped at the head of the stairs, not four feet from where I was standing, and asked Laura if she was okay.

She poked her head out of the room she and Brando were in and told him to get blown. He whispered: "Only by you, baby," probably remembering Crusher's black eye from the first week. Besides, Laura was holding her industrial razor in her hand.

Anyway, Carlos took off and I decided not to wait around for him to get back so I started wrestling one of those huge hunks of wood into the room. Then I found myself remembering that bowl of hamburger blood in Brando's fridge. Everyone brought thermoses to work, and on break you could always see steam coming out. But no steam ever came out of Brando's thermos. And he had one of those flip-up spouts, so he knocked the whole thing back like it was a giant tit.

Just as I got that hunk of wood where I wanted it, I heard Laura yelp and say "Shit." I looked up, but her and Brando were in a room diagonal from me so the wall studs blocked most of my vision. Then I heard her say something like: *"What the–"* and then a crash.

But the crash wasn't the only thing I heard. There was another sound with it– so quiet I'm not sure I heard it at all. Sounded like ripping twenty sheets of sopping wet paper towels at once.

I yelled out: "You all right?" and got no answer.

All of a sudden I started to get scared because it's so quiet over there and between the studs I think I can see Laura's denim coveralls lying on the floor, and I think Brando's red and black flannel shirt is right on top of her.

I took my hammer. Walked down the hall real slow, trying to give Carlos time to come back because I really didn't want to go over there alone.

I think I was starting to figure it out even then. Even before I saw.

I didn't tell the cops the rest of this. I only mentioned that Laura was holding her knife and said she was forever cutting towards herself. When McGruff backed me up, I think they accepted my theory as actual fact.

Not that I think she *didn't* slip. She did. But that was only the beginning of what happened. I think when she slipped her arm flung up and she cut her own neck, because when I got to the room my first thought was that they had dropped a can of paint. There was red everywhere and Laura was right in the middle of it. She was staring up like she'd seen her own ghost shoot away.

I hope she had. I hope she *was* dead by then.

Because... Brando...

Shit.

❖

Brando was lying on top of her like they were screwing. He looked up at me when I walked in. His lips... his whole *mouth*... was painted with Laura's blood. He was *drinking* it.

That's when it all clicked in my head. The lip chewing, the hamburger, the way Brando gnawed on his thumb that day.

He said to me: "I killed her," and then he made a horrible wounded-animal sound in the back of his throat. "I didn't want to. I tried not to."

I remembered him telling me that Ramona made him what he was, and I must have said that out loud because he looked up at me and said: "Ramona said I wasn't strong enough. She was going to... to...."

I try to ask him '*What?*' but he said: "When I cut her head off she *burned.*"

I tried to decide what to do, what to say, but I just stood there, working my mouth like a moron, not knowing whether to scream, run or shit my pants.

Then Brando squinted really hard and said the sunlight hurt his eyes. He said he killed so now he's *dead.* I tried to ask him what he meant, but suddenly he was *changing* and the words wouldn't come. He had looked really pale that morning, but now it's like his skin is becoming invisible. Squiggly blue lines which had to be blood vessels started popping out on his face. I could even see some between splatters of Laura's blood– and *that* was still spitting up like a goddamed water fountain.

Then Carlos slammed me out of the way, screaming something in Spanish and waving *his* industrial razor.

Brando flew to his feet. And no, I don't mean *climbed* or *scrambled,* either. It looked like he was on a string and someone yanked him to his feet from above. That's exactly what it looked like.

Carlos lunged with the knife like he was going to try to impale Brando on that tiny blade, but Brando was *quick.* Quicker than anything I've ever seen.

The next thing I knew Carlos was on his knees with his arm folded up behind him just as neat as you please and he's screaming like a woman– all high-pitched and out of control.

I moved as quick as I could, thinking I could separate them before someone got killed, but Brando shoved Carlos' chin way the hell back and then slapped his face onto the exposed neck. By the time I got my hands on Brando's shoulders, blood was gushing down the poor spic's shirt.

Somehow, Carlos got his knife into his other hand.

I was trying to pull Brando away by the hair when Carlos swung the knife up. The little triangle blade disappeared into Brando's head with a *chunk!* followed by a *snick!* and then the knife fell away without a blade.

I screamed, then, and Brando moved, and some of his blood flicked onto my tongue.

I swallowed it. What the hell else could I do?

Then Jimmy was there, too. I don't know if he saw Laura or not. I think maybe all he saw was Brando attacking his precious Rican wet-dream and he went ballistic. And then suddenly Crusher's there too.

I was fucking dizzy.

Might have been the gore, but I don't know. I've never been squeamish before. The time I put an axe blade in my thigh I didn't even look away. Only this time that little *snick!* was too much and I passed out.

But not before I saw Jimmy and Crusher stomping Brando's head into the floor.

I didn't know they were all dead until McGruff came to see me in the hospital. "Richard disappeared," he said and I didn't know who the hell he was talking about until I remembered that Brando was just a nickname. He told me that the address on Brando's application form led the cops to an apartment that belonged to someone named Ramona Childress. He said they broke into the place and found her body all burnt up. Like a spontaneous combustion thing. Only the ashes were in two unequal piles, like her head was cut off.

"Weird shit," he said.

Soon as McGruff left, I bolted. The cop outside in the hall didn't even *try* to stop me. There was another one waiting outside to tail me, but I ditched him quick enough.

You see, I hadn't used Brando's address card when I robbed him. I'd followed him.

❖

I picked the lock same as I did the night I busted him. The place was dark. Darker than it should have been.

I called out: "Brando?" but there was no answer. I flicked the lights on, and the place looked almost exactly how it did after I busted it. The diary was still open on the table, so I went over and checked it out. There was a pile of ashes on the floor and the pages I'd seen before were gone, so he must have burned them before he split.

The top page of the notebook was written on, and it started with my name. His writing was really clear, so it took me almost no time at all to read. He said I'd be okay if I locked myself into a room by myself for seven weeks. He said the blood thirst would last that long.

"Ramona was right," he'd written. "I am weak. I have too much compassion to have to kill in order to survive. If Laura hadn't slipped with that knife – if I hadn't *smelled* her blood – I would have been freed of the curse by tomorrow afternoon. But now I am trapped.

"If you don't kill – if you drink no blood but your own until the thirst passes – the full power will not take you.

"You are stronger than me. You can beat this. When you do, come and find me. Kill me. I will watch for you.

"Until then, gays and I are both God's population control."

Next to the notebook was a bloody metal triangle.

❖

You know if you listened to all this that I have very little of that *compassion* shit. I wasn't five minutes out of that apartment when the first real thirst hit. I don't know how Brando lasted so long sucking his own cheek blood, but I didn't last one hour. There was a pristine business lady, maybe forty-one years old, walking down the street in front of me. I followed her until she opened her apartment door, then left her corpse inside.

If Brando wants me to kill him, he'd better come find *me,* because I've got plans of my own. After I sell this tape to one of those supermarket rags, I'm moving out to Arizona. They do construction at night down there to escape the heat.

Then I'm going to start studying a whole *new* set of coworkers.

REDEMPTION

The Alberscine's Vigil

By Thomas J. Strauch

The whole place reminded Maddy of Stateville.

She taught eighth grade for three semesters near Stateville Federal Prison, and it was a hard place to forget.

Or Alcatraz, maybe. She'd seen it last year, but only from a tour boat when she was in California for the Baltimore Catechism Eclesiology Seminar, though why a conference on that outmoded dogma was held in San Francisco, she never knew. Maddy just remembered how frustrating it was to know that every other nun with one foot in the twentieth century was finagling their way to Rome for Vatican II, while she endured lectures on new ways to teach young minds the finer points between Actual and Sanctifying Grace.

Alcatraz.

Stateville.

She even remembered hearing about Fort Leavenworth from Sister Mary Gerianna, her roomie at Five Blessed Martyrs. Gerianna came from northeast Kansas, and had part timed in that federal prison's administrative office while she saved for convent school. Told some hair raising stories about life on the inside. Or at least, the life on the inside that a seventeen year old bookkeeper could observe from the warden's office.

Gerianna's real name had been Julie, of course. Julie McDermot. But she gave that up once she finished her novitiate. Maddy missed Sister Gerianna. Missed Julie McDermot even more. They'd done some good work at Five Blessed Martyrs, the two of them. But then, Sister Mary

Gerianna hung herself in the band room in '61, and took Julie McDermot with her.

The fact was, the Good Sisters Of The Alberscinian Order were doing that sort of thing all the time.

Stateville.

Alcatraz.

Fort Leavenworth.

Maddy bet none of them had a thing on *this* place. The Alberscinian Retreat House out in the Minneapolis boondocks outdid them all.

The Alberscines favored bad pastiches of faux-Gothic for their facilities, like the Mother House in Cleveland where Maddy'd done her obligatory four years. She took her final vows there in '58, but in the five years since, *this* place, this "retreat house", had only been a rumor, rarely mentioned by the more sensible nuns, and only in hushed whispers by the hard liners. It was someplace they sent you if you really messed up. If you were really bad.

Really, *really* bad.

Right now, the Alberscine Retreat House Prioress perched behind her boat sized desk, pince-nez barely clinging to her skinny nose, her head bowed over a pile of reports. On the other side, Maddy shifted in her wooden chair, her eyes roaming the Priorate, even though there wasn't much to linger on. Whitewashed walls. Rugged stone floors, oozing a damp chill right through Maddy's shoes. There was the Prioress, her desk, the crucifix on the wall behind. That was about it.

That, and the one, portal sized window, drapeless, leaking September sun, and just a feeble strip of light at that. Gray clouds hung over the grounds outside, just as they did when Maddy'd hiked in from the front gates to the retreat door.

Part boredom, part impatience, part nerves – Maddy juggled each of those and gazed out that little window, watching Minnesota prairie winds whip the last leaves around on browning grass, then kicking them up and over the Alberscine Retreat walls. They were quarrystone walls, ten foot tall at least, ringing the entire compound. The walls were crowned with rusty spikes, intimidating enough to keep anyone from prying into the cloistered world of the Alberscines. And just as sure to keep the cloistered from going over the wall and back into the real world.

Out there, one last, little brown leaf lingered in the breeze too long. It fluttered, fell, and was spiked on the wall.

Maddy checked her watch, glanced at the Prioress, and waited to be sentenced.

It would be a long wait.

Half an hour, an hour, all silent in that spartan office, except for Maddy's and the Prioress' breathing. With nothing else to do but wait on the old woman, Maddy kept staring out the window, like it was a waiting room television set. She watched the sun hover above that quarrystone wall, watched a nun cross the grounds with the wind lashing her layered robes. The nun was dressed just like the Prioress, in the old fashioned Alberscine vestments. A voluminous floor length shift, cinched at the waist with a knotted rope and a wood bead rosary. A black chasuble layered over that. A rigid white cowl encased the nun's head like a knight's helmet. A long black veil topping it all.

Maddy'd switched to the new vestments as soon as word came down from the Mother House after Vatican II that they were approved. Grudgingly, but approved. A crisp A-line dress, black, wool, and long sleeved, but so normal and liberating after five years of dressing like a pilgrim. She went in for sensible, low heeled pumps – nothing too shiny or spiky – even regular nylons. And just a short, simple black veil pinned loosely over her hair, more like a scarf, actually. It let Maddy's whole face show, let her ears poke out from under her hair, let her unruly, reddish brown bangs trickle over her forehead.

Right now, that spot of henna color almost seemed a rude intrusion in the Priorate's austerity.

Out there on the grounds, that nun trudged through unmowed grass, a missal tucked under one arm, the other dragging a huge cross – four foot tall and heavy looking. The nun disappeared behind leafless trees as the sun sank completely below the quarrystone walls.

Maddy turned away from the window to find the Prioress staring at her with pinched eyes. Intimidation 101. Maddy had seen her share in convent school. House Mothers all interned in the death camps, or so the novitiates always said.

"Sister Mary Madalena," the Prioress began. Her face barely moved inside the starched white cowl. Only her thin lips wiggled, wrapping themselves in a sneer around each word. "You know why you've been sent to us?"

"I was told that I'd be transferred to the order's retreat for a short stay, which would afford me an opportunity to reflect on my role as a Bride Of Christ."

The Prioress smirked, then produced a manila envelope from her desk. Two books slid out on top of her neat stack of reports. "Sylvia Plath," she read off a paperback with a torn cover. "You've read this book,

Sister?"

"*The Bell Jar?* Yes, I have."

"And yet, having read it, a book condemned by your diocese' Archbishop, and by the Mother Superior, you still felt it was appropriate to assign to your students?"

Maddy had gone over this a hundred times back at St. Basil's – with the principal, with the parents, with the Holy Name Society officers. "I assume those reports document everything," Maddy said, doing her best to maintain the defiant edge in her voice. "If you've read them you know I didn't *assign* the book. I simply recommended it to a couple of bright girls with inquiring minds."

The Prioress nodded. "And this one as well?" She held up a hard-bound Baudelaire, *The Flowers Of Evil.* "This also was suitable for seniors in a Catholic young women's high school? An Alberscinian school?"

Maddy sighed. "I don't mean to be impertinent, Prioress, but again, I didn't assign Baudelaire to anyone. A group of girls were working on a literary project, and –"

"*Whore!*" The Prioress flew out of her chair, leaped on top of the desk and flung the paperback at Maddy. It just missed. "Filthy whore of Babylon!" She hurled the hardbound Baudelaire then. Maddy dove to the floor, but the book caught her at the edge of her mouth.

"*Sister* Mary Madalena," the prioress shrieked, crouching there on her desk. "'Madalena'. Oh, how very appropriate. Just like *Magdalene,* whore of Jerusalem. Our Lord Jesus Christ may have saved *her* soul, but you, Sister, you are beyond redemption for your sins." She scooped up a report off her desk. "Impertinence? It's the least of your transgressions," and she showered papers down on Maddy, one by one. "Obscenity. Corruption. Debauchery. A thousand good women have worked and bled and died for over two hundred years for this sacred order. And you – *you* think you will shame us now? It's not so very long ago that you'd have been flogged for even bringing this retched trash into one of our holy convents."

Maddy grabbed the chair and started to drag herself up off the rough stone floor. Her knees were bruised, her nylons shredded. She tasted blood in her mouth. But she swallowed it and fought back the tears welling up in her eyes. "With all due respect, Prioress, this is 1963. The order can't dictate what we read or –"

"*Cannot?* The Holy Mother Church is not a republic, Sister Madalena. The Good Sisters Of The Alberscinian Order are not a democracy. Forget whatever vile blasphemy you've adopted from the 21st Ecumenical Council. Vatican II has never happened as far as we're concerned inside these walls." The Prioress climbed off her desk and towered over Maddy. "Those books are only a small sign of your true wickedness, Sister Mary Madalena. Your Mother Superior's reports tell the whole story, don't they? You know why you're really here, don't you?"

"Y-yes, Prioress."

"Get up off the floor, then, Sister Madalena. Get out of my office. Sister Ursillina will escort you to your chambers. Get used to them, Sister. I think your stay with us will be a long one."

Maddy got up and tried to salvage some of her dignity. She turned to go, pausing by the Priorate door just to straighten her veil, to brush some grit off her dress.

"And you will hand those whore's rags over to Ursillina as well, Sister," the Prioress said. "We'll burn them along with these vile books of yours."

Maddy dragged her wooden rake through another mountain of browning leaves. The handle chafed her broken blisters, and her back winced with each stroke. But it was better to keep raking. If Ursillina or the Prioress caught her resting, they'd just dream up some new torture for tomorrow. It was getting late, though. The little bit of autumn sun that appeared earlier today was fading now, and Ursillina and the Prioress were almost certainly on their way to vespers.

Anyway, if she continued to rake, she stayed warmer. A dreary September had chilled into a frigid October. Maddy longed for her black topcoat, the nifty one with the zip-in zip-out lining she bought at J.C. Penney last year. And her black wool gloves. Gerianna knitted those.

But they were gone, of course. The gloves, the coat, all her things. Even her wristwatch. Ursillina made her toss them in the incinerator that very first evening. Maddy had stood there, stark naked in the basement, her embarrassment painted orange by the firelight, watching her few possessions consumed by the flames.

They made her walk back to her room like that, naked, shivering, mortified when the other Sisters filed past on their way to dinner. She found her new clothes waiting for her on her bed: the traditional Alberscine vestments, along with clunky, Grandma style shoes, some coarse, grayed underthings, and black cotton stockings she had to roll over her knees to keep up. There was a pile of white rags there too, rank with the stench of lye soap and bleach. At first, Maddy couldn't even guess what they were for. Then she remembered that her period was due in a few days. She'd raced back down the hall to the communal bathroom, naked as she was, to throw up.

"We'd better hurry with this section, Sister Madalena." It was Sister Sidiellus, raking up a huge leaf pile a few yards away. Maddy barely heard Sidiellus' whisper. It was the first thing the young nun said in their three long days raking the grounds together.

"What are you whispering for, Sister?"

Sidiellus glanced over her shoulder. "We're not supposed to...you know."

There was no talking in the retreat. None. Only with the Prioress herself, or with one of her minions. The good Sisters could only lift their voices in prayer, before sunrise, at the noon Angelus, at vespers, each prayer a plea for absolution.

"Sister, no one can hear us out here," Maddy said.

Sidiellus shook her head. "Still." She raked some more, then spoke again, louder this time. "How long will you be here?"

Maddy shrugged her aching shoulders. "I don't know. I suppose that's part of the punishment. Not knowing. It's been three and a half weeks so far. Feels like forever."

"I've been here a year," Sidiellus said.

Maddy stopped raking. "A year?" Sidiellus didn't look old enough to have taken her vows a year ago. A skinny figure lurked under her layers of robes. She had a scared little teenager's face wrapped up like a mummy in that starched cowl and veil. It was the kind of face Maddy had seen on dozens of girls back at St. Basil's, the ones the popular girls always picked on. "What did you do?" she asked her.

Sidiellus started to answer, then shook her head and clawed her rake through the leaves.

Though it was getting dark, Maddy was in no mood to hurry. She knew if she missed vespers she could forget about dinner. But she'd already had her share of the kitchen's mystery soup and rye bread. Anyway, there had to be another three acres waiting for tomorrow. At least it was better than scrubbing the bathrooms. She'd done that for the first two weeks.

Maddy wondered what the Prioress had in mind for winter.

Out of the corner of her eye, Maddy spotted a nun crossing the grounds, missal in one hand, dragging a huge cross with the other. It was the same every day, just around dusk, though not always the same nun.

"Sister, where's she going?" Maddy asked.

Sidiellus looked up, saw the nun vanishing into the darkness by the walls, and looked right back down at her leaves. "Vigil."

"Vigil?"

Sidiellus nodded.

"So, what's that?"

"One of the Sisters sits Vigil each night."

"Okay," Maddy said. "But what's *vigil*?"

"I'm not sure, Sister. But it lasts all night. And it's the worst punishment."

"How do you know?"

"I *don't* know. And don't ask," Sidiellus said. "Quit talking, Sister. I want to finish and get my dinner."

Maddy leaned on her rake and watched where the nun disappeared. There, near some old, gnarled trees clinging to the west wall, their dark trunks merging right in with the shadows.

"Sister, please, let's just finish," Sidiellus said. "All I know is that some are chosen to sit Vigil. Sometimes it's just for one night. Sometimes for many nights. And sometimes..."

"Sometimes?"

Sidiellus stopped raking. She looked all around her, sure someone was listening. But there was no one, not a sound except for the cold breeze tickling the leaves.

"Sometimes they sit Vigil," Sidiellus said, "And never return."

Maddy thought about Kevin.

There wasn't much else to do during the long nights in her room. The first few nights she was so bone tired she fell asleep before she hit the bed. But now she was getting used to the gulag hours, the regimen, her room.

Room? Cell, more like it.

It was an oversize closet, really. A low bed that was even lumpier than the stone floors. A wall-mounted hurricane lamp, lamp oil refilled only once a week. Maddy learned that the first week after she lit hers two nights in a row. Two books were left on the bed with her vestments that first night: a nineteen twenties vintage Bible, and the Alberscinian Press' own edition of *The Life Of St. Alberscine*. Maddy knocked off the Bible, cover to cover, the first two weeks. She was saving the biography of the order's founder till she was really desperate.

Mostly, it was like tonight. She undid the Alberscine combat boots, freed her head from the helmet cowl, dragged her fingers through her hair and rubbed her ears till they bent back into shape. Then curled up on the bed, drew her knees up to her chin and endured the minutes dragging like hours there in the dark.

She would think about Kevin.

Father Kevin O'Connell, Assistant Pastor at St. Basil's Parish, coach of the girl's volleyball team, occasional sub in Civics class.

Father Kevin, with the curly black hair of the dark Irish, with eyes bluer than the royal blue cardigan he wore so casually over his clerical shirt. Kevin, with the perpetual grin on his unlined, thirty year old face. A smile for everyone, especially the girls, who giggled and blushed when he made inappropriate jokes. Those girls sometimes flirting with him. Kevin sometimes flirting back.

Maddy thought about Kevin, thought about that day he drove her in his Pontiac – his very own Pontiac, priests could *own* things, after all – drove Maddy downtown to pick up some new textbooks. Treated her to dinner at a real restaurant afterwards. He had a seven and seven before the meal, and ordered a bottle of burgundy with dinner. Played the radio in the Pontiac on the drive back, folk songs, the Lettermen, the Righteous Brothers, rock and roll.

Kevin...

Maddy barely heard the knock on the door.

"Sister?" It was more a breath than a whisper. Maddy knew it wasn't Ursillina or the Prioress. They never knocked. They just barged in.

Maddy opened the door as quietly as she could, and Sister Sidiellus tiptoed in, bare feet silent on the stone floor, standing there with a bewildered look on her face, like she'd just leaped into danger without a clue what to do next.

"You know," Maddy said, "If they catch you in here, they'll probably make us scrub the floors with our tongues or something."

Sidiellus nodded. She turned back towards the door.

"No." Maddy touched her arm. "Stay. It's okay."

"You...you're different," Sidiellus said. "You're not like the other Sisters."

"Oh? How's that?"

Sister Sidiellus crept over to Maddy's window and looked outside. A half moon lit the grounds. "Why don't you seem scared?"

"Scared? Of what? Of them?" Maddy plopped down on her bed and tucked her legs under herself, indian style. It took a little doing with the tangle of chasuble and robes.

"What did you do, Sister?" Sidiellus asked. "I mean, to get sent here?"

Maddy shrugged her shoulders. "I broke the rules, I guess."

Sidiellus nodded. "I heard Ursillina say that you were selling pornography to your students."

Maddy laughed, too loud she suddenly realized, and slapped her hand over her mouth. It was the first time she'd even cracked a smile since the bus dropped her off at the retreat's gates. "Yes, well, there just wasn't much money in bootlegging, and I don't have the figure for the burlesque. So it was pornography for me." She laughed again, but quieter this time.

Sidiellus stepped away from the window, glanced at the door with a worried look.

"I'm kidding, Sister," Maddy said. "Don't you remember how to joke?"

Sidiellus nodded tentatively. Then she smiled half a smile, as much as her starched cowl would allow. She looked at Maddy's red hair, short, wavy and free. Touched trembly fingers to her own veil and cowl. She nodded again, and her smile widened.

Sidiellus pulled a long pin out of her veil. She unclasped her cowl. Long blonde hair tumbled out, and Maddy could see she'd once been a pretty girl, perhaps before a year 'on retreat' drew dark circles under those innocent eyes.

Sister Sidiellus tossed her veil and cowl aside and plopped down on the bed right beside Maddy. She tried to arrange her legs like Maddy's too, but three days of raking in the autumn cold just wouldn't let her. "Please tell me Sister, what did you do?"

So Maddy told her.

Maddy told her how it wasn't *The Bell Jar* or even the Baudelaire. Maddy weathered flaps like those before. She hadn't been assigned to five Alberscine schools in the five years since her final vows just for a tour of the country.

Maddy told Sidiellus about Kevin.

Told her about the burgundy wine and the songs on the radio and the wide seats in Kevin's Pontiac. Told her about the feel of the summer breeze blowing in the car's open windows, about Father O'Connell talking on and on about how the world was changing and how the clerics had to change with it too. How he talked about the protests down in the south, the beatnik clubs downtown, the Peace Corps, and all the books the kids were reading on the college campuses.

Maddy told how Father O'Connell kissed her, and how she didn't protest, didn't say a word, didn't tell him to stop, even though she knew she should, knew it was wrong. How she didn't tell him to stop when he kissed her again, but kissed him back instead. Didn't tell him to stop when his hand slid under her dress, that brand new just-below-the-knees uniform that showed off her legs. It was scandalous, Mother Superior said, and would make men think about sex when they looked at a nun and that was wrong, and there she was in the front seat of a Pontiac with Kevin, beautiful, handsome Kevin, with his hand under her black wool dress, with his hand rubbing across her bare thigh just above her stockings, and Maddy knew she had pretty legs, she just hadn't thought about them for years. But she thought about them then, thought about them as Father O'Connell's hand slipped higher, as he took her hand and placed it between his legs, where she found his pants undone. And there he was and she held him and squeezed him and stroked him while Kevin's hand still crept higher up her bare thigh, crawled under her drawers and slipped inside to where it was suddenly so warm and so moist and so...

"I should have stopped him, Sister Sidiellus. I knew I should have stopped." Maddy sat there beside Sidiellus on the lumpy cot, staring straight ahead at the patch of moonlight reflected on her whitewashed wall.

"Y-yes," Sidiellus stammered, her voice breathy, tense. "It was a sin...the sin of fornication."

"No," Maddy said. "That's not what I meant. It wasn't a sin. It was stupid. He was just so...only I didn't know then."

She didn't know that old Mrs. Kolinsky was peering out from behind her two flat's chiffon curtains, late as it was. Mrs. Kolinsky, treasurer of St. Basil's Mothers Club and head of the Ladies Sodality.

Father O'Connell denied it all at first. But Maddy stood up to the Mother Superior and told the truth, even when Kevin accused her of leading him into sin, said she'd tempted him with lewd words and actions, even then. "The banned books were just gravy, Sister," Maddy said.

"What about Father O'Connell?"

"*Father* O'Connell's teaching US History at a college in Vermont, last I heard. A girl's college. He should be very happy there."

Neither of them said anything for awhile. Maddy could taste that burgundy wine like it was yesterday. She wished she had a glass right now.

"So, what about you?" Maddy asked. "Who'd *you* murder?"

Sister Sidiellus hopped off the bed. "I – I didn't..." She ran for the door, stopped, ran back and scooped up her veil and cowl. But back at the door again, she paused. "What was it like?"

"What was *what* like?" Maddy asked.

"What was..." Sidiellus slipped through the door.

Maddy sat there on the bed for a long time, thinking about Father

Kevin O'Connell, thinking about Sister Sidiellus. The patch of moonlight crept across her wall while she thought, till her eyes grew heavy.

Before she went to bed, Maddy stood by the portal window and looked out on the grounds. A faint haze of fog sifted across the grass, swirling on a westerly wind, pungent with decaying leaves. Her eyes tracked along with the fingers of fog, to where it curled towards the west wall, to where it vanished into the darkness by that copse of leafless tress, and she wondered who was sitting Vigil tonight.

Since Maddy and Sidiellus managed to earn all the worst chores over the next two months, they spent less and less time with the other Sisters. Which was just as well, they decided. The others nuns rarely spoke.

They had separate duties this day. Maddy had to wash the stained glass windows on the retreat's tiny chapel. Inside and out, with vinegar and water that kept turning to ice when the cold wind blew. Snow flurries fell in the late afternoon, speckling the glass, and Maddy suspected the Prioress would have her back on the rickety ladder washing them again tomorrow. Her hands were still numb during vespers, and she had trouble gripping her spoon at dinner. She assumed Sidiellus went through something similarly barbaric. She saw Ursillina leading the girl across the grounds with a broom and a bucket in the afternoon.

Sidiellus didn't knock anymore. She'd just slip in through Maddy's door most every night now, around midnight, Maddy guessed. They agreed that knocking was too risky. Someone was bound to hear, and most of the other nuns were born tattletales.

"It's a graveyard," Sidiellus said, leaning against the door.

She stood on tip toe, dancing one black stockinged foot, then the other off the cold stone floor. The rooms were chilly in the autumn. With a Minnesota winter looming, the cells could be iceboxes at night. Sidiellus never wore her veil and cowl to Maddy's room anymore. Tonight, dank and chilly as it was, she only had on her white cotton shift, the shapeless slip the nuns wore under their habits; rough, but not as coarse and scratchy as the thick robes.

"*What's* a graveyard?" Maddy sat on her bed, her blanket wrapped around her legs. "And get over here before you freeze."

Sidiellus scampered across the room and jumped on the bed, snuggling up close, shivering. Maddy wrapped the blanket around the both of them.

"Vigil. It's in a graveyard. By the west wall, under those old trees."

"But I thought the Alberscine cemetery is at the Mother House?" Maddy said. "I know it is, I've seen it."

"Sister Ursillina told me about it today. I had to go there to clean up. It's where they bury the Sisters who die while they're – you know...*staying* here."

"That's crazy."

Sidiellus' cold feet wormed their way under Maddy's thighs. "No, it's true. The Sisters buried there died before they could complete their penance. They haven't atoned for their sins yet. So they can't be interred in consecrated ground."

"No," Maddy said. "The Church would never go for that. Not anymore."

"Oh yes, and that's what sitting Vigil is for. A nun must sit Vigil every night to pray for the souls of the Sisters buried there. To beg indulgence, so they can leave Purgatory."

Maddy thought it over. "It doesn't sound like such a harsh punishment. Sitting Vigil, I mean. At least, not for this place. A little cold in the winter, maybe, but it could be kind of nice in the warm weather. 'Course, it *is* a graveyard. That would be a little gruesome." She felt Sister Sidiellus' feet tucking further under her legs. Felt Sidiellus' head lean against her shoulder. She thought about inching away. It felt funny. "So what's with the big Crucifix then? You see them dragging it over every evening. It's big enough to – "

Sister Sidiellus giggled. "They're not all *in* Purgatory."

"Oh, and where are they then?"

Sidiellus shrugged, still smiling. Her shivering stopped. "Some of the nuns who've died were sent here because they were very bad. Very, *very* bad. Ursillina told me. The Sister sitting Vigil *needs* the Crucifix."

"That's just crazy, Sister. Angels and miracles – the Church is trying so hard to sweep all that business under the carpet. Demons and devils – it's an embarrassment – witches and exorcisms, burying suicides at the crossroads, vampires and revenants. That went out with the Inquisition. I didn't buy all that stuff in Saturday matinees, and I didn't buy it in catechism classes, I'm sure not going for it now. Not even here." Maddy got off the bed. She looked out the window, towards the west wall. But the afternoon's flurries had turned into real snow, and the grounds were veiled in windblown white. "That does it," she said.

She turned away from the window. "I've been thinking it over for a few days now. I suppose I was thinking it over even before I was sent here. I'll do my time 'on retreat'. I'm not going to let them think they broke me.

But then...I'm leaving the Order."

Sidiellus sucked in her breath. "Don't even say that. You can't leave the Order. You took vows. You're a Bride Of Christ. You'll be excommunicated, you can't —"

"*My* God wouldn't send nuns to concentration camps, " Maddy said. "*My* God doesn't care about Angelus' and vespers and all this ridiculous ritualism and all these inane rules. That can't be all there is, Sister, it just can't."

"That's paganism," Sidiellus said. "It's blasphemy."

"No it's not. You know it's not." Maddy plopped down on the bed and took Sidiellus' hand. "Come with me. There's a whole world out there, Sister. It's changing, it's — it's *happening* without us. "

"No. I couldn't. It's a sin."

"So? We're all sinners. Especially us, right? That's why we're here, isn't it?" Maddy was tempted again to ask the other nun, wanted to ask Sidiellus once more what she had done to be sentenced to the retreat. Sip the sacramental wine? Whistle a banned tune in the convent? Sneak a peek in the boy's locker room?

But Sidiellus always evaded her before. And Maddy didn't really care anymore.

"I don't know," Sidiellus said, shaking her head. "I'm not as brave as you are. I don't know if I could." So Maddy didn't press her. She'd let the nun wrestle with her own demons. Let her snuggle there on the cot, let Sidiellus leave her feet tucked under Maddy's legs, her head on Maddy's shoulder. They sat there in the dark for a long time, saying nothing.

"Sister," Sidiellus finally said, "You've still never told me."

"Told you what?"

"What it was like."

"What was *what* ...oh."

Sidiellus lifted her head from Maddy's shoulder. With her face just inches away, only their fogged breaths hovered between them. "Was it...was it like this?"

Sidiellus closed her eyes, leaned forward and pecked Maddy's lips.

Maddy was too stunned to react at first.

Sidiellus edged closer, and kissed her again. Longer this time. She wrapped her skinny arms tight around Maddy. Her tongue probed at Maddy's lips.

And familiar bells rang warnings in Maddy's head: *No, stop, it's a sin, this is wrong, no Kevin, we really shouldn't do this, no...*

But it felt good.

Wrong, but good. The touch of another person, so human, so real, so forbidden here in the hellish underworld of the Alberscine retreat. It was the front seat of Father O'Connell's Pontiac all over again, only the air was chillier, the lips were trembly and unsure, and softer. But the pounding in Maddy's chest and her temples and her belly – that was the same. Sidiellus started to ease Maddy down on the lumpy mattress.

"No." Suddenly, Maddy pushed the girl aside. She leaped off the bed. "I don't want to."

"Oh God," Sidiellus whined. "Oh God, oh my God, what have I done? You'll tell. I'm damned now, damned for good."

"No, Sister," Maddy said. She reached for her, but Sidiellus slipped away. "Sister, it's okay. Really. It's just...just that I don't want to do this. Not with – "

"With *me,* you mean," Sidiellus sobbed. "I'm evil. I'm wicked and evil and ugly and you're repulsed by me."

"No, Sister, not at all. You – you're beautiful. But very young, I think, and very confused. There's nothing wrong with what you did. It's just...not for me, see?"

"I'm going to burn in hell. For all eternity." Sidiellus made for the door.

"You're not," Maddy said. But the other nun cried uncontrollably now. Sidiellus flung open the door...

...And shrieked.

The Prioress stood there in the hallway.

Maddy didn't see Sidiellus for days.

Didn't see anyone, actually. Though she was ready for the Prioress or Ursillina to rip into her that very night, nothing was said. Not a word. Sidiellus had just skulked out of Maddy's room, and the Prioress had just glided away behind her. That was it. The next morning, and the two mornings after that, Maddy never even saw the Prioress, or Ursillina. No toilet scrubbing, no gutter cleaning, no jobs at all. So she kept to herself, hid in her room, mostly. She was sure they'd get to her once they were ready. They were probably too busy browbeating Sidiellus over a washbucket or worse. It made Maddy cry when she thought about that frail, frightened girl down on her knees, dodging slaps and more from Ursillina and the Prioress.

It was late afternoon now, the third day after the big scene. Maddy snuck into the kitchen and wolfed down some bread and milk. She passed no one on her way back to her room, concluded the other nuns were all busy on their various duties, and hoped the showers would be empty. She hadn't bathed in three days now.

She showered quickly. Drying off, she wondered if she should just sneak back to the kitchen and load up on more food. Maybe today was as good a day as any to leave this place. She'd said she wouldn't let the Alberscines think they'd beaten her. That she'd stick it out till her time "on retreat" was up. But maybe they *had* beaten her after all. Maybe today was the day to leave. To escape.

But she had no money. Not a penny. They'd taken all her things. She didn't have a purse, not even a coat. And if she remembered, the bus had driven a good hour out of the last town before it dropped her in front of the Alberscine Retreat House gates. Could she walk all the way to town, wherever that was? Or would she just wind up frozen to death along a wintry Minnesota backroad?

And what about Sidiellus? She couldn't just leave Sidiellus here, could she? Could that skinny little wisp of a girl hike through the snow with her? *Would* she, anyway?

Hair still damp, cowl and veil in hand, Maddy crept down the hall to Sidiellus' room.

The door was wide open.

Inside, it was as empty – emptier, perhaps, than Maddy's own cell. The bed was made. And other than the bed, there was nothing, absolutely nothing in the room. Maddy crossed the stone floor to the window. Stared out across the grounds, where a cold looking wind blew out of gray, winter skies, blew dustings of snow into whirlpools and shimmery sheets of see-through white. Maddy stared all the way across the grounds, all the way across to the band of leafless trees, and the quarrystone walls. To the dark shadowy spots there, that were veiled under wisps of snow. Was that where Sidiellus had been these past nights? Sitting Vigil?

"She's dead."

Maddy whirled around, and there they were, the Prioress in the doorway, Ursillina hovering behind in the hall. "W-who's...?"

"Your whore," the Prioress sneered. "Sister Sidiellus."

"D-dead? When? How?"

The Prioress removed her pince-nez and polished them on her robes. "Sitting Vigil last night. The worst sin of all, the most hideous transgression against God. Took her own life, evidently. Ursillina found her this morning. We only finished burying her before the noon meal."

"It's a good thing," Ursillina chimed in from behind. "The weather's turning colder by the day. The ground will be frozen soon." There was a trace of a giggle in her voice.

"No," Maddy cried. "You're lying. She can't be dead. She wouldn't have killed herself, not Sidiellus."

"Oh yes, Sister," the Prioress said. "Perhaps if you weren't so determined to lead another soul down your own sinful path, the poor girl would still be alive. But no, not you, *Sister* Mary Madalena. You're not content to fornicate with priests, you'd see our holy retreat turned into another Sodom, laying with other women, doing things, doing things with your sinful mouths and your wicked hands."

"No, it wasn't like that," Maddy sobbed, "Mother, it –"

"Enough!" the Prioress screamed.

Sister Ursillina stepped into the room, dragging that cross, that four foot long metal cross. She thrust it at Maddy. Stuck a missal in her hand.

"Enough, Sister Mary Madalena. We have no intention of listening to you heap one sin on top of another. You can confess your evils while you pray to God for mercy, pray for Sidiellus and for the others. All the others." The Prioress grabbed Maddy by the neck and pulled her towards the door. "It's growing late, Sister. *You* will sit Vigil tonight."

The gray sky grew grayer still as Ursillina and the Prioress led Maddy out of the retreat house and into the cold. Maddy's crying didn't stop, she babbled to herself as the two nuns held her tight and dragged her through snow that was already blowing into low drifts.

"You're surprised your little whore killed herself?" the Prioress said. "Why? You knew her sinful past. You were drawn to it, like a moth to a flame. All sinners cling to one another."

Maddy tripped and tumbled in the snow, but they hoisted her up and dragged her along. "What are you talking about?"

"Your little whore's done this before. Don't pretend you don't know that's why she was here. I'm sure you two shared your filthy little secrets. She'd done it before, with a student, no less. Caught in the act, right in the supply room in her school." Across the grounds. Into the trees. Closer to the quarrystone walls. "The girl's father was so ashamed, of course he beat her. The girl died. But who could blame the man?"

"Oh God," Maddy moaned. "Poor Sidiellus, she –"

"The whore tried to kill herself then," the Prioress screamed over the wind. "Sick without her vulgar little slut, shamed about what she'd done. Your Sidiellus stood right in the blessed Sacristy of her church and slit her wrists. Shed her tainted blood all over the altar. Sacrilege! But the other Sisters found her. Saved her. Sent her to us. Like all the sinners, they sent her to us."

They threw Maddy down into the snow, cross, missal, cowl and veil scattering.

"Now pray, Sister Madalena," the Prioress shrieked. "Pray for the souls of the wicked and the damned. Pray for your precious little Sidiellus, pray for all of them." She and Ursillina turned to go. "And pray for yourself. Pray, so some other Sister will have the goodwill to pray over *you,* when your sinful flesh wastes away here under this heathen dirt."

The wind kicked up stronger, whipping a curtain of snowflakes off the ground between Maddy and the two nuns, who turned and walked away. "Keep the cross close, Sister," Ursillina called as they disappeared into the dark and the snow. "You may find you'll need it before morning." Maddy distinctly heard Ursillina giggle now.

And then they were gone.

❈

By the time Maddy finally pulled herself up out of the snow, the little copse of trees was shadow dark. She stood up and wiped her face, her tears falling off now in flakes of ice. She brushed the snow off her robes, then clutched them tight around her. It was so cold. The wind slapped her face, the snow pelted her eyes, the cold snaked its way right up and under her billowing robes and froze her skin.

She looked to the west and saw a sliver of orange in the sky, low under the blanket of gray, just a ribbon of color hovering there along the top of the walls, pierced by jagged silhouettes of the spikes poking out of the quarrystone. The band of light was shrinking fast.

Maddy didn't pray. She knew she should, should pray for Sidiellus. But somehow, Hail Mary's and Our Father's and Glory Be's seemed almost...silly now. She couldn't bring herself to mouth the words. Not a one. She left the huge cross half buried in the snow. Left the missal where it fell, where it's black cover was dusting white now. Let her cowl and veil blow where they would.

There was a bench there. A rough old stone thing, and Maddy sat down on it. At her feet, the snow piled over little mounds. Graves, she figured. The graves of the poor girls and women who took sick and died "on retreat," who couldn't take the punishments the Prioress and her minions handed out, who gave up and died. No markers, no tombstones. Nothing to mark who was there, good women who couldn't – or wouldn't – buckle under to the Alberscines.

But one of those mounds wasn't quite covered with snow. The dirt was dark and moist looking, *fresh*...freshly black dirt, blackening more as the last of the sunset glow vanished behind the walls, and the shadows buried the graveyard.

Sidiellus.

Maddy screamed.

Screamed all high pitched and crazy, screamed one curse after another. Screamed up at the darkening sky, screamed at the Prioress and Ursillina and the all the Alberscines, screamed in rage at Father Kevin and the whole church and heaven itself, screamed until her throat was too dry and frozen to scream anymore, her last wail just an exhaled breath. Then she pulled her robes tight around her, curled up on that bench, and cried.

The cold finally made her stop.

Shivering uncontrollably, Maddy uncurled herself and sat up on the bench. Her eyes were sore from crying, her vision blurred, and the stinging snowflakes just made it worse.

She blinked.

Her eyes were playing tricks on her. The snow, the wind, the frozen tears, they were playing tricks on her.

White snow curtains twirled into shapes above those mounds. Gossamer sheets of transluscent white, twisting, turning...

Forming.

Maddy rubbed her eyes, ground her fists into them then.

No, it's just a trick of the wind and the shadows, just...

Shapes hovered above the mounds.

Above the graves, above *their* graves. Hovered there, then glided right over to the newest mound, the freshest grave, Sidiellus' grave.

The shapes floated there, and now the wind played tricks on Maddy's ears too. It howled with each gust, whined in the leafless trees, moaned its way over the shifting drifts.

Maddy thought she heard voices in the wind, voices...

"Sister."

No, it was just the wind, just –

"Sister, come out."

"No," Maddy shouted, all hoarse, but louder than that wind, than those voices. "No, this isn't real!"

The snow-curtain shapes swirled into gauzy robes, crystalline veils. They knelt beside Sidiellus' grave. *"Sister, come out, it's time."*

"No!" Maddy shouted, "No." She dove behind the bench. "No. Leave her alone!"

"Sister, come out. Join us, Sister."

Maddy clamped her hands over her ears, tried to shut out the howling wind, tried to shut out those voices.

"Sister..."

"M-Maddy?"

"No," Maddy whined. "No, this can't, just can't – "

"Maddy?"

It was Sidiellus' voice. It was, but it wasn't. It sounded hollow, far away, part wind, part words.

Maddy let her hands fall away from her ears. She raised her head. Peeked over the top of the bench.

Sidiellus stood there, on top of her grave. Flanked by six figures, white as the snow, but solid now. Solid and real, and frighteningly close.

"Maddy, don't be afraid, " Sidiellus said. "You've come to sit Vigil for me, haven't you?"

"You're not real," Maddy shouted. "You're just a dream."

The Sidiellus-thing looked down at herself, at her white skin, white like ice. She touched herself, then looked back at Maddy. "No, not a dream. Don't hide from me, Maddy. Don't hide, not from me. Not from us."

Maddy backed away from the bench, back till she bumped into a tree. "You're dead, Sister."

"Yes," Sidiellus said, and the other figures giggled, the sound all broken glass and tinkling windchimes. "Yes, I am dead." She glided towards Maddy, her feet floating over the snow. Barely an arms length away, she finally stopped. "You see, I've been bad, Maddy. Very, very bad." A pale, cold hand reached out and stroked Maddy's cheek.

The touch of Sidiellus' hand sent a shiver through Maddy's body. It was frigidly cold, but it burned too, burned like the touch of dry ice.

"Sister Sidiellus, did you...did you really take your own life?"

"I tried, Maddy. Oh, I tried. Hung myself, with my rosary beads. Right from that tree you're leaning on. I really was very bad."

The other figures started to prance around. Maddy glanced at their faces, and clamped her eyes shut. They were white faces. White faces with hollow cheeks and sunken eyes. Black eyes. Dead eyes. They started to chant.

"Sin. The worst sin. The worst..."

"Oh, so very bad, Maddy. It's the very worst of sins, suicide. Despair. Forsaking God's greatest gift. Much worse than anything else. Worse than anything you and I did, Maddy."

"No, Sister," Maddy cried. "We didn't...I didn't..."

"But they saved me. My sisters. They came out of the snow and they saved me." Sidiellus leaned in close, her long, blonde hair slapping Maddy's face. Maddy's nostrils wrinkled at her scent, like dead flowers and sticky sweet cordials and burning incense. "You were wrong, Maddy. All wrong. Angels and demons. Miracles, it's all true. I had to sin the worst of sins to find out, but it's all true." Sidiellus' cold hand drifted down from Maddy's cheek. "And they showed me." Pale fingers danced across Maddy's chin, traced a line down her throat, and stroked the pulsing skin there. "They showed me. Showed me everything I ever wanted to know."

The Sidiellus-thing smiled now, and Maddy felt her knees buckle. Sidiellus' sunken, frightened little girl eyes darkened, from opal black, then flaming into a fierce, red glow. Her frail, frightened, little girl smile widened, red lips on a pale face, red lips parting, red lips leering open around a mouth full of ugly, white sin, and the vulgar smells of death and Hell and worse washed all over Maddy.

Sidiellus reached her other pale hand to Maddy's throat, turned Maddy's head aside. "Come, Sister. Join us." Her tongue lolled out and rolled over those lips, tickled the tips of her long teeth, and she pulled Maddy closer.

"No!" Maddy screamed. She twisted away, flung Sidiellus' icy hands off her neck.

"Join us, Maddy," Sidiellus said, following Maddy as she backed away. "It will be so much nicer than Father Kevin."

"No!" Maddy stumbled and fell face first into the snow.

"Join us, Sister," the other figures chanted. *"Join us on Vigil, join us."*

Sidiellus glided closer. "Join us, Maddy. You're already one of us. You're a sinner, just like us. You can sit Vigil with us, Maddy."

Maddy clawed through the snow, trying to get away. Clawed right over one of those graves, face scraping across a frozen drift. Clawed till her hand bumped something cold, and hard and metallic. She could feel Sidiellus' robes brush her legs.

"Sit Vigil with us, Maddy," Sidiellus said. "It's not your prayers we want." That vulpine face and those grinning teeth leaned over Maddy once more. "It's your blood. Your blood and your soul we want."

"No!" Maddy screamed. She clutched that four foot long crucifix, then whirled around to face Sidiellus.

Sidiellus' eyes flickered – hungry red to frightened black – and for a second, just a flash, Maddy saw those same, innocent, frail little girl eyes she'd known before, and they looked like they were pleading, *'Save me, Maddy. Pray for me, Maddy.'*

But that look vanished, and Sidiellus' eyes glowed thirsty, sinful red again, and her white fanged mouth plunged down.

Maddy flung the crucifix at her. Shoved it as hard as she could, hard and deep into Sidiellus' chest. It plunged in with a hiss, sparks glinting off the metal. Sidiellus fell backwards, that huge cross sticking out of her chest. She flopped down on the snow, and it sizzled and streamed all around her.

Maddy's hands were burned raw. She let go of the crucifix. Turned and saw those other figures approaching, their black eyes glowing red now too, their red mouths gaping open, drooling over their ugly fangs.

She leaped across the snow, grabbed the missal she'd dropped before, and flung it at the figures. They shrieked and dodged the black book. Maddy didn't wait to see what they'd do.

She was at the quarrystone wall in a flash. Her fingers clawed the mortar, hands wrapped around those jagged spikes, her feet pawed at the stones. She felt cold breaths on her back, cold fingers tearing at her robes. Smelled that rancid, dead flower smell drenching her.

She flipped over the top of the wall and landed in a snowbank on the other side. Didn't stop, didn't catch her breath, just ran, on all fours at first, then flat out across the snow and down the dark road.

But even with her heart thundering in her ears and her breath blasting steam out of her mouth, she swore it wasn't the wind, could have swore she still heard Sidiellus' voice.

'Pray for me, Maddy.'

Carting platters of ham and eggs to truck drivers was a lot different from teaching English Lit. at St. Basil's. She just about laughed her head off the first day on the job, when they handed her the uniform, a black shift and a white apron. A private joke, she told them, the colors were so familiar.

Her walkup apartment was only a few blocks away from the diner, just off the main exit for Duluth, Minnesota. It was a dump – cramped, drafty, radiators clanging like cathedral bells all the time. But it was hers. Tips were pretty good at the diner, especially once you caught on to the routine. Shorten the hem a few inches on the uniform skirt, bend over a lot where they could see you real good, bat your eyelashes and laugh at their jokes. There was always an extra dollar beside the plate when they were gone.

Tips were pretty good, enough for the apartment, even enough for a down payment on the old Pontiac. It was more rust than metal, and if she didn't bring in twenty five cash every Friday afternoon they'd take it back, but it was hers too, and the radio worked anyway. And the music was good these days.

Her landlord never asked, but figured she had family downstate, seeing as she subscribed to the Minneapolis papers. She'd scour them every morning before heading off to work, even the mornings when Jeff slept over, and that was getting to be more and more often, now that his route took him through Duluth twice a month.

Jeff never asked either, not about the mounds of newspapers cluttering the apartment, not about the articles she clipped out and kept in a manila folder locked in a drawer, not about the crucifixes she had nailed all over the walls and the doors and hanging over the windows. He'd asked once, asked her if she was the church going type, and how could she be such a tiger in bed if she was so all-fired up religious. But he only asked once, because a laugh was the only answer he got, and it was kind of a scary laugh, so they went back to their original agreement of 'no questions, no talk, just sex'.

So Jeff sure wasn't going to ask when she said she'd be away for a couple days, heading downstate, and that was okay anyway because Jeff knew he should be spending more time at home, the wife was really getting on his case about the kids. He just told her to be careful, just because it was springtime didn't mean the roads weren't still slick. Minnesota backroads were tricky in the spring; they could go from wet to ice in a blink.

Maddy sipped little brown bottles of Stroh's and drove with the windows wide open, even though it was kind of chilly. Sipped Stroh's and lit one Kool Filter King off another. It was Jeff that started her smoking. But she preferred the menthol to his filterless Luckies. She had the radio blaring all the way, rock and roll and Motown, and the sweet smells of green things sprouting up alongside the road reminded her of summer breezes sifting in another Pontiac's window, with those same songs lilting out of the radio, and the sweet touch of insincere lips and hands.

The wind was crisp this Friday afternoon, crisp and cool as it blew in her window and tugged at the manila folder beside her on the front seat, blew the cover open and tickled neatly scissored newsprint. The clippings blew all over the interior of the Pontiac, some right out the window. *'The Alberscine Mystery'* one article was titled, *'Brutal Slayings Discovered At Rural Convent'* it went on to say. *'Sheriff's Office Reports No Leads On Mysterious Disappearances At Alberscine Retreat House,'* another said. *'Services Tomorrow For Alberscinian Prioress and Assistant'.*

Maddy pulled the Pontiac to a stop right alongside those quarrystone walls. She downed the last of her Stroh's and shut off the radio, staring ahead at the gates. Then she stepped out of the car and lit another Kool. Smoked it, still staring at the gates. They hung open, quivering in the wind. Yellow and black striped sawhorses were overturned in the brush beside them. Official investigations ended months ago.

Maddy ground out the Kool with her tennis shoe, then reached inside the Pontiac. She pulled a little crucifix from the visor. Brushed aside whatever newspaper clippings hadn't blown away, and pulled out a missal. She'd bought it at a religious store in Duluth, and Maddy read that missal every night, even when Jeff stayed over, once they were done and he would be snoring away. She read it while she sipped beers and chain smoked Kools, read it over and over again.

With the sun dipping low across the farmland to the west, it was cold, and getting colder. Maddy zipped up her jacket. She tucked the missal under her arm, shoved the crucifix in the back pocket of her jeans and headed for the gates.

It was almost time.

Almost time, and she wanted to read from that missal, read over Sidiellus' grave. Maybe the Prioress and Ursillina too.

She was going to sit Vigil tonight.

Reconciliation

By Michael J. Arruda

"Bless me Father, for I have sinned. It has been 200 years since my confession."

The priest, 62, thought his ears had betrayed him. Leaning over, he pressed his left ear and the left corner of his mouth against the screened window which separated him from his visitor in the darkened confessional.

"How long has it been?"

"Two hundred years," the dry male voice repeated.

"I'm afraid I don't under – "

"I am a vampire."

"A vampire? You mean one of those things from the movies?"

"Would that I were just a Hollywood creation," the man said grimly, "then I wouldn't need to be here."

"Why are you here?"

"To confess my sins."

"Then perhaps I should hear your confession."

"Thank you, Father."

The vampire took a deep breath and began.

"I am disillusioned with the world, Father. It used to be, way back when, that the worst crime, the worst sin, was murder. Then we had Nazi Germany, and the world went crazy. They paved the way for the madness we have today with their attempts at obliterating an entire race, an innocent race, and nearly succeeding. The Nazi legacy is all around us. Look at Bosnia and its 'ethnic cleansing.' The tribal wars in Africa, where families are slaughtered daily, where babies are beheaded in front of their mothers. If I were a horror fiction writer I'd be told by my editors that the things I just described were too sick for print, but these are true atrocities, having happened not in the dark ages, but here and now in the 20th century!

"And things are no better in this gun-happy country of ours," the vampire continued, "where we lose 16 children a day and 40,000 adults a year to people wielding guns, from disgruntled men who take out their frustrations on the world by shooting into crowds of innocent bystanders, to playing children who accidentally blow their best friends' brains out. Children! I feel for them most of all. Abused, sexually assaulted, forced to – I won't even go there. Damn pornographers. Sex and violence, Father. We're a nation addicted to both. How else can you explain the fact that women here are raped every day? *Every day!* What kind of a world allows these sorts of things? The kind that makes the types of sins I have committed in my lifetime fodder for a Disney movie!"

The priest shifted in his seat. The vampire noticed.

"But I digress. You must think me crazy."

The priest did not comment.

"I did not come here today to ramble about generalized atrocities, but I cannot help myself, I am so sickened by it all. I ask you, how can I not be horrified by the world in which we live, a world gone mad?"

"Yes," the priest agreed. "The world is a difficult place to live in these days. But, the world is not in this confessional with me. *You* are. Is there anything that *you* have done that you would like to be absolved for?"

The vampire hesitated before responding.

"Yes. There is something. Some things. That I need to ask forgiveness for."

He did not elaborate.

"Go on," the priest prompted, "and rest assured, that whatever these things are, if you are truly repentant, the Lord will forgive you your sins."

"Yes, the Lord will forgive – it makes sinning so much easier, doesn't it? When you can say you're sorry and have your sin washed away as if it never happened. Very convenient."

The priest opened his mouth to disagree with this cynical comment, to make the point that reconciliation is not about condoning sin, but getting past it, when the vampire beat him to the punch and spoke first.

"I have never harmed a child, and I'm certainly not a rapist. But I *am* a vampire, and as such, I have done things that I am sorry for. *Terrible* things."

The priest rubbed his chin. He was disturbed.

Disturbed by his visitor's repeated assertion that he was a vampire.

It was an assertion he did not believe. However, it was quite possible that this man believed it, and in all sincerity thought himself to be a vampire. If this were the case, then this man may have committed acts which he might be sorry for, which would explain his need to seek God's forgiveness. For this reason, the priest listened.

And waited.

Waited for any indication that this was merely a joke. And if and when he received such a sign, the confession would be terminated.

The vampire declared, "I have lied to women. Promised them anything they wanted. From money to marriage to simple companionship. I even promised one young lady a book contract."

"Why did you make these promises?"

"Why? So that I could become intimate with them. So that I could hold them, kiss them, sleep with them."

"Are you married?" the priest asked.

"No. I'm not confessing to adultery, Father. I'm confessing to the reason I wanted to sleep with them."

"What was the reason?"

"I needed their blood."

For a moment, neither the priest nor the vampire said a word.

"Father? Are you still there?"

The priest answered with a question. "Are you confessing to having murdered these women?"

The vampire paused.

"I do not like the term, 'murder.' It makes what I have done seem less from necessity and more from passion, and this, Father, is certainly not the case."

The priest ignored the comment.

"Have you committed murder?"

"I have taken lives, yes," the vampire admitted.

"How many?"

The vampire hesitated but then responded, his voice deep, dark, and threatening, "More lives than you have touched with your sermons, Father. Many more lives."

The vampire's voice suddenly choked with emotion, "I have been drinking the blood of innocents for 200 years."

The priest was unimpressed. "Let's call it quits, hmm?"

"Excuse me, Father?"

"With this performance. I'll give you two thumbs up, and then we'll call it a day, hmm?"

"What?"

"Come on. I know why you're here."

"What do you mean?" the vampire asked, sounding very uncomfortable.

"I mean, I know Halloween is just two nights away," the priest answered, sounding angry for the first time. "The joke's over. Go home!"

"You disappoint me, Father. I thought you a wiser man."

"Oh, I'm wise, alright. Wise to the ways of the wicked."

"No doubt," the vampire quipped under his breath. "You do not believe me then when I say that I am a vampire? That I need to drink human blood to survive? That I have drunk the blood of women the world over for 200 years?"

"Let me tell you what I believe. I believe that if you don't leave this confessional in the next 10 seconds, I'll sound the silent alarm by my side, and the police'll be here before you can say Bela Lugosi!"

"A silent alarm?" the vampire questioned. "I had no idea."

"Obviously," the priest responded. "Some people may consider the sacrament of Penance a matter for the dark ages, but our security advisor isn't one of them. Now, will you please leave? While you still can."

"I assure you, I am being completely sincere," the vampire said, his voice indeed resonating with a clear and honest authenticity. "I was born in the 18th century, and I am a vampire. Do you have a light in there with you, Father?"

"A what?"

"A light. I would like you to look at my face. Please, indulge me, and do not yet sound your alarm. I need the forgiveness of God. Please."

The priest remained silent.

The vampire squirmed, shifting his position for the first time since the conversation had begun.

"I beg of you, Father. Look at my face before you pass judgement. Keep your finger on the button if you so desire. But, before you press it wait until your eyes have seen the likes of which few men have seen and lived. If only for a moment, if you dare."

The vampire heard the rustling of the priest's frock in the darkness; he was moving his arm, reaching for something. The silent alarm, the light switch, or both.

Click.

Both rooms of the confessional were suddenly bathed in light.

The priest, seated in a comfortable chair, turned to his left and gazed into the screened window. He gasped.

The face staring at him was chalky white, and the pale flesh of the man on the opposite side of the partition contrasted drastically with his combed forward dark hair, hair as black as ink. His eyes were wide and red, as if the whites had been cracked open like egg shells, spilling bloody yolks into the empty sockets. His nose was long and straight, like a nail, and his lips were coal black.

"Please extinguish the light now," the vampire beckoned. "It pains me. My eyes. Please."

The priest's habit rustled again, and once more the confessional was draped in darkness.

"Do you believe me now, Father, after having seen my face?"

"Nice make-up," the priest quipped, "although, frankly, I've seen better. Must have bought your stuff at Wal-Mart, huh?"

"Do not joke!" the vampire raised his voice, for the first time losing his composure. "Please, Father, you must believe me!"

"Why? Why do I have to believe you? Is that part of the prank, huh? Get the old priest to admit he believes in vampires? So you can broadcast it to all your friends?"

"No. It's not that way at all."

"Well, what *way* is it, then?"

"*I – have sinned! I – need – true forgiveness from God!*"

The confessional nearly shook. The vampire's body was vibrating with anxiety.

"True forgiveness from God," the priest repeated. "That's a curious statement coming from a *vampire*. I thought vampires abhorred churches and crosses and all things religious? I'm surprised you could even enter this building, it being a church. I'm confused. You say you're a vampire, but you're not acting like any vampire I've ever seen in the movies. Or, are *real life* vampires a different breed altogether?"

The vampire huffed.

"Will you promise me absolution, Father?"

"Beg your pardon?"

"If I tell you more, if I explain myself more – put myself at risk, if you will – will you promise me absolution?" the vampire repeated.

The priest considered the question.

"If you are truly sorry for what you have done, then yes, of course I will give you absolution. But I'll tell you right now, I don't believe you.

Drop the vampire act and come clean with me. Tell me what it is you are sorry for. Do this, and I shall offer you God's blessing. Refuse, and I'm afraid I'll have no business offering God's forgiveness to you."

"You'd withhold that blessing which you alone can give me?"

"No. But if a man comes in here, tells me he's Superman, and he's sorry for loving Lois Lane and losing his super powers in the process, you think I should dignify this man by offering him God's blessing? Super heroes, monsters, there's no difference. It's all the same to me, son. Stuff for school yards. Not the confessional."

"I see," the vampire muttered with a tone that implied disappointment. "You asked me a moment ago if real life vampires are different from the ones you see in the movies. I ask the same of you: are real life priests different from the ones we see in the movies? There, you have your answer now.

"Vampires are not devils, Father," the vampire continued. "We do not partake in black masses or satanic rituals. Granted, some of us may, but so do some humans. It's just a choice. Are we repelled by holy things? Yes. Because we are spawned by Satan? No. Why, then? I will tell you why: because we have sinned against God. That is why it pains me to be inside this building or to look closely at a crucifix. We, by our very existence, have broken God's law. We who were dead have come back to life, a power supposedly reserved for Christ Himself; He does not look kindly on those who, in His eyes, unlawfully share in His life-conquering abilities. Worse yet, we take the lives of others. As a result, we are scorned by the heavens."

"Are you blaming God for your supposed condition?" the priest interrupted.

"Not at all, Father. Only that, in God's eyes, we are unholy. That thought has haunted me for ages, but never more so than now. You see, I've begun to look at the world differently. As I told you from the outset, I see the world as a terrible place in which to live, especially for the children. I no longer want to be a part of these horrors. I want to make amends. And I firmly believe that in order to do so, in order to change, in order for me not to be contributing to this madness, I need God's help. This is not a fleeting thought, one that I have casually dreamed up. Nor is it something I'm taking lightly. You must know that! Seeking God goes against my very existence. Believe me, Father, I have thought long and hard about this visit. I've had years to do so, don't forget."

"That's right. You were born 200 years ago," was all the priest could say. It was evident he was patronizing his visitor.

"You don't believe me," the vampire said, his voice dropping down to a decibel more deadly.

"That you were born 200 years ago? Of course not! Where were you born?" the priest asked quickly, as if to catch his visitor off guard.

"In Boston, Massachusetts, on May 29, 1758. Do you know, that I knew Paul Revere? Have you ever read the novel, *Johnny Tremain?*"

"No."

"It's about a young boy who grows up during the Revolutionary War in Boston, and he meets and works for Paul Revere. My childhood was not unlike that boy's. I – died in 1783. On September 4, 1783. Do you know the significance of that day, historically?"

"No."

"It was the day after the final peace treaty between Britain and the colonies, except I didn't know that at the time. I found out later, when I – returned. I never knew peace in the colonies – as a human," the vampire said, suddenly pausing, as if to consider the disappointment. "At the time, I was working in a shipyard in Boston. A foreigner, from one of those ships, asked me for directions to a local pub. He said he was hard of hearing. I had to speak directly into his ear. I can still feel his bony fingers even today as they poked my back, bringing me close to his body, into that alley, out of sight and sound from the rest of the dock. He made me what I am today."

Again, the vampire paused.

"And you're only feeling sorry for your sins now? Two hundred years later?" the priest questioned.

"I see things differently now."

"Yes, you've developed a conscience. Isn't that what you said?"

The vampire did not answer the priest directly.

"I do not drink the blood of women, thus murdering them, because I am an evil entity. Nor do I do it for the enjoyment, although I must admit the process *is* enjoyable. I do it for nourishment. It is how my dead body and mind continue to function in this world. I didn't ask for this fate. It was given me.

"Although I have always been saddened by the lives I have taken," the vampire continued, "it is only within the past decade or so that I've begun to feel – pained. Grief stricken and pained. It's like I told you, Father: it is because of the world around me that I feel this pain, the world which commits acts of evil far worse than my own. Yet, I know that I contribute to this evil all the same. I lure young women. I lie to them. I kill them.

"I have tried, in recent years, to be more selective with my victims.

Women with cancer, for instance," the vampire explained, "who are going to die anyway. Women who have AIDS."

"I don't mean to interrupt yet again, but wouldn't blood contaminated with AIDS give you the disease as well, since you claim that you drink blood?" the priest inquired.

"I am already dead. I cannot succumb to physical illness."

"How fortunate for you. Forgive me for being so blunt and cold, but I would not expect a man who is unable to die to be interested in God's forgiveness," the priest commented derisively.

"Would you also not expect a wealthy man to be interested, a man blessed with family, friends, money, material wealth; would you not expect such a man to still seek God?"

"Such a man as you describe is still mortal," the priest answered. "He must still reckon with God on judgement day. But you – you can do whatever you like without ever having to worry about what God thinks since you will never have to face Him, since you cannot die. I find it amusing that you would worry about God."

"Amusing? Have you not been listening? Why must you treat me with such disrespect? Why must you mock me?"

"Because I do not believe you. I do not believe your story. If it were true, you wouldn't be here."

"No?" the vampire questioned. "You don't believe that a man can be sorry for sins committed against other human beings merely because of the pain felt when wronging those human beings? You believe a man has to fear God to be sorry?"

"No, that's not what I am saying. Men can be sorry for their sins without fearing God, but for a man to come here, to seek God's forgiveness here, such a man must fear God, or else, why bother? Do you fear God, sir?"

"I fear –" the vampire fumbled for words momentarily. "Yes, I do fear God."

"Why?" the priest asked directly.

"You mean, since I cannot die, why do I care about God? You realize, you're implying that people only come to you and your church because they're afraid of dying and going to Hell. I should think a majority of your parishioners would find that attitude insulting."

"No, I don't mean that at all. You're misinterpreting my words," the priest argued. "People practice their faith because they *love* God. I simply find it difficult to believe that a man like you claim to be – a vampire – would love or even care about God. You can't kill women weekly and claim to love God!"

"And therein lies the reason for my visit to you today. You have hit the nail on the head, Father!" the vampire proclaimed. "For I *do* love God, and that is the paradox which wounds me. Because I live a life that God must obviously shun. Yet, I believe in Him and in the goodness of people."

"So, what would you like me to tell you? That God will love even a vampire?"

"Yes!"

"If you were a murderer, the answer *would* be yes, but a vampire? Come on. Like the ads say, *get real!*"

The vampire groaned.

"You're not going to admit that this is a joke?" the priest questioned.

"It's not a joke! Believe me, how I wish it were."

A minute ago the priest had been convinced that his visitor was a prank. Now, he wasn't so sure. There was something in his voice, a grave sincerity, that gave the priest cause to wonder.

"Alright," the priest said, trying to accommodate his visitor, sensing how distressed he had become, "let's move away from the vampire concept if we can. Something is obviously troubling you. Tell me which sins you would like God to forgive, and we'll take it from there."

"Which sins? All of them! I've murdered countless women."

"Let's start small, okay? How about last week? Did you take a life last week?"

"Did you eat dinner last week? Of course I took a life."

"You murdered someone last week? You would like to confess to murder?"

"Yes!"

The priest leaned forward in his seat.

"Go on."

"Last week, I killed a woman. A cancer patient. She was terminal, but I suppose that does not matter."

"How did you do it?"

"How do you think? I punctured her flesh and her veins with my teeth, and then I drank her blood. Drank until she was dry. Until I was young again."

The priest sucked in a deep breath. Yes, the man did seem just on edge enough to be taken seriously, but there was one fundamental flaw in his story. If this man was the murderer he claimed to be, the crimes would have been reported in the news; and like they had done so many times before, the police would have come to his church and informed him that such a killer was on the loose. They hadn't.

Furthermore, this meeting was dragging on forever with no apparent end in sight, and he was growing tired. The priest quickly made up his mind: the man was a fraud. Granted, he may have been a delusional fraud, but he wasn't a murderer. Absolve him, and get rid of him.

"In the name of Jesus Christ, I hereby forgive –"

"Just a minute, Father," the vampire interrupted. "I wasn't finished. There's one more sin I must confess to, the most important of all. A *future* sin."

"A future sin?"

"A sin I have not committed yet. You see, Father, I have a friend who is a priest. A young priest. I bet you find it funny that *I* have a priest for a friend – then again, you probably think it strange I have *any* friends – but let me tell you that my relationship with the church goes back centuries, and I have always respected and admired priests. They've been kind to me. None kinder than this young priest I know today.

"He has as his mentor, an older priest, a man he loves and admires like a father," the vampire continued. "Last week, my friend made a horrifying discovery: his mentor has a – how shall I put it? – a problem, a problem that, frankly, I find so revolting that I cannot even bring myself to say it. Me, a vampire! But let me just say that this older priest is, like myself, a predator, but he does not prey on women. Do you understand the problem of which I am referring?"

The priest did not answer. His mouth had suddenly become dry. His hands trembled.

"Father?"

"Yes, I believe I do," he said very softly.

"My priest friend is torn between his love for his mentor and his duty to report him to the Church and to the authorities. I ask you right now as a man of God to intercede on my behalf to God, to ask forgiveness for my reaching out and doing my friend a favor, a very huge favor."

The priest reached with his sweaty palm for the doorknob.

A mist flew through the screen separating the confessionals, choking the priest's nose and throat. He coughed and then gagged. Waving his hand in front of his face, he tried to dissipate the mist, but it had already vanished.

The priest felt a presence behind him.

The vampire wrapped his bony hands around the priest's neck and squeezed, forcefully blocking the man's windpipe. The priest's fingers stretched desperately towards the doorknob but fell inches short of their destination.

The priest gasped, his throat tightening, his eyes rolling, his feet dangling.

The vampire constricted his grip, and the priest breathed his last.

Licking his fangs, the vampire tilted his head and brought his face down into the man's neck, where his incisors pierced the old priest's dry flesh.

Even in the darkness, the vampire could see the blood as it began to drip. He slurped the first few drops with his tongue, and then he pressed his lips against the dead priest's neck and drank like an infant at its mother's breast.

The vampire immediately received a coffee-like high. Smiling, he let the priest's body slump quietly to the floor. He removed a handkerchief from his pocket and wiped his mouth thoroughly, making sure not a drop of blood remained on his face. He then adjusted his clothes so that he would not look disheveled.

Before looking down at the dead body, he gazed at his own hands, which just a moment before had been so bony and wiry. Now, they were beefy and brawny. He smiled, rubbing his plump fingers together, enjoying their warmth. He eyed his fallen victim.

"I told you I did things differently now, Father. No longer do I contribute to the madness. On the contrary, I am battling the madness. Battling the true evildoers of the world. People like yourself, Father. Predators who are truly unholy. The world is a better place today, without you. You will be mourned, most certainly, but the altar boys of this parish will not miss you, Father. They will not miss you."

The vampire opened the door to the confessional, let it close softly behind him, and calmly walked away.

The Covenant of Il Vigneto

By Julie Anne Parks

Il Vigneto, Italy, 1984

Lucien Castille didn't have long to wait.

The young woman hurried around the corner, her shawl draped loosely over her head, its end tossed over her shoulder. Her heels tapped a staccato rhythm on the cobbled street.

The gossips whispered that she'd been involved in a scandal – a romantic liaison with her village priest – and her horrified parents had thrown her out. "Can you imagine, Signor Castille," the old biddies cackled, "a young wench seducing a man of God?"

Now shunned by all, Serafina Calabria eked out a meager living at a tawdry bistro, serving wine to patrons whose hands were permanently stained by the vineyard soil and the grapes themselves.

Lucien stepped from the shadows and into the wash of a streetlight. "Signorina Calabria!"

Foolish woman. She stopped and looked up. Her muscles tightened visibly when she saw him. She drew her purse tight against her side as if she thought he might be a thief.

"Serafina, I have a message from your father," Lucien said, hurrying toward her.

She watched him approach, eyes wary, as if deciding whether to run or hear him out.

"My father? Wh – who are you?" she called.

"Lucien Castille," he answered. He stepped into range.

The prey looked into her predator's eyes and he pulled her into his spell, draining her will. He caught her as she crumpled, and carried her into a deeply shadowed doorway.

The street was still deserted.

Cradling her with one arm, he pulled away her shawl and blouse, then traced an "LC" with the razor sharp edge of his thumbnail down one breast. Monogramming his dinner was his single petty indulgence.

Ah, she's lovely!

He'd have preferred a virgin, but those he'd seen in Il Vigneto had either been too scrawny or were already turning to fat. And he couldn't wait any longer. He needed to feed.

Thin lines of blood peeked from the slits his fingernail made, bubbled up, then ran down her breast and dripped onto her skirt. He swiped at the initial with his finger, licked it clean, and found it pure. He pushed her head gently to the side, brushed back her thick, wavy hair, lowered his head and sank his fangs through the lovely white skin at the base of her neck. The first taste filled him with a pleasure that shuddered up and down his spine, then spread through his groin in a warm glow of ecstasy.

He fed slowly, deliberately, checking the urge to gulp his dinner like a half-starved peasant, so he might maintain the pleasure that was so much more than a mortal orgasm.

Strength flowed back into his body. His power began to surge and – *Something else.*

He stopped, extracted his fangs from Serafina's neck and dropped her. Swallowing, he ran his tongue over his teeth and across the roof of his mouth.

What was that sudden bitter taint in the deep aortic flow?

He dabbed a drop of blood from the corner of his mouth and licked it, smacking his lips together as he tried to identify the unexpected burst of tartness.

The bitch was pregnant!

Just barely so, but pregnant nonetheless.

A burst of anger tapered to tentative excitement.

He'd thought about it, toyed with the idea over the long, lonely centuries, played the "what if" game many a night. Was fate offering him a chance to make his one dream come true?

He knelt and leaned back on his haunches, then pulled her across his lap which would be his work table. He pushed her head backward, pried open her mouth, then sliced a quick, clean slash across his wrist with his thumbnail. Quickly, he laid his forearm – wound downward – into the cradle of her gaping mouth.

Within moments, she started to sputter and gag. Lucien removed his wrist, pressed her lips together and rubbed her throat like a mortal impelling their dog to swallow a pill.

When she quieted, he force-fed her his blood again and again, repeatedly sealing and stroking her as necessary, until he began to feel slightly weak from blood loss. Summoning his powers of self-healing, he fused first his vein and then his wrist, gathered her into his arms and carried her back to his villa that overlooked the village of Il Vigneto.

❋

Lucien waited on Serafina hand and foot for the eight remaining months of her pregnancy. He had fresh fruit and vegetables brought to her daily. The finest red wines passed her lips as he attempted to stabilize and enrich their mingling blood. He personally inspected every morsel of food his staff prepared for her consumption. He wheeled her onto the terrace every evening so she could fill her lungs with clean, country air. And he force-fed her his blood once a week.

It was a horrible pregnancy. Serafina seldom kept down the foods he brought her. Too weak to stand, she had to be carried or wheeled to her bath. She cramped, spotted, ran fevers and shivered under chills. Nightmares tormented her from which she awoke screaming, her body covered in sweat. She seldom spoke and gazed upon Lucien with vacant and lifeless eyes.

Yet in June she bore a son – a puny, scrawny infant, as pale as a trout's belly. The weakling slept little, spat up constantly and mewled like a kitten, annoying Lucien to no end. And no matter how deeply he looked, the child whom Serafina had named Enrico showed no trace of his surrogate father's power or strength.

At the end of the child's first month, exhausted from the infant's constant whimpering, repulsed by Serafina's haggard, drawn face and stony silence, disappointed by his apparent failure, he lost heart and put them out.

"I'll check on him from time to time," Lucien said, stuffing Serafina's pocketbook full of lira for food and lodging.

"No," she said.

"Take it. The child must be fed and clothed."

She paused for a moment, then lifted her chin. "Very well, I'll take your money. But don't you dare come near him. He's not your son, no matter how much of your blood flows through his veins. I won't let him be your son. I'll give him to the priesthood."

"Don't do that," he warned. "Keep my son away from priests."

She clutched Enrico closer to her breast.

"If you do," he said, gripping her arm tightly, "the responsibility for what happens will be entirely yours. There would be no place on earth you could hide. And when he comes of age, I shall come for him. I swear this on his life."

He nipped his forefinger with his fangs, squeezed out the blood and smeared it on the infant's forehead. "Baptized in blood. This is my covenant with my son."

She wrenched her arm free. "He's not your son," she screamed, starting to run. "He's mine. Mine and God's."

***

Three weeks later, as the priest lowered Enrico's head into the baptismal font, the church began to tremble.

"I baptize thee in the name of the Father ..."

Statues of the saints shuddered on their shelves.

"And of the Son ..."

The sunlight streaming through the stained glass windows dimmed.

"And of the Holy Ghost. Amen."

The priest's thumb, anointing the crown of Enrico's head, trembled as he made the sign of the cross in holy chrism.

The infant screamed.

Everyone stared, horrified, as the child's scalp bubbled and roiled where the chrism touched it.

Serafina caught Enrico Ernesto Calabria just as the priest crumpled to the ground with blood streaming from every orifice, seeping from his pores, and his tongue lolling from his mouth.

***

San Rafael, California, 1998

"Are you sure you're up to it, Ricky?" Father Mike asked. The child was even paler than usual, blue veins throbbing close to the surface of his snowy skin, his eyes bloodshot. If Ricky was too ill to serve the Mass, there'd be no harm done: three other altar boys were there and ready.

Ricky Calabria nodded, and helped him into his vestments. "I'm okay, Father. Just tired."

"More nightmares?"

The boy nodded again, sighing like an old man.

Father Mike sat down in his chair so he could be closer to Ricky's eye level. The boy was fourteen and already past puberty, but his stature was more like an eleven-year-old.

"Have you been playing outside like I suggested? Playing sports in school?"

The child shrugged. "I try, Father. Honest. But I don't have the energy to run and I can't kick the ball. I miss it, and the other kids laugh at me." Ricky hung his head. He always lowered his head when he thought he'd disappointed Father Mike. "They don't like me."

The priest bit back his anger. "Will your mother be attending Mass this morning? I want to talk to her."

Ricky nodded, and headed toward the church, presumably to tell his mother.

Father Mike tapped his fingers on the arm of his chair. What more could he possibly say to Serafina? He'd tried every tactic he could think of, yet Ricky's life never improved. She refused medical treatment for the child. She wouldn't allow a psychologist to evaluate the source of Ricky's violent nightmares. She kept him inside at all times, forbidding him to play with other kids, and limiting his life to St. Michael's School and his role as altar boy.

"My son is destined to be a priest," she'd said on the several occasions Father Mike tried to speak to her. "He doesn't need to play baseball. He only needs to study. And to grow closer to God."

"Ricky will make a wonderful priest, if he has the calling," Father Mike had explained at his last meeting with Mrs. Calabria. "But he's not healthy enough for the priesthood. It's a grueling vocation. A candidate for the priesthood must be both physically and mentally strong. It takes endurance to sit up all night with an ill parishioner, then celebrate three or four Masses the next morning."

"God will provide it."

"God helps those who help themselves."

"Enrico's a child!" she said.

"But you're an adult. His welfare is your responsibility. He needs a physical. He needs counseling to get to the bottom of his nightmares. Mrs. Calabria, normal fourteen-year-old boys do not dream about death and violence and blood, night after night."

"There's no money for doctors, Father Mike," Mrs. Calabria had said, softly. She clenched her hands into fists which she laid on her lap. Her knuckles gleamed white with tension.

"*I'll* pay for it!" Father Mike cried. "The child needs tending."

For a moment, her resolve appeared to waiver. Then she straightened her shoulders and said, "No."

Perhaps he should do the unthinkable. Perhaps he should contact Social Services. He would speak to the Monsignor about it, and follow his counsel. Right now there was a Mass to celebrate.

He rose, gathered his entourage of altar boys around him, and nodded to the organist.

❁

Serafina Calabria sat in the second pew, gazing proudly at her son, Enrico, as she did every Sunday when she watched him perform the rituals of the Mass with appropriate devotion. There was a softness about him, a purity, that spoke to Serafina's heart.

Father Mike lifted the chalice over his head. "And Jesus said to his Disciples, 'Take this, all of you, and drink from it. This is the cup of my blood, the blood of the new and everlasting covenant. Do this in memory of me.'"

This was the holiest of moments, the transubstantiation, when the wine was transformed into the blood of the Savior.

Serafina, and all the devoted, closed their eyes and touched their breasts, while Enrico rang the altar bells and Father Mike genuflected.

Father Mike served himself Communion, then turned to the other celebrants, saying "Body of Christ" as he held up the Communion wafer in front of each, then "Blood of Christ" as he offered them the chalice.

But when he reached Enrico, the child grabbed the chalice and lifted it, as if *he* were the priest performing the transubstantiation. Enrico almost drained the chalice, and wiped his wet lips with the sleeve of his chasuble.

Serafina frowned.

Suddenly, the sunlight pouring through the stained glass windows dimmed just as if the sun had disappeared behind a cloud. Lightning cracked outside the church, and a sudden draft of air blew in from nowhere, snuffing out the candles throughout the sanctuary with a "pfft." A sulphurous odor seeped into the church. A sudden movement caught Father Mike's eye.

There – at the baptismal font – a tall man, pale complected and dressed all in black, smiled, then vanished.

Father Mike wiped his eyes.

He turned to Ricky, who still held the chalice in front of him, waiting patiently for the priest to take it.

Ricky was ... *changed.* The child was glowing. His eyes shined bright and luminous, his cheeks looked plump, filled out, and his waxy complexion was now as rich as heavy cream. A rosy flush bloomed on his cheeks. The child's sudden transformation made it diffiicult for Father Mike to tear his gaze from Ricky's face, but he did, reluctantly, to serve communion.

The first communicant sputtered, clamped his hand to his mouth, then shoved through the waiting parishioners and bolted out the back of the church.

The next communicant screamed, gagged and fainted. Two ushers scrambled to pick her up, but the usher closest to Father Mike looked up, his face gray. The woman's prone, rigid body thrummed the floor in convulsions, and her lower face was dripping with blood.

Did she hit her mouth on the altar step when she passed out?

A third screamed, "Blood! Blood in the chalice!"

For a fraction of a second, everyone seemed frozen in some grotesque diorama. Then the shock was replaced with panic.

Parishioners frantically shoved their way out of the church, sobbing, looking around fearfully. Any semblance of order was forgotten.

Father Mike looked down into the chalice he held. It was indeed blood.

How? Why?

He fell to his knees, his heart hammering in his chest as if it were a prisoner demanding to be released.

The church was empty now, but for Serafina Calabria, her son and Father Mike. Serafina's eyes scanned the choir loft, the balcony, her gaze raking left to right and left again. She rushed to Ricky, pinning him protectively to her bosom.

The church trembled. The statues in their niches shuddered, and the racks of vigil lights sizzled, sputtered, and went out. The flowers on the altar wilted and drooped. Then the back doors of the church burst open and a cold blast of air rushed in.

Father Mike watched, mesmerized, as the stranger from the baptismal font strode toward him down the center aisle with studied dignity.

He was an impressive figure of a man. Massively built and immaculately groomed, his face was shadowed angles and planes above the pristine white of his pleated shirtfront.

The stranger held out his hand to the boy. "Enrico," he said, his voice soothing and gentle, "come to your father."

"Get out, Lucien!" Serafina cried. "You're not his father. He's not of your kind!"

Lucien smiled. "Of course he is. Look at him! What other proof could you need?"

Ricky's eyes still glowed. A trickle of dried blood tracked from the corner of his mouth to his chin.

"It was Enrico that turned the wine to blood," Lucien said. "I just gave him a little boost. Come to Papa, boy." Lucien wiggled his fingers in a 'come here' gesture.

Ricky took a step forward.

Serafina scrambled around the boy and stood between the child and Lucien. "No! This is not your father! He transfused his blood into me while I was pregnant with you. He thought that would make you his. But it doesn't. It can't."

"Get out of the way, Serafina," Lucien warned.

"No. You can't have him." She turned to Father Mike. "Father, help."

"Bitch!" Lucien roared. "How dare you defy me!" His eyes turned into red, glowing embers in his dark face. He spun around, his right arm extended in a sweeping motion.

Suddenly, Serafina was airborne, hurtling down the center aisle like a missile and slammed into the statue of Joseph on the back wall. She sank to the floor, bringing down the plaster statue. It smashed into chunks and slivers as it crashed on top of her.

Serafina lay motionless.

"Mama!" Ricky screamed, and started toward her.

Father Mike leaped toward the child. He encircled the boy with his arms, his white vestments draping around the child like a shield. "Get out of this church!" Father Mike shouted. "You defile it with your presence!"

Lucien glowered at him.

"But I thought my father was dead," Ricky wailed, his voice muffled by the priest's garments.

"*Un*dead is more accurate," Lucien laughed. "Come here, boy. Before I lose my patience."

"Is my mother okay? I need to help her."

"No," Father Mike said. "Don't go to her yet. Trust in God, Ricky."

Lucien laughed again. "If your god is so powerful, why did he let this happen?" He stepped closer. "I grow tired of this mortal minutiae." He snapped his fingers. "Enrico, come!"

The child slipped from Father Mike's arms and began walking toward Lucien.

"No, Ricky! This...this *thing* isn't your father," Father Mike shouted.

The child stopped.

"The priest offers you vows of poverty, celibacy and servitude." Lucien leered at the boy. "I offer you immortality. And infinite power."

Ricky glanced at Father Mike over his shoulder, uncertainty written on his young face.

The church gave a great groan as if her rafters were being pried apart. Plaster dust drifted from the ceiling.

The lights snuffed out. The air turned bitterly cold.

Red sparks erupted at Lucien's feet and traveled upward and outward, encasing him in a semi-transparent vortex of energy. Lucien took a few steps, then stopped at the base of the altar, flashes emanating from him like a child's July 4th sparkler.

He broached the first step.

Up the second.

Crept onto the third – his sparking, evil energy mere feet in front of Ricky.

Then Lucien stepped onto the altar itself.

A dazzling white light flashed. The air shimmered with tiny glimmering crystal motes drifting down from the beams and carrying on them the scent of summer roses and spring showers.

Father Mike opened his mouth and roared, his suddenly powerful voice resonating off the vaulted ceiling and swirling around like a living entity, stirring the crystal motes into dancing drafts, "How dare you desecrate my altar with your filthy presence? You exist only because I allow your existence, because I gave you the gift of free will. You chose freely, and you now pay the consequences of that choice. As this child will do if he chooses you."

The light softened, became less glaring and gentler on the eyes. Father Mike dropped to his knees. The fluorescent sparkling around Lucien diminished, then winked out altogether as Lucien retreated from the altar.

The voice spoke again, softer now. "The choice is yours, child. Purity or power. Life with all its wonder, or living forever – if you consider sucking blood like a leech and hovering in the shadows, living."

Lucien looked diminished somehow, as if his power and self-confidence had eroded. Even his appearance seemed duller.

"A son belongs with his father," Lucien pleaded, extending his hand toward Ricky.

"You're right," Ricky said.

Lucien smiled. He stood taller and his eyes glimmered with satisfaction.

Ricky spun around and embraced Father Mike, drawing the priest's arms around him so that the white vestments again enveloped him.

Lucien's smile faded, then snuffed out altogether. His eyes became steely. His forehead pleated into a scowl.

Then he was gone. Evaporated. Disappeared into eternity in the wink of an eye.

"I love you, Ricky," Father Mike said, hugging the boy closer to him. How calm he was! No trembling, no fear, no bewilderment, none of the jellied knees that close calls usually leave behind, only a vast sense of peace, of knowing justice had been done, his faith exonerated. "Everything's going to be okay now. Let's go see to your Mother."

"Okay, Father," Ricky said, pushing away from the priest's chest.

Father Mike felt a cold stickiness as the child pushed away.

He looked down at himself. His white vestments dripped blood where the child had pressed against him.

Ricky grinned up at the priest. Trusting. Loving.

From the back of the church, a deep, resonant laughter erupted. Lucien's sinister form materialized, shadowy at first, but growing brighter by the moment until he was almost blinding in intensity.

Father Mike felt as if a strong hand clenched his heart, wrapping its fingers around the organ and squeezing tighter. Harder.

His breath burned his throat and nose.

Nausea spilled across his stomach and backwashed his mouth with bile.

Ricky licked the tips of his newly sprouted fangs as he spun around and scampered down the altar steps toward his fallen mother, and his eyes were a bright, spellbinding red.

Nocturne a Tre in B-Double-Sharp Minor

By Robert Devereaux

Late one summer night, up through a rectilinear glow of cityscape into sprawling affluence, Mischa drove. That morning, at the Balfour School, he had taught his yearly master class. At two, he and the orchestra had taken a spin through the Mahler Fourth with the latest young star of the classical circuit, a captivating, ego-ridden mezzo with a fetching eye but no intent to follow through. An inspired performance that evening in packed Philharmonic Hall ensued. Mischa lost himself inside Mahler's persona, as he did with every composer he tackled. Drenched in sweat, he drew upon all his sensate knowledge about the music, delivering it from the podium with conviction, his background in ballet allowing him the utmost in nuance and bodily inflection.

Now for the capper to a busy day.

Bethany had received a routine hug – everything about their marriage had become, alas, routine – on his way out their penthouse door.

"A little nightwork?" she asked, her eyes tiny wet saucers holding no love.

"Yes," he said.

"Make it special."

"I always do."

Truth be told, Mischa was expecting nothing much of consequence tonight, aside from his fee of course, steep by the standards of most people. But the ultra rich – those few who knew the maestro was available to conduct the odd activity in need of heightening – felt the drain of a few thousand dollars as but a single drop lifting from a lake.

By now, he knew well the ritzy neighborhood passing before him. He and Bethany could surely afford, if they so chose, to purchase one of the more modest mansions, the sort the young heiress hiring him tonight lived in. But now that their daughters Roxie and Isadora were out of the house and on their own, and given the international and whirlwind nature of his commitments – by tomorrow, he would be in Vienna to resume his latest Bruckner cycle for DG, then on to Tokyo, and New Zealand after that – such extravagance made no sense.

Mischa parked on the street. Katherine Frye, the heiress who had hired him, had asked him to do so. No doubt she had dismissed her servants, as on his earlier visits; sent even the resident ones away till morning. At the wrought-iron gate, he punched in the code she had given him. Approaching the front door, he felt as calm and collected as a high-class burglar. These performances he especially loved. No matter what he was asked to conduct – dinner party, love tryst, an infirm matron being given a spongebath by candlelight – he delighted in the intimacy most of all, in being close to people who knew how to live well, but not being *of* them. He loved too the sheer privacy of these events, their close-kept nature in such sharp contrast to the glare of his public life.

The mansion's porchlight was off.

Mischa rang the bell. At his side he carried a portable podium and, in its protective case, the olive wood baton given to him ten years before by the Israeli Philharmonic. To judge from her past hirings, the bubble-headed heiress would want him to conduct undressings, fondlements, kisses, *und so weiter.* Katherine Frye was young and healthy, yes, but not at all to his taste in women – too short, too slight, just a touch off, her mind (so like many born into wealth) a thing of mush. But that was all to the good. He found only a glimmer of prurient pleasure in watching her and her evening's companion writhe and moan; and yet, he counted it a privilege to witness such doings and to partake in them at a safe remove.

A muffled rustling flurried inside.

That would be Miss Frye, of course, dressed in sheer nightwear, a pewter candleholder in one hand. A pert simple rich pampered thing she was, young enough to be his granddaughter.

The gilt handle began to turn.

Genevieve awoke simply, abruptly, as always, raising her eyelids with a silent snap.

If breath had been necessary, she would have taken in nothing but foul air. But her lungs were used only for speech and to help take in the fluids that sustained her. For centuries, those functions alone had they served.

In the worn plush, barely discernible above her, she pictured her little aperitif, her rich wide eyes open, her neck bared for the tasting. Katherine Frye. It was good to decoct blood from such a savory decanter, a delicacy after slumber. Had it only been a month of midnights since her lips had first touched Katherine's flesh? Addicting, the warm flow of life in that succulent little package of skin and bone. A few sips to draw the idle young heiress farther along toward eternal companionship; then, leaving her in a languid swoon, a maraud, a frenzy of bloodspew, of suck and swallow in the miserable streets of the city below – these were the doings Genevieve craved tonight.

And tonight, her diminutive lover had said she would meet Mischa Vrublevsky, the flamboyant maestro she had seen conduct in Berlin in the seventies. He had been in the prime of his youth then, still trailing the mantle of wunderkind, a man in his early thirties who had, not many years before, fled the Soviet Union and a promising career in ballet. That night, Mischa had been a pinpoint of life, the sharpest she had seen in a long while, the mad whirligig sounds of Liszt's *Faust Symphony* surging through his tight athletic body. In anyone else, the way he moved would have been called flamboyant, the flailings of a dilettante too full of himself; not so in the young Mischa, who, without yet an orchestra of his own, had taken the musical world by storm.

She hadn't sought him out then. Too many people swirled about him. His recent bride had slept beside him that night.

Tonight would be different.

Genevieve tasted anticipation.

Artists, those thoroughly immersed in their craft, always boasted such rich blood. The bloom that greeted her nostrils as she broke skin was almost sufficient in itself to reinvigorate her.

Time to stir. Time to mist into Katherine's life, love her, cover her, reopen the wounds upon her neck, drink deep the night's libation.

And then there was the maestro.

What, she wondered, would he make of her?

And she of him?

She willed herself into scatter and shift, the old form yielding to the new. It was easier than lifting the ponderous lid, this misting. She seeped between the imperfect joins of rosewood to rosewood, her dark effervescence held intact by will. Thus diffused, she drifted along damp concrete, into a sultry summer's night.

※

Katherine, trying to remain calm, drew open the front door. There stood her new toy, her bought artist, in a professional slouch. Mischa. That's how the press referred to him. Chummy. First name. They had done so for as long as she could remember. What had she been, nine, when an oil rendering of him, brash and brooding, had appeared on *Time*'s cover?

"Ah, my handsome maestro!" she said. He was tall and naturally imposing, his white hair almost silver. "Dear Mischa!"

He nodded. "Miss Frye." Such a challenge, this one. He pointedly yielded nothing (except, she was pleased to note, his time and talents) to riches. Nor did he let his eyes leave her face, though her silk cream nightgown was so thin as to be transparent. "So what's it to be tonight?" he asked. A subtle twist of irony, familiar from his TV lectures, enriched his voice.

"Come in, come in." She switched the candle to her left hand and walked beside him, slipping her fingers under his arm. "Tonight?" she said. "The usual, but with a twist."

"Do tell." His light baritone danced, made her thighs move smoother on their joints.

"Yes, I think you're going to like tonight's companion very much."

"I like the ones you've picked so far. What were their names again?"

"No, I mean *really* like," she said. The maestro was just making conversation, as he had done before. Even when he conducted the most intense of couplings, as sweeping as his passions were, he always held himself in reserve.

"My dear Miss Frye," he mocked her, knowing she would accept his mockery with a smile, "you have impeccable taste in lovers. My interest is duly piqued."

The white of the walls and furnishings ovaled by in the gliding corona of her candle, gilt trim gleaming, then going dull, as they passed. Their bodies whispered across the plush carpet to the winding staircase. "Follow me," she said. There was, of course, ample room for two on the stairs. But from their first meeting – it was a joke they now shared – she did her best to entice him, the contrived sway of her buttocks exaggerated by the candle's shadows as they ascended.

"Oh, Miss Frye, how delectable you are."

Tossing a coy look over one shoulder, she paused midway up. "Mischa, my darling," wishing just once her allure might snag him, "you are such a suave bullshitter."

"My stock in trade, pretty one."

It was absurd. He was what, sixty-two, and she was twenty-one. All the society boys wanted her. Ambitious lawyers and politicians-to-be catered to her every whim. But they were wet pups. Mischa was a man, nothing to prove, a sharp sensuality in his every look. And he cared not a whit for her, not even as a momentary distraction.

Oh, the crock the universe sometimes served up!

But he would go wild over Genevieve, of that she was sure. Genevieve would lure him to their bed, and at last she would enjoy him.

"In here, dear boy," she said at the doorway to her chamber. The candlelight bloomed upon her dressing table, doubled in movement by the mirror. It caressed the drapes to her balcony, the spread upon her bed. Carefully she placed the holder on her nightstand's smooth marble top. The candle's flame winced and steadied.

Behind her, Mischa flourished one hand and placed the portable podium at a sharp angle to the bed. Poor man seemed perturbed tonight. He passed through the drapes and out onto the balcony.

Katherine joined him, her arms wrapped about his waist. Without pulling away, he seemed, as usual, distant. "Something's bothering you," she said.

His fingers, massive and sure, brushed the stone balustrade. "Oh, I was just – " he said. An idle pause. Then, eluding her, "It's my schedule, I suppose. I'm constantly on the move. Doesn't allow for much of an anchor. Except in the music. In finding, how might one say it, a familiar truth beneath continual surprise." He waved it away. "So where's our new friend?"

She followed him inside, the temperature the same but somehow more confining than before. "She'll be along soon."

"Ah, it's a she again. Like the first time." No condemnation, nothing of that sort. Katherine knew that, in artistic circles, sexual latitudes tended to be generously wide.

"Yes," she said, "but someone different."

"So I gather."

"Her name's Genevieve."

Mischa, raising his eyebrows, corrected her pronunciation, giving it that impossible French lilt.

"Whatever. And you know, Mischa . . ." she teased.

"Yes?" he asked, taking the bait.

Slowly she raised her nightgown, swaying as she bunched it. Up rose the whisper of silk, past legs and thighs, past waist and breasts, over her head. She flung it aside. "My lover gets to taste this sweet pretty, um, *everything* of mine. Wouldn't you like to do the same?"

"Ah. We're being blatant now, are we?" He cracked a smile. "Listen, my dear, you're quite lovely." He said it by rote. "But my wife is all I can handle, has been for some time. It's best if I decline, regretfully, your offer. Please don't take offense at that."

She stretched out on the bed, the comforter's initial coolness turning to warmth. Her fingers glided down her body, sculpting it. "As you like. But if you change your mind, you'll let me and my Genevieve know, won't you?"

"I will indeed," he said, unlatching his baton case.

"Oh, good, you're going to start."

"Yes," he said. "I only wish I had begun at the front entrance. You put on quite a show, as always."

She laughed. "Next time?"

"Next time."

✦

Mischa bounded onto the podium and was transformed. There wasn't much sparring room, a mere postage stamp compared to his four-by-four square of carpeting onstage. But these intimate settings didn't require much in the way of flare and gymnastics. In the concert hall, flamboyance reigned. But here, Mischa counted on economy, on concision of movement; a study in miniatures, his baton work in private.

He wondered just how the latecomer would get in. Usually the bell would ring below, he would wait, directing the room's emptiness, the night sounds, the play of light – and the lover of the moment would at last appear behind Miss Frye at the bedroom door. But the spoiled young heiress, a poor man's Salome, was already naked, pulling a corner of thick soft bedding up so as to slide herself beneath it, turning it down coyly at the waist, as her head nestled into the pillow's deep trough. Her perky little breasts, nippling out from an invisible harness, boldly proclaimed that they were going nowhere.

No matter.

How the mystery woman found her way inside was none of Mischa's concern.

He was here to perform.

No doubt Katherine Frye had sent his fee to the charity he had named – something he would have his accountant check after New Zealand.

He laughed. Conducting sex for charity. Why not? He had done stranger things in his career. In the sixties, a time of great experimentation among classical upstarts, he had conducted a naked cellist frying an egg, a stage full of silent Steinways in Carnegie Hall, an Easter sunrise from the south rim of the Grand Canyon. A time long gone. But those wild excursions into the heart of conducting had led directly to these private sessions.

His eyes swept the room, his baton moving in stately fashion, grandly, slowly, warming to the task. He cued the diaphanous drapes, the flare of an unlit brass torchere, the rolltop desk (what an odd item for Miss Frye to have in her bedroom, but there it was), the shadows defining its slats, the woodstained highlights touched by candlelight, by moonlight. Then he nodded to the rapt tufts of carpeting, close and tight as the clipped coat of a wheaten terrier, and brought them in – scurrying about him like seas of caught foam – with a gesture of grand affirmation.

"You're marvelous," said the naked woman, her eyes piercing him with a sultry look.

"Thank you, Miss Frye." Decades before, at Tanglewood, Mischa had learned that there were no dead moments in music, that what happened between the beats was of no less importance to the conductor who knew his art than what happened on the beat. Later, he had taught *himself* that the idea of an inanimate object was an illusion, that everything lived if awareness gave it life and that music, even music which bore the misnomer silence, informed all.

"I mean," she said, "there are no words."

He thought to answer, "Then kindly shut up, Miss Frye." In the midst of formulating a more diplomatic way of conveying the same message, the air changed. A sharp whiff of ozone invaded the atmosphere. Could moonlight, could candlelight, suddenly brighten? If they could, that's what happened – and so his baton strokes implied, a hint of *The Sorcerer's Apprentice,* an upsweep of piccolos, invigorating the light.

The balcony drapes danced upon another soft breeze; brilliant spanglings, like abrupt aches of the eye, tangled in them. But as he fixed on the spanglings, as he acknowledged their role in the visual symphony, they became a muddle: part glint, part flesh. Mistake. His mind abruptly corrected itself, then was forced to do so again. *Entirely* now a thing of flesh. Tall, naked, monstrous, the creature by her sheer presence made his breath lull, his mouth go dry.

It walked. It floated. Mischa's baton sped up to fend off insanity.

Acknowledge it, cover it with art, *keep* acknowledging it, the white on copper sweep of hair, the red bloom at its pubis, the sick Munchlike clay-white marshmallow cloy of its flesh, repellent yet desirable. Two leathery nipples, tan mouse snouts, capped the creature's breasts. Even this, his mind said, as he caught its wild music; accept, acknowledge, even this.

A fever wracked him, then passed.

The thing must not look his way. If it did, if it turned those mad eyes away from its supine victim, he would surely snap. He was conducting a tarantella, the fastest most frenzied spiderdance he had ever drawn out of an orchestra.

Halfway into the bedroom, the creature turned its head and captured his eyes.

And he did not go mad, but rather all serene, his baton suddenly cut to a quarter of its beat, as love blossomed in his brain – a love eternal and unconditional.

※

When her foot first touched carpet, Genevieve looked away from her intended and drank in the man on the podium, seizing him, sizing him up.

What Katherine had told her was true. In an intimate space, the maestro's sheer presence, the sway of his frame, his hands, those deep eyes and the intelligence behind them enhanced the scene he conducted.

Her entrances always satisfied. But this one bore a special quality, a sharpness and a delight, as though she had never made an entrance before, not even the ghost of one. Her lover gasped at its beauty. Genevieve felt a mingle of emotions, and Mischa at once picked up on them and drew them out. She felt, on the one hand, appreciated, her grandeur recognized and celebrated; her body, as always, flowed grandly in, yet each moment was fixed and fascinating, captured in the maestro's deft gestures. On the other, she was not used to, liked not in the *least,* sharing the spotlight with anyone. In bringing out the sweep of her power, the brilliant conductor, feigning mere artful observance, displayed his own.

Ah, but what a sensual nature was his, this Mischa, this Slav in a black turtleneck swaying on his little platform. She smelled the richness of his blood, beating just beneath the surface of his skin. Before the evening was out, she had to taste it. She had him by the eyes, but he had her too. He refused – not by will but by nature – to succumb to her proffered illusions. He saw what was in her, and she saw him see it: the monster, the lover, the dream.

She glanced toward the bed. The thing lying there was a trifle. How could she have imagined her as anything more? Allure blinded one, brought out what was sublime, suppressed the rest. All it took to open one's eyes was to sample the presence of something better. Of Mischa. Not that she had to snag him. No. He would be wrong for that. But he pointed her the way, corrected her vision.

Thirst nipped at her.

Her mouth craved blood. But more than that, Genevieve wanted to witness her own feeding as it filtered through Mischa's sensibility. The carpet tufts tickled her toes, her soles, her heels, as she slid toward the bed. Lifting off, she glided through candlelight, feeling almost as if Mischa's conducting carried her into the air above the bed. Zen masters spoke of effortless doing. That was how she felt now, a witness to an act involving her whole self. The Frye girl's eyes widened into dark pools of acceptance. Like a trusting child's, her arms opened. Her smooth white neck, its wounds brown as bruises, lay bare and inviting. Genevieve tasted saliva, swallowed it, drifted down, brought her fingers beneath the skull of her next meal, caught Mischa in her eye.

The maestro reflected her beauty. Her grandeur. Her depravity. She felt . . . an old feeling she had long thought dead . . . moist toward him. Drool brimmed between her thighs.

Keeping her eyes on the sweating Slav, she parted her lips, sited the sharp slick tips of her fangs, and drove them home.

❊

At first, Katherine felt creamy.

There was Mischa, of course, making her bedroom glow with his awareness, catching the odd sound – nightjars outside, the rustle of her body on the sheets – delighting in the sights.

Then there was Genevieve's entrance: The mist always sparkled in such beautiful patterns, like a storybook opened by Disney animators. And up from its depths, or within its swirl, floated the perfect rebirth of Katherine's lover. Her eyes blessed what they fell upon. Her teeth cooled and stung. The night before, in a yawn that was no yawn, Genevieve had grazed their pinprick points across her own lower lip, raising stipples of blood, whose wine-dark taste she had allowed Katherine to savor. The bitter tang had stayed with her the next day, like the lingering buzz of repeated orgasms.

But now, after the heightened entrance that was Mischa's doing, after Genevieve had fixed him in her eyes, the look on her lover's face brought terror home to the young woman.

Her gaze, no longer soft, bit like teeth.

And her beauty had fallen away. Katherine recaptured an erased memory, her first glimpse of the monster rapping at the window glass. She woke in shock. Some hideous thing stood on the balcony then. Through her fear it lured her, so that by the time she reached to open the way, it had become beautiful, losing all ugliness.

No longer. No need. It descended upon her and sank its teeth into her neck as if they were thick rude spikes, not the numb insertion of tiny needles she had grown accustomed to. Katherine panicked, struggling against the assault. But the vise of Genevieve's arms tightened about her. Her heart thundered. She felt life rush out of her feet, her hands, her brain, numbing them, leaching them white, a numbness that spread to arms and legs as her mind fizzed in a wildfire of tight bubbles.

No, she said, in her head. But her mind had gone white too, swimming, buzzing, as if she were being rolled on a gurney under harsh lights. And when, with a round thud, it blundered against the doors to an operating room, Katherine fainted away.

Once in Kiev late one summer's night, Mischa had passed through a ghost on the stairs of an old house where his ballet troupe was encamped. He hadn't believed in ghosts. He didn't particularly believe in them now. But when, that summer, going over the day's choreography in his head, he walked through a fog of resistance on those steep steps to his room, he knew at once and without question what had happened.

So now, although the thing defied gravity and its face, once human, was no longer so, it claimed its place in the natural order as if it had always belonged there. He conducted that naturalness, as it snagged him yet again with a look.

Not it.

She.

Genevieve.

The thing was womanly, its gaze hungering for his sex. He was stiff as a trowel handle, wanting her, yet horrified at his desire. But he refused to succumb. As blood sheeted along Katherine Frye's throat, out from beneath the sucking lips, as the heiress struggled naked and helpless in her death throes, Mischa acknowledged his lust, his refusal to yield, the burning power of those deep hard eyes. He was conducting a death. Save for the elder Sanborn, Gavin the last (a lavish patron of the arts and a saint among millionaires, whose terminal moments he had agreed to direct),

Mischa had conducted no deaths, had vowed indeed never to do another, Gavin Sanborn's death had so wrenched his heart.

But he conducted a death now. It was quick with ravin, sensual, violent, but there was in it an acquiescence so peaceful as to render the whole scene – it did so now and he followed suit with his baton – sexual, the insistent pounding of one body against another in a clutch of mutual desire.

The creature's eyes kept to him, becoming now the focus of his baton. They had to. If he tried to evade them, they would claim him. He dove deep into them, knowing he could only sustain control by matching them, glare for glare. Maelstroms of hunger swirled in them. She dropped the drained corpse to the mattress, audible the vacuum of her lips unsticking. Through the air she slinked, her face aglow with monstrous beauty.

Mischa was erect.

His body twisted this way and that in the frenzy of his art, confident but trapped.

There wasn't a thing he could do to stop her, so he continued etching her approach upon the air, slicing it, stabbing it, prodding it, pointing it up, beat crowding upon beat.

✦

Abandoning the bloodless corpse, Genevieve drifted toward the dancing man. Mischa's power awed her even through his trapped-rat terror. He captured, expressed, transformed the vast depths of feeling between them, the hunger, the fear, the powerplay that so fiercely bonded them.

The poor man was sweating like a pig about to be plunged into boiling water. Gesturing with two outstretched fingers, not touching him, she parted the thin black cotton at his neck, his shoulders, along his arms. The material clung as it peeled off, darker at the chest where his exertions had painted an amoebic sweatstain. He didn't miss a beat. Downward she drew her fingers, curving them around his baton's insistence, severing the belt, unthreading the weave of his trousers, watching fabric fall away, panel by panel. His briefs parted at the bulge, fell floating like a damp coffee filter, until, captured within a heap of cloth that skirted the podium, the maestro stood naked and erect.

Kneeling in the air above the carpet, her hair stringy about her face, she felt his heat, sniffed the fluid waiting for her tongue. Like an engorged loaf of dark rye, the drained clottings of the dead heiress lay heavy on her stomach. But her hunger would not be stilled. Before her, the maestro's upthrust member threw off the greatest heat, clutched and fisted the greatest concentration of blood. The thing bobbed to his rhythm, a bloodpacked baton of flesh. Like an angry coelacanth it swayed. As her eyes swept his body, her hands wove to its rhythm. His skin, slick with sweat, shimmered like baked blacktop, vibrant wherever she looked, not like the flesh of her victims nor the morgue chill at her heart.

The stiff thin fang of his baton stabbed the air. His eyes burned with life. Intent sat upon the narrow tip, a dipstick downthrust and dancing. In antic counterpoint, his aroused flesh rose and swayed, thick, taut with blood, the focus now of her fascination. Against the muscled gyration of his hip-lyre, above powerful thighs, the thing stiffly tick-tocked. She drew ever closer to it, pulled in tight, the better to watch it dance.

※

Breaking into consciousness, the first sound Katherine heard was the maestro's breathing. He was the only one breathing in the room. Opening her eyelids, she let deadlight in. The bedroom, an ancient memory, smelled like a tomb.

It was odd not to be breathing, as though a preternatural cunning had shut her down, as though she crouched in a corner with her senses entangled in terror. Yet she was dead calm. A lassitude lay about her limbs, and a strength. Her head sat at an odd angle, yanked up by sheer power, then dropped. But she lay still, letting her eyes rove.

There he stood, there he danced, her silver-haired maestro, wearing not a stitch. He was a god, a goat-hoofed faun, tempting, without wanting to, the nymph who knelt before him. To no sounds but the puffing and blowing of his own exertions, he wrestled with attraction, with repulsion.

Katherine, as though she dreamed, recalled wanting him just like this, muscular, a sheen of sweat making his skin glow, the lift of his sex tempting her lips, her labia. Now, that craving had been subsumed by another.

Keep quiet, must keep quiet. Surprise would gain her what she craved.

Her every atom and fiber shivered with thirst. Gathers of strength bunched beneath the quiescence of her limbs, a strength that grew in tandem with her need for nourishment.

The aroma of her lover's dead-rich blood invaded her nostrils, the same bouquet that had stirred her into waking, propagating through her veins. Far more tantalizing, she smelled the man's blood – the sizzle and aroma of sunshine breakfast, sausage steaming next to scrambled eggs – and deep down in the empty gape of her soul, longing rose and billowed, a bloodlust that would burst her at any moment from the bed, propel her forward, urge her to imbibe at his exposed neck.

Quiet, she thought. Not yet. Not yet.

❈

He was a dead man. He knew that. As long as he remained focused, however, on delineating with baton and body this softly lit death chamber, the creature's blood hunger, and his own terrible mix of arousal and repulsion – so long would she leave off attacking him, so long would he live.

But she had all night. He had not. Not soon but eventually, his endurance would flag, he would falter, and she would take him.

That fear too he wove into his art. Her eyes never left his sex, her head and hands matching its movement like a cat watching a cornered rat, ready to pounce. Fear typically trumped sex, abating all lust. But within this fear burned desire, yes as well as no. Waves of light swept the bed, the desk, the dresser – moved by breezes that held and lifted the balcony drapes. That light, playing upon his unclothed body, flooded and tickled his insides with sensuality. Liquid gold dabbed his skin, inside and out, a blush of blood raised there and there, pale scarlet patches on golden apples. Despite his terror, his body felt free and beautiful, moving with a music only he heard, but which his insistence made others fancy they heard too. She heard it, the ancient young-looking one whose longevity hung about her like the odor of parchment. Her every headbob, her unblinking eyes, the dance of her hands told him so.

His testicles strained tight. Above them, the empurpled shaft felt as if it would burst its skin. Could such a thing rupture? He wanted to let fly, to come. But it was impossible, a thing she was drawing out. Then, abruptly – he *had* to stay focused, not drop a stitch, not let the beat blither away in passion – his sperm flew forth, in jets, in spews. Not the white of tapioca but pink as lobster bisque. Blood tainted it, as had once happened in his youth. Inches away, the creature, ducking and weaving, caught the erratic spurts in her mouth, as a golden retriever prancing before a lawn sprinkler might catch beaded blasts of water.

Mischa shuddered. "Oh God," he thought. But his baton held steady, triumphing over the power of his orgasm by sweeping that power too into its infinite purview.

He had to hold her off. He would.

❈

Genevieve engorged what he tossed, gulping between surges, tasting always. His whole body danced in mastery. As his sweat flicked off in the rhythm of his limbs, so too his seed caught the sprung rhythms he cross-conducted.

Gorgeous man.

The blood was the life. The sperm as well. The mixture? An ichor divine.

Too many men and women, like the dead bauble on the bed, played it safe, hid their life behind barriers of meekness, never cultivated it, never proclaimed it, never set it free. They were the contemptible masses of might-as-well-be-dead. But here was a human being who walked and joked like the rest of them, but who, when he unleashed his power, did so with boldness, swept it over the edge, a man who dared all, defied all, who opened himself completely and displayed what lived inside with joy, and rage, and glory. All his life, she could tell, he had been doing that; and what lived inside, because he had nurtured it so long, was huge and beautiful and to be envied.

Too late for her to attain.

She could only suck the momentary glow, the off-flung life that died in the flinging.

But the juice she had just imbibed, that and a tiny drop of the pure stuff, would sustain her for days. She'd take no more than that. He was a precious vial. He belonged not to her but to the world.

The brilliant man, panting still, conducted as he regained himself. She would have to touch him now, still his baton hand, halt the glorious show he had given her, was giving her even now, tap his jugular and be on her way, rolling his life on her tongue as she went.

A flurry at her back took her unawares.

❖

Lying head askew, her need for the maestro's blood growing unabated, Katherine had only enough room in her mind to watch her identity seep away.

Hunger – ravenous, true, and deep – had been unknown to her. In twenty-one years, she had never been more than a servant away from food. Even when she had run away at age ten, her backpack of Doritos and Crackerjacks had only been half depleted when the gathering darkness changed her mind.

But now the hunger was there all right, and growing. Had she been alive (*I'm dead,* came to her matter-of-factly), her stomach would have growled and given her away. But that, like her other organs, lived on only as an idea. Her hunger centered elsewhere, everywhere, not a thing of gastric juices but of pure need.

There on the podium swayed the source of her nourishment. His skin was fully revealed, every point of entry made available, so easy to rush in and feast, the patches of heat where blood flowed just below the surface, pulses pounding at wrists and armpits, at the sinewy place his inner thighs met, in his sex, and most surely beneath the flesh of his throat.

With no upshift in heat, her fever grew. In that beautiful moving canvas, there interested her more and more but one tiny patch. The rest loomed in her sight and fell away, as lust magnified the vein she craved. She saw the interstices of his skin, the mottling, the subtle rise and purpling of the jugular – not so subtle now, as though he had tied off his neck, made it bulge, readied it to receive the needle, the *twin* needles in her mouth whose hollowness burned and craved.

When movement finally came, she was too far gone in hunger to realize she was moving. There was simply food and a maw that would brook no delay in being filled. The bedclothes flurrying by had no name, nor the furniture, nor the swaying body she quickly closed upon. There was "food" and "obstacle," but she had no time even to name these.

She gaped and bared her sharpness, ready to sink into the place of engorgement.

Something flickered upon the bed. But before Mischa could fold it into his batonwork, the air on his left whooshed aside. Katherine Frye's dead body, eyes open, mouth wide, rushed toward him as swiftly as a hand recoils from an oven burn.

He jerked back.

Iron fingers wrenched his chin up.

Something huge sprouted below it, as if a goiter had ballooned upon his neck, the bubblegum swell of an inner tube. The dead woman's head. Twin piercing pains slid into him, deep stings. He winced. The corpse clung like a frightened spider monkey to him, cold but lightweight, not toppling him off-balance.

But he was falling, set off-balance more by shock than momentum.

Below, the creature he could no longer see, the one called Genevieve, steadied him with cold repellent hands that swept up from his buttocks and left his body. At his throat, a chill wet rubber mouth, dead, demanding as any infant's, rounded and pulled.

His baton hand faltered, his art abruptly at an end. Then a claw came about his hand, and he saw Genevieve rush in on the right.

The bitch was fast. And cagey.

In Genevieve's haste to drain her, in her concentration on the maestro and his power, she had forgotten the heiress's taste of ancient blood the night before.

Now the little nullity was back, with teeth.

Her speed was the speed of the undead. But it was crude and unpracticed. Genevieve's, on the other hand, had been honed over centuries.

She kept the man from toppling, applying just enough pressure in the right direction to counter his fall. His beautiful fingers, wrapped around the cork-bulb of his baton, relaxed their touch. Against the maestro's chest pressed the woman's dead left breast, white and bloodless. Behind it lay her heart.

Genevieve caught Mischa's hand, tightened his grip, and jammed the baton tip in below the woman's breast, angling up between the ribs to impale her. At the same time, she grabbed a fistful of black bloodmatted hair and snapped the heiress's head back. Her virgin fangs angled out like a pair of wasp stings expertly extracted, clean, minimally damaging the pierced skin.

Now Genevieve snatched at her throat, gripped it, squeezed it, wrenching the head back so that her spine snapped. Squeezing and twisting until the bloodless head came off, she tossed it across the room. The body, losing its hold on the conductor, thudded to the floor.

Mischa felt twisted, wrung dry.

Katherine Frye's corpse fell and with it his baton, sunk deep into her chest.

"You're all right," Genevieve said.

He watched her, dazed.

She beaded to the bed and wrenched off two feet of post. It came away as easy as balsawood, its end splintered and white. She homed in upon the corpse. When she drew out the baton, the limbs began to shudder awake. Swiftly she jammed in the broken bedpost, and serenity reclaimed the headless corpse.

Genevieve's tongue flexed about the baton, drew along its length, two, three times, until all trace of gore was gone. Then she was beside him, placing the bulb end in his hand.

"You're all right," she repeated.

Her body touched his, her skin supple but nubby, holding him up, though her feet never met the floor. I'm dead, he thought, and he thought it again with greater certainty as her full cool lips O'd upon his throat, where the other's mouth had been. He pictured not Bethany his wife, nor his daughters, but his beloved Philharmonic and flashes of other ensembles he had guest-conducted. He pictured lovers he had kept at a distance: Jade, the cropped-blonde sculptress in Paris, whom he hadn't allowed himself to fall in love with; the bright-eyed translator on his last trip to Hungary, her name gone already, but he would never forget her tenderness and what might have been if he had given back what he got; others, a handful each year for the past many years. People called it being faithful, but Mischa knew in his soul, and for himself, that it was simple cowardice and romance denied.

But now, as he surrendered to the monster who grasped him, he felt not the piercing of fangs but a cold wet sandpaper tongue scraping along his neck, smoothing it, closing his wounds. Ice on nipples. He thought he might pass out from the sudden shuddery delight. Twice he felt the impress of sharpness; then, despite the creature's soft swoon, it withdrew.

Abruptly he was free. Genevieve dropped down upon the body like a spider, grabbed it by one underarm, hauled it up as if it were stuffed with newsprint.

She fetched the head.

He was afraid she would fly at him.

"You're not going to – " he gasped out.

She turned, her monstrosity as repellent and alluring as ever. "My way is beautiful." She laughed. "It is. It's a joy. Getting used to it isn't difficult. And once you're there, it has its rewards." He sensed a "but" in the offing. Then, changing course, she craned her neck at him. "Care to come along?"

"Please, no."

She nodded. "I didn't think you would. Your way is different from mine. Your immortality will come in its own time. Carry on. Grow. That's what you need to do."

He felt bereft, the tingle of her mouth still on his throat.

"Wait, I – "

But she sped toward the balcony, tossing the body and head before her. They tumbled into the night. He heard a dull thud below as the larger mass struck. Genevieve, not looking back, broke up into pointillist fog, then nothing.

The secret of his art had at last opened to him. He could detail what was – and at the same time let people in, let them be as intimate with him as they liked. There was no clash, none at all, between vulnerability and power.

Mischa faltered off the podium, feeling as if the whole world beneath his feet were now nothing *but* podium, his every gesture a sweep of the baton. He gripped the nearest bedpost. Could he conduct his alienation from Bethany? Could he stop hiding it, bring it out in the open, not harshly but with kindness and truth?

He must.

He would.

There was clothing to gather, fingerprints to smear. None of that mattered. He doubted they would ever find her body, nor that he could be traced here. A B-movie dither crowded his brain. But through it all, through the pulling together and a half-dressed stumble to his car, he felt Genevieve's chill lips on his neck and saw his wife's vacancy, saw how she had looked, so vibrant and happy, in their earliest years together.

Things they had had.

Things they had lost.

He saw how it all fit together and how, out of the seeming jumble of his personal life, he could bring final resolution, a sad kind of sense, and a moment that would segue – smoothly, with needful sorrow – into new life.

For The Love Of Vampires

By Deborah Markus

"I don't think I was the only little girl in the world who wanted Dracula to win," Laura began, rising from her comfortable seat and pacing restlessly across the room. It was her favorite lament, her theme song.

"You know very well you weren't," Caroline said. From anyone else the words might have sounded reproachful, or at least impatient, especially if that anyone had heard Laura's complaint as often as Caroline had. As Caroline's voice was, by some happy accident of nature, incapable of sounding anything but serene, the phrase was only cheerfully accurate. "If you were, your books wouldn't sell nearly as well as they do."

Laura glared out the window, refusing to be consoled. At moments such as this, she wished that there were some non-fatal habit that could play the same dramatic role for nonsmokers that cigarettes did for the addicted. How satisfying it would be to pull out a silver case now and blow a puff of smoke in lieu of answering the unanswerable. Many of her characters were fond of doing exactly that at carefully timed intervals, though of course none of them had to worry about anything as nasty as lung cancer. They would all die young or not at all, and nothing they could do would change things; that being the case, why fret over a little tar?

Even if Laura had such an assurance to fall back on, she hated the smell of smoke. She contented herself instead with folding her arms and frowning as hard as she could. The night was cold and stormy, which might have helped matters if it hadn't served instead to show her apartment up as the beautiful, cozy place it was. It was difficult to keep a bad mood going when one was surrounded by color and light, but Laura was a determined sort.

"I mean, come on," she continued, as if Caroline had not just agreed with her. "Why would people read and write so much about vampires if deep down – not all that deep down – they didn't admire them?"

"I don't think that follows, necessarily," Caroline said. Her tone was serious, but she was smiling at her friend's back. Every time they had this conversation, Caroline tried to insert something new into it, both as a test of her own creativity and to make Laura happy. Laura might be a little repetitive herself – some critics said that was the secret of her success – but she couldn't bear others to be. "Look at Fate, or Death. How often have they been anthropomorphized? They've even popped up as characters in *your* work. But no one likes them. They respect and fear them, that's all."

Laura sighed. Caroline was a classics scholar, and Laura always felt she had pulled off an amazing feat when she managed to drag her away from some musty tome and engage her in something as mundane as conversation. Not that Caroline ever minded Laura's need for attention; on the contrary, she appeared to enjoy it. But Caroline always seemed to be forcing herself to step out of another world, one infinitely more pleasant and well-ordered than this. Trust her to mention Fate and Death as casually as if she'd had tea with them that afternoon.

The view from a tenth-floor apartment on a rainy evening was of limited interest no matter how bad one's mood, and Laura abandoned it to flop down again on the overstuffed couch across from Caroline's easy chair. "Carrie, give me a break," Laura said. "People read about those things, just like they read about crime and punishment and car chases, but they don't read about them for the same reasons, and they certainly don't seek them out in the same way that they do vampires. Vampires have charisma. They have sex appeal. Why else would so many Dracula remakes be presented as love stories? Stoker would die again if he could come back to life and see what people have done to his book."

"I think he'd understand," Caroline said in her soothing voice, though who she might have been soothing was difficult to say since the great man himself wasn't there and Laura was buried too deep in her own private anger to care for verbal caresses.

They sat in silence for a moment, Laura ruminating, Caroline content to wait for the other to speak first. The contrast between them was as great as that between Laura's bristling personality and her coldly controlled, well-selling prose. It was just this contrast that allowed their friendship to thrive as it did.

Caroline was unselfconscious golden loveliness. She had all of the grace of the Greek heroines she wrote about so joyfully and well – in her own way, and in her own field, Caroline was as successful as Laura. They were both self-made women, though Laura's humble beginnings couldn't hold a candle to the grinding poverty that had been Caroline's childhood and youth. The difference between their separate successes was that Caroline genuinely loved her work and was driven only by her own pleasure in it. Laura resented the novels she finished with such effort and speed, and regarded her own talent without false modesty as a burden she often wished had been given to someone else. Yet her dark hair was cropped short and her spacious apartment was cared for by someone else's hands and her social life was limited almost exclusively to Caroline, all in the name of giving herself more time to devote to her work.

"So what am I doing wrong?" Laura burst out.

Caroline looked at her without surprise. This, too, was a question she had heard many times before. "Who says you're doing anything wrong?"

"I do, damn it! I work my ass off, and for what?"

"For a great deal of money, last I checked," Caroline said, allowing a hint of asperity to trickle into her voice. "For the people who love your books."

"Oh, please."

"Look at all the letters you get."

"You look at them," Laura growled. This would have been the time to throw her cigarette down, or at least grind it out savagely on a valuable piece of furniture. That twenty-something vampire brat who was finally, finally going to die in the very novel Laura was working on now (wouldn't her fans howl at that!) had ruined quite a few antiques that way.

"Don't they mean anything to you?" Caroline pursued.

"Oh, they mean something, all right," Laura said. "They mean that my readers are a bunch of vampire groupies with too much time on their hands who all seem to think that I have the home address of every guy with fangs they've ever heard of!"

Caroline laughed. The rain began to beat with particular force against the windows; Caroline stood up and pulled the curtains shut. "So, they're fools. Most people are. Why take it personally?"

"Because I wish they were right," Laura said. From the intensity of her voice, anyone would have thought that she had never spoken this wish before. "Because I'm tired of hearing from the fakers and the wannabe's. I want the real thing, and no matter what I do, I can't find it."

That was Caroline's cue to haul out the tea and comfort. Laura stocked plenty of the former, but Caroline felt less confident than usual in her abilities to dole out the latter. She left Laura to muse bitterly over her fate and went into the kitchen to boil an extra-full kettle. She needed time to think.

It was strange, she pondered as she filled a bright baroque teapot with hot water to keep it warm in preparation for the brew, how indifferent Laura was to the costly, lovely things that surrounded her. If Laura had been born to money, Caroline might have been able to understand it, but Laura's family, left coldly behind long ago, had been quite poor. That was what had driven her to work with such single-minded ferocity from the very beginning. Yet wealth brought no joy. Laura barely seemed to notice it.

Caroline had chosen and decorated this apartment, occupying the same building as her own, almost entirely by herself. She had taken joy in every corner and cupboard that needed filling, and continued to look after some of the smaller regions – keeping an eye on the tea caddy, for example. As she took out a tin of dark fragrant leaves now and spooned some into a perforated silver egg, she checked automatically that there was plenty left for her next visit. Laura would never want for life's little comforts as long as Caroline was a regular guest here. But for all the pleasure her home gave her, Caroline knew, Laura might as well have been back in the one-room apartment – luxuriously furnished with bed, table, typewriter, and hotplate – in which she had lived when Caroline first met her.

Caroline sighed, watching the rapidly heating kettle for the first hint of steam. What, after all, had drawn her to Laura in the first place and continued to attract her long after another person would have thrown up her hands in despair, if not that neediness that couldn't be filled by mere material objects, a longing not for a mother or a lover or even a friend by any ordinary definition, but for a rock to cling to, a cave in which to hide? The opposite of a moth to the flame, Caroline thought, pouring hot water out of the tea pot and boiling water in. She loved Laura exactly for the darkness that repelled everyone else.

And tonight Laura was burrowing into that darkness, again. It was cropping up more and more frequently, this bizarre notion that Caroline knew kept Laura up not only nights (which was when she usually worked anyway) but days, too. Wonderful for her work, which grew stranger the less sleep its author had; less than healthy for Laura herself. Caroline refused to harbor doubts about Laura's sanity even in the privacy of her own thoughts, but she was growing quite concerned. Laura looked more despondent than usual tonight, and she was much too pale.

Well, most artists had their obsessions, ones that might seem foolish to the outside world but were quite real to their creators. This was, after all, directly related to Laura's work, and might fuel it even as it fed. Caroline smiled at her own sloppy terminology and piled cups, saucers and other tea necessities onto a tray. Tonight she would do more than just listen. If she asked enough pointed questions, perhaps Laura might tire and change the subject herself.

Laura was still sitting huddled on the couch. That was odd, at least for her. Generally, Laura couldn't stand doing nothing at all; she paced or read or turned on music when left to herself even for a few minutes. Now she was glaring at the wall opposite as if it had wronged her.

Caroline set the tray down on the table and poured tea in silence. She knew that look, had even seen it on her own face. It wasn't anger. It was fierce concentration, reflecting an effort to force words together in just the right way.

"I know we've been over this before," Laura said after reaching for a cup of tea, as if prompted by the warmth between her hands. "You must be getting sick of it."

"Don't be silly," Caroline said, settling back in her seat. She pressed her teacup gently to the side of her face, enjoying the heat; Laura always kept her apartment too cold, whether from absentmindedness or because she preferred it that way Caroline had never figured out. "I ranted for a week about Helen of Troy when I was working on that paper, remember?" From force of academic habit, Caroline always referred to whatever she was working on at the moment – book, chapter, or essay – as a paper. "You didn't complain once, and you had to listen to every word."

Laura smiled grudgingly. "You never rant, Carrie."

"Call it what you will, I go on and on when I've got something on my mind. And I reserve the right to let you do the same."

"All right," Laura said. She shifted restlessly, almost spilling her tea in the process. "I just don't understand what I'm doing wrong."

"I ask again: why must you be doing anything wrong?"

Laura looked at her. "Caroline, have you ever wondered why I write about what I write about?"

Caroline shrugged delicately. "Not really. If I gave it any thought at all, I guess I figured your reasons were the same as mine: you like it and it's what you're good at."

"It never struck you as odd? My material, I mean?"

"No odder than being as crazy as I am about people who died

thousands of years ago and plays no one else reads or cares about."

Laura sighed, took a sip of her tea and made a face. The tea was too strong, as usual. "Things are so simple for you," she said; it sounded like an accusation. "You have your work and you love it and that's that."

"If you're considering a change of field," Caroline said tartly, "I'll be thrilled to start your Greek lessons first thing tomorrow."

"I'm sorry," Laura said. Caroline smiled at Laura's pained expression. Laura hated to apologize. "I didn't mean to make it sound as if your work isn't difficult. It's certainly a lot more worthwhile than mine is," Laura added glumly, stirring sugar into her tea.

"None of that," Caroline said briskly, frowning over the ruin of yet another perfect cup of tea. She wondered why she bothered measuring the leaves so carefully, when Laura treated the drink as if she would be happier with a cup of molasses. "I don't think about things that way, and neither should you. Now, why did you ask me if I wondered about your choice of subject matter?"

"Everyone seems to assume I have a Gold Rush mentality," Laura began. "I don't mean you. You know me better than that. But the line of non-reasoning seems to go like this: a few people have made a lot of money writing about vampires, and a lot of people have tried to make a lot of money writing about vampires, so anyone who writes about vampires must therefore be trying to make a lot of money. Period. Not exactly a valid syllogism."

"Even if that were true about you," Caroline murmured into the delicious steam from her cup, "and I'm not for a moment saying that it is, what would be wrong with it? You do what you do well, and you're well paid for it. If you had any other kind of job – a non-creative one, I mean – and you were 'only' doing it for the money, no one would care."

Laura laughed. "Excuse me," she said. "Your subject matter is so romantic, I keep forgetting that at heart you're just another die-hard capitalist."

"Don't insult me," Caroline said, smiling. "If you think what I do is romantic, I suggest you go back and read a little Aristophanes."

Laura rolled her eyes and shook with a mock-shudder. "Perish the thought."

They sat for a moment in silence, and then Caroline said, "All right. You're waiting for me to ask, so I'll ask. Why do you write what you write?"

Laura didn't answer immediately. She abandoned her tea, which never seemed to have more than a symbolic value to her anyway – Caroline had never seen her finish a cup, or even half a cup – and stretched out full-length on the couch.

"The first one," she said meditatively, staring at the ceiling, "was for money. I admit that." She darted a defensive glance at Caroline, whose serene expression hadn't changed. "I had to do something," she added. "I mean, it wasn't as if anyone was volunteering to let me quit my day job and just type whatever my little heart desired. I knew what would sell, and it did. The same with the second one."

Caroline nodded noncommittally.

"I could have done anything after that," Laura continued. "I don't mean that anything with my name on it would have sold – I wasn't *that* big. I'm not sure anyone ever is, no matter what people say. I mean that I could afford to branch out a little, if I really wanted to. Even if people still expected 'horror' from me, I could have moved on to, I don't know. Mummies. Witches. Cthulhu. Whatever."

"But you didn't," Caroline said, as Laura hesitated.

"No. I didn't." She sat up abruptly and looked at Caroline. "Do you believe in vampires?"

In spite of her good intentions, Caroline had to bite back a smile. Laura often spoke of vampires as casually, or as purposefully, as she would have anything that had the blessing of knowable, tangible existence. Laura had more than once – more than a hundred times, if the truth were to be told – lamented that the letters she received were all from admirers of vampires, never from the creatures themselves. Laura had never come right out and asked Caroline if she shared Laura's seeming belief. Either she assumed that she did, or, more probably, assumed that she didn't.

"I suppose," Caroline said carefully now, not wanting Laura to think she was laughing at her, "I hadn't really given the matter much thought."

"Well, I have."

"Apparently."

Laura narrowed her eyes. "I don't mean my writing," she said. "Or if I do then only indirectly." She stood up and moved to the large book-case near the window. From it, she gathered several books, all of which appeared to be well-read.

"Look," she said, spreading them out on the low coffee table and sitting down again. Obediently, Caroline looked. *The Annotated Dracula. In Search of Dracula. Carmilla. Varney and Other Vampires. An Unnatural History of the Vampire. Vampires, Burial, and Death.*

"Do I sense a recurring literary theme here?" Caroline asked, smiling.

"Do you know why all of these exist?" Laura asked, laying her hand protectively over one fragile volume.

"Tell me."

Her dark eyes gleamed, as if with some secret joy. "Because people believed in vampires. They did. Some still do."

"People," Caroline said cautiously, "have believed in a great many foolish things throughout the ages. Many still do."

"Yes," Laura said, smiling. "And why is that?"

"You tell me."

Laura leaned back, suddenly looking more relaxed than she had all evening. "Think about God," she suggested. "Think about ghosts. Think about Hell."

"All at the same time?"

"Carrie!"

"All right, all right. I'm thinking about them. Now what?"

"What do they have in common? Or, rather, what do they all have in common both with each other and with vampires?"

Caroline frowned. "Well, if you hadn't insisted on throwing in the vampires, and if you change the ghosts to souls or spirits – I guess that's what they're supposed to be anyway – I'd say they're all religious beliefs. With the vampires, say superstitions instead."

Laura nodded. "Now," she said, an edge of triumph in her voice, "do you know the big difference between vampires and all the rest?"

"Nothing leaps to mind." Several things did, actually, but that wasn't important – hearing what Laura had to say was.

"There are two, actually. The first one is obvious. Lots of people believe in God and Hell. I think even more people believe in ghosts, spirits, souls – call them what you will." Laura tapped her long nails together. Her voice had softened progressively until she seemed to be talking to herself rather than her friend.

"And the second?" Caroline prompted.

"Is qualitative, rather than quantitative." Laura's words sounded carefully chosen, as if she were recording rather than speaking them. "God and ghosts and Hell were all created to fill empty spaces. They were philosophized, not observed. Why are we here? Who made us? Who'll take care of us when Mommy and Daddy are gone? God. What happens when we die? We don't, really; we have ghosts, spirits – God was nice enough to supply us with those, too. Where do all the bad spirits go after their bodies die? They're not just thrown in with all the friendly ghosts to make trouble, are they? Oh, no. That's what we have Hell for. Funny how so many people seem much more set on having a Hell around than a

Heaven."

"People like to believe in justice," Caroline reminded her. "They can't find it here, so they hope it's somewhere else."

"Exactly. Just my point. They hope. They think. They decide." Laura was fairly rocking back and forth with excitement.

"I have to admit I'm not quite seeing your point," Caroline said. Laura had spoken oddly or angrily before, but she'd never detailed a cosmology to Caroline.

"It's easy. Having all those other things around, or not, was a conscious decision. All the rest – all the 'I know there's a God because one day he came down and told me so' – came later." Laura smiled at her hands. "But not vampires. Not whatever we're describing when we use that word. People didn't come up with them. They were forced to believe in them, after they saw evidence."

"Laura, I don't think –"

"No, wait. I'm not talking about those idiots on the talk shows who say they're vampires because they like to watch other people bleed." She laughed a grim little cough of a laugh. "Do you know how many of *them* have written to me? Some just want to touch bases. Some are looking for a relationship. One even wanted me to write his memoirs, for God's sake. Do you know, that one actually had me going for a while? I really thought I might have found the real thing."

"You never told me about that," Caroline said. "What happened?"

Laura shook her head bitterly, and a cold rage tightened her lips for a moment. "I was embarrassed to say anything. He was crazy. I mean really crazy, certifiable. That's part of why he was so convincing. But it wasn't just that he really believed it – his story was fantastic! If he could have held himself together enough to write it out and sell it, I think I'd have a rival."

Caroline set her cup down on the table, not too close to the books. "Laura, this is all very interesting, but I have to say I don't find it completely compelling. It just doesn't add up."

"But it does!" Laura didn't sound angry, only determined. "Don't you see? If God had half the tangible evidence on his side that vampires do on theirs, the whole world would be theistic by now. *I'd* go born again." She leaned forward, surprising Caroline. Laura didn't usually like getting too close to anyone. Now she seemed unconscious of the small space separating them.

"Think about it," she said. "Vampires have always left traces – more than traces. It's not like with faeries or elves, where stories circulated but the only person who ever saw the creatures was some friend of a friend who disappeared right after. Vampires have names! They have histories! No, not Dracula," she added as Caroline glanced skeptically at the books on the table. "That whole story's a mess. Interesting folklore, but nothing really cohesive. I'm talking about other ones – vampires you've never heard of. They existed. They used to be human, or at least the people who knew them thought they were, and then the truth came out." Laura stabbed her finger emphatically on a blue paperbound volume, the one about burial and death. "There are real names in here. Real people, not just myths and fairy tales."

"I remember reading something you might have missed," Caroline said as Laura paused for breath. "Something along the lines of there being a disease or condition that simulated some of the most common characteristics of vampires – not being able to go out in the sun, craving blood..."

"I've read references to that," Laura admitted. "It's an interesting theory." She seemed subdued now, almost sullen.

"Laura, I'm not trying to shoot you down. I just want to say that there may be some perfectly natural explanation –"

"Well, of course it's natural," Laura said. "Whatever vampires are, they exist in nature. I'm not saying they're like the ones I write about, necessarily. In fact, I hope they aren't."

"And here we are, full circle," Caroline said, pouring herself another cup of tea while there was still some warmth left in the brew. "You made me ask you why you write what you write, and you still haven't answered me."

"I thought it was obvious," Laura said, looking at her friend with an expression Caroline decided not to try to interpret.

"Well, it isn't," Caroline said, refusing to be nettled. "So tell me."

Laura ducked her glance away. "Have you ever read something that really spoke to you?" she asked. "Someone writes about women or scholars or whatever group you identify with most and hits the nail right on the head, seems to know exactly how you feel and what you want? Or just the opposite – some writer thinks he understands what 'real women' like and want? And he couldn't be further wrong if he'd never met a woman in his life? I'm not just talking about male writers. I mean anyone writing about any group, whether they belong to it or not, and doing a just great or just lousy job."

"Yes, of course."

"Well, now do you understand?" Laura looked at her almost pleadingly. "People who consider themselves members of a special group respond when they see their group written about. If they think the writing is good they can't shut up about it, and if they think it's bad they're ready to invite the author to a necktie party."

Caroline smiled. "A necktie party?"

"Isn't that the expression? I thought I heard that somewhere – must have been an old movie."

Caroline set her cup down and stretched. "So you're telling me," she said, and her voice was as sweetly reasonable as ever, "that you write your novels because you're hoping someone who knows whereof he speaks will send you a letter saying, 'Hey, you've got this all wrong here,' or, 'Nice job! And here I'd spent all these centuries thinking no one understood me'?"

Laura stood up, hands clenched. "I thought you'd understand," she said. "You of all people ought to know me better than that."

"Laura, I didn't mean to sound sarcastic." Caroline stood up as well and risked placing a hand on Laura's shoulder. Laura didn't shrug it off, but she looked as if she'd very much like to. "I guess I don't understand after all," Caroline added, pressing gently on her friend's arm. "Come on. Sit down and tell me more."

"Why?" Laura asked, letting herself be coaxed back down to the couch. "So you can tell me how ridiculous I'm being?"

"I didn't say that. I never would, because you never are. But you have to admit, this isn't the kind of thing one hears every day."

"I know they're out there," Laura said. She leaned back, away from Caroline, tacitly rejecting any comfort that might be offered. "I don't care what they think of my writing, either. It's just a tool. How else can I reach so many people at once?"

"Laura," Caroline said. "Let's ignore the question of why you'd want to hear from – this particular group. You still haven't told me why, and I'm not sure it matters."

"It does," Laura said sullenly.

"All right, it does. But forget it for a minute, please?"

"Fine." Laura had edged herself away from Caroline until they were sitting at opposite ends of the couch. She was curled up with her arms tight around her knees.

"Remember what you were saying before, about what people think about people who write about vampires? They're all in it for the money, right?" Caroline watched her friend's face closely. "I'm not saying it's true, but that's the idea most people have, right?"

"Well?"

"Well," Caroline said, "why wouldn't vampires think that, too? After

all, as you pointed out, some writers are making a fortune off this particular subject."

Laura looked at her coolly, but her voice betrayed definite interest.
"So you think that they'd just write me off as one more gold-digger?"

"Something like that. Is the idea so unreasonable?"

Laura shook her head. To Caroline's surprise, she was smiling.

"Not bad, Holmes," she said. "There's just one thing you're forgetting."

Caroline smiled back at her, relieved that the storm seemed to be over.
"And what is that?"

Laura gazed at the window, neatly covered in its yellow curtain.
Caroline's color scheme, of course – she loved color and light and thought
that everyone else in the world must, too. "My writing is different," she
said. "Not to toot my own horn or anything, but I took the modern idea
of vampires and took it one step further. They'd already become genuine
main characters, interesting enough to be sympathetic, or at least no one
really cares if they're not. Well, *I* make them real people. Everyone else
seems to want to draw them as saints or demons, nothing in-between. But
if they're of human origin, or even if they've just lived among humans for
a long time, they're bound to be fairly recognizably human in a lot of ways,
and at the same time uniquely themselves."

"Dracula, warts and all," Caroline suggested. "Don't look daggers at
me, I'm not teasing you."

"It doesn't matter," Laura said wearily. She seemed sick of the subject.
"Nothing I've done works. The wrong people eat my work up, and the rest
ignore it."

Caroline sighed. So much for helping. If anything, Laura was more
depressed than before. "I'm going to be brutally honest with you,"
Caroline said. "In spite of everything you've told me, I don't see any
reason to believe as you do. But even if I did, I can tell you a perfectly good
reason why you haven't made any friends worth keeping, so to speak, in
spite of all your efforts."

"And what's that?" Laura sounded as if she were on automatic pilot;
not really listening, but responding because it was expected of her.

"Really, Laura," Caroline teased, "I'm surprised it didn't occur to you
before. Or maybe it did, and you dismissed it too easily."

"All right, already," Laura said. "I'm listening."

"We're talking about a group at risk here," Caroline said. "You may
genuinely admire them, and a lot of people like them just fine as long as
they're on paper, but that's about as far as it goes. In order to survive,

they'd have to keep their very existences a secret. Think about how many people are still in the closet. Would you come out of the coffin, so to speak, if you thought it might mean death, no matter how much of a relief it might be?"

Laura was silent. "Besides," Caroline added practically, "there isn't any way for someone to find out how you feel about this. It isn't exactly intuitively obvious, you know. Even assuming someone...like that...had the courage to make the first move, wouldn't they think you'd just dismiss them as some crackpot?"

"I see," Laura said. Her voice was very low, almost toneless.

Caroline looked at her quizzically. "Won't you tell me why this is so important to you?" she asked against her better judgment.

Laura only shook her head. "It doesn't matter now," she said. "If you're right, you're right. If you're not – well, you don't believe in any of this anyway, remember?"

"I'd still like to know," Caroline said. "It's important to you. You're important to me."

Laura sat in stubborn silence.

"You want to be one, don't you," Caroline said rather than asked.

Her friend glared at her. "I don't know," she said defiantly. "Maybe."

"And would you stop writing if you were?"

Laura looked at her, startled. "That's a strange question."

"I didn't mean it to be."

They sat in uncomfortable silence for several minutes.

"Well," Laura said at last, getting awkwardly to her feet with the idea of looking to see if her kitchen contained anything stronger than tea. "Maybe I should get back in touch with what's-his-name, let him pay me to write those memoirs. I kept his letter, you know. Thought – oh, I don't know, that I'd want to show it to you sometime or something." She smiled crookedly. "Anyway, I might as well cultivate him, right? He's the closest I'll ever come to the real thing. And like I said, he had some great stories."

Caroline rose and stood next to Laura, ruffled her sparse hair with a gentle hand. Caroline knew she was the only person on earth privileged to take such liberties with Laura, and even she didn't push her luck too often.

"Why not?" Caroline said. "In this world, we take what we can get."

※

Caroline didn't stay much longer. Laura didn't come right out and say so, but she clearly wanted to be alone after such an unusually, wordily revealing night. It was early for them, quite late for the rest of the world.

Caroline could tell someone had been in her apartment as soon as she opened the door. Had been, and still was – the only person in the world with whom she spent more time than she did Laura. Gods above, she hated it when he did this.

She sighed quietly, shutting the door without bothering to turn on the light. "This couldn't wait?" she inquired in a language no human being had spoken for a very long time.

The darkness next to her thickened, became substantial. "You said we could hunt tonight," a voice she wished she didn't recognize said.

"Might," she snapped. "I said we might." He was like a child – always mistaking possibility for definite intent.

The solid eagerness next to her didn't melt away at this demurral; if anything, it pressed closer. "You're here now," the voice pointed out, wheedling.

"All right, Holden." Caroline gave in. If she didn't, he would bother her all night, and the next night, and the next. Worse, he might disappear for a time. Let her think about being completely alone, a stranger in a strange land. Repulsive as he was, he was the closest thing Caroline had to family.

"Let me just set something down," she added, shrugging his presence off and moving through the darkness to her room. Holden didn't follow her, for which Caroline was heartily grateful.

Carefully, she set her parcel on the nightstand. She touched the large envelope wistfully, wishing she didn't have to leave just now. This was the first three chapters of Laura's latest work, which Caroline was allowed to see before any editor, just as she was all of Laura's work.

A fairy tale. Something to while away the time before sleep.

Caroline thought about the night's conversation and her mouth tightened painfully. She had never knowingly converted anyone in her entire existence, wasn't even sure she could if she wanted to. And here was someone so very close, practically begging her to try. Someone she loved.

Someone who wrote the stories Caroline treasured so much because she was as lonely in her own way as Caroline was in hers. Messages in cardboard bottles, no longer necessary once rescuers arrived.

Caroline forced her mind away from useless contemplation and went to meet the thing in the other room. She had survived by her strength of will and fine mind. Holden took great pleasure in reminding her that brute force was just as good, if not better, in a pinch.

Well, she reminded herself as they moved together through the heavy night, in this imperfect world, we do take what we can get.

The Authors

Michael J. Arruda has been a fan of horror and vampires since the age of three after viewing an 8mm version of Hammer Films' *Horror of Dracula*. His most satisfying professional experience has also involved vampires: directing the St. Gabriel's Drama Club production of *Dracula* in Charlotte, North Carolina. A former middle school English teacher, Michael now works at home, writing horror tales in New Hampshire with his wife, Michelle, son, Lucas, and two dogs.

Edo van Belkom has authored over 120 short stories published in a wide variety of magazines and anthologies. His first novel, *Wyrm Wolf,* was a finalist for the 1995 Horror Writers Association Bram Stoker Award. Other novels include *Lord Soth* and *Mister Magick*. He has also been a nominee for the Aurora and Arthur Ellis Awards. His first short story collection, *Death Drives a Semi,* and a book of non-fiction, *Northern Dreamers: Interviews with Canadian Science Fiction, Fantasy and Horror Writers* are 1998 titles from Quarry Press of Kingston, Ontario. Edo's home page is located at http://www.horrornet.com/belkom.htm

Sue Burke of Milwaukee, Wisconsin, has worked for years as a reporter and editor for newspapers and magazines – which has provided an inexhaustible supply of material suitable for science fiction and fantasy, especially the stint covering suburban governments. In addition to hundreds of non-fiction articles in print, she has had short stories and poems appear in several publications. She is a member of the Milwaukee Area Writer's Guild and a 1966 alumni of the Clarion writing workshop.

Margaret L. Carter is the wife of a Navy Captain, currently living in Annapolis. They have four sons and two grandchildren. She received English degrees from the College of William and Mary, the University of Hawaii (M.A.), and the University of California, Irvine (Ph.D.). Her first book was a vampire anthology, *Curse of the Undead* (1970). She has published several books and articles on vampirism in literature, including *Dracula: The Vampire and The Critics* (an anthology, 1988). Her stories have appeared in various small press publications, in Marion Zimmer Bradley's *Darkover* anthologies, and in *The Time Of The Vampires*, edited by P.N. Elrod and Martin Greenberg. She edits a semiannual fanzine, *The Vampire's Crypt*. In her "day job" she works as a proofreader for the Maryland General Assembly.

Stirling Davenport has been writing fiction since she was a child, preferring dark fiction in which her imagination has free reign, and characters can work out philosophical problems without the ordinary constraints of reality. Stirling has completed four novels and numerous short stories, and is a member of the Six Foot Ferrets Writing Group. Among her unpublished works are a dark elven adventure saga, tahe tale of a rebellious priestess, and a modern Tibetan love story.

Robert Devereaux works, writes, and thrives in northern Colorado. His short fiction has appeared in numerous periodicals and anthologies. Robert's first two novels, *Deadweight* and *Walking Wounded*, were published by Dell Abyss. His latest work, *Santa Steps Out: A Fairy Tale for Grown-Ups* (Dark Highway Press), which presents the erotic misadventures of Santa Claus, the Tooth Fairy, the Easter Bunny and select mortals, features introductions by David G. Hartwell and Patrick LoBrutto and a full-color cover and interior illustrations by Alan Clark.

d.g.k. goldberg received an honorable mention in the 1997 Thomas Wolfe Fiction Prize Contest, her work has appeared in *EternityOL* and *Tangents*. A chapbook of her dark fiction *The Edge* is scheduled for mid-1998 release by Eternity Press. She lives with her spousal unit, who is the most tolerant human on the planet, and several personal demons. In addition to a series of unrewarding and stressful jobs, she foolishly attempts to garden. When she was a little girl she wanted to grow up to be a queen – she still thinks it's a rather nice idea.

Scott T. Goudsward is from Massachusetts, where he works full time as a data analyst and lives with his family and cat. First inspired to write at age 10 after hearing his first Edgar Allan Poe story *The Tell-Tale Heart.* Scott has been a contributing member of the Essex Writer Guild since 1992, with horror, fantasy, science fiction, mainstream fiction and young adult stories, novels and screenplays in circulation.

Barb Hendee's short fiction has appeared in numerous paperback anthologies such as DAW's *Year's Best Horror Stories XX, Young Blood, Realms of Infamy,* and *GhostTide.* Her first novel, *Blood Memories,* will be published in May, 1998. She lives just outside of Boulder, Colorado, and teaches writing at the Metropolitan State College of Denver. She's a firm believer that life is just too short for cheap coffee.

Kyle Marffin is a midwestern commercial copywriter, railroading fan, and part time wildlife and nature "nut". Kyle's articles and short fiction have appeared in a number of zines, periodicals and journals. Kyle's first novel, *CARMILLA – The Return,* a modern day retelling of J.S. LeFanu's classic vampire novella, is currently published by The Design Image Group.

Deborah Markus manages an apartment building in Santa Monica, California with her husband, writer Dominick Cancilla. *For the Love of Vampires* is her first published story, but she and Dominick have collaborated on a joint creative work due out in February, 1998. At press time, they still didn't know whether it was a boy or a girl.

Paul McMahon has created stories all his life but only started writing them down in algebra class when he was sixteen. His stories have appeared in numerous small press magazines, including *White Knuckles,* and *Outer Darkness.* He lives in Massachusetts with his wife Michele and their two cats, where he organizes *The Nightwriters Shadowgram,* a nation-wide writers' critique group, by mail. His first novel, *The Trough,* is due out mid-1998 from Commonwealth Publications. He will be writing his second novel as soon as he finds another algebra class that will accept him.

Julie Anne Parks turned to fiction after several years as a New England news reporter. Now living in North Carolina with her husband, Chuck, and children, she is a member of the Horror Writers Association and the Writer's Group of the Triad. Her most recent novel, *Storyteller,* is currently being shopped and her short stories have appeared in several genre and mainstream magazines. Julie extends special thanks to her good friend Janice McDowell for the brainstorming sessions that fine-tuned *The Covenant of Il Vigneto.*

Rick R. Reed is the author of the Dell Abyss novels, *Penance* and *Obsessed.* In addition to the U.S. and Canada, both books have been published in translation in Germany and Russia. His short fiction has appeared in the White Wolf anthologies, *Dark Destiny, Dante's Disciples* and *Dark Destiny III: Children of Dracula* and numerous magazines. Upcoming publications include the short story, "Moving Toward The Light" which will appear in the anthology, *Shattered Lives and Broken Dreams,* edited by Edward Kramer and James O'Barr, published by Random House. Reed is currently at work on a new novel and lives in Chicago.

Thomas J. Strauch is a Chicago area artist and marketing communications business owner, who writes, as he says, "recreationally" much to his wife and daughter's amusement. An avid Horror Writers Association helper, Tom is also the publisher of this anthology. No one on the Editorial Committee volunteered to issue him a rejection slip.

William R. Trotter has been Senior Writer for *PC Gamer Magazine* since 1987, and has published more than 1,000 reviews, articles, and columns about entertainment software. He is the author of 11 published books, ranging from novels to biography, and is an internationally recognized military historian. His history of the Russo-Finnish War, *A Frozen Hell,* won the 1992 Finlandia Foundation Arts and Letters Prize. His genre stores have appeared in "Deathrealm", "Fantasy Book", and "Night Cry", and his 1996 novella, *The Siren of Swanquarter,* was a finalist for the Bram Stoker Award. He lives in Greensboro, NC, and his wife, Elizabeth Lustig, is also a noted author of horror and dark fantasy.

THE NEW VOICES IN HORROR

Night Prayers   by P. D. Cacek

Bram Stoker Award winner P. D. Cacek's NIGHT PRAYERS is a wryly witty romp that turns the conventions of traditional vampire fiction inside out. You'll meet Allison Garret - thirtysomething, biological clock loudly ticking and perpetually unlucky in love - who wakes up in a seedy motel room after a three day binge...as a vampire without a clue about how to survive! In a rollicking tour through the seamy underbelly of L.A., Allison hooks up with a Bible-thumping streetcorner preacher, and it will take more than prayers to save them both from the clutches of a catty coven of strip club vampire vixens.

ISBN 1-891946-01-3
5.5 x 8.5 trade pb, 224 pg $15.95 US ($19.50 CAN)

Carmilla - The Return   by Kyle Marffin

Kyle Marffin debuts with a provocative, modern day retelling of J. S. Sheridan LeFanu's classic 19th century novella. CARMILLA - The Return reintroduces Gothic literature's most notorious female vampire, the cunning Countess Carmilla Karnstein. While revealing glimpses of her unwritten history, Carmilla seduces an unsuspecting victim, stalking glittery city streets, the desolate northwoods and back to her haunted Styrian homeland in a series of events that mirror the original tale, with a decidedly contemporary twist.

ISBN 1-891946-02-1
5.5 x 8.5 trade pb, 304 pg $15.95 US ($19.50 CAN)

Support your local bookseller.
If unavailable, ask them to order your copy today by calling toll free
1-800-563-5455

The Darkest Thirst